A FLIGHT TOO FAR

By

Tony Blackman

A Flight Too Far

ISBN 978-0-9553856-3-6 / 0-9553856-3-6

First Published September 2006
© 2006 by Anthony Blackman.

Published by Blackman Associates
24 Crowsport
Hamble
Southampton SO31 4HG
UK

Previous books by same Author

The Final Flight
ISBN 0-9553856-0-1 / 978-0-9553856-0-5
August 2006

Flight Testing to Win (Autobiography)
ISBN 1-4116-4825-0
September 2005

To Margaret, without whose ideas, enormous help and continuous encouragement this book would never have seen the light of day.

This book could not have been completed without the support of Rob Foulkes. He gave me specialist advice which was of enormous help. Any errors remaining in the book must be laid entirely at my door. I also received advice from many other people in the aviation industry and hope I will be forgiven for not naming them all.

Anthony L Blackman OBE, M.A., F.R.Ae.S

About the Author

Tony Blackman was educated at Oundle School and Trinity College Cambridge, where he obtained an honours degree in Physics. After joining the Royal Air Force he learnt to fly, trained as a test pilot and then joined A.V.Roe and Co. Ltd. where he became Chief Test Pilot.

Tony was an expert in aviation electronics and was invited by Smiths Industries to join their Aerospace Board, initially as Technical Operations Director. He helped develop the then new large electronic displays and Flight Management Systems.

After leaving Smiths Industries, he was invited to join the Board of the UK Civil Aviation Authority as Technical Member.

Tony is a Fellow of the American Society of Experimental Test Pilots, a Fellow of the Royal Institute of Navigation and a Liveryman of the Guild of Air Pilots and Air Navigators.

He now lives in Hamble and spends his spare time writing books and designing and maintaining databases on the internet.

CONTENTS

DRAMATIS PERSONNAE

Peter Talbert	**Aviation Expert, Narrator of Book**
Jim Akers	Aeronautical Correspondent of Financial Times
Sir Robert Applegate	Chief Constable of the Metropolitan Area
Mandy Arrowsmith	Peter's Solicitor Girl Friend
Bill Baker	Chief Training Captain, NWIA
Humphrey Barton	Tower Controller, Heathrow
Tip Brewster	NWIA Shift Supervisor
John Chester	Chief Pilot, Royal World Airlines, wife Jane
Jack Chiltern	Managing Director, Royal World Airlines
Janet Crowburn	Chief Counsel for the Attorney General
Dora	Peter Talbert's Domestic Help
Evan Evans	RWA Expert on 798 Landing Systems
John Fairlane	Counsel for CrossRisk Insurance
Liz Fairlane	John's Wife
Dick Falconer	Captain on Royal World Airlines flight to Sydney
Tim Forrestal	Solicitor for CrossRisk Insurance
Martin Foster	Senior Inspector, Air Accident Investigation Branch in charge of crash investigation
Paul Franconi	Daily Mirror Air Correspondent
Jane Franklin	Times Air Correspondent
Bob Furness	Head of Air Accident Investigation Branch
Tom Gardner	American Airlines Training Department
Harvey Gates	Approach Controller, Heathrow
Tony Giles	RWA 798 First Officer
Harry Hodgson	Captain of crashed aircraft, killed on flight
Jack Lawrence	NWIA/United Electronics Engineer
Justin Lockyer	RWA 798 Captain
Fred Longshaw	First Officer on Royal World Airlines flight to Sydney
Mike Mansell	Partner in CrossRisk Insurance
Jock Mansfield	NWIA Training Captain
John and Julia Marchant	Peter Talbert's Neighbours

Prof. Charles McGuire	Inquiry Assessor, Prof. Software Engineering at Imperial College
Jim McIntosh	Peter Talbert's solicitor
Catherine Mercer	Frank Mercer's Wife
Frank Mercer	Surviving First Officer on fatal flight
Anne Moncrieff	Surveyor with Safety Regulation Group, Civil Aviation Authority
Tom Nesbitt	En route RWA Captain to Sydney
Michael Noble	Seattle Editor of Aviation Week
Roger O'Kane	Avionics designer, Independant Transport Aircraft Company
Chuck Osborne	Daily Telegraph Air Correspondent
Bob Parnell	President, Independant Transport Aircraft Company, builder of 798 airplane
Ted Richmond	Senior Operations Staff, NWIA
Robbie Robson	En route 798 Pilot of Royal World Airlines
Jill Stanton	John Chester's secretary
Lance Stephens	NWIA Electronics Engineer
Jack Templeman	Inquiry Assessor, Chief Engineer, Britannia
Francis Thomas	Royal World Airlines Engineering Director
Lord Justice Thomas	Head of Commission of Inquiry
Matt Thompson	Head of Maintenance, NWIA
Dick Tremlett	En route RWA First Officer killed on flight
Carol Trentham	Wife of Richard Trentham
Richard Trentham	Deadheading Cathay Pacific Pilot killed on flight
Frank Trotter	Chief Ground Instructor of NWIA
Roger Tucker	Flight Magazine Air Correspondent
Charles Tumbrill	First Officer of crashed aircraft, killed on flight.
Liz Ward	Operations staff, NWIA
Bill Wentworth	Captain, Royal World Airlines
Jack Wilson	En route First Officer to Sydney
Roger Williams	John Chester's deputy, wife Margaret, daughter of Jack Chiltern

ACRONYMS

Acronym	In full
AAIB	Air Accident Investigation Branch
ACARS	Aircraft Communications Addressing and Reporting System
ATIS	Automatic Terminal Information Service
ATC	Air Traffic Control
BAA	British Airports Authority
CAA	Civil Aviation Authority
DERA	Defence Evaluation and Research Agency
DGAC	French Directorate of Civil Aviation
DME	Distance Measuring Equipment
EASA	European Aviation Safety Agency
FAA	Federal Aviation Administration
FMS	Flight Management System
GAPAN	Guild of Air Pilots and Air Navigators
GELAS	Galileo European Local Augmentation System
GESS	Galileo European Satellite System
GLOSNASS	Russian Satellite Positioning System
GPS	Global Positioning System
HUD	Head Up Display
ILS	Instrument Landing System
IRS	Inertial Reference Systems
INMARSAT	Not acronym but an international telecommunications company
ITAC	Independant Transport Aircraft Company
LAAS	Local Area Augmentation System for GPS
MMR	Multimode Receiver
NWIA	New World International Airlines
PAI	Pacific Aerospace Insurance
RVR	Runway Visual Range
RWA	Royal World Airlines
SAE	Society of Automotive Engineers
SRG	Safety Regulation Group, UK Civil Aviation Authority

Manufacturing Firms

Marcovitch	Makers of Galileo European Satellite Receiver
Microspot	Makers of the MMR in the 798

Great Circle Route Sydney—London
Flight RWA 573

From	To	Distance
SYD (33°56'46"S 151°10'38"E)	LHR (51°28'39"N 00°27'41"W)	10573 mi

Map produced using Karl L. Swartzmapping web site

A Flight Too Far

PROLOGUE

Richard knew he was dying. He could feel his consciousness slowly slipping away. The whole thing was like a nightmare. One moment he was sitting in the jump seat on the flight deck of the world's most advanced airplane about to land at Heathrow and then next moment he was in terrible pain, lying in hospital, with the world spinning around. He tried to remember what had happened but nothing seemed to make sense.

He could not see the room clearly. He was glad Carol was there, though he could barely say a word to her. What a homecoming. He was aware of people rushing in and looking after him but he realised it would not be for long.

Though everything was a blur, the flight somehow kept coming back to him. He remembered Harry arranging for him to travel back from Sydney as supernumerary crew. He had been wanting to see the 798's advanced flight deck ever since it had gone into airline service and so he had leapt at the chance when Harry invited him. The 747s he was flying were quite new, but were archaic compared with the 798. He had read about the aircraft in the newspapers and magazines, especially those articles by his old colleague Peter Talbert.

Carol had just come into the room again but she seemed far away, behind the flight deck. He could feel the pain in his shoulders from the shoulder straps and he tried to loosen them. It had been a wonderful flight until the hijackers arrived. How on earth had they got on board? And onto the Flight Deck past the marshals? They had somehow forced their way through the flight deck door, both carrying guns, pointing them at Harry and at Charles, the first officer. Harry had been magnificent controlling the madmen and the aircraft at the same time.

The hijackers had a crazy scheme of getting the Government to give them some al-Qaeda prisoners and then take-off again for the Middle East. Ahmed, the leader, was talking about blowing the plane up if the prisoners were not released. Surely they had not got a bomb? Perhaps it was all bluff. Richard had known, and surely Harry must have done, that they would never have been allowed to take-off again but Harry played along with Ahmed, the leader, arranging the refuelling on the runway. As if to make matters worse, the headwind from Sydney had been stronger than forecast so they did not have too much fuel and the weather at London was freezing fog. Richard had felt so sorry for Harry to have to carry this burden but he was powerless to help.

11

Suddenly he felt he should tell Peter about the flight. Someone needed to know. He felt himself saying "Peter Talbert. Get Peter. I want to tell him …"

Now Carol seemed to be walking through the instruments towards him and bending over him. He tried to move but he couldn't and he knew it wasn't really the shoulder straps stopping him. He seemed to hear air traffic control talking. Harry had turned the speakers off but Ahmed had insisted that they should be turned back on again. He remembered wondering if it was going to be possible for Harry to fly a Cat 3 approach and landing, in freezing fog, with the hijackers interfering, without the aircraft crashing. He knew the autopilot would be flying the aircraft but the system was not infallible.

Poor Harry, he seemed only to have one display in front of him and he was continually having to switch from the vertical display to the horizontal one. Charles, on his other side, seemed to have no problem. Richard remembered that he also had had a display and some instruments in front of him but they did not seem to be much use for finding out what was happening. Air Traffic had told them they could not use the ILS on 27L which had concerned him. But Harry had known it was permitted to use the new European satellite navigation system for the landing. He heard Ahmed talking to Harry and Harry telling him to be quiet.

Richard woke up with a start. He must have dropped off into a coma. The pain in his leg was terrible. Carol was still there and so was the flight deck. They were close to landing. He remembered feeling worried as his experience with GPS for navigation had not been all that good but Peter Talbert had written that the latest satellite system was first rate and very closely monitored for errors. He knew that he had felt that there was no way that Harry was going to be able to manage with Ahmed standing there with his gun, talking. Harry and Charles had seemed very confident but Ahmed kept interfering. They were down to 100ft now and he looked again at his instruments and then at the hijackers. He tried to yell 'Pull up, Pull up' felt himself bracing, there was a crash and he realised that he was being moved from his bed.

Sometime later Richard woke again. His right leg was completely numb. This time the flight deck had gone. He could see Carol and there was Peter standing next to her. He made a supreme effort to talk.

"Peter. The hijackers…"

Peter was leaning forward.

"I tried to tell …"

He felt himself slipping away.

CHAPTER 1

"Heathrow broadcast – the airport is now closed. I say again, the airport is closed. Speedbird 6328 route direct to Ockham, climb flight level 100 and join the hold."

I was driving in thick fog, trying to get home from Bournemouth. I didn't have far to go to my house in Kingston and I was looking forward to getting back. As I often did, I was listening to the conversation between aircraft and ground controllers on my VHF set. I had had the receiver specially fitted to my rather elderly BMW at what was, in my view, an extortionate cost but I reckoned I could offset the cost against my tax. The transmission from London Approach was only just audible, even though I was only a few miles from Heathrow.

"Climbing level 100 to Ockham to hold, Speedbird 6328. What's the snag? We are Cat 3"

Clearly the fog I was experiencing covered Heathrow as well. Like the British Airways pilot I wondered what the problem was and why the aircraft was not allowed to land.

"Speedbird 6328 understood. Call Director on 119.2 with cleared level"

"119.2 Speedbird 6328"

It was strange that Approach did not advise the aircraft of the reason for diversion.

"RWA 372. Please advise your desired alternate."

"Roger. Royal 372 calling company."

"Royal 372 thank you – quick as you can please."

I switched to Royal World Airlines Operations frequency.

"RWA Operations this is 372. Just been told Heathrow is closed. Why? What do you want me to do?"

"Ops to 372. Confirm Heathrow is closed. Request clearance to Stansted. We are arranging a gate for you."

It was odd that RWA operations did not tell 372 what the problem was either. I would have liked to have known as well. The fog if anything was getting worse and there was now ice on the road. Perhaps the airport authority had decided that they needed to treat the runways.

"Operations, this is 573. Have you arranged the refuelling?"

"We're still doing that. You are being refuelled by tankers instead of by hydrants on the stands and we are making sure that they have enough fuel for Karachi and that they can get to your parking position on the runway."

"573 understood."

If the reception had not been absolutely clear I would have thought I had misheard the aircraft transmission. It did not make sense.

"RWA Ops This is 573. I have been asked to establish whether the prisoners have been released and are waiting at the airport?"

"573 please stand by. Will advise."

There was only one explanation I could think of. The aircraft must have been hijacked. But that was virtually impossible these days with such high security at the airports. I wondered where 573 had come from. What a dreadful situation. If the aircraft was going to land at Heathrow it was no wonder the airport was closed.

There was a short pause.

"RWA Ops I have been told to remind you that the hijackers are going to blow up the aircraft if there is any delay to their instructions which I passed to you"

"573 This is RWA Ops Copied."

I wanted to retune my VHF receiver to London Approach but I was frightened I might miss something. However there was nothing more on the RWA Ops channel so I switched to the Approach frequency just as I was entering my drive. I decided to stay in the car until 573 had landed. I left the engine running to keep warm.

"Speedbird 756 Heathrow now closed. Do you want Stansted or Gatwick?"

"Gatwick please 756"

"Speedbird 756 maintain flight level 70 and turn left heading 240 degrees. Maintain 220 knots. Expect to hold at Biggin."

Clearly there was a real emergency for this hijack. I wondered how many other people besides me were hearing this appalling situation unfold.

"Director Royal 573 reaching 4,000."

"Roger Cleared procedural GESS final approach 27 left"

"Royal 573 we'd prefer the ILS"

I sympathised with the pilot. I always preferred radio beams physically defined in space to virtual centre lines calculated by software.

"Sorry Royal 573 the ATIS is incorrect. The ILS is no longer approved for Cat 3 approaches and is out of service. What are your intentions?"

There was a distinct pause.

"Royal 573 Request GESS approach 27 Left."

"You are cleared for GESS approach cleared to descend on the procedure. Maintain heading and call the Tower on 118.5"

"118.5 Royal 573"

I switched to the tower frequency just in time to hear 573's call.

"Tower Royal 573 ten miles 27 Left. Confirm GELAS OK."

Chapter 1

"Royal 573 hello. You are clear to land 27 left, wind calm RVR 20, 30,20 GELAS showing OK"

"Roger Royal 573"

The weather was definitely Category 3B. The three transmissionmeters measuring the runway visual range along the length of the runway all agreed. I just couldn't imagine what it must be like doing an automatic landing in fog while being hijacked, presumably with a pistol being held to my head. Furthermore, I did not understand why the aircraft was having to use the Galileo European Satellite System, GESS, instead of the Instrument Landing System, ILS. The pilot was very sensible to recheck that the GELAS system, which augmented the accuracy of the GESS satellites, was working correctly.

"Heathrow Tower RWA 573 please check wind speed."

The Tower did not answer immediately then,

"573 from Tower, the wind is calm."

Another pause.

"573 you appear to be low on the glide slope."

There was no answer. The controller sounded worried and so was I. There were no more transmissions. I wound down my car window and I thought I could hear sirens in the distance. I looked at my watch. It was 10.30. It had taken me over three hours to get home from Bournemouth instead of my normal two. I was undecided what to do. It was too late to ring Mandy, my girl friend who I had just left. I knew she went to bed early when she was working the next day. Her train left at 6.30 am. That was why we had had a very early meal and I had left soon after seven having lingered much longer than we had planned and had very nearly broken our unspoken resolution about where I should stay the night.

I had driven back to my house in Kingston on an emotional and sexual high, trying to listen to some of Andrew Lloyd Webber's older songs on my CD but having to keep switching the CD off in order to concentrate on the almost impenetrable fog, made much worse by the freezing conditions. It was a very scary drive trying to allow for the vagaries not only of the weather but the other foolhardy drivers on the road and I was very thankful for my GPS navigator. In the end I had switched the music off and decided to listen to my VHF receiver to hear how the fog was affecting the Heathrow traffic.

I collected my things from the car, unlocked the front door, cancelled the alarm and went into the house, full of trepidation. Something terrible had obviously happened. It would have been pointless rushing to the airport. I dropped everything and switched on Radio 5.

As usual Radio 5 was talking about soccer. It was obviously a subject that was of great interest though I found it difficult to understand why. Suddenly the guy leading the discussion said there was breaking news and passed us over to the newsroom.

"It has just been reported that an aircraft has crashed trying to land at London Airport. Apparently, the aircraft has crashed on the A30 to the east of the airport."

There was nothing more and soccer once more reigned supreme. I turned the volume down slightly so that I would hear the inevitable upgrading of the news on the crash. I was horrified. The accident was clearly a terrible disaster. Goodness knows how many people had been killed, on the ground as well as in the air. Already people would be wondering how the accident occurred. The hijacking was clearly a critical factor.

Automatically I went into the dining room, which I had turned into an office, and turned on my computer. I had one of the latest machines on the market but it still seemed to take a long time for it to load the software and be ready for use. It was rather like the Flight Deck Computers on aircraft; however fast they were they were never fast enough for the job the pilot wanted to do. This was what I immodestly called Talbert's first law of flight deck computing.

Aviation was my business. I had spent the first fourteen years of my working life flying for Britannia Airways, until the doctors discovered a heart murmur which had never troubled me but which they considered made it impossible for me to keep a licence. I tried everything I could at the time to appeal against the judgement of the doctors at Gatwick but to no avail. I had had to settle for loss of licence insurance which hardly compensated for being unemployed and I was attempting to earn my living as a consultant in airline safety matters, having done some crew training in the classroom as well as various other things to make ends meet.

I went to the Royal World Airlines web site and found the flight details of RWA 573. It had taken off from Sydney at 0930 local time and was due in at 2230. There was no other information on the web site.

I thought about the conversation with air traffic. The voice sounded very familiar. I felt I should have recognised it. Perhaps the voice, presumably the Captain, was a member of the Guild of Air Pilots and Air Navigators, as I was, and we had met.

It was puzzling that the aircraft had been allowed to land at Heathrow. The standard Air Traffic Control instructions were to divert all hijacked aircraft to Stansted. Not that there were any hijacked aircraft these days. Security was always far too good. I wondered again how the hijackers had got on board since the Sydney security was extremely tight. It was going to be important to discover not only why the accident happened but how the breach of security occurred.

Chapter 1

I heard the news reported again on Radio 5.

"Further details have emerged on the accident to an aircraft that occurred trying to land at Heathrow. The weather was extremely foggy and very icy. The aircraft was a Royal World Airlines' Independant Transport Aircraft Company 798 flying non-stop from Sydney to London. There are believed to be about 500 passengers and crew on the aircraft. The situation is confused because it is understood there was a hijacking alert coming from this aircraft."

The news reader had said that the aircraft belonged to Royal World Airlines and was one of the new super jumbo four-engined Independant 798s. I knew the aircraft well because I had written a technical article on it for the Financial Times when it was first certificated. The 798 had a capacity of about 750 people when flying on the Sydney-London route against the normal headwind. It was made by the Independant Transport Aircraft Company based near Seattle and could carry over 1,000 people when flying short distances with the maximum number of seats, a fact which I found slightly disturbing imagining the understandable panic if there was ever a need for rapid evacuation.

Independant was a relatively new airplane manufacturer started by ex-Boeing engineers and marketing executives. As the competition from the European Airbus company had increased, Boeing had found it harder and harder to compete. The launch of the Airbus 380 accelerated the decline of Boeing and the firm had had to lay off an enormous number of engineers in the Commercial division of the company. These engineers, realising that the Boeing overheads were crippling the company, had persuaded some venture capitalists in the State of Washington, many of whom had made a lot of money locally out of Microsoft, to start the Independant Transport Aircraft Company. The new firm had managed to get a lease of some ground on the airfield at Everett, where the large Boeing aircraft were assembled, and had built a huge new hangar. The design office was in a rented building in Renton near the Boeing facility and nearly everything was subcontracted so that all the parts came together for the first time at Everett. The headquarters of the new company was in Kirkland, just north of Bellevue. Almost every facility they needed was rented to avoid the need for excessive amounts of capital and this was made possible because of the surplus capacity available in the United States commercial aerospace industry. This technique really kept the costs down and Boeing were having a hard time to compete with the new company. Even Airbus in Europe, with the subsidized launch costs from the various national Governments concerned, was feeling the strain. This was the first major accident to an Independant manufactured aircraft and would be an enormous blow to the company.

It was 11.30 by now and I was feeling tired. It was tempting to stay up and listen to the details of the accident unfolding but I had just decided that I might as well go to bed when the phone rang.

"Peter, Jim Akers here."

Jim was the aeronautical correspondent of the Financial Times. It was thanks to him that the FT had commissioned me to write the article on the 798 some months earlier. "Have you heard the news?"

"Yes, Jim. I was actually listening to the aircraft talking to RWA Ops as it was coming in. I couldn't believe what I was hearing on the hijacking."

"What do you mean? You actually heard the aircraft talking to the ground?" Jim was a newsman, through and through. I think he felt he had struck oil. "What happened?"

"Well, apparently the hijackers had asked for some prisoners that they wanted to be released and taken to the airport, ready to be loaded on to the aircraft. It was then going to take off again for Karachi."

"How do you know all this?"

"I just heard the aircraft requesting confirmation that the prisoners would be available and that the refuelling arrangements were in hand."

"Was it confirmed?"

"The refuelling was. The Captain said that he had been told to remind Ops that the aircraft would be blown up if there was any delay to the carrying out of the hijackers instructions."

"Peter, perhaps that was what actually happened? No wonder the aircraft crashed." Jim paused. "It was Cat 3B weather wasn't it? That must have made matters worse."

"Yes it was. The ILS was out of service and the aircraft was making a GESS approach."

"What do you make of it all?"

"I don't know. We shall have to wait until AAIB investigates the matter. The real issue at the moment, Jim, is what is happening at the crash site. Were there any survivors? How many people were killed?"

"You are quite right." Jim sounded slightly chastened. I think he realised that his curiosity for the cause of the accident had got ahead of the mayhem and carnage that must exist on the A30. "I understand that there are some survivors, Peter."

We didn't carry on much longer. I guessed that Jim, having listened to me, wanted to update his article on the accident in the FT. I couldn't resist listening to Radio 5 again. It sounded as if the soccer had been kicked into touch and the accident had taken over.

The announcer said that the situation was completely confused because apparently some terrorists had somehow got on board the aircraft with weapons and overpowered the crew. The story was that the hijackers had been planning to get the Government to release some prisoners, believed to be al-Qaeda, and then to take-off again for somewhere in the Middle East. They were going to blow the aircraft up on the ramp at Heathrow if their orders were not obeyed. Consequently, the police, army, and fire services had all been alerted, ready for the landing.

The point was made that the accident couldn't have happened at a worse time. The roads had been very busy as it was the Monday night at the end of the Christmas/New Year holidays and people had been returning to start work the following day. Making an approach to Heathrow, the aircraft had apparently dived into the ground before reaching the airport. The visibility had been reported as less than 30 metres. It had crashed on the road causing a lot of casualties to people travelling in cars, before sliding into a cargo shed just to the left of the approach lights; this had caused the whole front of the aircraft to concertina, but it wasn't clear whether there had been an explosion, either before or just after the impact. There were several hundred people in the aircraft, the exact number was still being investigated. A lot of the passengers had been killed though there was a significant number of survivors near the back of the upper cabin, who had either been thrown clear or had managed to scramble out of the wreckage. Nearly all the survivors had had to be taken to nearby hospitals. Work had already started in identifying the victims.

The news reader went on to say that it was probably the worst air disaster ever in the history of UK aviation, worse even than the accident to the Pan American 747 at Lockerbie many years earlier, though of course not to be compared with 9/11 in New York.

The newscaster explained that because all the Heathrow rescue services had been on stand-by in the airport next to 27L runway, it had taken only a few minutes for the crash crews, fire engines and police to get to the crash, though they were hampered by the appalling visibility. The rescue teams had been working non-stop, assisted by the armed services who had been drafted in to help, but everything was complicated by the fog which was still very thick. Things were made even more difficult by the need for the security forces to cordon off the area and check for weapons and bombs. Even the survivors had to be security checked which made things harder for the ambulance crews and the hospitals. It was going to take a long time dealing with all the injured. The Army and the Air Accident Investigation Branch inspectors, AAIB, were already on the spot looking for the crash recorders and examining all the wreckage and they were getting specialist help from the security experts who had apparently appeared on the scene from nowhere.

I switched the radio off. It was well after midnight. I went to bed and went straight to sleep. It seemed only moments later when the phone rang,

19

waking me up before I was ready. I stretched out, rolled over and lifted the phone off its hook. Even after four years it seemed strange not to feel Diana's warmth on the other side of the bed. I sensed through the thick curtains that it was still very dark outside.

"Peter?" It was Mandy, her voice vibrant, urgent, catapulting me from deep sleep to extreme awareness. "There was a terrible accident last night. An aircraft landing at Heathrow crashed on the road outside the airport. I've just heard the news on the radio. The passengers included the Foreign Secretary and two or three of his staff. Apparently the aircraft had been hijacked in some way and all the emergency services at the airport had been alerted and were waiting for it to land. Did you hear about it last night on your way home?"

"What time is it? I've only just gone to sleep."

"It's alright for some! It's 6.30 already. I'm on the platform waiting for the train."

"Mandy. Yes, I did know about the accident. I was listening to the VHF in my car. But I didn't know about the Foreign Secretary." I told her about my journey home and the Jim Akers telephone call.

"Look I've got to dash. The train is coming. I'll call you later. Bye."

There was what might have been a perfunctory kiss and she was gone. I rolled over and switched on the radio, the announcer was just giving the headlines. There was to be a statement on the accident by the Prime Minister on radio and TV at 9 o'clock. Telephone numbers to call were given out so that worried families could find out if their relatives were on board, whether they were in hospital, whether their bodies had been found or if they were still missing. These same families might well be needed to help in identification so it was very important indeed that all people who were concerned rang in.

Listening to the news reader, it was clear that the Police, the British Airports Authority, the Fire Services and the local hospitals had all done a marvellous job dealing with the horrendous problems caused by the accident. The Police had set up an Accident Operations Room, conceived and planned several years previously by the Department of Health and Safety with the help of all the local authorities, the British Airports Authority and the rescue services and this Operations Room seemed to have been extremely effective. Less immediately obvious to the uninitiated was the speed with which Air Traffic Control had reacted. The announcer said that Heathrow was now open again using the northern runway but that the weather was still very foggy.

The rest of the news followed and then the producer went back to the accident story. In the middle of the night one reporter had managed to find a survivor who was not injured badly, though the reporter remarked that the man had a bandage on the side of his head. The man sounded dazed and it seemed to me that he should have been in hospital, not talking to the reporter. I always felt that no-one should be expected to give an interview in such a situation but the reporter clearly had no such reservations. I wanted to switch the radio off but the survivor's description was so graphic and heart rending that I found myself listening.

"The flight from Sydney was fine." The man sounded very hoarse. He coughed. "I was sitting in a window seat in the middle of Upper Class. We could see the ground most of the way and then the stars as it got dark."

He stopped again and we could hear him spluttering. Why he carried on I could not imagine. Perhaps talking about what had happened helped him.

"I heard a strange noise up front like a muffled explosion of some sort and then about four foreign looking people got up and went through the curtain. Almost immediately afterwards the Captain announced that the aircraft had been hijacked and that no-one was to move from their seats. He said that we were going to land at Heathrow and the situation would then be sorted out."

There was a pause and the man started coughing uncontrollably for a few seconds. Surely this interview would be cut short. I found it hard to be believe that, apart from anything else, the security people would allow the interview to be heard. The survivor tried again.

"We were told to remain in our seats, I could see everyone around was as worried as I was. Two swarthy looking men with beards appeared at the front of the two aisles carrying what looked like pistols of some sort. Then cabin staff appeared from the galley behind us and tried to quieten some of the passengers who were panicking."

Another long pause and sirens could be heard in the background. The man seemed to pull himself together.

"No more announcements were made. The cabin staff made certain we were strapped in for landing. Everything was very smooth. As we descended, I heard the landing gear go down and then we suddenly went into cloud. Then, just before the crash I saw some lights, caught a glimpse of a house incredibly close, then a car and an enormous bang."

We could almost hear him shudder. He coughed again, this time very loudly. I was certain that must be the end but somehow the man struggled on.

"The next thing I knew I was lying on the side of the road. I could hear cries for help and frightened shrieks of pain from the wounded and the ringing of mobile phones. There were flames coming from what I took to be the wreckage. It was like a nightmare. Everything was in fog. I could smell burning and there was ice on the ground. I felt numb, lying on some grass. I thought I was in Hell already."

We could hear him bursting into tears. Apparently someone had helped him into a nearby house immediately after the crash. The interviewer started to say something but I had had my fill and I switched off the radio. Nobody should be subjected to that sort of interview.

I knew from the experience of listening to the media dealing with other disasters that there would now be ill-considered discussions purporting to give an in-depth analysis of the situation. The producers would have been scouring the country for expert witnesses and the interviewers would then be bullying the eager interviewees, asking what they thought had happened. Sure enough, when I turned the radio on again there were experts on hijackings saying that this was the first time for many years that terrorists had hijacked an aircraft instead of blowing it up or destroying something on the ground like the Twin Towers in New York. The experts were not clear why the hijackers wanted the aircraft to go to the Middle East, but guessed that they wanted to take the released prisoners to some safe country. They gave their opinion that this was a strange thing to want to do, since even militant Muslim countries would not be keen to accept the aircraft with the hijackers and al-Qaeda people on board. However, if the airplane still had passengers they might be forced to let it land though it was most unlikely that they would free the hijackers and the terrorists they had rescued.

A security expert was then interviewed and he made the point that even if the aircraft hadn't crashed it would never have been allowed to take-off again from Heathrow. Another security consultant speculated on how the hijackers had got on board with weapons, and wondered whether the weapons and bombs had been loaded by a member of the ground staff at Sydney. The interviewer asked whether it was dangerous to use a gun in an aircraft and he was told that the weapons were probably the very special small calibre pistols now used by aerial hijackers which could kill but, because the bullets were very soft, the range after coming out of the body was very small, thus making it unlikely that the bullet would affect the aircraft significantly or go through the aircraft skin. It amazed me that that sort of information was allowed to be broadcast for everybody to hear.

One thing was obvious in all the confusion. It was clearly going to be necessary to find out exactly how the hijacking caused the crash. Of course there might be some other explanation but the coincidence of a freak accident whilst a hijacking was taking place seemed unlikely. Since almost all the leading players, flight crew, hijackers, and witnesses would almost certainly be dead, it was going to be incredibly difficult to establish what had really happened. This accident sounded dreadfully like the one that those of us in the business had hoped would never occur, but finding out the how and the why it had happened was going to be even more difficult than anyone might imagine. Luckily, the emergency services had planned for the worst case scenario and their work had to be done regardless of the reason for the crash. For them, the cause of the accident was irrelevant.

I forced myself to stop listening to the radio and to start getting up. The windows were covered with condensation in spite of the double glazing. I cleaned a patch of moisture away and could just see the house next door where there were some lights in the windows where John and Julia Marchant were clearly already dealing with the new day. It would not be long before John got the car out and headed for Reading closely followed by Julia taking their two children to school. I did not envy them driving in the fog. At least there was some benefit for me working from home, even it was very lonely at times.

I got dressed into some casual trousers and a pullover, and wandered downstairs. In the kitchen the coffee machine was full of grounds. Tuesday was one of Dora's days and hopefully my invaluable but rather loquacious help would deal with all the mess from the week-end. Ideally, I would have liked her to come more than twice a week but I could not afford the money to pay her nor the time she seemed to need to discuss her family problems. I made myself a drink and the smell of fresh coffee was reassuring of normality. I wandered into the hall to get the paper.

The Times was by the front door and I picked it up. 'HIJACKED AIRCRAFT CRASHES' was right across the front page and 'DISASTER IN FREEZING FOG' headed another column discussing the weather. It seemed to be a fact of life that every time an aircraft crashed, the eyewitnesses said the aircraft had exploded or was on fire just before it hit the ground. Perhaps in this case for once it might even be true. Just below the headline the page was filled with a foggy picture of the burning aircraft in the middle of some just discernible cars and people, possibly survivors, wandering near the wreckage. I scanned the paper rapidly. Clearly, at the time the newspaper was going to press there was still so much confusion that the reporters had been unable to get a full understanding of the situation but it was expected that at least three hundred people had been killed. The papers had managed to discover somehow before they went to press that the Foreign Secretary had been a passenger and that the airport had been on security alert just prior to landing. The survivors of the crash had been rushed to hospitals by ambulance but the paper said that it was still proving extremely difficult in view of the very thick fog. It was obvious that the reporters had not been able to get particularly close to the wreckage themselves due to the weather and the security cordon which the army had managed to get round the crash site fairly soon after the accident. Because of the fog, helicopters could not be used to rescue the wounded. It must have been a horrendous situation though the police seemed to have had excellent liaison with the security forces. I shuddered involuntarily. What a terrible mess and how appalling for the all the dependents and the survivors.

I went into the front room and turned the television on. The Chairman of the Civil Aviation Authority was being questioned and doing a very good job of standing up to the grilling he was receiving. I always admired the way politicians and public figures kept their temper when being subjected to probing from interviewers who, it seemed to me, were as much interested in making a name for themselves as for informing the public. Presumably in the current situation the Civil Aviation Authority Chairman could not refuse to be interviewed and, as usual, he did a first class job. He pointed out that it was going to be very difficult to establish the cause of the accident since it was known that there must have been at least one hijacker on the flight deck giving instructions to the captain during the approach and landing. He added that the Secretary of State for Transport was of course responsible for investigating the cause of aircraft accidents in this country and no doubt he would be making a statement.

The interviewer asked if the 798 was really safe and the Chairman patiently explained that questions like that had no meaning since safety in any field, be it aviation, nuclear power stations, food production or indeed in any industry, was a matter of acceptable risks and probabilities. The only certainty in life was that we were all going to die. With regard to the 798, the aircraft had a valid UK certificate of airworthiness but it had actually been certificated by the relatively new European Aviation Safety Agency, EASA, based in Cologne. In the unlikely event that safety questions of the 798 needed to be addressed, then questions would have to be addressed to the EASA since aircraft certification was no longer the direct responsibility of the UK Government and the Civil Aviation Authority; European law made the ratification of the EASA type certificate mandatory.

The newscaster gave up trying to get incautious statements from the CAA Chairman. Because of the fog the TV reporters had been unable to get any eyewitnesses. Luckily, the survivor from the aircraft who had given the interview in the middle of the night had seemingly gone to hospital or to bed. They did manage to find one or two people who had arrived on the spot just after the accident. Their stories were horrific and I was not sure that getting these people to tell their experiences on TV actually helped in any way but merely encouraged the ghouls. Luckily when the security forces had cordoned off the whole area, the media producers and their reporters had been prevented from raking over the details. Of course it was understandable that this crash, as with other crashes in the past, was a subject of great interest but in reality nothing was ever gained by trying to guess instantaneously the cause of an accident before it had been thoroughly investigated. In this case, with the Foreign Secretary on board and with terrorists as well, it was clear that the actual sequence of events that led to the crash was going to be even more complicated than usual to determine, since there seemed little chance of there being a survivor who would know what had happened. Because air transportation was so safe, it was only occurrences like hijacking or an unlikely combination of circumstances which resulted in aircraft accidents and it usually required great detective work by the accident inspection experts to discover what had actually gone wrong.

I turned the television off and went into the office, still thinking of the evening before. Mandy, my current girl friend, had produced a splendid meal and we did not hurry. I had planned to leave much earlier but it was after seven by the time I had got away. For the first time I realised that Mandy must be playing a much larger part in my life than I had previously thought, or indeed cared to admit even to myself. We had met a few months earlier travelling across the Atlantic to Seattle when I was visiting Boeing and the Independant Transport Aircraft Company and she was going to Portland to deal with some business on behalf of one of her clients. We were gradually getting to know one another but were being very cautious in developing a relationship as we had each been hurt by affairs in the past. I think we both felt there was a possibility that our increasingly frequent meetings could develop into something more enduring. We had not yet consummated our relationship but clearly the time could not be too far away.

Mandy was a hard working partner in a small firm of solicitors in the City but she lived in Bournemouth because she liked sailing in her spare time. She travelled up to London every day by train leaving at 6.30 and was lucky if she got home before 8 o'clock in the evening.

Mandy was not dissimilar physically from Diana, but then in my experience men often chose a second partner rather like their first and I was no exception. She was quite tall, maybe 5 ft. 7 in. but still comfortably below my 5 ft. 11 in. She was very trim, not running to fat and her breasts jutted out provocatively, the way I liked in any satisfactory sexual relationship, though my alter ego was always reminding me that lasting relationships are in the mind, not in the body. Mandy's hair was light but not blonde. She kept her hair short and businesslike, as one would expect in a solicitor's office. She wore glasses most of the time since she was long sighted, but I noticed that she always wore contact lenses when we were going out.

It was now 9 o'clock and I switched on the television set on the shelf over my computer. The Prime Minister came on and briefly repeated the details of the accident. He confirmed that the loss of life was indeed the worst in British aviation history, worse even than Lockerbie.

"We are still investigating the exact circumstances of the flight but we know that some people who we have reason to believe were terrorists, attacked and killed two passengers in the upper sleeping compartment of the 798. The Foreign Secretary was on board returning to London and his body has now been identified. The hijackers seem to have entered the flight deck area together with the Foreign Secretary, held the crews captive, and then Captain Hodgson was ordered to land normally at Heathrow. After landing, the aircraft was to be refuelled and the terrorists demanded that the six named al-Qaeda terrorists we captured two months ago were to be released from prison and taken out to the aircraft. The terrorists then intended that the aircraft would take-off again for somewhere in the Middle East where all the passengers would then be released. As a result of this message which was sent by satellite to Royal World Airlines flight operations, all the security and crash services were either standing by for the aircraft to land or on their way through the fog.

"As you all know the aircraft crashed on the A30 and then caught fire. There may have been an explosion either just before or just after the impact and this is being investigated. I have declared a state of emergency in view of the security aspects of this crash and because the aircraft has crashed on the A30, very close to houses and vital airline operational buildings at Hatton Cross. I hope to be able to relax the emergency very quickly once the fog has cleared and the police and security forces have the situation completely under control.

"As usual the Air Accident Investigation Branch will carry out its normal function to discover the real cause of the accident, helped in this special case by the security investigators. I need the co-operation of all who are involved to help the families who have been so tragically, unexpectedly and suddenly bereaved. There is no need for anyone except the people concerned with the accident to go to the accident site and I have asked the police to use their emergency powers to remove summarily any people near the accident who have gone just to look or to take pictures or videos. I must remind you that many of the victims came from overseas and I have sent a personal message of sympathy to the Australian Prime Minister since I understand there were many Australian nationals on board. I want you all to co-operate with the police and the authorities to get the situation back to normal.

"If anyone has any special information about the accident which might help the investigation of its cause, would he or she please call this special number at 10 Downing Street, since I am personally committed to finding out exactly what happened and to ensuring that nothing like it can ever occur again."

The telephone number appeared at the bottom of the screen. I sympathised with the Prime Minister. This accident was going to make his normal heavy workload even heavier. It would be a testing time for him and inevitably he would be judged by how he responded to the crisis. I remembered in the USA, when the Twin Towers were destroyed, how President Bush went up in people's estimation as he gave voice to the pent-up feelings of the population and took all the necessary action to discover what had caused the explosion. In all probability this accident would have been caused by interference in some way from the hijackers with the flight crew during the landing in fog. Hopefully, the crash recorders would yield some vital clues.

Of course, it was all very well for the Prime Minister to be determined that a similar accident would never happen again but it would depend on the accident investigators finding out what had actually occurred. Aircraft always have accidents however hard the manufacturers, certification authorities and regulators try to prevent them and planes were liable to have hijackers and bombs on board, however rigorous the inspection.

Aircraft were always at their greatest risk from accidents when they were landing and having hijackers on the flight deck was bound to be a recipe for disaster. Everything had to be right for a safe landing and, however hard the regulating authorities tried, one could never allow completely for the unpredictability of the human pilot in the control loop. In this case, the weather conditions were clearly at the limit for a safe landing so the presence of hijackers would have made the situation that much harder for the crew. Thankfully, judging by the number of people reported killed, the Independant 798 had not been full since it could carry many more on inter-continental flights, much more in fact than the previous world's largest aircraft, the Airbus A380.

For me every aircraft accident was very important. When I had stopped flying two years previously and become a consultant to the airlines, I had decided to specialise in giving training courses on the modern airliner flight deck. It seemed to me that it was necessary to emphasise the need for the pilots to keep a critical awareness of the aircraft's control systems and not get lulled into a false sense of security by the superb flight deck displays and computers which had taken the place of the specialist navigators, flight engineers and radio operators. After the second World War it took five flight crew to take forty or fifty passengers across the Atlantic; now two pilots could take nearly a thousand people across the world much more efficiently and safely. However, the modern aircraft was incredibly complicated and the job could only be done by relying on computers, both to fly the aircraft efficiently and to manage the systems.

Most of the time nowadays pilots had very little physically to do actually flying the aircraft, after the computers had been loaded with the flight plan, but watch the aircraft being controlled automatically half way round the world along the planned flight path until it had landed and was rolling along the runway. The pilots' main task en route was getting the clearances that were required to enable the aircraft to follow the optimum flight path. The problem was that there were more and more aircraft flying the routes, not at identical speeds, and chasing the local air traffic centre for a new altitude or for a change in routing was a considerable task.

It was very difficult earning a living trying to persuade the airlines that their pilots needed to do more training than the minimum amount required from the aircraft manufacturer and the regulating authorities. I had to convince the airlines that I understood more about the aircraft systems and the way their crews reacted than they did and that spending money with me would improve the total airline performance. Safety was always a difficult thing to sell because achieving it was seen as a cost, spoiling the airlines' profits. To be fair, good airline management realised that it was vital to have a reputation for safety, since there was always plenty of airline competition to take the travellers elsewhere if there was a feeling that an airline was unsafe. The airlines knew that discounting the ticket prices would never make western world passengers travel in aircraft or with airlines that had an unsafe reputation. The problem for me was always that the flight training staff in the big airlines did not like having outsiders doing their work or telling them what to do. Still, I was managing to get some work from some of the large flag carriers.

The telephone rang. It was the Chief Pilot of Royal World Airlines, John Chester, on his direct line. Understandably, he did not waste any time in coming to the point. He wanted us to meet as soon as possible, but not in his office. He had to come into London to brief his Chairman and I suggested we met in the Royal Ocean Racing Club for a sandwich. He said that he would probably be able to get there sometime after one o'clock and rang off. Though I was very curious as to the reason why he wanted to talk to me, I decided not to add to his problems by wasting time asking questions.

I had got to know John well some years back when we were both members of the Technical Committee of the Guild of Air Pilots and Air Navigators, GAPAN, and also of the Society of Automotive Engineers S7 Flight Deck Committee. He had had to leave the committees when he was promoted within the airline but we kept in touch and I think it was largely because of him that his training staff gave me some work, particularly in specialist areas of navigation and in the difficult design task of managing the systems, that is trying to get the right relationship between the pilot and the computers which controlled the aircraft. We had both seen coming this very important human factor problem and we had both been nervous of very clever technical pilots who encouraged the aircraft designers to make too many fancy alternatives available to the line pilot. John and I belonged to the 'keep it simple' school of thought.

I tried to finish the proposal I was writing for American Airlines to provide training in Dallas to their senior training personnel but my mind kept returning to the accident and my conversation with John Chester. I could not stop trying to work out what had happened to cause the disaster. I switched on the television set again. The newscaster was interviewing the Chief Constable who was explaining about the emergency Accident Operations Room and the co-ordination required to deal with the fire brigades, the traffic handling, the army, the security people, the AAIB investigators, and the ambulances which were getting survivors to the hospitals and the dead to the mortuaries, all in the fog.

The interview was followed by a talk with the Chief Airport Fire Officer. He gave a very low key understated description of the devastation and carnage at the scene of the accident which somehow, because of its very restraint, was the more disturbing. The TV cameras had at last managed to get on to the airfield's southern perimeter road so that it was just possible to see the scene of the accident through the fog over the top of some buildings. The pictures were unbelievable. Wreckage of parts of aircraft could be seen everywhere, one of the engines was standing on end.

There were still a lot of fire engines and ambulances on the scene. The cameras zoomed in to show a body without a cover being carried away to the back of a nearby ambulance. It was a terrible sight and must have been immeasurably worse for those people actually there and for the anxious relatives and friends watching and waiting at home. I switched the set off and almost immediately the telephone rang again. Mandy had reached the office and, despite all her appointments, she had found time to call to hear my reactions.

"I've made it but quite a few haven't. Some managed to get in from the south west by taking wide detours. I think the fog is clearing slightly and it isn't freezing any more."

She sounded breathless. I was not too surprised about the number of people who had managed to get into work despite the problems. Life is about survival and people are always very resourceful in times of difficulty. Because the accident had taken place the previous evening a lot of drivers had been able to make contingency plans.

"However," she carried on, "I expect the time-table in the courts will be affected. Many of the judges will not have been able to make it unless they lived in town." She paused. "But Peter, what do you think happened?"

I could think of nothing useful to say. I knew nothing and hated speculating.

"It's too early to say yet. Almost anything might have happened with hijackers on board. They could have shot the pilot, they might have exploded a bomb, the pilots could have had their attention diverted and made a mistake. The problem is that the accident will almost certainly be due to the hijackers in some way if not completely, but it may not be straightforward, which is going to make finding the exact cause very difficult. Aircraft are so safe that accidents inevitably occur only when there is a most unlikely combination of circumstances. I may know a bit more later on as John Chester phoned and we are meeting at the RORC."

She latched on to that straightaway.

"Be careful when you talk to John. Don't offer advice unless he is going to be your client. If he called you then there must be something worrying him which he knows and you don't. Listen and learn all you can. Don't volunteer."

"I'll do my best."

As usual she was giving good advice, but she was not so emotionally involved as I was. She was in a competitive business with her own clients but she had the enormous advantage of the support of her partnership. I was a one-man band, struggling to make ends meet and she was concerned that I was not commercial enough. She felt that in my eagerness to help to find the reasons for the accident I would offer gratuitous advice and might spend a lot of time helping John and others without any reward. She knew, faced with the need to find out what had gone wrong, that I would find it very difficult not to enter into long discussions to solve the problem and I appreciated her concern. However, in the case of force majeure, the normal sequence for investigations was difficult to apply. Lawyers were trained to be commercial, however harrowing the circumstances, but Mandy knew I found this a difficult concept.

"I'll call you later when I get out of court though I expect in the circumstances they will defer the hearing."

I finished my proposal to American, made an airmail package for the post office and then went in to the kitchen. Dora was probably on the wrong side of fifty and had been married twice. She had had two children from her first husband, who had died from a heart attack, and they were now grown up and both working somewhere in London. Fred, her second husband, had left home fairly soon after they got married but not before helping to conceive Jenny. Dora was having to bring up Jenny on her own and was not able to get Fred to send her money regularly. She looked after her figure and had not let her appearance run to seed though things were clearly pretty difficult for her. She worked long hours as a domestic help to make ends meet. Inevitably, Dora immediately started asking me questions about the crash but I avoided saying anything, since I knew that anything I did say would be noted and quoted at the Fox and Hounds later in the day while Jenny was doing her homework. I pleaded ignorance.

It was quarter to eleven by now but I had a little time in hand so I went back into the dining room, switching the TV on again while looking for some technical papers I had on the 798. The announcer was giving an update on the crash. The crash recorder with all the flight information had been found but the cockpit voice recorder was still missing. RWA were bringing Australian relatives of the killed and injured to London as quickly as possible. Independant had managed to get some specialist crash investigation engineers on the regular RWA flight out of Seattle the previous night, the moment they had heard about the accident. They had also chartered a special flight to bring more engineers to London and the team was headed by Bob Parnell, President of the Independant Transport Aircraft Company.

Like all aircraft companies, Independant had always responded immediately to the few incidents that had occurred previously to their aircraft. This particular accident would be especially important for them, even though it was bound to be due in some way to the hijacking. The aircraft type was comparatively new and did not have the millions of flying hours behind it like Boeing airplanes, the 737s, the 757s, the 767s, the 747s, the 777s and the 787s. RWA was one of Independant's biggest customers and only had a few Boeing and Airbus aircraft. Airbus were trying very hard to persuade RWA to support Europe and buy their latest A380 from Toulouse. Independant, and of course Boeing, were watching the situation closely and trying to match the Airbus salesmen. The cause of the accident had to be found straightaway to prevent Airbus or Boeing taking advantage of Royal World Airway's bad luck. No wonder Parnell was coming over to talk to the Chairman and Managing Director of the airline.

I turned the TV off and found the papers which Independant had given me when I was writing my article on the 798. There was a magnificent data dump of material weighing about 10 lb. which, splendid though it was, unfortunately made it very difficult to find anything. Realising the problem, Independant had thoughtfully also provided me with a summary book. The 798 was fairly conventional in design though using a lot of carbon fibre in the structure. The only new development on the flying side was that the electrical cables connecting the flight control computers to the control surfaces had been replaced with fibre optic cables, but this technology was now well established on military aircraft. It had the great advantage of reducing the effect of the computers, telephones and radios that some passengers brought on board the aircraft and used illicitly, despite the warnings of the flight crew, determined apparently to see if they could make their flights kamikaze missions. The design and inter-linking of the computers, called the system architecture, made sure that no conceivable electrical failure would result in loss of control. I could see nothing unusual in the 798 which might give cause for any concern. I devoutly hoped that the accident had been due to the hijacking and it clearly was the most likely cause. I guessed that that would be the prayer of the whole of the aerospace and airline industry.

I put the papers in my brief case with a writing pad and went up to the bedroom to change into a standard grey suit, white shirt, blue tie and black shoes. Formality was essential to enable an efficient interchange of information to take place without getting side-tracked into other matters. Soft shoes, slacks and a polo necked pullover might keep the wearer warm and comfortable but I always felt that such informal dress did not create the right atmosphere for important exchanges of information. Everybody had to have a uniform to inspire confidence and to enable work to be done as quickly as possible. It seemed to me that offices that had relaxed the rules, certainly when dealing with other organisations, regretted it later.

The phone rang again.

"Peter, it's Carol Trentham. Remember?" I remembered alright. She came straight to the point. She hadn't changed in that at least during the years since we had last met.

"I'm worried stiff. Richard hasn't called me. Can you find out if he was on the plane?"

For a moment I was speechless.

"Peter, are you there?"

"Yes, Carol. I can hear you. Tell me what has Richard been doing?" I first knew Richard Trentham when we were both junior first officers on Britannia Airways. He had had the opportunity to join Cathay Pacific based in London flying the Airbus A330 and he had leapt at the chance. We had not seen each other for some years though he was also a member of GAPAN.

"He's been flying for ten days operating between Hong Kong and Sydney and he told me he was hoping to find a way of dead heading back to London for some leave. He should have left yesterday. I'm so frightened, Peter. I fear the worst. I'm sure he's dead. I took the children to school in Amersham this morning without saying anything. What am I to do?"

"Have you called Cathay in London?"

"Yes I did. I called flight operations the moment I heard the news at seven this morning. They're trying to find out but they have not called me back. Can you call Royal World Airlines to find out for me? I must know."

I hesitated again trying to make up my mind what to do for the best. I had known Carol long before I met Richard.

"Look, by chance I am just going in to London to meet John Chester of Royal World Airlines." I wasn't sure if she would know that John was Director of Flight Operations. "I'll have a word with him and call you from London. Will you be at home?"

"Yes. I'll be there until about three when I have to collect the kids. Forgive me for calling you but I know I can rely on you to help." She rang off.

I felt appalled. The accident was bad enough but suddenly to find I was deeply involved was devastating. I had not seen Carol for some time but some relationships can never be forgotten. I knew in my heart of hearts that Richard was dead, or seriously injured at the very least. He would have called Carol the moment he had heard about the accident if he had still been in Sydney. What a terrible mess.

I looked at my watch. I was going to miss my train unless I got a move on. It was no use taking the car as I might not be able to find somewhere to park. I collected my brief case, put on my overcoat and gloves, said good bye to Dora and almost ran to the station. The train was on time in spite of the fog and I only just caught it. It was not full and I was able to do some more thinking about the 798 as the train travelled to Waterloo. I caught the Bakerloo line to Piccadilly Circus and then walked along Piccadilly in the grey mist until I reached Green Park. Walking was one of my favourite activities in order to keep reasonably fit and I enjoyed looking at the shops and the people. The park had the feel and smell of winter with the dead leaves lying on the ground as I went down the tarmac walk and then turned into the tunnel which led to the top end of St. James Place and the RORC. I entered the key code, pushed the door open and went upstairs.

John was not due for another twenty minutes and he could well be late. I ordered a tomato juice, picked up the Financial Times and sat down in the corner. The Club was not very full and nowadays I did not know many people there. I had joined in my youth when I was at Cambridge reading electrical engineering and spending all my spare time racing in the Channel. When I started flying for a living and got married, there did not seem time for racing and, anyway, Diana had never been very keen on sailing though we had sailed over to France once or twice. In fact, it was because I was not well known in the club that I thought it was a good place to meet up with John. I had avoided the Royal Air Force Club, full of mutual acquaintances who would have tried cross questioning John the moment they saw him.

Looking at the FT, I saw that Jim Akers had written a very good article about the accident and all the implications, perhaps not altogether surprising after our talk at midnight. Still, how it was possible to put together articles of such quality at such short notice always baffled me since I never wrote anything unless I had researched it very carefully. In his article Jim had suggested that the chances were that, because air transportation was so safe, the accident was almost certainly due to the hijacking.

Jim also touched on the legal issues. If the cause was due to some form of hijacking then the claimants might find it very difficult to get money from the airline, though they would try and prove negligence when the passengers were being loaded and, therefore, name the Sydney airport authorities as co-defendants in the case. If the cause was not due to hijacking, then of course it was the airlines and/or the aircraft manufacturer that would be sued in the event of an accident and, conceivably, the defendants could include the certificating authorities. However, one of the points made in this article amplified the point made in the interview I had watched with the Chairman of the Civil Aviation Authority. The 798 was one of the first large aircraft on the UK register which had been certificated, not by the Safety Regulation Group of the UK Civil Aviation Authority, SRG, but by the new European Aviation Safety Agency, and the Safety Regulation Group of the CAA had to carry out a mandatory ratification of the type certificate because of the European Commission rules. The effect of this change meant that passengers or their dependents could no longer make a case against their own Governments for failing to certificate an aircraft properly but would have to try to take legal action against the EASA, which might be difficult to do, or against the European Commission itself. Whether the cause of the accident was proved to be due to some form of terrorism or not, it looked like a legal minefield with rich pickings for the lawyers, but only time would show how things would work out.

Someone switched the television set on in the bar in time for the news headlines. The cockpit voice recorder still had not been found. The police were diverting all the traffic down the Causeway and along the A316 to the Clockhouse Lane roundabout. It was going to take a long, long time to collect all the wreckage from the A30 and the surrounding area. The death toll had risen to 383; it was very high in spite of the relatively slow speed of the aircraft on the approach because of the impact with the cargo shed. It was still not known if there had been an explosion. There had been 530 passengers and crew on the aircraft, mostly UK nationals but, as the Prime Minister had indicated, there were quite a lot of Australians. It was not known exactly how many people had been killed on the ground by the aircraft but it looked like somewhere between thirty and forty. The whole thing seemed unbelievable. It was indeed the nightmare accident that we had all feared, if for a different reason. Aircraft travel was now incredibly safe but, when an accident did happen to a large, long range aircraft, a lot of people got killed.

John arrived looking his normal distinguished self. Immaculately dressed, no-one would have guessed he had been up most of the night. How he managed it I didn't know. John was just over 6ft with very dark wavy hair which somehow had escaped any dilution with grey, notwithstanding he was on the wrong side of fifty. It occurred to me that he must be using some hair colouriser, but men I noticed never discussed these matters. I had decided the best thing to do was to ignore the suggestion of a sandwich and to take him straight into the dining room where I had booked a table at the far end, out of the way. John, not surprisingly, looked very serious and I decided to let him start the ball rolling. He did not want a drink and we both ordered soup and the grilled plaice. There was a couple fairly close to us, luckily seemingly more interested in themselves than in anything else. There was also a crew of four near the door way out of earshot.

"The exact cause is a complete mystery, Peter, but it's almost certainly due to the hijacking by terrorists." he started. "However, I wanted to talk to you because I am worried that the accident might be due to the pilots having done the wrong thing for some reason, maybe connected with the hijacking or maybe not. You're giving lectures to our training courses so you're probably as knowledgeable as anybody on the flight deck/crew interface. Harry Hodgson was in charge and he was one of the most experienced Captains."

I gulped. No wonder I thought I recognised the voice. We both knew Harry socially as well as professionally since, as I had guessed, he too was a member of GAPAN. He paused as the waiter, a new one I did not recognise, brought the soup over. John took a roll and buttered it but he did not really notice what he was doing. He was reviewing the whole situation and describing it to me with great precision. I listened carefully but did not comment.

"Nothing unusual had happened on the early part of the flight according to our flight operation department's log except that the Captain's Navigation Display failed. There had been the normal position reports from the crew, using the INMARSAT communication satellites, which backed up the automatic satellite position reports that the air traffic centre at Swanwick had sent to us as they got them. Harry flew the aircraft for the first six hours and then he went to one of the two pilot's sleeping cabins in the flight deck area and in front of the VIP area. His first officer Charles Tumbrill went into the other cabin an hour later. The other crew, Dick Tremlett and Frank Mercer, took over and flew across Asia and Harry then went back on the flight deck.

"Thank God Peter that we took your advice on making the crew enter their identification numbers and passwords into the Flight Management System before the 30 minute position report goes out. The FMS now enables us to track what is going on during these long flights. By the way, the aircraft had the latest type of cockpit voice recorder, so there should be a record of the last two hours of the flight when they find the recorder instead of the earlier thirty minutes of recording on older cockpit voice recorders.

"Charles came onto the flight deck an hour later. The weather en-route was reported to be good though they had been flying into a stronger headwind than had been forecast. They did not have as much fuel as expected when they flew over Warsaw but our operations department released them to go on to Frankfurt. The weather in London was Category 3B, indeterminate cloud base, freezing fog and a visibility of 20 metres. About one hour fifty minutes before landing Harry reported that they had been hijacked. He was being told to land at Heathrow as planned and then the aircraft was to be refuelled immediately so that they could fly on to somewhere in the Middle East. Meanwhile the Government were to collect the six al-Qaeda prisoners they had captured recently and take them to the aircraft. We did not know where the aircraft was supposed to be going and so we calculated the fuel to Karachi. Once the prisoners were on board the aircraft, it would depart straightaway. If the authorities tried to prevent the aircraft taking off then the terrorists said that it would be blown up on the ground. About the same time as Harry was talking to our operations, Eurocontrol advised London Approach that the aircraft was transmitting the emergency hijack code.

"Our operations then rechecked the fuel on board at Frankfurt and cleared the aircraft all the way to London. They should have had about 70 minutes fuel left as they started their final approach on 27L, just within limits for diversion to Manchester where the weather was good."

The waiter took our soup dishes away. I decided to keep my questions back so as not to disturb the flow.

"Charles made a routine report to Operations and then went back to talk to Air Traffic. About fifteen minutes before landing Harry said that he was being told to check that refuelling was available, that the prisoners were at the airport and that a flight plan was being prepared for Karachi. I had arrived on the scene by then and I told our dispatcher to confirm that all was ready, though Air Traffic would be able to advise on the whereabouts of the prisoners to be uploaded. There was no point in telling him what was really planned and in any event we didn't really know in detail, since the police were giving instructions to the British Airport

Authorities on where the aircraft was to be parked. Harry said that he would call after landing and the next thing our Operations knew was a report from Air Traffic that there had been an accident and Operations could get no reply from the aircraft, G-RWAGH by the way."

I knew from the time when I did some lectures to the first RWA crews that the Royal World Airlines 10 798s had been registered G-RWAGE to G-RWAGN so that G-RWAGH, Golf Hotel as it was colloquially called using the phonetic alphabet, was not particularly new. Clearly, there was going to have to be a lot of investigative work done correlating the communications between Air Traffic and the aircraft and between Royal World Airlines flight operations department and the aircraft.

"After Harry had said that they were going to land at Heathrow, were there any other communications about the hijacking?"

"No, none at all. From that point onwards during the approach the flight seemed to be routine. Harry presumably was concentrating on the landing, albeit in very difficult circumstances with hijackers there."

"Do we have any idea at all if anything unusual happened during the approach."

"Not really, Peter. The aircraft seems to have kept to the runway centre line but something must have happened to make it go below the glide slope. Our problem in RWA now is that all the communication tapes have been impounded by the AAIB and it is going to take some days before the whole flight path can be ascertained. But that's not going to tell us what happened inside the aircraft. Let's hope they find the cockpit voice recorder soon and that it is not damaged. We have to find out what happened."

"What sort of approach was he doing?"

"We don't know for sure, Peter, and Air Traffic won't talk to us but the Instrument Landing System, ILS, on 27L was out of service. Anyway it is no longer approved for Category 3 approaches so he would have had to select the Galileo European Satellite System to navigate down the approach, not really desirable in my opinion for Category 3 approaches, though it is certificated and seems to work well."

He paused expectantly, clearly waiting for me to ask some more questions. Mandy's advice was ringing in my ears and I decided not to probe too deeply.

"John, you don't need me to tell you that the problem here is going to be very different from most accidents because of the hijacking. Normally, if nothing obvious is found wrong then the simple thing is for everyone to blame the pilots but this time it could be the hijackers. Obviously pilots can make mistakes because they are careless or because they are misled by the information presented on the flight deck or, in this case perhaps, because they are being distracted from what they are doing. This investigation is going to be very difficult unless there is some stroke of luck to indicate the cause or it can be proved to be due to the hijackers. It could be a lawyer's dream."

"You're right of course," John said. He was hesitating and I wondered if he was hiding something from me. Since the cause must surely be due to the terrorist hijackers, why on earth had John called me to meet him? He must know something he hadn't told me. I felt sure that he had had second thoughts about what he was going to tell me. Perhaps his boss Jack Chiltern, Royal World Airlines Managing Director, had warned him not to discuss anything outside the airline. Perhaps there was a security angle to which I was not privy. The waiter brought our grilled plaice and the conversation stopped as we ate our meal.

"When did you eat last?" I decide to change the subject for a moment and noticed that John had started to eat as if he was very hungry.

"I had a sandwich at about midnight last night. We were just about to have a late dinner when the phone rang telling me about the phone hijack. Somehow I haven't had much time for anything else except coffee." He smiled, glad to get away for the moment from the worries that surrounded him. "I got three or four hours sleep in the office but the phone never stopped ringing. I had to speak to Marcia, Harry's wife, told her that there was still hope, but not much. She took it very bravely but it seems so hard." He swallowed for a moment and managed to compose himself again.

"Also I had to speak to the other families, all very difficult. The media have been terrible and we had to take our phones off the hook. The direct line to Operations came into its own. Mind you the MD wasn't too pleased when he wanted to talk to me and couldn't get through. I had to give him my mobile number." He grinned.

"The police at Hounslow with their accident centre are acting as the central reporting point and relaying the information on to us. We have a copy of the passenger/crew manifest which we are trying to keep up to date."

"Do you know which passengers were the hijackers?"

"No. We have no idea but the fact that they wanted to go somewhere in the Middle East suggests they were Muslim terrorists, almost certainly al-Qaeda. We believe that some of the hijackers were seated on the upper deck near the front, Upper Class. I've no idea if they were all killed but the security people will sort that out. Goodness knows how they got the weapons."

"You must have had a job getting here."

"Well yes. Luckily, my office on the North side of the airport is some way from the crash and so I managed to get out using the northern perimeter road, get home, see Jane, shower and change before coming into Town to see Jack. I hope I will be able to get back to the Office but it is going to be quite difficult. My driver is an expert on all the side roads so I suppose we will make it. How he got into work this morning I don't know. The A4 and M4 were completely blocked with traffic trying to get into London."

He came back to the present.

"Peter, I'm very worried about this whole thing, not just because of the accident but because I was one of the strongest advocates for the aircraft. If the accident is not due to the hijackers then I might be in some difficulty. You see, in order to keep the total package price to a minimum and the Independant bid competitive, I persuaded the Board that we should have almost the identical technical specification for the aircraft as United and American Airlines and this was not too popular. The Chairman seemed to want to be the launch customer for the latest larger version of the Airbus A380 on the grounds that we ought to be good Europeans and clearly the Department of Industry felt that this would be the correct thing to do. The MD, as always, wanted an easy life and would have gone along with the Chairman.

"I argued that all my pilots were used to the Independant flight decks and that the Airbus flight decks might be safe enough but were not as safe as the Independant aircraft. I really believe that Peter, but think how it would look if this was pilot error due to the Independant design philosophy. Francis supported me because the whole of the engineering maintenance system was based on the Independant concept. Changing to Airbus would have been very expensive and would have been confusing for the engineers. The operating economics of the two aircraft were very similar, so Jack and the Chairman couldn't very well overrule us. It was a very close run thing because Airbus were criticising the electronic architecture on the aircraft. At the final meeting a couple of the non-execs. started pushing the Airbus."

"Well John, the hijacking is bound to have had an influence on the crew when they were making the approach. I think you're worrying unnecessarily."

I didn't say anything more. Francis Thomas had been the RWA engineering director at the time the 798 decision was taken but he had retired two years ago. I knew that Roger Williams, John's deputy, would love to take over from John and the fact that Margaret, his wife, was Jack Chiltern's daughter would probably not spoil his chances. I suspected that Airbus had been trying to persuade Roger as hard as they could. Certainly he and his wife were always going to France on holiday and visiting Toulouse!

A Flight Too Far

I could visualise the Royal World Airlines Board meeting when the agenda item for the 798 decision came up for discussion. The Board would have already had all the supporting papers but there would have been a presentation by the finance director explaining the financial implications of purchasing a new aircraft. There would have been a summary paper highlighting the pros and cons of the A380 and the Independant 798 and the non-executive directors would probably have started probing. John and Francis would have explained why they favoured the 798. It was anyone's guess how hard Airbus had been influencing the various Board members but from what John said it was pretty clear that at least some of the non-executives had been talking to Airbus. Stories were legion on the way aircraft decisions were made by airlines all round the World.

In the Middle East, buyer's commission was an accepted way to proceed, decision makers expected to be rewarded for their choice. In the Western World such payments were frowned upon, but payments are not always made with money and it is unlikely that some form of reward had not been made for aircraft decisions in the past, both in the USA and the UK. The problem was that the prize for winning was so great, the cost of each aircraft so high and the value of the reward needed to sway the decision maker's choice was so very small. Of course with a large Board no single person ever made the decision, but that did not prevent the aircraft manufacturers from trying.

John took his telephone out of his pocket. He had it turned off but switched it on to get the messages. He listened for a few minutes as the waiter took our plates away. He made one or two notes and then he dialled a number. "Hello Jill? How's the office."

Jill Stanton at the other end, a devoted secretary of a certain age, started to give him a run down. "OK. I will be about an hour if the traffic permits." He turned his phone off.

"I just have time for a very quick coffee." he decided. We went into the bar and helped ourselves. There were a couple of seats free by the library. "Thanks for listening to me, Peter. I may have some work for you depending on how things are looking. We will just have to wait and see how things develop.

"By the way, you should know that we have just heard that one of the survivors miraculously was the off duty first officer, Frank Mercer. He's unconscious but let's hope he gets better and will be able to help."

I grabbed my moment. "Look John. I don't think you knew Richard Trentham. He's in the Guild and he works for Cathay. We were pilots together on Britannia. His wife has been on the phone to me. Richard was due home to-day dead heading from Sydney and he hasn't called. How can I find out if he was on the plane?"

Chapter 1

He looked really upset and passed me his card.

"Call my secretary, Jill Stanton. This is my direct line. She'll know what to do. I'm so sorry"

John collected his brief case and went downstairs to where his car was waiting. I watched the Jaguar drive down past the Stafford and turn left towards St. James. The problem for John, now that he was so senior in the organisation, was that he was under pressures which most of the workers didn't appreciate. I felt a bit mean adding to his burden by mentioning Richard. The pay at the top may be good but the hours are long and the responsibilities are enormous. John was good at delegating as much as he could, but he knew that in the end he was responsible. Of course some managers seemed to manage by delegating everything and never being responsible for anything. I always felt that Jack Chiltern came into that category, he was very adroit at making sure that the buck never stopped with him. In my experience, many chairmen and managing directors of large public companies, however competent they were, had qualities, in order to get to the top, which did not endear them to their fellow men.

After John left I helped myself to another coffee. I wasn't sure whether to ring Carol first or John's secretary. I had met Carol in my first year at Cambridge. We were both at Trinity but she was reading languages while I was doing my electronic engineering. I noticed her during dinners and started chatting her up. She was a very attractive redhead and I was smitten but it was clear to me that I was not her only admirer and she, very understandably, played the field. However, I discovered that she liked listening to classical music. I took her to several concerts and we had supper afterwards. Nothing developed, probably because we both shared rooms in college with other students.

She agreed to be my partner at the May Ball in June at the end of the year. About a week before the dance we were talking and she asked me what time the Ball finished. I said dawn. She looked me in the eye and said she would like to visit the new motel at Newmarket and why didn't we stay there for the night of the ball. Carol was my first real encounter with a girl. I had never made love before though I suspected she had. I could barely contain myself. We arrived at the hotel early. She had chosen well. The staff did not even look at the guests checking in.

We kissed slowly at first and then more seriously. I felt her hands undoing my belt, undoing my trousers and stroking me. She showed me how to excite her. We made love as we were getting undressed to change for the Ball, then used the shower together. It became touch and go whether we would get to the Ball but somehow we did. We danced all night in a dream and got back to the motel at 4 o'clock. We took all our clothes off and went to bed exhausted. The chamber maid knocked on the door at 10.30. I rang down and arranged a late check out. We took full advantage of the two hours extension and arrived back at College at three feeling rather tired. It occurred to me how marvellous it would be to be able to perform now as I did then.

In fact our relationship did not continue for much longer as I was committed to going sailing all Summer and, when we returned in the Autumn, I stupidly agreed to do some rowing for the college second eight which cramped my spare time. Carol was not too pleased and disappeared in a huff. I did not mind too much as I was having to work quite hard and there were other girls at college who were not so time consuming, even if they were not quite as exciting.

I came back to the present with a start. I decided I would try John's secretary and called her from my mobile when I got downstairs in the lobby. Jill told me she would look at her copy of the passenger manifest. I gave her Richard's name. She came straight back telling me that he had been on board the aircraft but that his body had not been found; he might be in one of the hospitals. She added that the bodies of Harry Hodgson, Charles Tumbrill and the other 798 Captain on the aircraft had been found. She sounded desolated.

I called Carol. The phone rang and rang but there was no answer. I tried Mandy.

"Where are you?" she said "I've been calling you and they told me in the RORC that you had left."

"I'm in the RORC, just about to go home."

"How did you get on with John? Did he ask your advice?"

I didn't feel like giving her a run down on the conversation just then. I needed to explain all the many nuances.

"Why don't you come round to my place to-night. It will save you a long journey and I need to talk. Have you got any spare clothes with you?"

"Oh yes. I always keep some in the office. OK. I'll be round about 6.30 to 7." She paused and then carried on. "I'm looking forward to seeing you." The phone went dead.

I collected my briefcase and caught a cab to Waterloo. The fog which had been thinning as I went into lunch had lifted into a mist and the visibility was about 800 yards. I felt a sense of urgency to get home and do some work but could not define what was driving me on. I was back by 3.30. Dora had left and the place looked spotless. I called Carol. A strange female voice answered. I gave her my name.

"Oh thank goodness you called. I'm Susan, a friend of Carol's. She has rushed off to Ealing General Hospital. Richard was on the plane and is very seriously injured. I've collected the children but I don't know what to do as we are all going away on a skiing holiday to-morrow morning."

Chapter 1

I seemed to remember that Carol's children were ten and eight years old.

"Susan, Carol is bound to call you. Doesn't she have any other friends locally? Try and get something organised for to-night and get them to school to-morrow." I gave her my number to call in emergency.

The news was still full of the accident. The dead had been split between Hounslow and Ealing mortuaries and the injured were spread amongst the local hospitals. The accident investigation authorities needed to collect every piece of wreckage and mark carefully where it had been found so that the flight trajectory of the aircraft could be worked out. It was going to take a long time since even the smallest piece of wreckage and electronics could be very important. They were getting a bit worried because the cockpit voice recorder had still not appeared. There was no way that the A30 would be open for a day or so, even though troops had been called in to help collect the wreckage. It was mentioned that the AAIB would be using a special hangar at Farnborough belonging to the Defence Establishment Research Agency, just for the wreckage.

Jill Stanton rang to give me the news I already knew. Richard was very ill at Ealing. I asked her how he was but she did not know. I rang the hospital. It took ages to get through. The lines must have been jammed with calls. I asked how Richard was. At first they would not tell me but I explained the situation briefly and the man told me that Mr. Trentham was critically ill. There was nothing more I could do but pray, something I did not normally do.

The phone rang.

"Peter." It was Carol sounding desperate. "He's alive but there is not much hope. I'm going to stay here over night. I've spoken to Susan who has agreed to look after the kids this evening and her eighteen year old daughter is going to sleep in the house to-night. They're off in the morning so I don't know what I am going to do. My mother lives in Edinburgh and is not very fit and Richard's parents are both dead. I will have to get back by end of school to-morrow whatever happens."

"Carol, call me the moment you have any news. Phone me to-morrow morning whatever happens and let me know how you are getting on." She rang off.

I did not know what I should do to help. I could bring her kids over here for a day or so but I had had no experience of children and anyway they really ought to be with their friends. Surely she must have other friends who could look after her children. Apart from our early infatuation, we had not kept in touch. I was shattered when Richard first introduced me to his new wife in the car park at Luton Airport but instinctively neither of us said anything at the time. Richard had met Carol when she was a management trainee with Britannia but she left when she had her first child. Carol and I had met several times while we were at Britannia but after Richard left we did not see each other again. I decided that Carol would have to sort it out to-morrow, by herself. She should get her mother down. I did not want to get involved again.

The afternoon mail had arrived. Mostly bills and computer companies selling hardware and software. There was an invitation to take part in a symposium on the modern airplane flight deck at the Royal Aeronautical Society, 4 Hamilton Place, which pleased me. It was six months off but it would need a lot of work.

On a shelf in the dining room I found my Jeppeson radio navigation approach charts. I took out the ILS and GESS approach plates for 27L at Heathrow and marked where the 798 crashed on the chart; it was actually right on the centre line for the runway but about 500 yards short of the correct touch down point. The instruments on the flight deck would have shown that the aircraft was on the runway centre line all the way down until it crashed. However, the instruments should also have shown that the aircraft was about 150 ft. below the correct glide slope. The weather of course was very poor but that should not have mattered. What really had happened? Surely whatever went wrong must have been due to the hijackers? It was difficult to think of any other explanation.

Though I could not stop thinking about the crash it was really not my business, but John Chester had drawn me into the action. He was keeping me on line as an insurance policy, possibly using me as a sounding board. Mandy told me not to listen. But Mandy did not know about Richard, or Carol for that matter. I realised that I needed to be careful how I introduced Carol into the conversation with Mandy. Least said soonest mended had always been one of my maxims. I was the world's worst dissembler.

CHAPTER 2

I must have dozed off in the sitting room. The TV was on, the local London news just finishing and there was a banging on the door. I recognised the imperious knocks. Mandy had arrived.

"You made good time. What train did you catch?"

"I didn't work overtime to-night, everything was so disorganised because of the crash. Clients didn't turn up or they wanted to leave early so, what's sauce for the geese is sauce for the goose. Anyway," she suddenly turned serious "I wanted to see you and hear how you're getting on."

"What was the weather like? Has it cleared any more?"

"The fog's still quite patchy but the Evening Standard says the fog will be gone completely by the morning."

I helped her off with her jacket and once again saw two of the reasons why I found her so attractive. She had a magnificent figure and knew it. She stretched knowing that I would immediately pull her towards me. I could feel myself pressing against her. Suddenly she broke away.

"Let's be sensible. We have a lot to talk about. What time did you book the table?"

She was right of course, about not rushing anything, as she was right about a lot of things, but from where I was standing it seemed a pity. On the other hand there was something to look forward to!

"Eight o'clock at Simon's. I ordered oysters, lobster and shrimps in that order!"

She grinned, took her bag upstairs to change and shouted down as she climbed up the stairs "To-day's only Tuesday and I have to work to-morrow. You'd better check that they've got salad and sole meuniere."

"You are not accompanying me looking like that, I hope," she added as she turned into the spare room. She always used the spare room and probably, whatever our future relationship might be, always would in this house. She felt that Diana was in my room there, looking on. I should have moved when it became obvious that Diana wasn't coming back but it hadn't mattered until Mandy came along.

Upstairs, I concluded that a shower might be a good thing in the circumstances, bearing in mind I could hear Mandy using her shower in the spare room. A slightly less formal suit than the one I had been wearing in London seemed also the order of the evening. After a quick shave I went downstairs to wait but not for long. Mandy would win first prize for a quick change act against all comers. Diana had always seemed to take an eternity to get ready. Perhaps Mandy's legal training and her ability to switch quickly from one subject to another was relevant. Anyway, whatever the cause the result was always very agreeable.

She entered the sitting room radiating a smell of some exotic French perfume. I could never tell which one was which since they all had the same effect on me. She was wearing a fawn cashmere dress, buttoned all the way down the front which showed her figure off to perfection. I hoped her clients were not affected the way I was. Of course they had to endure the severe spectacles which reassured me slightly. To-night however the spectacles were nowhere to be seen. Besides her other attributes, Mandy just had to hold the world record for inserting contact lenses.

"Where's my Kir?" she announced quickly as I approached her, almost as a defence mechanism. "It's the minimum reward for such a quick change."

"Good idea." I went into the dining room to get the drinks from the dresser and on my return she was watching the Channel 4 news. The accident seemed to be the only subject. Everything else in the world seemed to have been put on hold. A new Foreign Secretary had been appointed. The cockpit voice recorder had still not been found. The A30 might be opened on Thursday morning. Sadly, two more survivors had died.

There was one new piece of information from Sydney. A dead body, murdered by a bullet in the head, had been found in the Hyatt Regency car park. It was suspected that the body might be associated with the hijacking as the bullet was a special soft type found in the latest pistols that hijackers used. Significantly, there were no papers on the body to aid identification.

The news reader showed an interview that had taken place earlier with Bob Parnell. Bob started by sympathising with all the relatives and people affected by the accident. As befitted the President of the Independant Transport Aircraft Company his words somehow carried the conviction of someone who really cared, unlike a lot of politicians.

"At this stage clearly no-one knows for sure whether the cause of the aircraft loss was due to the hijacking. However, I can assure you all that my company will do everything in its power to help in discovering the true reason for this terrible accident and to ensure, as far as **we** can, that nothing like it ever occurs again."

The interviewer tried to get Bob to speculate on the cause of the accident but Bob would have none of it.

"Your AAIB is probably the best of its kind in the world and we must all help the AAIB to find out what happened. To try to second guess the cause would be very stupid. We must be certain that we find the right answer. Neither you the media, the travelling public, the world's airlines nor we, the world's airline manufacturing industry will be helped by rushing into the wrong answer."

The interviewer attempted to get Bob to agree that if Independant was to blame then they would meet all the claims.

"No useful purpose will be served by discussing the issues you are trying to raise. Claims are a matter for the courts, not for discussion on the television."

The interviewer kept on trying to speculate but was no match for Bob who had been trained in a hard school. Mandy switched the set off.

"If we get hooked on these interviews we will never get out."

"Did you notice the smooth way Bob tried to include Airbus and Boeing in the equation, suggesting that the cause may read across to all aircraft as well as to Independant."

"Tell me about it. These guys really earn their money. They don't run monopoly utilities. They know what true competition means. And look at the way he side stepped the issue of whether Independant would pay the claims. Which reminds me. We have a lot to talk about. Come on, Peter. Let's get the show on the road."

I had chosen Simon's because we would not need a car and could drink without worrying about whether we were over the limit. The downside was that we had to leave early to allow for a fifteen minute walk. We put on our coats, I set the alarm and locked the door.

As we walked along the street Mandy started to chat.

"I don't know whether it is significant for our relationship but our firm has been retained by General Electric."

"I shouldn't think so. They supply the engines of course, but it is most unlikely that the accident was due to the engines. Hijacking must be the obvious reason. If it was due to the engines then there would have been conversations between the crew and air traffic and the media would already know all about it. In my opinion, this accident is almost certainly going to be due to some effect of the hijacking."

"You should know. I hope you're right because somehow I feel you are going to get drawn into this thing. I don't want there to be a conflict of interest. It seems to me that my firm will have to be at the inquest for a start and who knows what will happen after that. There are bound to be claims because the old Warsaw Convention passenger insurance amount of $150,000 is still pitifully small. If there were any US citizens on board, the claims would start in the USA so Independant and GE had better be clean, let alone Royal World Airlines. This thing could rumble on for years."

Mandy must have been psychic about my involvement. She did not even know yet the detail of my conversation with John Chester and certainly not the Carol/Richard Trentham dimension. One thing for sure, I had no intention of mentioning Carol to Mandy unless I was forced to. Luckily we reached the restaurant and were shown to our table, conveniently to the side of a quite small dining room. Simon, the owner came up and asked what we wanted to drink.

"I'll stay with Kir," decided Mandy without hesitation, but I decided to have a Scotch since the Kir was a bit too sweet for my taste. Simon returned with the drinks, some water for my whisky and the menus. There was a complete silence as we studied the options. I looked round as I added the water to my Scotch. The room was quite full of diners which must have been good news for Simon.

"Have you decided?" I asked and shut my menu.

"Yes. I shall have crudités and grilled sole with sauté potatoes. What about you?"

"Salad niçoise for me and I'll join you with the sole." We put down the menus as a signal to the waiter.

"OK. Let's hear about John Chester."

I paused for a moment judging where to begin.

"John told me that the hijacking took place just under two hours before landing and Harry must have selected the hijacking code because Eurocontrol warned Heathrow fairly early on. The hijackers told Harry to organise the aircraft to be refuelled at Heathrow so that they could immediately fly to somewhere, unspecified, in the Middle East. In addition, they told him to send a message to the Government that the six recent al-Qaeda people who had been taken as prisoners must be brought to the aircraft and boarded as passengers."

"But the security forces would never have allowed the aircraft to take-off."

"Yes, the hijackers obviously realised that there would be a problem and so they told Harry to tell Heathrow that the aircraft would be blown up with everyone on board killed if they weren't allowed to go. From that point on the flight appeared to be normal, that is from a RWA flight operations viewpoint. The next thing that flight operations knew was that the aircraft had crashed. They've no idea of the cause and are waiting to hear from the AAIB after they have inspected the wreckage for evidence of a bomb explosion. Clearly the cockpit voice recorder is going to be absolutely crucial because, if there are no clues there, it really will be a mess. Let's hope they find it soon. I'm sure we are going to learn something from the crews' conversation.

"The weather was Category 3B, blind auto-pilot landing, so they would not have seen anything until they hit the ground. John is very worried because if the accident is not due to hijacking then he may be involved personally. He was one of the chief advocates for choosing the 798 over the new larger Airbus A380. He felt that the flight deck design was basically safer than the Airbus and he was supported by Francis Thomas who was Director of Engineering at the time. To cheer him up I told him that in the circumstances anything might have happened. The design of the flight deck would almost certainly be irrelevant.

"One problem for John is that at about the time of the Board Meeting, Airbus was saying that they did not like the electronic architecture of the 798. It was not in accordance with the latest specifications of the Airlines Avionic Committee."

"Who are they, for goodness sake? Does their opinion matter?"

"Well, the committee is very influential and is a collection of all the major airlines together with aircraft and avionic equipment manufacturers. There has to be a very good reason for a manufacturer to go against the committee's recommendations. Airbus felt the aircraft was designed to a standard that was less safe than the standard to which the Committee had agreed. Of course, at the time everybody dismissed the Airbus remarks in the immortal lines of Mandy Rice-Davies 'they would say that wouldn't they'. However, now there's an accident Airbus can say 'I told you so!'"

"But it's the hijacking."

"Maybe, but not proven yet. Remember some of the Board would have preferred the Airbus. If the accident is shown to be due to poor flight deck design, inadequate safety provisions or bad interfacing with the pilots then John's job could be on the line. Margaret Williams can't wait for Roger to take over from John."

"Surely all planes are designed to the same rules. Aren't they all equally safe?"

"You know it's not quite as simple as that. The rules are pretty well the same both in the USA and in Europe but manufacturers can meet the requirement in different ways and Airbus, Boeing and Independant are always looking for a competitive edge. On the flight deck, the new aircraft are full of digital computers and the pilots are really managers of all the different systems, electrical, navigation, auto-pilot, hydraulic, air conditioning and many more. The days of the pilot actually pulling and pushing the flying control surfaces himself are long since gone."

"But the flying controls are operated by the pilot when he, or she, is actually flying the aircraft?"

"Well yes, but the pilot is not actually strong enough to move the controls. The control surfaces are moved by motors signalled from the flight deck. The pilot can tell the controls what he wants by moving the control wheel but, depending on the actual flight conditions, the computers modify what the pilot selects so that there is not always a fixed relationship between the position of the pilot's controls and the position of the control surfaces. The computers know best."

Mandy pulled a disapproving face.

"What a horrible thought."

"Everything's fine when all the computers are working correctly, but it can be a very different story when things start to go wrong. Pilots are trained to deal with all the emergencies which the designers can think of, but I always get worried about how the flight crew will react to emergencies which no-one has thought of. The problem is that when things are going normally, the pilots don't have all that much to do actually flying the aircraft since all the routine functions are performed automatically. The pilots' biggest work load en route is probably dealing with Air Traffic, getting the cruising altitudes and routings that they want. From that point of view things are not getting any easier and the number of aircraft on the long haul routes is steadily increasing."

"You make it sound as if the pilots are just managers, not pilots at all."

"That's just my point, Mandy. They really don't have to do a lot of actually flying the aircraft and for well over 99% of the time the systems are working correctly.

"The difficulty is that the pilots have to be incredibly knowledgeable to understand all the systems, but the control of the systems is, most of the time, done automatically so they are not exercising their knowledge. For most of their working life the pilots are doing a very humdrum routine task and the real test only comes when things go wrong. These days, pilots can be trained on emergencies in flight simulators which are really superb and incredibly realistic but the problem here is that the pilots know that they are going to be given emergencies during the training flights so it is somewhat artificial and anyway, as I said, how do you practice for a real emergency that no-one has anticipated?"

I was getting too enthusiastic on my pet subject and speciality but luckily the waiter appeared with our starters and I was able to stop. Mandy however was clearly listening very intently, subconsciously filing the information away for her legal briefs. She started eating absent-mindedly and then stopped.

"Look. You're getting carried away. The aircraft was hijacked and crashed and you can't resist wondering if there was some abstruse fault in the aircraft design." She waved her finger at me. "I think it will be very interesting to see if the dead man found in the Hyatt in Sydney has any connection with the flight. It would have been better if the crew had been trained to deal with hijacking."

"They are all trained in dealing with hijackers. It's just another emergency they have to deal with."

She paused as she was about to carry on eating.

Chapter 2

"Tell me, what was John Chester getting at about preferring the Independant over the Airbus?"

"Well for a start, in the Airbus aircraft the engine throttles do not move when the engine power is being controlled automatically. You can have the throttles fully forward as you would when taking off but the engines can actually be at flight idle. The only way you can tell how much power is being applied is by looking at the engine instruments and possibly by the noise, but these days that's not much of a clue. Airbus made this change to save weight but both Independant and Boeing considered that the visual cues from the moving throttles actually helped the pilots control the aircraft more safely. So in the 798 the four throttle levers between the pilots are always in the correct position for the amount of power being applied and they move even when the speed or power is being controlled automatically. I think John liked that."

"But Peter, surely the government authorities who approve the aircraft must know if the Airbus system is alright and if it is, surely that's an end to the matter."

"You would think so, but some people think that the European regulating authorities, now the EASA, tend to support European industry."

"What does EASA stand for? You people talk all the time in acronyms. How anyone is meant to understand you I just don't know."

"I bet you are just the same in the legal profession. It's just not practicable to keep repeating whole collections of words to describe a single element, be it organisations like the European Aviation Safety Agency, the Federal Aviation Administration or a radio aid for navigation like the Global Positioning System which we call GPS for short. I know what, I'll give you a list of all the acronyms. Seriously though, you've made a very good point. You really will need my list if you get involved with this case.

"Anyway we digress. The point is that commercial competition between the manufacturers is intense, so the regulators really feel the pressure from their local industry. In the example I have given you, the French authorities approved the Airbus throttle arrangements and everybody else validated the approval, even the FAA. There have been one or two Airbus accidents which some people attribute to the throttles not moving, but all the accident investigators concerned have given the concept a clean bill of health. In my view the system seems to work and even if having the throttles moving does make for a safer aircraft, the Airbus system is safe enough and that's all that matters."

I paused. "Look let's hope all this discussion is quite irrelevant. The situation is that there were some hijackers on the flight deck. As Jim Akers wrote in the FT to-day, it would be incredible if some very unlikely rare fault occurred on the aircraft on the very day the aircraft was hijacked."

"You're almost certainly right. But it's going to be so difficult to sort it all out."

"Look if we carry on talking like this, my love, we will never finish the first course and our fish will be ruined. Let's have five minutes silence."

Mandy said nothing, ate the rest of her crudités as if it was grass though luckily she showed no signs of chewing the cud. She looked as if she wanted to ask me a load of questions but I kept on raising my finger to my lips which clearly did not please her. She finally ate the last mouthful and looked at her empty glass.

"I wish you weren't so rude. All I wanted was another Kir," she said primly. We both knew she was trying to needle me but for once I was sure of my ground and ignored her. I waved to the waiter who brought another Kir and I asked for another whisky to keep her company. The drinks arrived followed almost immediately by our soles, which clearly had been waiting for some time while we were talking. We started to eat but Mandy could not hold her questions back.

"Are there any other differences between the aircraft that I would notice if I went on to the flight deck?"

"Well yes. There is one big difference between the Boeing and Independant aircraft on the one hand and the Airbus fleet of aircraft on the other. The pilot on the Airbus uses one hand on a small 'side stick controller' to fly the aircraft while the pilot on the 798 has a conventional two handed control wheel. The point here is that all the latest aircraft including the 798 use either electrical or fibre optic cables, instead of steel cables, between the flight deck controls and the control surfaces, so the pilots' control forces can be very light indeed. As I said, the controls surfaces are actually moved by large motors situated at the surfaces themselves and so there is no need for a conventional and heavy control column. On an Airbus the pilot with a side stick has an unrestricted view of the instruments and navigation displays."

"Well if the side stick controller is so good why won't Boeing and Independant use it?"

"Good question. In my opinion for three reasons. Firstly, they are very conservative and the side stick controller is a relatively new concept which in their opinion has not been validated. Secondly, Airbus thought of it first and the others don't like being 'me too's'.

"The third point is that with a side stick controller the pilot not flying the aircraft has no idea where the other pilot has put his controller since the two controllers are not tied together mechanically. In other words he can't be certain what the operating pilot is trying to do. On the 798 the two wheels move together all the time so the 'safety pilot' is 'in the loop' which is very important in the opinion of the protagonists of the Boeing/Independant solution."

"But what happens in an emergency? Can you have an emergency in the flying controls?"

"Bingo. You have asked the $64,000 question. Airbus have put an enormous amount of work into ensuring that if anything goes wrong with the pilot flying on one side of the aircraft, the other pilot can take over. It is all done by computer logic. The regulating authorities including the FAA are convinced that the Airbus solution is safe but the US aircraft manufacturers and some airlines don't like or trust the idea. They believe in the conservative approach when dealing with safety issues."

As usual I could not help being impressed by Mandy's grasp of any subject she put her mind to. She was a historian for her first degree but she always grasped the key points straightaway, however technical the subject.

"As I said, Airbus was very concerned about the 798 avionic design. However, neither the FAA nor the EASA were convinced by the Airbus arguments and agreed to certificate the aircraft. Only time will tell if they should have done."

By mutual agreement after we finished our fish, we decided to have coffee back at the house. I called for the bill, helped Mandy on with her coat and we walked thoughtfully and slowly back home.

"Peter, you've told me why John is worried. Did you learn anything else?"

"Yes, two things. Firstly, the off duty first officer is alive and in hospital, unconscious. Let's hope he will be able to shed some light on the situation. The other thing is that I'm sure John didn't tell me everything. My guess is that he was going to give me a complete run down but, after talking to Jack Chiltern, he decided not to confide in me. Perhaps there is some security implication. I suppose I'll find out eventually what it is he's holding back."

We arrived home and as usual I went in first to cancel the alarm. I shouted to Mandy that it was safe for her to come in. I was always very careful not to set off the alarm inadvertently, ever since a friend of mine went into the living room before I had cancelled the alarm. I was connected to Central Station straightaway and they had rung the house to check, but the noise was so great we did not hear the phone in time before the answerphone took over. In no time flat the police were around and quite rightly gave me a hard time. This time there was no mistake and Mandy came in and went upstairs to her room. I went into the kitchen and started to make the coffee. My mobile phone rang.

"Peter, its Carol. Richard is alive but he has had to have his right leg amputated. I don't think he really knows what is going on. He is full of drugs." I could hear her choking at the other end of the line. I felt terrible. She had no real family to support her and with her mother not very strong, life was suddenly treating her very cruelly.

"Mother is managing to get here somehow, thank goodness and the children are staying with friends. I'm virtually living at the hospital. The people here are just wonderful. I barely know what I'm doing."

Mandy wandered into the kitchen to find out what was going on. She took over making the coffee but was clearly listening, certainly to my end of the conversation.

"Carol. Is there anything I can do to help?"

"Not really. I just had to talk to someone who understands. I'm not very optimistic. Anyway I'm not sure Richard could adjust to just having one leg and not being able to fly."

"Don't talk nonsense. Of course he'll be able to manage. Look at all the people who only have one leg and lead normal lives." I tried to reassure her but I don't think either of us was convinced.

"Carol, give me a call to-morrow when Richard has recovered from the operation and let me know how he is."

Mandy eyed me thoughtfully as the coffee drained through the filter into the pot. So much for my idea of not telling Mandy about Carol.

"Who was that?"

"Carol Trentham, Richard Trentham's wife. Richard and I were pilots together at Britannia before Richard went off to join Cathay. He is based in London but was operating Hong Kong - Sydney last week. He was dead heading back to London on Flight 573. Carol called me this morning worried as hell and then later she let me know that Richard had been found and was alive. You probably gathered that he has had to have one of his legs amputated and she is doubtful whether he will survive. What a mess."

"That's terrible." There was a pause. "You didn't mention that she'd called," she said almost accusingly. Nothing got by Mandy.

"I forgot. It didn't seem that important and everything else drove it out of my mind."

Mandy said nothing. By mutual consent we both knew that the matter was reserved for another time. We took our coffee into the living room and sat down, close together, on the settee. She must have put on some more perfume while I was talking to Carol. I put my mouth on her neck and smelled the fragrance. She turned towards me and took my hand in hers. Her hand followed mine as I turned the TV on to the News at Ten and then put it at the top of her thigh. Mandy immediately took her hand away and reached for the controller to turn the TV off but stopped suddenly as we both realised that there was an interview with Bob Furness, head of the Air Accident Investigation Branch. Bob was explaining the procedure for investigating accidents and how important was the analysis of the two crash recorders. We relaxed for a moment and started to drink our coffee.

"We have not yet found the cockpit voice recorder but it can only be a matter of time. We do have the other recorder with all the flight information. The 798 meets the very latest requirements for recording the critical flight data which can shed light on possible causes of accidents. However the analysis will take a long time. We need the help not only of the airline but also of the aircraft manufacturer and of course the security and explosive experts.

"In parallel with this work we are collecting every piece we can of the aircraft and looking for evidence of bomb damage. We are laying all the pieces out in a hangar we are using at Farnborough and we are 'rebuilding' the aircraft. We have had a lot of experience of similar work in the past starting with the Comet fatigue failure accident many years ago. The position of each piece where it hit the ground is important since this can show if the aircraft started to disintegrate before it hit the ground. We log the position of every part before it is moved and 'reassembled' in the hangar."

"But surely Mr. Parnell this is going to be a straightforward case of the hijackers interfering with the crew?"

"Possibly, but if so we still need to understand what exactly happened."

The interviewer raised the subject of voice recorders. Would the public be able to hear the conversations of the crew.

"You are quite right to mention the voice recorder. The remarks on the recording between the crew will be absolutely vital in helping us to find out what went wrong. Deciphering what has been recorded however is not as simple as it sounds." Bob paused to stress a point. "It is our policy in the United Kingdom only to let the absolute minimum number of necessary specialists listen to the recording. For a start it can be quite difficult to understand what is being said and a lot of what is said is very often quite irrelevant to the accident. If the recording got into the wrong hands a lot of unnecessary grief could be caused to the dependants of the crew and passengers."

For once the interviewer did not question this point as I expected.

"What would happen if you couldn't find the voice recorder?"

"We will find the recorder. It's just a matter of time. When we know the cause of the accident we will let everybody know. Meantime I would ask you to help us by not interfering with our work. You must realise that the work of inspection is incredibly harrowing and upsetting to my inspectors and they need your support."

I switched the set off.

"He must be getting a bit impatient, not yet having the cockpit voice recorder." Mandy remarked.

"You're right. It shouldn't be taking this long. It is a pity it is not underwater because it has a special beacon if it is submerged."

We sat up and drank our coffee. Mandy put her cup down and then took my cup and saucer from me and put it safely out of reach. She turned to me and as she came closer I could smell the fresh perfume again. Slowly and gently she made it clear that life had to go on in spite of tragic accidents. She ran her fingers through my hair and down my body and I could feel myself reacting. This was going to be our first time and we had to learn how the other would respond. I started to unbutton her dress and helped it off her shoulders. I realised why Mandy had gone upstairs. She was not wearing a bra, or anything else for that matter. I held her breasts in my hand and caressed her nipples as we started to kiss. We both froze as the telephone started to ring.

"Let it ring." she whispered in my ear. "The answering machine can deal with it."

"It won't. I haven't switched it on."

"Well it's your decision." But the way she stroked me made it almost impossible for me to leave.

Everything stopped while the phone seemed to ring for ever. The caller finally gave up and all was quiet. We both relaxed and tried to continue where we had left off but the noise started again. Mandy took her hand away and moved back slightly so that I could get up to answer the phone.

"Peter, its Mike Mansell here."

I sat down as I knew it would be a long conversation. Mike was a partner in CrossRisk Insurance and I had advised him before in an accident claim where pilot error might have been involved. Mike's firm had been retained by the airline concerned. It had been a tricky case and the engine manufacturer had been trying to say the crew drills had not been carried out correctly and a very expensive engine had been damaged. I had been able to show that the drills in the Flight Manual had not covered the particular case in question and that the airline was not responsible. I had saved Mike's company over a million pounds and they were very grateful. They even gave me a percentage bonus which had kept me going between other jobs.

I had got to know Mike quite well. He was slightly older than I was and he had never married. Not, I judged, that he had not had lots of opportunity with quite a few delightful girls, but he always seemed to shy away when he reckoned he might get caught.

My telephone chair faced Mandy who had not bothered to pull her dress back up. Her breasts seemed very prominent and I found it very difficult to concentrate. I put the phone down and turned the chair round so I could not see her.

"Peter, are you still there." Mike asked as I re-lifted the handset.

"Yes, its OK. I was just getting a chair and some notepaper. Go ahead. How can I help you.?"

"Look, I'm sorry I'm calling you so late. I hope I'm not disturbing you?" I made no reply. I did not dare look at Mandy.

"Are you there?"

"Yes Mike, please go ahead."

"You may know that we recently got the contract from Royal World Airlines to supply insurance cover for any passenger claims that might occur from flight crew negligence. RWA did not want us to insure the hull, that was already being done by Hull Claims Insurance but Hull Claims didn't want to be involved with claims resulting from 'pilot error'. They felt that pilot error was still the most frequent cause of accidents and required a specialist organisation. Well Peter, we have just had an internal company meeting and we are very concerned that the claims from this particular accident could bankrupt the firm. We laid off a lot of the risk of course but we feel that the magnitude of the claims will be unprecedented, particularly when all the legal fees are taken into account.

"Of course I'm not for a minute suggesting the accident was due to pilot error. The accident is almost certainly due to the hijacking. It's anybody's guess at this stage, but the nature of the accident suggests that if it's not a bomb or something like it then pilot error is clearly a possibility and we might then be liable. I recommended that we should ask you to advise us and everybody agreed. They hadn't forgotten the last job you did for us. What do you think?"

"Well, I think you're probably worrying unnecessarily. However I think you're right to be prepared. Mike, I think I'm free to accept your offer but I'll have to check with John Chester since he half hinted when I saw him at lunch to-day that he might have a job for me. To be honest I think he changed his mind about using me but I had better check with him in the morning. In any event his interests and yours should be identical."

"Great. I feel much happier already."

"Mike. Let's get one thing straight. If I help you I am only interested in finding out the truth, hijacking, maintenance fault, pilot error or whatever. This accident could conceivably have been caused by pilot error but of course, bearing in mind all the safeguards that are currently built in to protect modern aircraft, I feel that the hijacking must have caused something to go wrong. For example, the hijacker may have prevented the crew from flying the aircraft correctly. Clearly in that case it wouldn't have been pilot error. It's not going to be easy working on the job because as you know everything is in AAIB's hands at the moment. If they think it's pilot error, the chance of getting anyone to believe anything else is going to be very small and there are no witnesses, except possibly Frank Mercer if he survives. So in that case there would be precious little chance of my being able to help you. However, it certainly looks like a bomb or possibly pilot error and as far as the manufacturer, Independant Transport Aircraft Company, is concerned either would be an ideal solution.

"Another thing, if you do want me to help, you must realise that if I'm going to keep abreast of the situation I shall have to do a lot of work and travelling using all my contacts and it 's going to cost you. Your money will probably be wasted. I will do everything I can to help you but I don't want to mislead you."

"I know that and in this case my company is prepared to pay you not only your normal fees and expenses but a lump sum percentage bonus as we did last time if we judge by your actions that you have saved us from having to pay up the many millions of pounds that will be due if the fault is found to be due to pilot error."

"OK. I don't like being mercenary in situations like this but this accident is on a scale that no-one has encountered before and there are many ramifications that are going to complicate the legal issues. Send me the normal contract letter and also another letter which shows that I am acting as your consultant. I may need it to convince people that I have a right to be involved. I will confirm I can take the job when I have spoken to John Chester. Bye."

I put the phone down and stood still for a moment thinking about the conversation. I suddenly realised that Mandy had come over from the settee and I could smell her perfume again. I reconnected the answering machine. She was standing behind me and starting to remove my clothes so we would be on an equal footing. I turned to make it easier for her. Mandy came very, very close and Mike Mansell seemed to go a long, long way away.

***

I woke up with a start in Mandy's bed. As I had suspected she had not wanted to sleep in the room that Diana and I had shared, even though the bed had been changed a long time ago. The last thing I remembered before going to sleep was asking Mandy how she could have been so sure that we were going to make it that night. She murmured that I was being very silly, it was standing out a mile. I told her that as a solicitor she should not exaggerate. She told me not to be coarse. But she was right in one way. I was never very good at hiding my feelings.

There were noises downstairs. It was already 7.15. There was a smell of coffee and bacon. I leapt out of bed to find out what was going on. I got some trousers from my room and went downstairs. As I had anticipated, Mandy was sitting at the kitchen table tucking into a bowl of cereal, a plate of bacon under the grill, brown toast in the toaster and coffee already made in the pot. She was dressed in her lawyer's uniform but without her jacket. She was wearing her glasses and reading the Times.

"Good Morning, Ms Arrowsmith, did you sleep well.?" She said nothing for a moment but finished her cereal.

"Good morning, Mr. Talbert. I trust you had a good evening."

"It was like the curate's egg, thank you. Good in parts. I've come to consult my lawyer. Would you advise me to have some coffee?"

"Very definitely."

I poured myself a mug of coffee and moved another chair to the table. Mandy looked at her watch. It was nearly time for her to go.

"Peter," she said breaking the lawyer/client relationship "From what I heard on the radio they've found the voice crash recorder. The security people unearthed it while they were checking for bombs and it's now on the way to Farnborough for AAIB."

"Strange that it was not found earlier." I looked at the time. "You're going to be late. You must stop eating and run."

She agreed and dashed to get ready. She returned with her jacket and I helped her and kissed her neck on the way. She leant back to show approval but quickly turned round.

"For once I wish you were dressed. You could have taken me to the station. I must go home to-night," anticipating my next question, "I've some things to do. I'll call you from the office later on when I see what's happening."

She turned back again and kissed me slowly, on the lips.

"Oh Peter. While I remember. That was quite a night." She put her tongue in my mouth and then withdrew it rather hurriedly as I grabbed her and tried to agree.

She rushed out with her bag and I watched her hurrying down the street being barked at by next door's dog. I collected the clothes I was wearing last night from the living room and went upstairs to get dressed. It was just as well that Dora had not been coming to-day, though I supposed she would not have been surprised. I had no plans to go out and in some ways it was a relief that Dora wasn't going to come.

I logged on to the Internet and looked at the FT. Jim Akers had an article saying amongst other things that at the time the paper went to press the cockpit voice recorder had not been found. He pointed out how vital it was not only to find the recorder but that it should work properly. He also pointed out that if something had gone wrong then it must have been at the last moment. Jim favoured the crew being distracted by the apparent hijacker when landing in critical conditions. Without something of this nature it was going to be necessary to investigate how it was possible for the aircraft to be actually well below the correct flight path and the crew to take no action. Was there something wrong with the Landing System they were using? Why didn't the Air Traffic Controller warn the crew? There was an alerting system in the control tower if the aircraft was not on the runway centre line, why wasn't there one for the glide slope?

Jim discussed the procedure in the UK for dealing with cockpit voice recorders. He pointed out how everything on the recording was confidential and how normally not even the transcript was ever written down in the final AAIB accident report. In the United States the transcript was a matter of public record but even there the actual recording was never played publicly.

I decided to ring John Chester to ask whether he minded my being a consultant to CrossRisk Insurance. Jill Stanton answered his private number.

"Captain Chester is not available at the moment. Can I help you?"

I told her of the need to speak to him as soon as it was convenient and she undertook to pass on the message.

"How is your friend in hospital? Is he alright."

I explained about the loss of his right leg and that it was unlikely that he would survive. She sounded very sad. My story was just one of so many she was dealing with. She had a very difficult job. In my study I went through my letters and started tidying up. Doing nothing for twenty four hours always left a lot of odd jobs to be cleared up. The phone rang.

"Peter? It's Carol. Richard's not very well I'm afraid." She paused trying to get a hold on herself. "He is able to recognise me and remembers the flight and the approach but nothing else. He suddenly said he must speak to you. It was very strange. It seemed more important to him than anything else.

"Can you come over straightaway? I'm so afraid. If you don't come immediately it may be too late."

"Of course. Which ward is he in?"

"He is in the Hossack Ward. Park your car in the visitor's park and you will see the sign to the Ward. When you get there you must ask for sister. He is on the critical list but you are being allowed in because I have explained the situation to Matron. You may have to wait because he is in great pain and on drugs. Anyway you will see me there. See you soon."

I got the car out, locked up the house and drove as quickly as I dared to Ealing General. I managed to find room to park the car and went to the Hossack ward which was on the first floor. The swing doors must have operated a buzzer and a nurse came out of the side office.

"Can I help you." She looked me up and down.

"I've come to see Richard Trentham who is on the critical list. His wife has just called me and said that she had spoken with Matron and it had been agreed that I could go in when it was judged possible."

"Oh I don't know anything about that. Let me get sister."

She returned with another nurse, no older than herself but wearing what must have been a sister's uniform.

"You are Mr. Talbert?" I nodded. "Well Mr. Trentham is very, very ill but has moments of consciousness and he has been asking for you. You had better sit down in the waiting room but it may be a very long wait."

I did as she asked and picked up the papers. To be honest it was difficult to concentrate but I tried to make myself read an old copy of Country Life. There was an article on houses in Brittany and it all seemed a million miles away. I suddenly became aware that I was not alone. Carol had appeared. She was an elegant and striking woman in spite of the surroundings. She looked very tired but she had obviously taken care with her appearance in spite of the world falling apart around her.

"Peter. It's been a long time." She held both my hands in hers and looked at me. I felt slightly uncomfortable, perhaps unsure of myself. "Thank you for coming. To be honest I'm not very hopeful. He has been asleep for an hour or two. If he comes round and can talk they are going to call me. If it seems alright and he still wants to talk to you I will call you."

"OK Carol." We said nothing, perhaps both of us remembering happier times in the past. "Can I get you some tea, coffee? Have you eaten to-day?"

"A cup of coffee would be nice. There is a machine on the next floor. To tell you the truth I haven't had breakfast. I've got a few biscuits in my bag." She produced an unflatteringly large ladies' bag which obviously contained all her emergency requirements.

"Look. I'll get some coffee and we had better go out somewhere."

"Peter. I can't. I never know when Richard is going to come to. They bring me some food from the canteen when they can."

I went downstairs and managed to make the machine deliver some coffee with milk and without sugar. As I climbed up the stairs Carol rushed down to meet me. "Quick. Richard wants to talk to you."

We went into the ward and passed many patients. It was not visiting time and the nurses were doing all the various things which were needed in a very busy ward. At the far end we went into a room which I realised was reserved for patients who were critically ill. I was horrified when I saw Richard but I hope I did not let my feelings show. He had a bandage on his head and both of his shoulders seemed damaged. One arm was in a sling and the other arm was positioned for a drip. His eyes were open and he recognised me. I could barely hear what he was saying. I leant right up to his mouth.

"Peter. The hijackers..." He coughed and shut his eyes. I waited. He opened his eyes again. He had obviously forgotten he had spoken. He stopped and then seemed to make a supreme effort "I tried to tell ..." He coughed again and then he seemed to go into a coma. I decided to leave which obviously pleased the nurse. Carol stayed behind.

I went back to the waiting room and tried to escape once again to Brittany but somehow Country Life could not hold my attention. Presumably Richard must have been sitting in the upper deck and seen the hijackers. Had he seen the lights out of the windows? I began to sympathise with the AAIB inspectors who have to go to the accidents. When one is surrounded by death on all sides one takes a very different and sometimes emotional view of what needs to be done to prevent another accident. Safety may be a statistical matter to the aircraft designers and the regulators but if one is present at the statistical accident, it all seems very different. AAIB had a history of recommending modifications to prevent accidents but in truth the only thing that would prevent accidents would be to stop flying, and that would never happen. The fact is that people are prepared to accept accidents providing they are not too frequent and that they do not happen to them.

I thought about what Richard had said. It didn't make any sense. What did the hijackers do? Who did he try to tell? And what was it?

Carol appeared. It was all over. "He's dead". I put out my arms to comfort her and she burst into tears. I held her as she sobbed uncontrollably for a minute or so. Then she quietened down.

"I'll take you home."

"But I can't leave my car here."

"Don't worry. We can sort that out." I spoke to the sister to make sure she knew how to contact Carol. We went down to my car and I drove her back to Farnham where she lived. It seemed to take forever. The traffic was terrible. We said nothing.

When we finally got to her house she gave me the keys and I opened the front door. It was about 3 o'clock by this time. "Have you got any food in the house?"

Chapter 2

"There's some food in the fridge and also in the freezer compartment. But I don't want anything. I think I'll go to bed."

"Carol. Your best bet is to eat something. Get the children home. You'll have to go on living. After all Richard has been away a lot and the children are used to a life without him, most of the time." I knew I was being hard but I really believed that though she had to grieve, she must not give way.

She looked at me and nodded miserably. I found some bacon and eggs in the fridge and turned the grill on. Carol pointed to a cupboard which had saucepans and a frying pan. She went upstairs.

I checked my mobile. John Chester had phoned and also Mandy. Mandy was busy with a client so I left my number. Jill put me through to John Chester.

"John, it's Peter. How are things going?"

"Not too well. How I can help you?" He was obviously up to his armpits in problems.

"Only a quick one. Mike Mansell of CrossRisk Insurance wants to retain me as a consultant to help them. Is that OK? You mentioned you might want me to act for you."

There was a pause.

"Yes. That's fine. Whatever. After all RWA insures with them." He clearly was not too pleased at this development but could not really stop it. I wanted to know what was troubling him but it seemed he was not about to tell me. "Keep in touch. I'd like to know how you get on." He rang off.

I started cooking the bacon and scrambling the eggs. I found some rather stale bread but felt it would be OK for toasting. Half way through Carol appeared. She had changed into sweater and trousers and looked very smart in spite of everything. She had not let having two children spoil her figure. She laid the table and when it was ready we sat down to eat.

I think she managed to eat a lot more than she expected. In fact she cleaned her plate. There was some bacon left over but she refused to have any more. "You're right. I had better get hold of the children. They've got to know."

She went over to the phone and called the friend who was looking after her children. She had to explain about Richard first which obviously she found very hard. She managed to arrange for the children to come over after they had had tea.

"Carol. You need to get some food. I'll take you shopping and get you home before the children return. Then I'll get your car back from Ealing." She nodded her agreement.

We went to Sainsbury's and got a trolley. I had to prompt her to get the things she needed. I told her again, Richard may have died but life had to go on. The children needed to be fed. She bought bread, fruit, milk and a host of other things. She had very little money but paid with a credit card. I made her use the cash dispenser outside before we got back into the car.

As we got back my mobile started to ring.

"Peter? It's Mandy. Where are you?" she asked tersely.

"Mandy. I'm at Carol's. Richard has died. He wanted to say something to me and I went to the hospital. I was only just in time but he couldn't get the message out. I'm helping her get her life started again. We've been shopping and the children will be home in a moment. I've got to go by train into London and out to Ealing to bring her car back from the hospital."

"Where are you now?" She sounded slightly more understanding but suspicious.

"Carol lives in Farnham."

"Well I shall be here until quite late and then I shall be off to Bournemouth. Call me to-morrow and maybe we can meet up."

"Fine. See you soon." We said our goodbyes but they were not too extravagant.

I noticed Carol had been following the conversation but she asked no questions. I rang for a cab to take me to the station and got Carol to give me the keys of her car. The cab came within ten minutes. I waved goodbye and was on my way. It was a miserable journey. When I got to Waterloo I bought the Evening Standard and took the underground to Ealing, reading the paper to catch up with what had been happening. The Secretary of State for Transport had decided to call a press conference the following afternoon. This was unheard of but then so was the hijacking. It was an unpleasant journey what with the rush hour, standing up most of the way and the difficulty of getting a cab to the hospital. It was gone 8.30 before I got into Carol's car.

The drive home was uneventful and I got to Carol's house by 10 o'clock. The children were still up looking very subdued. There was not much I could say. I embraced Carol sympathetically and said good-bye.

"Keep in touch. Anyway I'll call you." I got in the car and drove off.

I got home about 11.30. It had been a long day but I didn't feel I had accomplished much. I went straight to bed and dropped off to sleep.

I saw Richard Trentham with all his bandages standing next to the bed. Carol was showing him yesterday's Daily Telegraph. He looked through me with sightless eyes and shook his head, frowning, saying nothing. I tried to speak and nothing came out. I reached to grab him and

Chapter 2

he disappeared. Carol bent over as if to kiss me and I tried to escape by rolling over. I woke up covered in perspiration. I felt afraid.

A Flight Too Far

CHAPTER 3

I didn't sleep very well after my dream. My mind kept thinking about what Richard had been trying to tell me and wondering how Carol was going to manage without him, with the children to look after. I finally dozed off as it was getting light.

My alarm went off at 7.30. It was set to prevent oversleeping though usually I was awake well before it went off. Thursday was Dora's second day and I always liked to be down well before she arrived at 8.45. I got up, showered and went downstairs. The phone rang.

"Peter, I've just got into the office. Have you seen the paper?"

"No, not yet Mandy."

"Well you'd better get hold of the Telegraph for a start. Their air correspondent, Chuck Osborne, has got a story about the crash recorder and the pilots' conversations. Apparently they'd been on a party at a beach the night before the flight."

"A leak? From AAIB? It's unheard of. There's never been a leak."

"Well there's been one now."

"Anyway even if the leak is accurate and they'd been out the night before it wouldn't matter. They would have slept on the aircraft before the landing."

"Well don't shoot the messenger. Get your bottom out of bed for a change and buy some newspapers."

Mandy rang off. The Times was there and I glanced hurriedly through it while I had breakfast. There was a short article by a reporter mentioning the story and saying how deplorable such a leak was. The news item went on to mention that it was strange that the crew had noticed nothing wrong on the approach before the aircraft hit the A30. I dropped everything, got the car out and bought the Telegraph and the FT at the nearest newsagent.

Back home I read the Telegraph. Chuck Osborne had a large article on the front page. 'DID PILOTS' PARTY CAUSE ACCIDENT?' screamed the headline. Osborne told how he had managed to get an exclusive chance to listen to the flight deck conversations. The quality of the recording was very poor, possibly due to damage to the recorder. Up to now everybody had thought that the accident was due in some way to the hijacker alert, but was there another explanation? Osborne went on to say that on the recording before the start of the approach there had been a discussion about a beach party the night before they left. The aircraft then carried out a normal approach. Apparently the first officer was calling out the heights and just below 800 ft. the Captain said 'we are on the glide slope but we seem to be descending rather quickly' but there was some more background noise. Then he called the control tower and asked for a wind check. At 100 ft. he said he still couldn't see the loom of the lights. The first officer said the instruments showed they were on centre line, at just below 20 ft. there was a 'Oh my God', a noise of engines and then a crashing noise and nothing.

I was appalled. How on earth did the Telegraph get hold of the story and, if it was anything like true, what had been going on? My mind was racing. It did not make sense in several ways. The paper was quite oblivious to the damage that might be being done by running the story. There was a leading article justifying the right of the public to know and saying thank goodness for the integrity of the media, conveniently not mentioning any dirty tricks that they had probably carried out in order to get the story.

I switched on the radio just in time to hear the news headlines followed by an interview with Flight Magazine's air transport correspondent, Roger Tucker.

"Presumably Mr. Tucker you will have read the story in the Telegraph this morning about the accident to the 798 and the voice recorder. Have you any comments?"

"Yes. I did read the article and let me say that if the story is true, the whole aerospace industry will deplore that any information that was on the voice recorder has become public knowledge. Accident investigation relies on complete confidentiality whilst the investigations are going on and it is quite improper and most unhelpful if anything leaks out. No doubt the AAIB will be investigating the source of the leak."

"But Mr. Tucker, the fact is that the news has leaked out. Can you understand why the crew did not see that something was going wrong?"

"We must all be very careful in accepting the Telegraph's story as being true and, equally as important, a lot of very important details will almost certainly have been missed, like what the hijackers were doing. The article said the quality of the recording was poor which underlines the problem. Only when all the pieces of information are assessed can any sense be made of the causes of the accident. We have no idea, for example, if a bomb went off which might have caused the aircraft to come down below the glide slope. Clearly, if there was not a bomb then it will be very important to explain why the crew thought they were on the glide slope and yet landed half a mile short."

"The story is that the crew had been out partying the night before. Would..."

Roger interrupted. "It is quite disgraceful that personal conversation on the recording should be discussed in this manner. Anyway what did or didn't happen in Sydney is quite irrelevant since the flight lasted 22 hours and the crew had had a long rest after take-off before coming on duty to land the aircraft. Bunks are provided in the flight deck area to ensure the crew off duty get a good rest. The last thing the crew would be thinking about would be about partying when there were hijackers on board."

The interviewer interrupted Roger. "But once the story is out people are bound to discuss it and consider what happened in Sydney. You must realise that."

"It is precisely for this sort of reason that it is so important that information on the cockpit voice recorder should be kept absolutely confidential. There has been a terrible accident and, whilst people are bound to speculate at this time, it does not help for the media to rake over private matters and it will be very hurtful to the families of those concerned."

The interviewer clearly didn't give a damn to any hurt he might be causing to Marcia Hodgson. I turned the TV off feeling sick with disgust over Osborne in particular and the media in general. Dora was in the kitchen and I wandered in to get some more coffee.

"Isn't it terrible about the accident? What did the hijackers do to make it crash?"

"Dora, we don't know anything about what happened. We've got to wait for the accident to be investigated properly by the AAIB."

"And the crew out partying the night before."

"Dora, the flight lasted 22 hours. Whatever happened in Sydney would not affect the landing in London."

"If you say so, Mr. Talbert" she said, completely unconvinced. I was sure that she was expressing what would be a general view. It would not make my job any easier convincing the courts that there was no pilot error, in the unlikely event that that proved to be the issue.

"By the way. There is no need to change the sheets on the spare bed. A friend stayed the other night and might be staying again."

"Very good sir. Do you want me to wash the underwear and stockings that she left?" I felt that I could detect her smirking under her impassive face.

"That would be a good idea and you can leave them on the bed."

It was 9.15 in the morning UK time. It would be 8.15 in the evening Sydney time. I looked up the number in my database of Bill Baker, Chief Training Pilot of NWIA. I had done some work for NWIA a couple of years before on the Boeing 747-500 and had met Bill Baker then, as he was Chief 747 pilot at the time. New World International Airlines was a very rapidly growing Antipodean airline very much in competition with QANTAS and, like QANTAS, seemed to be known only by initials. Luckily I had Bill's home number as well as his office number.

In no time the phone was ringing and a female voice answered. I asked for Bill explaining that I was calling from England.

"Oh I'm so sorry. Bill's not here. This is Mary, his wife speaking. Bill is still in the office."

"No problem, Mrs. Baker. I've got his number. I'll call him there." I rang off and tried the NWIA main number in Sydney. The operator put me through to Bill's office after giving me his direct line in case we got disconnected before he answered.

"Bill, you're working late! It's Peter Talbert here, calling from England. You remember I did some work for you some time back."

"Of course I remember. How are you doing, Peter? What's the news?"

"Bill, I am getting involved with this terrible accident at Heathrow. Were any of your people on board?"

"I'm afraid so. We've lost a Captain and two first Officers re-positioning to London. You know there were 49 Australian passengers on the flight, 35 killed and 14 survivors all in hospital, so it really is a national disaster. I must say that to us the whole thing looks like the hijackers interfering with the crew in bad weather. If it was a bomb it must have gone off very late on the approach. We've all heard about the voice recording of course. How on earth did that get out?"

"I don't know but I hope for Bob Furness's sake at AAIB that he's found and plugged the leak. Probably more people than usual heard the recording because of the security implication. I'm so sorry to hear about your people. We've got to find out what happened. By the way when do you get your first 798?"

"In about four months time. I've got two of my senior training captains in Seattle right now learning about the aircraft and our first course starts in one month. Somebody told me you're lecturing to the RWA training courses. Is that right?"

"Yes. The 798 has a very interesting systems configuration and flight deck."

"How would you like to come out and help plan the course in detail and give some talks on the significance of the latest crew/flight deck interface?"

"Are you serious, Bill? You know I'd like that very much. However I'm rather busy at the moment otherwise I'd come out to-morrow."

"To-morrow would be a bit soon anyway, Peter. This accident has got a lot of us thinking hard. We don't really believe that the accident was due to pilot error and we don't think there is anything wrong with the 798 design. Our current view is that the hijack was responsible in some way. However, we need to make absolutely sure that our pilots are as properly trained as they can be. We want to be quite clear about the latest pilot interface issues on the flight deck and the system design. I can't help feeling that your input will be well worthwhile. I need to talk with my captains when they come back. I'll let you know."

"Bill, that's fine, I look forward to hearing from you. But let me tell you why I called. NWIA does all the servicing for Royal World Airlines?"

"Yes we do. Why?"

"Do you think you could find out for me if there were any allowable deficiencies when the aircraft left for London? Did all the electronics work when they left?"

"You bet. I'll contact Matt Thompson, head of maintenance and call you back. Anything else I can do for you?"

"Not really. What is your media making of the story about the party the night before?"

"Not much so far, all the talk is about the hijacking. As I said the accident is really terrible for us since the death toll is so high, not to mention the injured. The papers are concentrating on the family aspect of the tragedy. Understandably they don't seem to be pursuing the party story, perhaps because they feel, as we do, that it's not relevant. Anyway, you know as well as I do that there are scores of beaches and restaurants in the Harbour. We've had a heat wave for the last few days and it would probably be easier to find what the crew had been up to if they had been downtown or had stayed in their hotels and hadn't gone down to the beaches!

"Besides, all people can talk about here, after the accident, is the cricket. There is a test series on with the West Indies at the moment and everybody feels that accidents will always happen and sport must go on. If there is going to be any investigation of night life and parties, it will be reserved for the two cricket teams."

"Well Bill, that's a bit of good news. Its bad enough for the families as it is without adding a sex scandal."

"OK Peter. No worries. I'll let you know the moment I get anything from Matt."

"Thanks. Call me any time, day or night. Leave a message on my answering machine to call you if I'm not in. All the best."

The phone went again.

"Peter? I'm in a mess. I'm going to need money and I don't know what to do. I called the Cathay Office. They were very sympathetic and said they would call Hong Kong but I must know how I'm going to be placed."

"Carol, don't you have a solicitor who can help you?"

"Yes, but he's in Hong Kong and he's Chinese."

"Well you had better get hold of a solicitor in London. Look I've got to call my girl friend who is a solicitor and I'll ask her who she recommends. I'll call you back as soon as I can."

Mandy was in the office but it seemed to be forever before she came on the line. I was pretty certain that we'd had eight of Vivaldi's four seasons on the tape before she answered.

"How's everything going?"

"Not short of work. I understand from GE that the inquest is starting immediately but the coroner is only interested in making positive identification of the bodies. He's not going to get involved in investigating the cause and second guessing the AAIB. Also he is determined not to get into the problems that have occurred in other accidents where a lot of people were killed and mistakes in identification were made."

"Well, my love, he may be lucky there because what fires there were, were put out very quickly. Of course if there was a bomb, that would make life impossible for the coroner but the fact that there were some survivors makes me think there wasn't an explosion. We'll hear soon enough. Just as well the Australian families are coming over to help. However, it is still going to take a long time with so many bodies. I'm afraid that there must have been a lot of physical damage due to hitting that building."

"The Coroner has also let it be known to the interested parties that after the identification he is going to adjourn the inquest indefinitely until the results of the AAIB investigation are known. That means we won't have to be involved for months."

"Well I can't wait until then. I need to keep ahead of the gossip and get some real facts. I'm not sure yet how to do that but I'm working on it. I spoke to Bill Baker of NWIA this morning and asked him to check on the aircraft serviceability state on departure.

"Australia is clearly treating the accident as almost a national tragedy. They're also assuming, as I think most of us are, that somehow the hijackers caused the accident. He did tell me some good news. Apparently there's a heat wave in Sydney and also a cricket test series so that the beaches have been crowded and the reporters are busy so that they don't seem to be pursuing the cockpit voice recorder story. Let's hope it stays that way."

"How did you get on last night.?"

"I managed to get Carol's car back and got home about 11.30. I went straight to bed and had a dream in the middle of the night. It was like a nightmare. Richard was next to me reading the Daily Telegraph. I tried to grab him and he disappeared." I stopped, deciding not to mention that in my dream Richard was not alone.

"I was soaked in perspiration. It took me ages to get back to sleep and..."

"Write down exactly what happened. The mind works even when one's asleep. It may be important."

"Look, I need your advice. Carol is very worried financially. Obviously Richard was insured but Cathay in London can't help her, goodness knows when she will hear from head office and their solicitor is in Hong Kong."

"She had better get a UK solicitor straightaway. I'm sure there won't be a problem but it needs to be made clear to Cathay that she is well represented."

"That's what I told her but who should she get? Should I give her the name of my solicitor? Or can your firm do it? Can you recommend someone?"

"No she had better not use your solicitor. To be honest with you I wouldn't like that arrangement. Our firm doesn't do that type of work. Where did you say she lived? Farnborough?"

"No. Farnham."

"Let me think about it. I'll call you back in a few minutes. I need to talk to you some more anyway." She rang off.

The phone rang again. It was Bill Baker.

"I spoke to Matt. He said I was the second person to ask him that question to-day. Someone from the AAIB had called him, it was an inspector but he didn't leave his name."

"Well what was the answer, Bill?"

"There were no deficiencies reported. The aircraft had landed with two defects. One of the Captain's main instrument displays, the Navigation Display was not working and one of the Multimode Receivers was giving a GPS System warning. The ground crew checked the display but could find nothing wrong. However NWIA doesn't allow a 'ground checked and found serviceable' entry in the log book and so they put a replacement display in the Captain's position. It worked fine and they sent the reported defective display to be checked in the avionics shop.

"The Multimode Receiver fault was more of a challenge. As you know the receiver controls all the alternative equipment that can be used for automatic landings. The fault was confirmed on the ground when the GPS was selected. The avionics engineer on duty decided to change the Multimode Receiver which proved to be the right solution. He ground checked the system and everything seemed to be fine."

"Thanks very much. If you hear anything else you think I ought to know, please call me straightaway."

"Peter, wait a moment. I told you this 798 accident has got us all worried. I've now spoken to my guys in Seattle and we would like you to earn a dollar or two and come out when they've finished their course in about a month to advise on our training courses. At the moment you're much more up to speed on the aircraft than my guys. You can put yourself down for some lectures as well on the initial courses. If you'd like to block off the last full week in January or the first week in February and we can decide nearer the time."

"OK. That's fine. We'll be in touch."

I sat down for a moment and thought over my conversation with Bill. For a start I could use the money working with NWIA though it was a pity in a way I wasn't going out right away since at this stage of the investigation I could probably spare the time. By going to Sydney I would have been able to talk to the servicing people who had dealt with the display on Golf Hotel and, who knows, I might have found out some more about the 'party'. I needed to know if it was important or not. The phone rang yet again.

"There's a firm in Aldershot called Trethowan and Parker. Tell Carol to ask for David Smith. I knew him at law school and have had some dealings with him professionally since. Tell her to mention my name.

"Incidentally Peter, when are we meeting next? In case you have forgotten it's Thursday to-day. Why don't you come down and spend the week-end with me? We could go sailing or something. It could be fun."

"That's sounds a super idea. What are you doing tonight?"

"I'm having a quiet evening with a friend."

"That's a pity. I was going to suggest you came round here."

"I'll need an awful lot of persuasion to change my mind but you've talked me in to it. I'll be with you to-night at about 7 o'clock, clients permitting. By the way we'd better not go out as I've got no clothes left."

"OK. That sounds exciting. It's definitely not a problem. I'll cook you a meal and, by the way, you can collect the clothes you left behind."

"Ah. I knew there had to be an explanation when I couldn't find them. They're not the sort of clothes you can leave around absentmindedly."

"I'm glad you said that. I wouldn't like to think that you leave your underwear all over London." I sighed. "Well, I had better deal with Carol."

"Can't you deal with Carol over the phone?" I began to think she did not want me to see Carol.

"Possibly, but I shall have to call her back to see. She's all alone with the kids and has no support."

"OK Peter. But she has been living in London by herself ever since Richard went to work with Cathay. She can't be that helpless."

I thought about that. Maybe I should be careful not to be dragged into helping Carol, but I felt I ought to do something.

Chapter 3

"Peter, are you listening to me?"

"Oh yes. Your advice is always good but I feel involved."

"Well, watch it." The phone went dead.

Carol's mother answered the phone when I got through, not sounding too strong.

"Is that Peter Talbert? Carol's told me so much about you. Thank you for helping her. This really is a terrible business. Carol's out shopping at the moment. I'll get her to call you. I don't think she slept much last night." She rang off.

My next call was to Mike Mansell. He was clearly worried.

"What about that business of the party, Peter? I know the crew had plenty of time to sleep on the plane but a lot of people won't like it."

"We don't know really if there was a party but I agree it won't help the cause. The problem is that we don't know what was on the recording and the AAIB are not about to help us. However, the chances are the hijackers interfered with the pilots or perhaps a bomb went off, though I must say it doesn't look like it at the moment."

"You're right. I'm probably worrying unnecessarily. Keep in touch."

Jim Akers came on the line. "How about lunch at Rules and then coming with me to the Press Conference? I've told them you'll be coming and I'll bring a press pass for you." Rules in Maiden Lane was one of my favourite restaurants. However my upbringing, what the Americans called 'Mid Western ethic', felt that a working lunch at a place like Rules was decadent. I normally went there for a pre-theatre dinner. Diana used to like it and Mandy did too though I never mentioned to Mandy that I'd been with Diana. I decided to be decadent.

"Fine. What time?" We agreed 1.15.

I went upstairs to change and Carol came on the line. I gave her Mandy's message.

"Why don't you come over for dinner this evening?"

"Carol, I'm sorry I can't. I've got too much on investigating the accident. I'll try and call you to-morrow. Have you enough money?"

"Oh yes. I'm fine for a bit but I need to know Richard's insurance position."

I did not like the way she seemed to be depending on me but I felt I had to do everything I could.

"Anyway call me if you need help. Bye."

"Yes, I will. Thanks so much Peter." She sounded dreadful.

I accelerated and just made Rules at the appointed time. They showed me straight to the table where Jim was already waiting. The place was absolutely full and nobody seemed to be dieting or on the wagon. If there was an economic recession, it wasn't at Rules.

A Flight Too Far

We read the menu. I chose vegetable soup and grilled salmon with salad. Jim ordered whitebait and Rules' steak and kidney pie. The waiter punched in the order to his computer which transmitted to the kitchen downstairs. I always liked places that had this system. It not only helped to produce the food quickly but also ensured an accurate bill. We both ordered Bells and water.

"Not much hard news about the accident, Peter. We don't know yet what the hijackers did or even if there was an explosion. The story about the party seems to be irrelevant."

"I hope you're right but I think it's too early to say. By the way, I liked the bit in your article yesterday on the 798 and the aircraft being one of the first certificated by the new European authority. I have a concern in this area since the European Aviation Safety Agency seems to be law unto itself. There's no outside technical body seeing if they're doing a good job, the way the Airworthiness Requirements Board in the UK used to interface with the Safety Regulation Group of the Civil Aviation Authority. In my experience an organisation that is a law unto itself and is not being challenged technically, gets into bad habits. Anyway that's for the future I'm sure, not to-day's problem."

"But Peter, the European Aviation Safety Agency works very closely with the Federal Aviation Administration and they can't get very much out of step without everybody knowing. Both authorities have to certificate the other country's products."

"Of course you're right, Jim. But the competition between Airbus and the US manufacturers is enormous and both regulating authorities get pressured by their indigenous manufacturers to relax the rules. In the UK we never used to yield to pressure. We had a reputation for being quite impartial in setting safety standards, wherever the aircraft was made. The UK authorities were as hard if not harder on the UK manufactured aircraft as on the foreign ones being imported into the UK. The UK used to insist on all sorts of special requirements for imported aircraft because they felt that the original certifications were not good enough. The facts are that standardising with the EASA has probably meant lower standards."

"I think you're fussing too much. In spite of this accident, look at the magnificent accident rate that has been achieved world-wide, not just on UK aircraft. We gave in on abolishing our special requirements because we could not justify having them from a safety viewpoint." Jim emphasised his point. "In fact the new Regulations are probably stricter than they need be due to the influence of the UK."

"It's not quite as simple as that. Certification authorities very often don't even apply their own rules properly. You know full well that the UK has, on many occasions, had to insist on special requirements for certain imported aircraft because they felt that the original certifications by the FAA and others were not good enough. The most famous case I seem to remember was when SRG said that the FAA let the Boeing 747-400 through without proper venting in the cabin floor in non-compliance with their own regulations. They said that if a cargo door had blown open in flight, the floor would have collapsed and the aircraft crashed. The UK imposed a special condition. Whatever the truth of the matter I am sure they are all OK now.

"Look, I'm not saying that EASA certificated aircraft are unsafe. I'm just saying that in order to harmonise, on occasions the UK has had to agree to lower standards and we can no longer add our own safety requirements."

"Well you may be right but unless the accident rate goes up sharply it looks as if the UK has been over zealous and is the odd one out."

I said nothing. Jim was almost certainly right. Perhaps the UK had been too strict. But I was aware that in order to get the maximum economic performance from modern aircraft the safety margins had been reduced in recent years. Nevertheless as Jim inferred, the proof of the pudding was in the eating and air travel was probably still the safest form of transport. It was things like hijacking that ruined the statistics, not bad certification standards. However I decided to raise another issue.

"Jim, forget what has happened in the past. I think the situation is more serious than people realise. This terrible accident should make the regulating authorities consider what should be the statistically acceptable level of risk for these large aircraft. Should a higher standard of safety be demanded for large aircraft? The unpalatable fact is that all aircraft crash but these large aircraft carry so many people that perhaps the current safety level is not good enough."

"The manufacturers won't like that and you can't very well change the rules now."

"Yes, you are right there but what could be done now is to consider whether there is any way of demanding safer operating rules. For example, should there be three flight deck crew instead of two on these large aircraft? Should Cat 3B landings be stopped until the new Enhanced Visibility Systems become available?"

"Peter, you've got a good point there. Do you mind if I use it in one of my articles?"

"To be quite open with you, Jim. I would prefer you would wait until the Inquiry. I am thinking of raising it in my evidence."

"Alright, Peter. But please warn me when you are going to use it so I can get it out first."

Our first course arrived. I wished I had ordered whitebait. Jim's looked very good and smelt delicious. However, my soup was excellent so I had no complaints. While the waiter was clearing away our first course Jim asked the point which was worrying us all.

"What do you think happened? Why did the aircraft crash? It just doesn't make sense to me. I'm sure the hijackers didn't want it to crash."

"Perhaps not, but when you start intruding on the flight deck during an automatic landing in freezing fog you're asking for trouble. Let's hope it was a bomb but if Osborne's story about the recorder is to be believed, it would seem unlikely. As I told you, I checked with NWIA and they said that the plane was fully serviceable when it left Sydney.

"Of course we can't ignore what is probably a key factor in the accident which is the weather when it tried to land. The fog was very thick but that shouldn't have been a problem for the crew or the aircraft. It was equipped with the latest blind landing equipment. However, I hope the British Airports Authority organised a check on the GELAS after the accident in case that was faulty, assuming of course that they were doing a GESS approach. For my money AAIB should have insisted that a flight test was done as well but everybody says the integral monitoring built in to the Galileo equipment is good enough so I don't suppose they did. Of course we haven't heard the recording ourselves but despite what Osborne's said, the hijackers were there and must have been talking to the crew during the last part of the approach. Perhaps the flight deck microphone didn't pick their voices up."

"Osborne said the recording was bad." Jim commented.

"It's a bit much when we have to rely on Osborne. It's strange isn't it, if Osborne is right, that the crew didn't know something was wrong with their approach? I don't believe in the bomb theory but it does make the bomb explanation more likely. Hopefully we will learn something this afternoon."

Jim changed his approach.

"Do you think that the crew really get a rest in those 798 bunks? They look very comfortable but it would not do for me."

"I suspect it depends on the person. It must be much harder for the cabin crew because their accommodation is less spacious but on the other hand their performance is less flight critical. The pilots are much better off up front and it should work. In my view, the crew that does the take-off should not do the landing but the senior Captain likes to do both and RWA management have gone along with it."

"What do you think of the 798? How does it compare with the A380?"

"You know I've only flown the aircraft in the simulator, but they both seem very good to me from a pilot's viewpoint. I can't speak for the economics. My concern is that the flight control computers are a vital part of the pilot's control function and are needed to get the required performance safely. Independant claim to rely less on the computers than Airbus but I'm not sure whether this is really true. We are completely in the hands of the aircraft and software designers just as much as the regulatory authorities, the FAA and the EASA, to ensure the safety standards are good enough."

The conversation stopped for a bit while we ate our main course. Jim's steak and kidney pie looked superb. I knew that if I had ordered it I would never stay awake during the press conference and anyway I had to eat again that evening.

Jim told me he was trying to get another article out to-night. He really needed a new slant and I could see he was disappointed I would not let him use the issue of higher safety standards for the new large aircraft. I told him to wait until after the press conference. We finished our meal and we were walking down to the Strand to get a cab when I saw a large headline on an Evening Standard billboard. 'MINISTER CALLS PUBLIC INQUIRY ON CRASH.' I bought two papers as we took a cab to Marsham Street in Victoria. Jim looked at his copy.

"So that's why the Secretary for Transport called the press conference. He's decided to call a Public Inquiry. Do you know what that means?"

"I'm amazed. There has been some fairly recent legislation from the European Commission which prohibits individual countries having their own accident inquiries. We used to be able to have them of course. Strangely, I think there was one on the Trident landing at Heathrow many years ago, clearly deja vue. The Commission are going to be very unhappy with the UK Government."

"Well, Peter, the UK is not particularly enamoured with the EC at the moment so it may be quite convenient politically to strike a blow for freedom. Anyway, what's the effect of having an inquiry?"

"The inquiry effectively replaces the AAIB, Jim."

"That doesn't seem very sensible. They're the experts."

"Well we're going to hear all about it."

We arrived at Marsham Street and identified ourselves. We were given our passes and then ushered into a large room that Jim told me was always used for briefings. The place was packed and I saw Chuck Osborne from the Telegraph on the far side of the room. The Secretary of State appeared at about 3.30 and to my surprise he was accompanied by an uncomfortable looking Bob Furness. The Minister looked very grave.

"I've asked you to come here to-day because this is the worst aviation accident that has ever occurred in the UK. As you will have heard, I have decided to call a Public Inquiry. The effect of this is that I shall be appointing a Commissioner and two assessors to ascertain the cause of the accident. The AAIB will stop their current investigation and will operate under the instructions of the Commissioner. Clearly, the expertise of the AAIB will be needed but because of the hijacking and the scale of the accident, the Cabinet felt that the AAIB inquiries should be masterminded by the Court. To help some of you in your research in this matter, I'm having copies of Section 8 of the Navigation Order prepared so that you will be able to see the procedure that we shall be following. They will be available to you when you leave.

"I'd like to leave that subject for the moment and talk about the accident. I believe that it is important to keep all of you as fully informed as we can. As you know the plane was hijacked. We have found the two bodies of the guards who were travelling with the Secretary of State and these bodies had been shot. The aircraft carried two captains and two co-pilots and we understand that at least two hijackers were on the flight deck threatening the crews during the approach and landing. The emergency services were alerted before the aircraft started the approach and I'm sure that you are all aware that the emergency rescue services have and are doing an outstanding job. In addition, the local hospitals have responded to the demands of this accident superbly. The total death toll so far is 385 passengers and crew and 38 people in vehicles and on the ground. There are 101 people still in hospital and of those 27 are still on the danger list. The total number of people on the flight was 530.

"With regard to the cause of the accident, we are still investigating whether there was an explosion on the aircraft, but we now think that it is most unlikely that the accident was caused by a bomb. We feel it is far more likely that the hijacking interfered with the proper performance of the crew and the AAIB have been investigating the matter and will continue to do so, but now under the instructions of the Court. I am, of course, extremely unhappy that there has been an apparent leak of information from the cockpit voice recorder and Bob Furness here, the Chief Inspector, is investigating how the leak occurred. The leak is particularly unfortunate because of the security implications. It is important that there are no more leaks and that we try to protect the bereaved as much as possible. I ask you all for your help.

"The facts on this accident are quite clear. The weather was very foggy, the aircraft was cleared for an approach using the Galileo European Satellite System, GESS. As you all know, it crashed half a mile short of the runway on the A30. Bob Furness will now give you some more details."

Bob went to the lectern, pulled out some notes and started his briefing.

"You will appreciate that we have a lot of work to do just to check the basic facts even before we try to discover what went wrong. What I am about to tell you is all preliminary information which will need corroborating."

Bob put up an approach plate for GESS on runway 27L at Heathrow on a large screen.

"We believe that the crew were properly licensed and current in their required proficiency ratings. The aircraft had been serviced overnight in Sydney by NWIA. The aircraft was fully serviceable as far as we know at the start of the flight but the Captain's Navigation Display failed during the flight. The aircraft was hijacked nearly two hours before landing but the crew carried on flying very professionally. The aircraft was equipped to carry out automatic landings and appeared to couple automatically to the centre line and glide slope correctly. The local air traffic controller at the time confirms that the aircraft was on the centre line and that no warning was given by the Approach Monitoring Aid, a software alerting routine which causes an alarm to sound if the aircraft deviates from the centre line within two miles of the runway. There is no equivalent warning device if the aircraft deviates from the glide slope. The Captain asked the tower for a wind check when the aircraft was at 800 ft. The controller passed the wind which was calm. The controller noticed that the aircraft height indicated by the secondary radar was slightly below what he was expecting. At approximately one mile the controller tried to transmit an advisory warning to the aircraft but unfortunately there was an aircraft already transmitting on the frequency and the controller's transmission was blocked. By the time he was able to transmit, the accident had happened.

"We are analysing all the radar traces, VHF radio transmissions and the like and this will take some time. All we can say at this time is that the aircraft was seen to be slowly going below the glide slope by the controller at about one mile out. You should be aware that the controller in fact has no responsibility to warn the crew in these matters though, once he was convinced that there was something wrong, he did try to give a warning.

"If it is confirmed that there was not an explosion, then the Court will have to try to solve the problem of why the crew thought the aircraft was tracking the glide slope whilst in fact it was well below the correct flight path. It is very important that we find out what was the influence of the hijackers. The investigation is in its early stages but we wanted to share with you the current situation.

"Regrettably in one newspaper there has been a report of what was said on the cockpit voice recorder. However, without giving you any more details I can confirm that the crew did notice a slightly faster rate of descent than normal which would easily have been explained by a light following wind. In fact it was Captain Hodgson's query about the wind speed that alerted the controller to notice the aircraft altitude on his screen being transmitted by the radar on the final stages of their approach.

"There is nothing more I can tell you at this stage. My inspectors are working flat out reconstructing the flight, trying to assemble all the wreckage and trying to understand what went wrong. We have not yet analysed all the recorder traces in order to check on the navigation equipment."

Bob Furness remained standing and was joined by the Secretary of State who took over the briefing.

"Ladies and Gentleman. We are prepared to try to answer questions as far as we can."

Jim Akers asked the first question.

"Secretary of State, I thought that the EC had altered the rules affecting the investigation of accidents and that member states were no longer allowed to have Public Inquiries."

"That is debatable. In this case there is more to be investigated than just the accident, which is why the Government has decided to call this Inquiry modelled on Section 8 of the Navigation Order."

Jim persevered.

"Secretary of State, can you tell us who the Commissioner is going to be?"

"I have asked Lord Justice Thomas to be the Commissioner and head the Inquiry and I am delighted to say he has agreed. We have not yet appointed the assessors and, of course, I want to consult Lord Justice Thomas when making the appointments. The assessors will be experts who have the appropriate knowledge and experience to understand all the likely issues to be investigated in this terrible accident."

Jim wasn't about to give up.

"Why couldn't you have left the investigation to the AAIB. They have an international reputation for their expertise and professionalism."

"As I said earlier, this accident has wide implications, and we feel we must leave no stone unturned to investigate all the threads leading to the accident and, of course, to find the cause. It is already very clear that the solution may be quite difficult to find."

Paul Franconi from the Daily Mirror raised a new subject.

"Secretary of State, I thought UK registered aircraft all carried marshals these days. Shouldn't they have prevented the hijack?"

"Paul," the Secretary of State was being unusually friendly I thought. Maybe they knew one another socially or, perhaps more likely, he didn't like the question. "It is not Government policy to discuss whether marshals are carried on aircraft."

Chapter 3

"But Minister," Paul was not about to be put down, "it is obviously very important to know if there were marshals on board and, if so, why they did not prevent the hijack."

"Paul, I think we should leave that to be investigated by the inquiry."

There was a distinct murmuring amongst the audience. The reporters obviously didn't like being fobbed off. The Minister clearly knew more than he was going to disclose.

A reporter from the Independent then asked if there was any connection between the body found in the Hyatt car park in Sydney and Flight 573. The Minister said he had no information on the matter and quickly took the next question. I thought he looked a bit uncomfortable and I made a mental note to pursue the matter.

The Daily Mail man, who was next, focussed on the new information about the air traffic controller and the indicated heights. Bob Furness showed a typical secondary radar plot on the screen and explained how the height shown was the height transmitted by the aircraft to the radar. He also explained that this height jumped every six seconds or so as the radar swept the aircraft. There was no easy way of determining if the aircraft was accurately on the glide slope but very large errors were discernible. In response to a question from Roger Tucker of Flight he said that there was some experimental work going on so that the controller in the control tower would be alerted if the aircraft went below the glide slope, but such equipment was some years away.

One reporter asked about the Navigational Display and Bob Furness mentioned that the Display was a brand new one and had just been fitted before the flight in Sydney. The reporter queried whether it was significant that the display had just been changed. Bob said that this point was being looked at since it was possible the problem may have been an aircraft fault. The same reporter went on to query if anything else was changed in Sydney. Bob said that a Multimode Receiver was changed in Sydney but as there were actually three such receivers, any single failure would not be critical.

Questions were then asked about the safety of the aircraft and how it was certificated. The Secretary of State confirmed that this aircraft was approved by the European Aviation Safety Agency and that the UK had no independent jurisdiction in this matter. There seemed to be some surprise when this was explained since, despite Jim Akers article in the FT, most of the reporters thought that because the UK had issued the Certificate of Airworthiness for the aircraft on the UK register, the UK was responsible for the 798 type certification. The Secretary of State explained that the UK had no alternative under European Commission rules but to validate the 798 type certificate.

One reporter tried to discover if there was a conversation about girls and parties on the cockpit voice recorder and the Secretary of State became extremely stern and told the reporter that any such conversation, had it occurred, could have nothing to do with the accident since the flight had lasted 22 hours and that the crew had rested in the middle of the flight.

The press conference came to an end after about hour without anyone really being any the wiser. Jim and I left and caught a cab to Waterloo.

"Well you've got a subject for your article in the FT to-morrow."

"Yes but I'm not sure about this Public Inquiry. It's likely to hinder AAIB's investigations, not accelerate them."

"Jim, I don't think the Minister had any alternative. He was getting bombarded with questions from MPs, the accident happened in the middle of a hijack and the leak of the voice recorder conversation cast doubt on the reliability of the AAIB. It's never happened before and let's hope it never happens again."

"You say that, Peter, but not releasing the voice recorder transcript enables the investigators to be secretive. We want to live in an open society with freedom of information and yet the recordings of the pilots' conversations are all hushed up. Let's face it, it's an unholy alliance between the Establishment and the pilots' unions."

"Well I admit there's something in what you say but you have to appreciate that there's bound to be a lot of stuff on the pilots' recordings which has absolutely nothing to do with flying but everything to do with private conversations, for example criticising the airline management, praising the attributes of cabin staff and, in this case, apparently talking about a party. If rules for the use of the voice recorder cannot be agreed then the pilots won't fly." Jim was shaking his head. "OK. You don't agree. It'll make another good discussion item for your article to-morrow." I carried on.

"Jim, are you going to mention the marshals. I thought the man from the Mirror had a good point."

"Yes, you're right. It is definitely worth a word or two."

We stopped discussing the Inquiry and started discussing the conference we'd just been to. We agreed that the new information about the air traffic controller was interesting but did not help in finding the cause of the accident. The analysis of all the recordings, not just the pilots' microphones, would be very important indeed and we would just have to wait until this had been done. I told him I was looking forward to reading the FT in the morning and got out of the cab. Jim carried on to Southwark Bridge. I bought some filet steaks, new potatoes and salad when I got to Kingston before going home.

Chapter 3

***

I met Mandy at the station at 7.15. She looked tired. It had obviously been a long day. We drove home in silence and she held my spare hand. That was the nice thing about having automatic transmission.

"I'm going to relax in the bath. It is breaking one of my principles but it will have to be your bathroom because I want the Jacuzzi. You can run the bath." She went upstairs into the spare room. The only luxury in the house was the en-suite bath which Diana and I had decided to have when we moved in.

I turned the grill off, put the plate with the steaks all prepared back into the fridge and went upstairs and ran the bath. Mandy duly appeared wearing the slip Dora had washed. Without any comment and before I could grab her she had taken it off and was relaxing in the bath.

"That's wonderful. What a day I've had. I've had to go to court twice and wait around for hours. Then I had a difficult client and then GE decided to appear and our senior partner wanted me in attendance. I thought I would never get away."

She turned the jacuzzi on and all conversation ceased. After about five minutes she turned it off and closed her eyes. She looked like one of the advertisements in Ideal Home except in the magazines the nipples are normally hidden. There was no way I could keep still. She sensed my movement.

"Why don't you go downstairs and cook the steaks? Leave the doors open to encourage me to come down. I've had no lunch. I could eat a horse."

"Well you won't have to unless the shop is liable for prosecution under the Trades Descriptions Act."

Downstairs I put the grill back on and got the steaks out of the fridge. While I was waiting I laid the table in the dining room. The wine, a Macon, was already breathing. We were not having starters since that would disrupt the flow of the meal. I put the steaks under the grill and cooked them until they were both medium rare. They looked and smelt delicious with just a touch of garlic.

Mandy must have known when to appear from the smell. She was wearing a very thin blouse and short skirt.

"I thought you didn't have any clothes."

"Well I haven't as many as you think."

I inspected her more closely.

"I see what you mean. How do you expect me to eat?"

"Well you can start off with the food and then we'll just have to see."

She sounded very confident, with every reason as far as I was concerned. She took the salad and I took the steaks and we went into the dining room and sat down, adjacent rather than opposite one another. I tasted the wine. It was good and I poured it out.

"Well what have you been doing to-day?" she asked.

"I had lunch at Rules and went to the Secretary of State's press conference."

"I don't know how you can sit there stuffing steak if you've had lunch at Rules."

"It's not easy but I'm doing my best. I did have the foresight not to make a pig of myself at Rules. I walked back from Kingston station which helped a very little."

"Well I didn't walk anywhere and I don't intend to. You'll have to carry me up to bed when the time comes."

"You're on. Let me know when."

"That must be your decision. I've made all the decisions I intend to to-day."

We ate our steaks and steadily drank the wine.

"Shall I open another bottle?"

"I said 'no more decisions' but my advice to you is that we might both regret it. I am liable to go straight to sleep."

"How about dessert or cheese."

"No just coffee. I'll help you clear up."

We went through into the kitchen with the dishes. I filled the dishwasher with the grill pan and put the dishwasher on. Mandy put the coffee on and I held her very close as the water went through the filter. We both realised that our lives were being drawn more and more together. The coffee was finished but we did not move.

The phone rang just as I realised that once again I had not taken the receiver off the hook. I unclasped an arm and was able to reach the phone.

"Peter, it's Carol."

Mandy suddenly stiffened and escaped, pushing me abruptly away. I looked at her face and it was clear that she was not pleased.

"Carol. It's late. I'm up early in the morning. Can I call you again later? What's the problem?" I hope I did not sound as cross as I felt. Mandy disappeared.

"It's Tristram. He's throwing temper tantrums and blaming me for Richard's death."

"Carol. This sort of thing is right outside my experience. You need psychiatric help. Why don't you go to your doctor first thing in the morning."

Chapter 3

"I'm sorry to pester you Peter. But there's no-one else I can talk to. You're right I'll do what you say." She sounded very unhappy and I felt I'd been rotten. "Good night."

I put the phone down and went into the living room. I felt very guilty being so abrupt with Carol. The living room was empty. I could understand Mandy's annoyance with the telephone call but surely she must know that all I was trying to do was to help Carol carry on living. I couldn't believe that someone as sensible as Mandy could be jealous.

I collected my things and went upstairs. There was no light in the spare room and I did not dare go in uninvited. I cursed Carol, but most of all myself for not remembering the telephone.

***

My alarm went off at 6.15. I got out of bed and knocked on Mandy's door.

"This is your wake up call."

"Thank you." That was all.

I went downstairs and put the coffee on and made her a cup of tea. I knocked on the door.

"Come in." Mandy was sitting up in bed watching me with the sheet firmly up to her chin as I entered her room.

"Thank you. You'd better get a move on." She sounded business like even though I suspected that she was completely naked under the sheet.

I went into the kitchen and prepared breakfast. Mandy appeared shortly afterwards looking like a smart solicitor, wearing her glasses.

"Can I leave some stuff for Dora to wash?" She sounded slightly less frosty. As if there might just be hope.

"Be my guest. It will give her something to talk about in the pub. I haven't done any bacon if that's alright with you."

"That's fine. We weren't short of food last night." She helped herself to cereal and I passed her the carton of milk.

"Don't start relaxing standards, Mr. Talbert. Where's the jug?"

"It needs washing."

"So?" She took the carton and helped herself.

I put the toast on and we settled down to breakfast. I heard the paper arrive, collected it, passed the main paper to Mandy and kept the business section. She looked at her watch.

"We'd better go. Can we leave the dishes for Dora?"

"Not to-day we can't. But there's another help here who may be able to manage. Go up and get your things. I'll get the car out."

I opened the garage, backed out to the front of the house and locked the garage door. Mandy came down and I put her bags in the car, then set the alarm and double locked the front door. We did not say much as we drove to the station. I got out and gave Mandy her bags.

"See you to-night, Mandy."

"Don't bet on it. Call me later."

Back at home I had a shower and got dressed. I had bought the FT and the Telegraph at the station and read Jim's article about the Inquiry and the press conference. He clearly had reservations about not being able to hear the voice recordings but on balance agreed that confidentiality was probably the correct approach. The article also criticized the Secretary of State for not saying if there were marshals on board the aircraft. I turned to Chuck Osborne in The Telegraph where he had mentioned the conference but then, incredibly as far as I was concerned, added that reliable sources close to the accident investigation were beginning to think that the accident might be due in some way to an error by the pilots and not due to the presence of the hijackers. Analysis of the Distance Measuring Equipment beacon, DME, showed quite clearly that the aircraft was very low on the glide slope. The phone rang and I went into my office.

"Peter, it's Mike Mansell. Have you read the papers?"

"Yes, thanks. You sound incoherent."

"Chuck Osborne has clearly got the AAIB building bugged. Bob Furness must be going mad."

"You're right. I cannot remember anything like this happening before. It's just as well the Secretary of State called a Public Inquiry. I should think Thomas will be reading the riot act to Bob. Amazing."

"What can you do, Peter? This could be very serious for us."

"I'm not sure at the moment. Things don't look too good, I admit. The only thing that gives me any hope is that Harry Hodgson was a first class pilot and wouldn't do anything stupid. It's so easy to blame the pilots but, in this case, perhaps there's a lot more to it. Don't get downhearted, Mike."

"I'll try not to but the omens are not propitious. When are we going to hear who are the assessors?"

"I would have thought we should hear to-day, before the week-end."

Mike rang off and I decided that I didn't know enough about the Galileo European Satellite System and how it was used for approaches and landings. I called Jill Stanton and asked to talk to John Chester. She put me straight through.

"Thanks for talking to me John. How are things going?"

"As well as might be expected. Did you read that rubbish by Osborne?"

"Yes I did but surely he's just reflecting the attitude in AAIB?"

Chapter 3

"I suppose so, Peter, though how he knows what's going on is beyond me. It's about time Bob took over the investigation himself instead of leaving it to the inspector. Obviously, there are lots of people in the AAIB who are concerned with the investigation and Bob can't find the leak."

"Anyway John, Harry wouldn't have done something foolish, whatever the pressure from the hijackers."

"I know that, you know that, but the aircraft has crashed and, if Osborne is to be believed, it was showing well below the glide slope and the crew did nothing." He stopped. "Anyway Peter. How can I help you? You're working for our insurers so hopefully we're on the same side."

"I'd like to learn a bit more about GESS. Could I talk to your expert?"

"Of course. The man you need to talk to is Evan Evans and if he does not know all the answers he'll put you onto someone else who does."

John gave me his number and told me to call him in a few minutes after he'd briefed Evans. I thought about calling Mandy but decided it might be better to wait a bit. The mail didn't look terribly interesting but I did a bit and then called Evans.

"You don't know me, Mr. Evans. Did John Chester call you and explain that I needed to understand certain details about GESS?"

"Yes Mr. Talbert. I gather you're representing one of our insurance companies. How can I help you?"

"Well if you're prepared to talk on the phone perhaps you could run through how the Galileo European Satellite System is used for making approaches and landings in broad principles and then I can question you as we go along. Assume I know absolutely nothing. Will that be alright?"

"Fine, though I suspect I'll be teaching my grandmother to suck eggs. Well as you know the old instrument landing system, ILS, transmits a horizontal centre line for the runway in use and a centre line of the glide slope for landing. The ILS radio receiver on the aircraft just listens to the signal modulation as it is called and can tell straightaway where the aircraft is, relative to the centre line of the runway and centre line of the glide slope. The desired centre lines, both vertically and horizontally, are determined by the siting of the ground antennae. OK?"

"Yes, fine. That's what I like about ILS, no software."

"Right. Now the Europeans decided they wanted their own navigation system and not be dependant on the United States Global Positioning System. They would have liked to have called it the Galileo Positioning System but obviously the acronym conflicted with the United States GPS so they were forced to use the words Galileo European instead of just Galileo so it became the Galileo European Satellite System, GESS."

"Evan, how incredibly confusing."

"Tell me about it. Lack of forward thinking, in my view. Anyway approaches using GESS, or any satellite system for that matter, are an entirely different story. The systems are riddled with software. The GESS is an avionic box with three satellite position receivers. The output from each receiver is fed into a separate Multimode Receiver, MMR and each MMR has a world database of airfields and runways."

"But Evan, how does that work? In the case of the glide slope, for example, there is no transmitter at the aiming point."

"Well that's the beauty of using satellite positioning for approaches and landings. There is no need to have transmitters for each runway at each airfield. The MMR, because it has a world database of airfields and runways, is able to calculate a synthetic runway centre line and glide slope. The deviations of the aircraft from the synthetic centre line and glide slope are then sent to the auto-pilot and to the displays in just the same way as for ILS."

"That seems very neat."

"Yes it is in concept but it will only work if the software works. It really needs to be of high integrity."

"Presumably there are three GESS receivers to get the required integrity for automatic landings just like there are three ILS receivers?"

"Yes that's quite right but the avionic manufacturers have convinced the regulators that the three receivers can be in one box. On the 798 the ILS is actually a card in the MMR so there are three ILS receivers to guarantee integrity. The pilot selects whether he wants to use the ILS or GESS for the approach and the MMR sends the deviation output, computed in the case of GESS, to the flight deck display and to the automatic flight system. The GESS signals of course have to be absolutely accurate and so, for precision approaches, the Galileo European Local Augmentation System, GELAS, has to be operating at the airfield. The point here is that the GESS is only accurate enough for Cat 1 approaches, down to 200ft above the ground and for approaches below that height the accuracy has to be improved using an augmentation system."

"If I understand you correctly the GELAS is the European or Galileo equivalent of the United States Global Positioning System LAAS, Local Area Augmentation System?"

"Yes, that's exactly right. Both satellite navigation systems need augmenting to get the required accuracy for precision approaches, particularly for Category 3."

"You make it sound straightforward but goodness knows how the experts ensure software integrity for the system. Presumably from what you say there is no reason why the United States GPS can't be used in an identical way for landing?"

"Yes, that's so. However, Royal World Airlines decided they didn't trust the GPS system and in any event GPS Cat 3 approaches were not certificated when the first 798 was delivered because the new GPS satellites were not yet in orbit."

"Are the Airbus and Boeing aircraft organised the same way?"

"No, Peter, they are not. Technology changes at a frightening pace, as you know and 798 took advantage of the latest technology. It is the first to have this method of organizing the satellite navigation systems. One good thing about the design is that it keeps the two different satellite systems in step."

"What about the Russian system, GLOSNASS?"

"Independant have taken the view that it is much safer to keep all three systems separate rather than average them all together. You see, however an aircraft's position is determined, a local area augmentation system is always required for accurate work. To calculate accurate positions with a common area augmentation system would be a nightmare. Anyway, there is not a GLOSNASS augmentation system so it can't be used for accurate approaches."

"What about for ordinary navigation, Evan?"

"Well in the case of the 798, again the three systems are kept entirely separate but, in this case, any of the three systems can be selected on the FMS for en route navigation."

I couldn't think of any more immediate questions though I knew there would be some the moment I rang off.

"Evan, thanks so much. I'm going to have to consider what you've told me."

"If you need anything more give me a call."

I reflected on what Evan Evans had told me. It seemed to me that whatever positioning system was used, satellite approaches could only work safely in the first place if the database for all the airfields and runways was absolutely 'immaculate'. The chances of this being so was not realistic though for the relatively few Category 3 runways and airports in the world it was probably acceptable, since undoubtedly extra checks would have been introduced. The other blindingly obviously point was that the whole system was completely dependent on software. I was used to automatic flight systems and Flight Management Systems using a lot of software but not to the idea that ordinary radio receivers also needed software.

I got myself some soup and wondered what to do next. The phone rang.

"Peter, I'm sorry I was unreasonable about Carol. You're quite right to try to help her. How is she to-day?"

I felt a wave a of relief that Mandy had realised the pressure I was under. But that was why we got on so well.

"I don't know. I haven't called her and she hasn't been in touch. Perhaps I should." But then again I didn't want to encourage Carol to depend on me. "Mandy, what are you doing this week-end?"

"Well that depends. I'm catching the 6.10 to Bournemouth and going home. After that I haven't decided whether to go to the yacht club, ring up a friend or wash my hair."

"I could help you wash your hair."

"I'm not convinced that would help but you could come round and try to convince me."

"I'll meet you at Waterloo at the platform entrance and if that fails I'll catch the train anyway and meet you at the station exit. Do I need to buy shampoo?"

"No, only dinner."

The line went dead and I decided to call a French restaurant that I knew she liked in Poole. If her car wasn't working we could always go by cab. It was close to the yacht club so we could have a drink there first if we wanted. I went upstairs to put a few things in a bag when Mike rang again.

"They've just announced the assessors. The first one is Jack Templeman, Chief Engineer of Britannia and the second one is Professor Charles McGuire, professor of software engineering at Imperial College."

"Good Lord. Templeman is OK but I'm not sure about a software professor. They always try to say that everything needs more testing. However, to be honest it's probably a very shrewd move to make him an assessor. I'm just beginning to realise how much software might be a factor in this accident, it seems to be everywhere. By the way do we know anything about the Inquiry?"

"That was the other thing I was going to tell you. The Court is going to have a preliminary meeting next Thursday to determine the procedure for the Inquiry with a view to starting the Inquiry quite soon. Everybody who wants to be party to the proceedings must notify the Treasury Solicitor if they have not done so already."

"Next Thursday? That sounds very soon. Have you told the Treasury Solicitor you want to be there?"

"Yes, we have. You're right it seems incredibly early but the Court wants to get things started. The Inquest starts on Monday but that is going to be confined to identification at this stage but, of course, with so many dead identification is going to be a real problem. The Coroner is taking special measures to speed things up. Obviously the Coroner and Lord

Justice Thomas have been talking and there seems to be no reason why a lot of the facts can't be established and recorded in the first part of the Inquiry even though the reason for the crash is not known."

"What about AAIB? What are they doing?"

"Presumably they're now under orders from the Court and continuing with their investigation. Now Peter, we need to have a meeting with our solicitor, Tim Forrestal, and our counsel John Fairlane. Can you manage Monday at 11.00?" I said that would be alright. "Fine, come round to my office and then we'll go round to John's."

I looked at my watch after Mike had gone and tried to speak to Carol. Her mother answered the phone, Carol was collecting the children. I said I'd call sometime over the week-end but that I was not going to be at home. I finished packing, remembering to put in the stuff that Dora had done, and went downstairs just in time to pick up the phone.

"You won't know me, Mr. Talbert. My name is Anne Moncrieff." The voice was very French but the English was perfect. "I'm currently employed by the Safety Regulation Group at Gatwick as a surveyor but at about the time of the certification of the 798 I was attached to the EASA certification team from DGAC. I had some reservations on the way the EASA team were handling the certification."

"Ms Moncrieff, how did you get my name?"

"Because of my job I know a lot of the electronic engineers in the airlines and I had discussed my reservations with Evan Evans some time ago. I wanted to talk to someone and he suggested I talk to you."

"Have you spoken to AAIB?"

"I tried to but I didn't seem to be getting anywhere so I've written to the Chief Inspector."

"That's good. Bob Furness will contact you, I'm sure."

"I read your article some time ago about the aircraft in the FT. I know you've been retained by the insurers. Is there any chance that we can talk?"

"How are you placed on Monday?"

"Well I'm working at Gatwick."

"Well could we meet at lunch time. No, that won't work. How about at the end of the day?"

"If you could come down to Gatwick station we could meet at the meeting point at 5 o'clock."

"Fine. I'll be wearing a grey suit, carrying a black briefcase and I'm in the mid thirties."

"I shall be wearing a blue jacket and trousers and I'm some years younger than you."

"Good. We should be able to recognise one another. But give me your mobile number in case I need to cancel."

The phone rang as I put it down. Mandy was on the line.

"Very bad news, I'm afraid. One of my clients in Edinburgh is in trouble with the police and needs to see me this evening and then I'll have to go with him to-morrow to the police station. If I don't stop I can get the 17.30 shuttle."

"But what about our week-end?"

"We've got something to look forward to."

"But what about your hair? It needs washing."

"It's going to have to wait. I'll call you when I know what's happening. Must fly. Bye."

She was gone and so was our week-end. I wondered whether it was a wealthy client or an altruistic mission. I called the restaurant and cancelled the meal and then went upstairs to unpack. It had been quite a week. Perhaps a restful week-end doing nothing might be a good thing. There seemed to be no way I could help Mike Mansell which was worrying me. I secretly agreed with Osborne's alleged view of the AAIB. The chances were that with hijackers in the cabin the pilots' attention was diverted and didn't notice the approach was going wrong. It was strange Ms Moncrieff calling me. I wondered what she wanted but it would have to wait until Monday to find out.

CHAPTER 4

The week-end passed very slowly. I'd made no alternative plans following Mandy's unexpected departure. I did some work and tried to catch up with the many periodicals which I received. It was vital for me to keep up to speed on what was happening or the march of technological progress would pass me by. New ideas were always occurring and it was important to watch which ones fell by the wayside and which were adopted by the industry. I'd recently subscribed to cable TV and tried to find something decent to watch but apart from sport there was mainly a choice of old films. Mandy called on Saturday afternoon.

"I've finished at last. I'm catching the 7.30 shuttle and I'm going straight home."

"Shall I come down?"

"To be honest Peter, I shall have to spend to-morrow sorting myself out. Give me a call to-morrow afternoon and we'll try and get our diaries together."

"It wasn't our diaries I had in mind."

"You're at it again. You're being coarse." There was a pause. "Never mind, looking forward to hearing from you to-morrow."

On Sunday the papers arrived and I scanned the Times. Not much about the accident so I decided to go out and buy the Telegraph. Sure enough Osborne was giving the readers the benefit of his views on the accident. In fact, apart from reiterating the alleged AAIB view that the accident was probably due to pilot error, there was nothing particularly new.

I pondered over the dead body at the Hyatt in Sydney. The Secretary of State looked uncomfortable when he was questioned and there was no mention of the body in the Sunday newspapers. It may have just been a coincidence but the description of the bullet did suggest a hijacking pistol had been used. I wondered whether there had been a security clamp down on the media. If there was, then I needed to know. I called Jim Akers.

"Jim, I've been thinking."

"Peter, it's Sunday and I'm at home resting."

"Come off it. You guys never rest if there's a story."

"A story, that's different." Jim suddenly sounded interested.

"Well I wouldn't call you on a Sunday to pass the time of day.

"The dead body at the Hyatt…"

Jim interrupted me.

"Oh, I knew you'd notice the Secretary of State's rapid reply." He paused. "Go on."

"Well I wondered if the media was having it's future read by the Government? A D-notice perhaps?"

"You're quite right of course. The guy was meant to be on the plane but we have been told not to mention it."

"Why not?"

"That's just what we would like to know. I wanted to chase it up and investigate who the fellow was but my editor told me not to."

"So much for freedom of information. I smell a rat."

"So do I but there's not much we can do."

I rang off. If Jim wasn't going to do anything then I would have to. The explanation of the murdered man could significantly affect the hijacking. Perhaps Mandy would have some ideas on where to start digging for information.

After lunch I called Mandy and we agreed to meet the next day at the Archduke next to Waterloo at 6.30. I'd be back from Gatwick by then and Mandy would have finished work.

It wasn't too bad a day for January and I drove down to the river and went for a walk. On Monday I went up to town and arrived at Mike Mansell's in plenty of time.

"What sort of a week-end did you have, Peter?"

"Very quiet, unfortunately. My girl friend had to work in Scotland. How about you?"

"I went down to my little cottage in Wiltshire. Also very quiet. A change from London."

"What's the plan for to-day?"

"Well we need to brief our counsel John Fairlane and also Tim Forrestal our solicitor. Tim of course will be going to the preliminary hearing on Thursday and I thought we should give them some background to the accident. What did you think of Osborne's piece in the Telegraph?"

"I don't think it said anything new, did it?"

"I agree but from our point of view it's very bad news if that is the AAIB view. Anyway, let's go and see Tim."

We walked along to Lincoln's Inn and we were shown our way to John Fairlane's chambers. We waited briefly and then Fairlane appeared and introduced himself. He was 6 ft. 2 in., grey, thin and very distinguished. He spoke precisely and slowly as I expected from a QC.

"Let's go into my office and talk this thing through. Tim Forrestal, your solicitor is here already." We followed into a large room which had a partner's desk covered with papers in an orderly manner. He invited us to sit at a conference table where Forrestal was already in position. We shook hands. Tim was a bluff man, 5 ft. 10 in. wearing a brown suit and not my immediate idea of a solicitor. He started to summarise the situation.

Chapter 4

"We have a unique legal situation. This is the first aircraft accident since the EC altered the accident investigation procedures when the Secretary of State for Transport has directed that a Public Inquiry shall be held and replace the normal investigative procedure carried out by the AAIB. This is against the latest EC rules. The investigation is still proceeding but is now under the control of the assessors."

"But why couldn't the AAIB carry on, Tim? Aren't we going to be in trouble from the Commission?" Mike couldn't stop himself asking the obvious question.

"I shouldn't think so. We're only doing the sort of thing that the French are doing all the time. When our self interest is threatened it's quite unreasonable for the EC to think that nation states will defer to them. The old Section 8 rules lay down quite clearly that when an Inquiry is called, the AAIB investigation must be discontinued and the Secretary of State has decreed that this procedure should be followed. Of course, the Chief Inspector and his staff have to help when requested, but the responsibility for determining the cause is shifted from the AAIB to the Inquiry, or the Court as it is called. In order for this to be done the Lord Chancellor has appointed Lord Justice Thomas as the Commissioner to lead the Inquiry and has appointed two technically able assessors to help the Commissioner; as you know they are the Chief Engineer of Britannia, Jack Templeman, and a software professor, Charles McGuire from Imperial College."

John Fairlane interrupted. "Tim, I'm still not clear why the Secretary of State called the Inquiry, especially as the EC rules don't permit it. Why couldn't he have let the AAIB carry on as normal?"

"Well the reason for the Inquiry being called is not of course relevant to our discussion, but the generally accepted view is that the Secretary of State was forced to have the Inquiry because of the fact that hijackers got on board the aircraft and that information was leaking from the AAIB, which has never happened before. Both these circumstances need investigating and it is very convenient, with such public interest in such a terrible tragedy, to have a public inquiry. The Attorney General has given notice that the Inquiry shall start next Tuesday."

"But that's ridiculously soon." John interjected.

"Yes, it is. But the Court wanted to get the non-critical evidence out of the way while it was still fresh in the witnesses' minds. The inquest will still be on but it won't matter. It will be adjourned once all the identification of the bodies is complete but of course with so many bodies to be identified the inquest is going to be a very long one. As you know, the Inquiry preliminary meeting is being held this coming Thursday to determine the procedure and to check who wants to be represented and thus become a party to the proceedings.

"The obvious organisations who will be parties to the proceedings will be Royal World Airlines, Independant, the aircraft manufacturer, the National Air Traffic System which provides aerodrome control at Heathrow and the ground installations for the Instrument Landing System, ILS. Then there will be the two consortiums who manufacture both the Galileo European Satellite System, GESS and the local augmentation system, GELAS; also General Electric who make the engines. I suppose the pilots' and controllers' unions will also wish to be there. We shall be making an application to be a party to the proceedings because we are so involved financially and because only by so doing can we cross examine the witnesses. In addition, we shall probably wish to call witnesses as is permitted in the legislation. We cannot rely on Royal World Airlines to protect us since the hull is insured elsewhere and we need to look after own interests. I imagine their hull insurer will be present. I anticipate that Microspot, the maker of the multimode receiver, MMR, and Marcovitch, the maker of the Galileo European Satellite system receiver, may also wish to be represented. I suppose that the Police and the Emergency Services will ask to be represented as a matter of routine but really it is unnecessary for them since it is quite clear that they did a magnificent job.

"The order of the Inquiry will be determined at this preliminary meeting and also a likely calendar to be followed. I anticipate that I will be at this meeting and the current discussion we are having to-day will enable me to make the necessary request for time and witnesses. I expect that the first few days of the Inquiry will be spent hearing evidence from the Police and the Emergency services in order to satisfy everyone that everything that could have been done was done. After that it would seem logical for the chief inspector of the AAIB to be called followed by the senior inspector allocated to the accident. What the Inquiry looks at after the AAIB evidence may well depend on us. By the way, the Inquiry will almost certainly be in two parts. The first part, as I said, will just be to establish what really happened. The second part will be to permit the assessors to get further evidence to establish why it happened, and to determine the true cause of the accident so that the Court can write its report to the Minister. This report ought to include how the hijackers got on board and how the leak got out from the AAIB."

I indicated that I wanted to speak and Tim nodded to me.

"Tim, the way the plane was hijacked could be important. Apparently the media are under a D-notice over the body that was found in the Hyatt car park in Sydney. He was on the passenger list. We really need to find out who the person was."

"What do you suggest."

"I'm not sure, but if John threatens to ask some questions, we might be let into the secret."

Chapter 4

John Fairlane joined in.

"That's exactly right. Tim, I've scanned through Section 8 of the Air Navigation Order and it seems to me that the Court may well want some of the evidence held in private in view of the hijacking. As you say, they must discover how the hijackers got on board, what weapons they were carrying and how these weapons escaped the inspection of the ground staff in Sydney, but they may not want all that information to be public knowledge."

"Yes, John, I'm sure you're right. I expect they'll tell us on Thursday how the Inquiry will be organised. With any luck, by the time the AAIB evidence is over it may be an open and shut case of hijacker interference."

Listening to this, I made it clear that I was uncomfortable with relying on that happening.

"Peter here clearly doesn't agree with that rather optimistic hope and he may well be right. So what I think we have to do this morning is to review what we believe happened to Golf Hotel and to decide the witnesses we need. We need to judge what the AAIB and other expert witnesses are likely to say and whether we feel there is going to be a conflict of opinions."

"Thank you Tim." John Fairlane took over the running. "That's very helpful. It seems to me listening to what you've just said that it is going to be very important to know what we expect the AAIB to say and so I think we should start there. Mike, any views?"

"Well, there have been a succession of inspired leaks about what the AAIB have been thinking in the Daily Telegraph, who seem to have a source giving them information. The first leak was the voice recorder transcript and the significant point here is that if the Telegraph report was right, there was nothing really to suggest that the crew should not have been able to carry out and complete the approach and landing. After that first leak, the report stated that it was the view of the inspectors that the accident was due to pilot error. Presumably, the inspector is going to tell us why they think it might be pilot error."

John turned to me. "Peter, I think it is time you explained to us the procedure that the pilots would have adopted in making the approach. I would have thought that the aircraft should have been designed so that pilot error just is not possible."

I started slowly. This discussion was clearly going to take a long time but there seemed no alternative if John Fairlane was going to get up to speed.

"Well, we have to recognise that unfortunately there will always be accidents for a variety of causes. In a way I'm reluctant to get too involved technically in this accident because the balance of probability suggests that hijacking is the prime cause. However, we must be prepared, so here goes. We have to accept that pilot error will always be a possibility as the cause of an accident but pilot error is not as simple as it sounds. There are cases where the pilots make stupid mistakes or do not fly the aircraft very well. These cases are very rare these days but of course interference from hijackers might cause the pilots to make mistakes and not monitor all the displays properly. More common are the so called pilot errors due in part to poor aircraft design. These pilot errors are mainly due to a bad interface between the pilot and the displays or instruments on the flight deck. Sometimes errors are due to a lack of understanding of a too complicated aircraft. Perhaps the pilot does the wrong thing because the displays on the flight deck do not tell the whole story or mislead him. Normally these errors occur only if there is a malfunction of some type. We always have to be on our guard in these situations that we really understand the cause of the accident. It may be that the manufacturer of the aircraft, for competitive commercial reasons, may try to say that a particular accident is caused by pilot error alone and will not acknowledge that the aircraft itself could have been designed better.

"The problem is complicated because not all pilots have equal ability. An aircraft has to be capable of being flown by the world's worst airline pilot. The facts are that there is a huge range of ability and modern aircraft are incredibly complicated. Who is to judge when an aircraft is so complicated that it is unreasonable to expect the below average airline pilot to fly it? Notice we are all the time catering for the below average airline pilot, the worst pilot, not the average pilot and certainly not the test pilot."

John butted in as he realised I was about to continue.

"Come on Peter. Answer your own question. Who is to judge what is satisfactory so that pilots will not make mistakes?"

"In the short term the regulation authorities. That is the Federal Aviation Administration or the European Aviation Safety Agency. There is of course a bible of Airworthiness Requirements with which the designer has to conform. However, life is not that simple. Things are not just black or white, right or wrong. When the aircraft manufacturer applies for the aircraft to be certificated, judgements have to be made on acceptability, decisions have to be made on whether the aircraft is too complicated for the below average airline pilot. There is of course a wealth of background experience behind the decisions that are made and, in general, the system works very well. However, if a wrong decision is made then accidents will almost certainly occur due to the poor design. That is why it is so important for every accident to be investigated wherever it happens in the world and for the real cause of each accident to be established." I looked around at them all. "This is easy to say but very hard to do because when an accident happens in a remote place it is invariably the aircraft manufacturer and the regulation authority of the country that issued the original type certificate who are asked to help the local accident investigation authorities. Consequently, it could be that commercial pressures prevent the true cause of the accident from being established."

John came in again.

"Surely it is in everyone's interest to establish the truth?"

"You know much better than I do, John, that truth is a matter of opinion, depending on where you happen to be sitting. Wasn't it Pilate who said 'What is truth?' except he wasn't jesting. If the true cause of an accident is not established then the chances are that there will be more accidents of the same type until the real cause is clear for all to see and, very importantly, all the necessary modifications are carried out."

"I'm not sure I understand what you are saying about modifications, Peter."

"Well the normal situation is that if there is an accident due to bad design then changes will be required to prevent the accident re-occurring. Obviously, manufacturers have mixed feelings over this since they will invariably have to pay for any changes and of course they don't like that. The modifications could be very expensive and it could spoil their firm's competitive edge. On the other hand if they don't admit that changes are required then more accidents could take place. The regulatory authority must watch this situation closely and declare any necessary modifications mandatory."

John indicated that he had got hold of this point and had finished taking the note. I carried on.

"I want to leave this general discussion on the reasons for accidents, very important though it is, and consider now the non-contentious points on the accident to Golf Hotel. The aircraft had flown all the way from Australia and had enough fuel, but only just enough, to meet the minimum requirements of being able to divert to Manchester where the weather was good, being able to fly in a holding pattern near the airfield for 45 minutes and then land. They told the captain to carry on to Heathrow as planned where the weather was bad, in that there was an indeterminate cloud base and the visibility was 30 metres. This sort of weather is classified as Category 3B for landing and, in the case of Golf Hotel, this meant that the approach to the runway, 27L, and the subsequent touchdown and slowing down on the runway had to be made by the automatic flight control system. The pilots had a supervisory role so that if anything went wrong they would initiate what is called a missed approach procedure and the automatic flight system would apply power to the engines and climb away from the airport. Yes, John?"

"Surely the pilots have to take over sometime during the landing?"

"Yes, the procedure is that the pilot flying the aircraft disconnects the automatic flight control system when the aircraft is going sufficiently slowly to be able to steer the aircraft by reference to the centre line runway lighting. Remember, the pilot will not be able to see the lights very far ahead in fog conditions. Of course what is really needed is a so called 'enhanced visibility system' which can see through the fog and which displays on the Head Up Display, HUD, but there isn't one available yet. The 798 does have a HUD but that only repeats some of what the pilot sees on his head down Navigation Display.

"Returning to Golf Hotel, according to the press conference the other day Hodgson apparently did all the correct checks and coupled the aircraft to the Galileo European Satellite System for an approach. However, for some reason the aircraft went below the correct 3° glide slope and it crashed. I'm not sure whether we're going to be allowed to listen to the recording but the AAIB have and, according to Osborne in the Telegraph, they think that the accident was due to pilot error. This means that they have discounted the effect of the hijackers. I'm very unhappy about that because it is bound to be difficult to judge what effect having a knife or pistol held at the pilots' throats will make on their ability to perform correctly."

John looked at me. "Surely we're going to be able to hear the recording?"

"A good question. I believe Tim must insist that we be allowed to hear the recording, possibly at Farnborough or possibly at the Inquiry but I can't believe that the Court would want that because the recording would then be a matter of public record and that would not be acceptable in the UK."

"Would you be satisfied with the transcript, Peter?" Tim was obviously reviewing how to play his input at the preliminary hearing. "It ought to be possible to get hold of that."

"I'm not sure you will be allowed to have it but to answer your question, the transcript may be good enough but it obviously would be better to hear the recording played in real time." I looked at John. "Can you press the Court to play the recording?"

"We can try. Whatever happens we'll use the first part of the Inquiry as a fact collection opportunity." John was summing up. He obviously needed to get on with some other work. "I'll get everything we need from the witnesses and then Peter, you'd better advise us what you consider is our position and what else we need to establish. Tim, let me know how things go on Thursday."

The meeting was over and we chatted in the lobby before going our different ways.

Chapter 4

"I'll call you on Thursday Mike and then you can tell Peter how I got on." Tim was complaining, half to himself. "I can't see why, if the Inquiry goes into private session, we can't listen to the recording."

I butted in.

"As long as everybody is searched for voice recorders before they go in, Tim, it might be alright. If the press were there it definitely would be a non starter."

Mike and I went back to his office.

"What do you think?"

"I don't like the feel of this thing, Mike. As we said earlier, the chances of having a pilot error accident at the same time as a hijacking is extremely slight unless the two events are inter-related. How would your policy stand up if the pilots made a mistake because of hijackers pressure?"

"I don't know but I would have thought we would get away with it. However, it would be expensive because we might be taken to court." He paused. "Come on, let's go and have a sandwich."

We went in to Covent Garden and watched the world go by.

"I didn't tell you Mike. A lady called me up on Friday in connection with the certification of the 798. Apparently there was a problem and she wants to tell me about it. Perhaps it might be relevant. She sounded French with a very English name."

"When are you seeing her?"

"I'm going to Gatwick in a moment to see her. She's employed by the Safety Regulation Group down there."

"Well good luck. We need a break."

"It's early days yet, Mike. We don't know what the hell happened on the flight deck. We've got to hear the recording for a start. If Osborne can hear it, we certainly should be able to."

I went down to Temple and caught the circle line to Victoria. At Gatwick I was a bit early and went to international arrivals and had a cup of coffee. At ten minutes to five I wandered over to a position where I could watch the meeting point. Looking around I could see a lady dressed as per specification with a brief case, also watching the meeting point. She looked over, saw me and grinned. I went over to her.

"I'm Anne Moncrieff." I suppose I looked surprised.

"My family name was Delange but my husband's name is Moncrieff."

I gave an inward sigh of relief. Mrs. Moncrieff was not unattractive and I wanted no complications with this witness.

"How pressed are you for time, Mrs. Moncrieff? Can I get you tea or have you time to go over to the Hilton for a drink or a meal."

"Anne. Well my husband won't be home until 8 o'clock to-night. We live in Croydon." She looked around. "It will be quieter at the Hilton."

I led the way and we walked through the car park to the Hotel.

"Drink or food or both?"

"Let's sit by the bar. We can talk there."

We wandered over and sat down.

"Anne, I used to be a pilot and am now a consultant on flight decks. I have been retained by an insurance company to help them over the recent 798 accident."

"You are a journalist as well, Mr. Talbert. I read your article some time back on the 798."

"Peter. Well not a journalist, though I do occasionally write for the FT and other periodicals on technical matters."

The waiter came over. She chose a glass of wine and I asked for a Scotch and water.

"I know of course that the 798 was hijacked, Peter, and that therefore the accident could be due to that. However, the weather was very bad and it occurred to me that it was just possible that the hijacking was irrelevant."

"You are quite right to be concerned. Until the Inquiry gets under way we'll have no idea of why the accident happened."

"Let me tell you a bit about myself. I have a masters degree in electronic engineering, specialising in aircraft electronics obtained at the Paris École Polytechnique. My first job was with DGAC in Paris, you know like your SRG here at Gatwick. I was sent to Hoofddorp in Holland to get experience. I was attached to the EASA team certificating the 798 and I was lucky enough to be sent over to Independant in Seattle with the certification team. We had endless presentations and I was particularly interested in the satellite navigation and landing systems and, in particular, the way they were installed." She paused, picking her words carefully. "To be blunt, having heard the presentations, I did not like the way the Galileo European Satellite System and the Global Positioning System were installed, I did not like the standard of the software inside the Multimode Receivers, I didn't like the RWA approach selector switch and I did not like the way the flight path deviation was presented to the pilots."

I couldn't help grinning.

"That's seems fairly comprehensive, Anne. What did you do?"

"Forgive me, but I am now going to have tell you a lot of information that you probably know already in order to explain the problem I had with the EASA certification team."

"Don't worry about it. Just tell me the story as it happened."

Chapter 4

"Well, firstly the Global Positioning System and the Galileo European Satellite System. Both the satellite receiver boxes provided by the manufacturers had provision for three separate receivers on three separate cards within the box and the output from each card was fed into a different Multimode Receiver. Each MMR then computed the necessary steering commands to drive one of the three channels of the autopilot. This arrangement was to give the required integrity for automatic approach and landings. I felt that the three satellite navigation receivers should have been segregated into three separate boxes to achieve the required standard of safety but the manufacturers of the boxes had convinced both the FAA and the EASA that it was not necessary because of the particular power supplies being used and the way they had been arranged within the box. One of the reasons they did this, I am sure, was because they had to have a local augmentation system receiver to verify the satellite positions and they only needed to have one augmentation receiver if all three navigation receivers were in the same box."

Our drinks arrived which gave me time to make some notes.

"Very well. My next problem related to the Multimode Receiver. As you well know the box is full of software to calculate the steering command to the autopilot and this software has to meet a certain safety standard which is set by the regulation authority, in the case of the 798 by the EASA. This standard had been agreed with the FAA to be category B for the software of the Multimode Receiver. I felt this was not of a high enough level since the Multimode Receiver did all the computation for the autopilot during a blind landing and a failure could be catastrophic. In my view, the software level should have been set at Category A. but I suspect the box manufacturers did not want the extra cost of preparing the documentation."

"That's all very understandable but what was wrong with the RWA approach selector switch Anne?"

"Well unlike all the other airlines, RWA didn't want to be able to use the United States Global Positioning System for landing. Royal felt that the United States satellites were of an older design, based on Department of Defense requirements and not safe enough for Category 3 landings. It was true that newer satellites were coming along but GPS would always fundamentally be a United States military system. So Independant fitted a special switch so that different airlines with different requirements could all have the same layout on the flight deck instead of rewiring the aircraft. I felt that it was a cheap and nasty alteration. You see the whole thrust from Independant was to make a minimum change and, therefore minimum charge, between the airlines built to the RWA aircraft standard and all the other 798s instead of rewiring the RWA aircraft completely in this area."

"They must have loved you when you told them that."

"It's true they were not too pleased but the mere fact that they reacted so strongly confirmed me in my opinion. Being rather cynical, you must have noticed that the more violent the protestations that are made when something is said that is very embarrassing, the more likely that what has been said is very close to the truth."

"You're absolutely right. You can see it happening time and time again on the media. What about your last point?"

"Well it is all to do with the display of the deviation information to the pilots. In the case of the 798, the pilots were shown the same deviation from the desired flight path on the approach as was passed to the auto-pilot. If it was incorrect for the auto-pilot then it would be incorrect for the pilots looking at the displays. The fundamental point here is that there was no independent method for the 798 pilots to check if the deviations being calculated for the auto-pilot were being done correctly and, therefore, for the pilots to check if the aircraft was on the correct glide slope and centre line. I had real reservations about doing it this way with the satellite systems, because of the enormous amount of calculation that needed to be done at high speed. I felt that the pilots must not be completely dependent on the auto-pilot software, but I was told to shut up and stop raising difficulties."

"Anne, let me be the devil's advocate. There are three Multimode receivers, not one. Doesn't this deal with some of the problems you are raising?"

"No, Peter, I'm afraid not. Only a completely separate reference system would give adequate safety in my opinion, such as looking at the glide slope deviations independently using a different method when the auto-pilot was flying on the GESS. Of course as you are well aware, a forward looking device that could see through fog, displayed on the head up display, would be the ideal solution but they don't work very well yet and no such equipment was fitted to the aircraft."

"But there is an ILS indicator which the pilot can look at on the left hand side of the centre instrument panel."

"Yes, Peter. That's just what Independant said but the pilot has so much information on the electronic displays, there is no way that the ILS, displayed off to one side, would be monitored closely enough. And anyway, as this accident has shown, if there is no ILS what can the pilot do?"

"What happened after you made all these comments?"

"In the evening I was told that I was an observer, fresh out of training, no experience and I was not a contributor to the technical discussions. If I had any comments I could write them down and give them to the team leader when we got back to Cologne. So I stopped asking questions and continued making copious notes during the briefings. When I got back I did write a report showing that, when all my concerns were taken together, the RWA aircraft could not meet the overall required safety standard. I pointed out that in my opinion Independant had only done the display installation the way they had because it would have been very difficult to present deviation information on the displays independently from the auto-pilot without a lot of extra complication and expense. The way they did it made it very simple for the pilots to understand but in my opinion it was potentially dangerous.

"I was called in by my team leader and asked to withdraw my report and I refused to do so. The next thing that happened was that I was called from Paris and they said that they had been reviewing their manning requirements and how would I like to go to Gatwick and become an electronics surveyor. It was obvious that I had caused great embarrassment to the certification team of the EASA and they wanted to get rid of me.

"My English needed a lot of practice so I decided that I would not make a fuss and accepted the posting to Gatwick. In fact it was not long after that that I met my husband to be and we got married quite soon afterwards. He is an executive with Britannia at Gatwick so it was all rather convenient."

"Anne, did you keep copies of your correspondence?"

She smiled at me as if I was out of my mind and opened her briefcase.

"Here is a copy of my report and another letter asking them to confirm that they had my report on file. Needless to say there were no replies."

"Did you do anything when the 798 crashed? You must have been very concerned."

Again she gave me another look as if she could not believe I could be so stupid.

"Here is a copy of the letter I wrote to the AAIB the day of the crash. Again I have had no acknowledgment. In fact I sent the letter again, recorded delivery to the inspector in charge of the 798 accident and the letter was delivered."

She gave me another set of papers.

"As you know, Anne, there is going to be a Public Inquiry fairly soon. Are you available as an expert witness if you are needed?"

"Yes. I would be delighted. You and I know that for some reason the crew were below the correct glide slope and because of the installation they were unable to see this."

"Anne, I believe your comments may well be very relevant. We'll know a lot more when we are allowed to hear the flight deck voice recorder and know what the hijackers were doing. Like you I do not believe what we are being told in the press, that the accident was due entirely to pilot error. Apart from anything else the hijackers must have been influencing the proceedings. We need to find out what really happened and, if necessary, convince the Judge and the assessors. Anyway hopefully the Inquiry will soon be under way."

Anne gathered up her things and I gave her my card.

"If you change jobs or move please let me know."

She gave me her card and we said goodbye. I caught the next train back to Victoria, went to Waterloo and went upstairs to a table in the Archduke. Mandy appeared a few minutes late. We embraced.

"Sorry if I still look like a solicitor."

"You look lovely and you know it. And your perfume is exquisite as usual."

"You noticed."

"I notice everything about you. It's lovely to see you, I've been looking forward to it all week-end."

"I should hope so. If we're being honest, so have I." She squeezed my hand underneath the table and then moved her chair next to mine and not opposite so she could rest her hand on my knee. "Where have you been, Peter."

"I've been having a drink with a twenty five year old attractive young lady."

"I'm not sure I like the sound of that."

She drummed her fingers on my knee.

"Well she managed to find time for me between leaving SRG at Gatwick where she works and her husband's return. She's French but she married an Englishman who works for Britannia called Moncrieff."

Mandy relaxed and the fingers stopped drumming.

"Where did you two have this adventure?"

"It wasn't an adventure, it was in the bar at the Hilton. You're so suspicious."

"And don't you forget it." She moved her hand slightly up my leg which I found disturbing.

"Stop it, I'm trying to concentrate."

"I'm enjoying my supper."

"We haven't started yet."

"I have. Alright let's order."

We placed our order.

"Peter, did what Ms Moncrieff tell you help in any way?"

"It's too early to tell yet. It may have done, depending on what actually happened on the aircraft. I thought all her points were very valid. Before she worked at Gatwick she worked for DGAC in Paris and was attached to the EASA certification team for the 798. She told me all about her misgivings on the 798 avionic installation. She had had a row with the EASA after visiting Seattle when the aircraft was being certificated."

"Why did she have a row with the EASA?"

"Because she was a new girl and the EASA engineers were hypnotised by Independant. She raised the very fundamental point that the pilot only sees what the auto-pilot sees so it's very difficult to monitor the approach independently, which is important if the approach paths are calculated by software."

Mandy considered this and then remembered I'd met Mike Mansell.

"How did you get on this morning?"

"Well we were briefing John Fairlane, the QC CrossRisk Insurance are using, and Tim Freemantle, their solicitor. Tim is going to the preliminary meeting on Thursday to meet with the Court. I expect you know him." She nodded.

"I'll be there, Peter. It should be quite a short meeting."

"Are you sure? One of the issues will be whether the Inquiry will be in private or not when it comes to the flight deck voice recording, will everybody be allowed to hear it? Is anybody going to be allowed to hear it? Does the recording indicate how the hijackers got pistols and a bomb on board? Shouldn't all this be in private? My bet is that there will be a lot of argument but I'm hoping that some of the Inquiry will be in private so that we can hear the recording."

"Won't they produce a transcript?"

"They don't even do that normally, but because of the Inquiry I think they will. That's why the meeting might take longer than you think. Deciding on the procedure." I looked at her. "And there's another problem. There's a D-notice out on the dead body they found in Sydney. Apparently he was due to be a passenger."

Mandy looked at me in amazement.

"A D-notice? That's ridiculous. It had better not apply to the Inquiry."

"Jim Akers, and of course Tim, are both trying to sort that out. But any ideas of what we might do to find out what is going on would be very welcome. We need to know who he was for a start."

I could see Mandy considering the matter.

"Have to think about that." She looked at me. "When do we meet next?"

"How about Thursday? You can stay with me and tell me all about your meeting."

"Is that wise. We might rush the debrief in the excitement."

"We could have supper first to be on the safe side."

"OK. You can take me to Café Fish at six when they open and then we can go home. Pick me up from the office."

"Done."

Our meal arrived and we had a pleasant supper together though that night the meal was a gastronomic experience which didn't merit frequent repetition. But then the pub didn't charge Rules' prices.

"Now you're sure you won't stay?"

"I'd better not. I've got a lot to do and nothing to wear. Alright I know, but I've still got a lot to do. See you Thursday."

I saw her off to her train and then caught mine. When I got home I decided I'd better call Carol.

"I'm so glad you phoned, Peter. My solicitor has heard from Cathay and they have wired me £50,000 while they sort out the exact lump sum and pension due to me. It's a great relief. Please thank your solicitor friend for helping me."

"I will. At least that bit is good news. How are the children?"

"Tristram has gone very quiet. Wendy talks a little about the accident and her father. I think I am going to take them away to somewhere warm and have two or three weeks holiday. What do you think?"

"Carol, I think that's a very sensible idea. Why not go somewhere with lots of activity for youngsters? It doesn't have to be warm. You could take them skiing. The sooner the better. I'll call you in a couple of days."

We chatted a bit more. I rang off feeling rather guilty that we had not talked longer. As I went round the empty house doing this and that I reflected on the 798 accident. I hadn't really found out anything though the conversation with Anne Moncrieff might be important. The AAIB as directed by the assessors would be working at the problems and getting data twenty four hours a day, whilst other people like myself who were vitally interested, would be completely in the dark except for what was leaked in the Daily Telegraph. It looked as if the truth about the hijacking was being blanketed by the D-notice. What a ridiculous situation.

***

For the next three days I prepared some lectures, read some technical papers and wrote some letters to airlines trying to get more work. I left very early on Thursday and was at Mandy's office in plenty of time. She appeared looking like a girl who was being taken out to dinner and looking forward to it.

"I hope you didn't look like that in the office."

"Why not? You're a spoil sport."

"Well I know how I feel. I wouldn't like your clients feeling like that."

110

"You're jealous."

She looked pleased to see me and I hailed a cab for Panton Street.

"How did it go?"

She clearly wasn't in a hurry to tell me.

"I'll have a Kir Royale please, with plenty of attention."

The waitress, probably French, came over and took our order. We looked at the menu and made our choices. The girl returned with our drinks, bread and paté and I ordered salmon for Mandy and trout for myself.

"You were right, Peter. The meeting took a lot lot longer than I was expecting. The Treasury Solicitor people seemed to be in charge of the arrangements and of course there was endless discussion on how the Inquiry should proceed. In the end it was decided that the relatively non-contentious stuff like the police and firemen should start followed by the Air Traffic controller who was on duty.

"We then debated for hours about whether we should listen to the recording. AAIB said that it was unheard of for interested parties like us to hear the recording except for very special technical reasons. We countered by pointing out that this was not an AAIB investigation but an Inquiry controlled by the Court and we needed to hear the recording as evidence. AAIB then changed tack and said that we wouldn't be able to understand the recording because it was very noisy. We then asked for a transcript which was refused but, after a long battle, the Court decided that a few people nominated by the interested parties could hear the recording and the transcript would be available for the second part of the Inquiry.

"The recording would be played at the Inquiry in private session without the press. A complete list of attendees for the private session was made, each organisation saying who they wished to be present and why. While still in private session the Court would hear from the UK security experts and all of us would be excluded. It would be a very private session."

"Does the legislation permit that?"

"It refers to 'public interest' and presumably the Court has every right to decide who will be present. Anyway, since the legislation is now outdated and this is a special inquiry they can almost do what they like. It was agreed that after the private session the Inquiry would go back into public session for some preliminary questioning of the AAIB inspectors. We all insisted that there should be a twenty four hour gap after hearing the recording before resuming the first part of the Inquiry so counsel could be briefed, which suited the Court anyway because of their private security session. After the AAIB evidence had been heard, the first part of the Inquiry would be stopped. It would only be reconvened when the

Court felt that they were ready to take the rest of the evidence from the AAIB specialists and from the witnesses provided by the interested parties, RWA, GE, Honeywell etc. When the second part of the Inquiry was over, the Court would prepare their findings for the Secretary of State, referring to likely causes and with recommendations for avoiding future occurrences."

"Well that's pretty comprehensive. They'll have to go to Sydney I should think to investigate how the hijackers got on to the aircraft with their weapons, though I'm not sure whether they can do that legally. I suppose they could get some people to come over. Of course, we don't know anything about the Hyatt body yet and the impact on the hijacking but I suppose they may have been told something. It's good news about hearing the recording. We should be able to understand exactly what happened."

"Isn't it rather unusual for everyone to hear the recording?"

"Well yes. But this Public Inquiry is unique and after all it isn't everyone who is hearing the recording. It's only the experts of the parties who are directly concerned and they all should be responsible people."

"The recording will get leaked, Peter."

"I'm not so sure. After all, the people who will hear the recording are known to the Attorney General." I paused. "Will you be at the closed session?"

"I don't know. I shouldn't think so. We may want to nominate an expert to listen."

We discussed it a bit more then I got side tracked looking at Mandy and she noticed I was noticing.

"I think we're ready for a night cap at home."

I wasn't going to argue. We held one another in the cab to Waterloo and in the train to Kingston. I decided it would be an anticlimax to walk home and we caught yet another cab. Mandy went upstairs while I made the coffee. This time I remembered to make sure the answering machine was on and I altered it to make it answer after one ring. Mandy appeared and we took our coffee into the front room and we sat quietly for a bit enjoying the moment. I looked at her.

"You're making it very difficult for me to drink my coffee."

"You can have coffee any time. I thought you'd be pleased."

The phone rang for a moment and then the answering machine took over.

"Well you got one thing right but it's a bit bright in here."

I turned most of the lights out and put our coffee safely on the dresser.

"Wouldn't a bed be more comfortable?"

"Don't be so conventional. We've got to get to know one another." I didn't argue. She whispered in my ear "That's very nice."

***

We had to move quickly in the morning to get Mandy to the office on time. Dora wasn't coming until Tuesday so I didn't mind leaving the house looking a bit the worse for wear. I packed a few things for the week-end and we rushed for the station. I saw Mandy safely to the office, left my bag with her and went on to have a coffee and croissant in my favourite breakfast spot waiting for Mike to arrive. Insurance executives didn't start work at eight.

The Telegraph was full of the programme for the Inquiry and complaining of the iniquitous procedure of having a part of the Inquiry in private without the press being present to look after the public interest. Jim Akers in the FT said how necessary it was to have private sessions to prevent hijackers learning from the mistakes and successes of other hijackers. I finished my breakfast and went round to Mike.

"Have you heard about the Inquiry, Peter?"

"Only what Mandy told me. The private session sounded good because we'll be able to hear the voice recording.

"Yes that is good. As you know the AAIB strongly resisted playing the recording or even providing a transcript but the Court overruled them. Perhaps it was a judgement against them for leaking the recording. We need you there Peter because I'm sure you'll get more benefit from hearing the recording than Tim will. We put your name on the list as our technical expert."

"Won't John Fairlane be there?"

"No, I don't think so. We need him for cross-examination of the witnesses after we've briefed him. We shall need to have a meeting with John immediately after you've heard the recording."

"Will I have to give evidence, Mike? At the moment I've got nothing to say."

"Not for the first part of the Inquiry but you may learn something from the recording. I hope you'll have something to tell the Court when the main part of the Inquiry starts."

"You and me both."

After leaving Mike I went to the Royal Aeronautical Society to read some articles I needed from their library, which took the rest of the morning and some of the afternoon. After that I went to the Royal Air Force Club to catch up with the periodicals and time my departure to be at Mandy's office at 5.30. She didn't keep me waiting long and we were on our way in a taxi to Waterloo.

Mandy looked a bit weary but there was something else as well which I could not place. I knew she was pleased to see me and we leaned towards one another but I found I got the cheek and not the lips.

"Where are we having dinner?"

"I've booked a table at that place you like in Poole. The food's always good and they always look after us well."

"Lovely." She held my hands, looked at me carefully, thought about saying something, changed her mind and then carefully kissed my cheek.

We caught a fast train and then a cab to Mandy's flat.

"I need a shower and change and so do you" she said sternly. "Let's have a quick drink before we go out. I want to catch up with what you've been doing. Put your things in the other bedroom. I've missed you, Peter."

"Since this morning?"

"Since last night."

Mandy had first shower in the single bathroom and I showered while she dressed. It might have been quicker the other way round though I shaved while I was waiting. In fact I was ready just before Mandy and shouted through her door, asking her what drink she wanted. "I'll have a gin and tonic as it's Friday." came the muffled reply.

I prepared two gin and tonics, just in time before Mandy appeared.

"Call a cab will you, otherwise you won't be able to drink at all. Not that you drink much, I'm glad to say."

I obliged and asked the driver to be along in twenty minutes.

"What have you been doing to-day, Mandy?"

"Do you really want to know? It's so tedious in some ways but so important to the clients. How about you?"

"I saw Mike who didn't tell me anything new. Then I've been working at the Royal Aeronautical Society."

Mandy paused and again looked as if she was going to say something, but didn't. The taxi driver rang the doorbell.

"Come on, darling. Drink up, we need to leave for Poole."

It was only a small place and we were put at a table near the back. We were not late but the place was quite busy. I ordered two more gin and tonics. We started talking of all sorts of things not connected with our work and again I realised how our lives were getting more and more involved. I thought that when this investigation was over I might ask Mandy to come away for a holiday and perhaps we needed to talk over the future. Perhaps I should sell the house for a start to lay the ghost of Diana. However, I sensed there was something on her mind which needed flushing out.

We decided to have coffee before we left since we were in no hurry. We got home soon after eleven.

"Peter. Let's have another drink. I want to say something."

Chapter 4

I returned with two fairly stiff gin and tonics.

"Sit down over there." I complied with her request, wondering what was coming.

"I've had a client visit me to-day and it made me think about where you and I are going. We like one another a lot and we now know that we enjoy having sex together. But I'm not sure we should be making a habit of it. We need to decide whether we have any future. Peter, I see so many cases in my office of people who get into a tangle and I don't want it to happen to us. I know you like to forget all about it but we don't know whether Diana is alive and likely to reappear, or not."

She stopped and looked at me.

"Peter, you look as if I've hit you"

"Well you have really, metaphorically. You know I've done all I can trying to find Diana. I think the world of you and I thought our relationship was developing well. I feel a bit shattered. This is all rather sudden."

"Well let's sleep on it. I'm going up now and we can talk some more about the problem in the morning."

She came over, kissed me on the cheek and then went to her room. I never did understand women, or maybe I did.

***

In spite of Mandy's worries we had a lovely week-end together. The weather wasn't too bad for January and we managed to walk in the New Forest on Saturday. On Sunday I made breakfast and took the papers into Mandy's room. When we'd finished she got me to clear all the dishes away into the kitchen.

"Why don't you read the papers next to me in the bed?"

"It might spoil your New Year's resolution."

"Nonsense. Don't boast." There was a pause. "However I've decided I don't mind your trying."

I brought the papers over and lay on the bed. Mandy removed them carefully, rolled over and held me tight. She felt me responding but she didn't seem to mind. She whispered slowly in my ear, kissing my ear, kissing me gently.

"I don't want you to think that we haven't got to sort out this Diana problem. It's very important for both of us. However, I think the way I feel at the moment it'll have to wait for a bit."

We savoured the moment; we both realised that we were having more than just a casual affair. When it was over I held her close for a long time.

Mandy murmured what was clearly worrying her above all.

"Didn't you ever find out where Diana went?"

"No. We'd been quarrelling for a long time and I was away a lot flying. I began to suspect that she was seeing someone else. After she disappeared, I went to the police but they didn't seem too interested. Her parents had not heard from her but she very rarely contacted them anyway. It was and still is a complete mystery."

"But you do see? She may come back. We can't ignore that."

"You may be right but I can't spend the rest of my life waiting for something that may never happen, and I don't want to lose you just waiting."

She rolled over in the bed and looked at me.

"Well it certainly is a problem." She thought a bit. "Peter, why don't you go on up to London now and get yourself organised for the Inquiry on Tuesday? If you come up with me early to-morrow morning you'll be rushing all day to-morrow."

Subconsciously I had been wondering how I was going to get everything I needed to do done on Monday and Mandy had come up with a sensible solution. I nodded my agreement and got up and had a shower. Mandy got her car going and took me the station. We held each other for a bit and then I left to catch the train.

"Keep in touch, Peter." She waved as I disappeared up the steps.

The ghost of Diana which had stood behind us and which we had tried to put out of our minds was now out in the open. There must be a way of dealing with it legally. Surely Mandy must know. Why didn't she say? I was sure we both felt that there might be a real prize if we could find a way through. When we had said good-bye at the station we each had more confidence in the other than we had before the week-end. I went home feeling unjustifiably optimistic but realising that Mandy and I would have to have a serious talk. Perhaps I should talk to my solicitor to find out how long one had to wait before the presumption of death. He had mentioned something to me at the time of Diana's disappearance but I had not taken it in. On balance I felt the week-end had been a success.

On Monday morning I called Jim McIntosh, my solicitor.

"I've been thinking about Diana. If she does not reappear is there anything I can do about getting a divorce? I seem to remember a year or so ago you mentioned seven years. It seemed a long time then, it seems much nearer now."

"Well Peter, let me ask you first has anything happened to change the way things were when we last spoke? In other words have you heard anything from her or have you heard anything from anyone else that leads you to believe she might be alive?"

"No I haven't. I left her to do a Britannia trip to Australia and I have never seen sight or sound of her since. As far as I could see at the time she had not taken anything with her. The jewellery that I had bought for her was still in her drawer and our bank account was untouched. I can only assume she died or was killed in some way, though how there was no trace is inconceivable to me."

"Well you've put your finger on it. You are presuming that Diana is dead. The law says that if, after seven years from when she disappeared, there has been no change to the situation you may make a petition to the court to have it presumed that Diana is dead and to have your marriage with her dissolved."

"What happens if she reappears some time later and I have remarried?"

"You don't have to worry about that. Once you have gone through the necessary legal proceedings relating to death and divorce and your decree has been made absolute, then it does not matter if Diana reappears. It is the same as any other divorce that has been made absolute."

"So you're telling me to be patient and everything will work itself out?"

"I suppose I am really. Any way keep in touch and you may think it sensible to check again about now to make certain that her parents have not heard anything."

I rang off. Presumably Mandy knew all the solicitor had told me by heart and I guessed she was nervous of Diana suddenly reappearing. I decided to call Diana's parents in Newcastle under Lyme. I think they secretly blamed me for her disappearance but we continued to have civilised conversations. Her mother answered.

"No, Peter. We've heard nothing at all. I've tried the police recently to recheck the unidentified bodies list from the time when she disappeared until now but there still does not seem anything that matches up. How are you managing?"

"I'm OK, but I must admit losing Diana is still a great strain and I find the uncertainty very upsetting. How about you?"

"Well we get along, but losing our only child is a great loss."

"I understand. Let me know if anything happens? Bye for now"

There was nothing more to be said. There never was any common thread between us except Diana and she had gone. In the evening I called Mandy and brought her up to date. I went to bed thinking of the Inquiry. At least I would have a chance to hear what AAIB had been up to and to discover what had happened on the last few minutes of the flight of Golf Hotel.

A Flight Too Far

CHAPTER 5

The weather was not very kind, raining hard and a strong wind. Still it was reasonably warm for the middle of January. I got dressed in plenty of time and went up to Town and Mike Mansell's office. I was early and had my normal breakfast of croissant and coffee. Mike had arrived by the time I returned. There was really no need for me to attend the Inquiry but it was obviously a good idea to go to get used to the atmosphere of the court. We left in plenty of time to get to the Queen Elizabeth Hall at 9.30, half an hour before the Inquiry was scheduled to start. The organisation of the Inquiry seemed good and we signed in as people who were parties to the proceedings. We went in to the hall and sat in the space specially provided.

The place was already filling up and I identified the area reserved for the public, the press, the places occupied by the counsel, the witness box and the Court itself, placed on a fairly high dais. I saw Tim Forrestal but there was no sign of John Fairlane. Presumably he would only appear when there was something for him to do. At 10 o'clock prompt we all rose and Lord Justice Thomas appeared with Charles McGuire and Jack Templeman, the two assessors. I looked for Chuck Osborne but he was nowhere to be seen. There were a few pressman but not as many as I expected.

It was always difficult at first to judge the age of someone wearing a wig but to my surprise Thomas seemed comparatively young for someone in such an eminent position, probably just less than fifty years old. He was quite short but had not run to fat, perhaps because he was abstemious or perhaps just lucky. It must be very difficult to keep fit and trim as a judge, sitting long hours in court. Templeman looked a tough egg, six foot, heavy in build but not fat, slightly red in the face; I guessed the Chief Engineer had a drink or two during the day. McGuire looked very different from the other two, short, definitely running to fat, untidy suit, peering through thick glasses, every inch the stereotype of a professor. Time would tell how these three members of the Court would perform and behave.

The Court sat down and so did we. The proceedings opened with a statement from the Attorney General himself. He started by explaining that the accident was unprecedented in the UK bearing in mind the number of people killed and the location of the accident. The aircraft had crashed in the middle of a hijack and it was important to discover how the hijackers had managed to get on board the aircraft at Sydney. It was also vital to discover whether the hijack had caused or had contributed to the accident or whether the accident was due to some completely unrelated cause. He had consulted the Court and, mindful of the great public interest in this matter, the Court had decided that the Inquiry would be in two phases. This first phase would establish what had happened and, possibly, try to establish some indication of the cause of the accident. The Inquiry would have to go into private session when the security aspects of the hijack were being discussed and when the voice recording was being played to the expert witnesses. There would then be a gap while the assessors discussed with AAIB and others what extra work might be required and the Court could decide what additional witnesses would be needed. The Inquiry would then reconvene and hear the latest developments, if any, in establishing the cause of the crash; the information would come from the AAIB and other witnesses who might be requested to appear by the parties to the Inquiry or by the Court itself. The Inquiry would then be closed and in due course the findings of the Court would be announced. He intended that the Inquiry would review all aspects of the accident, on the ground and in the air, to enable the Court to find the cause, to ensure that all the necessary lessons were learnt, and to make sure that such an accident was unlikely ever to occur again. He anticipated that this first phase of the Inquiry would last a week.

The Attorney General then explained that the Court would hear first the reports from the emergency services to ascertain how well they had performed and to see what improvements, if any, were required. It was the intention then to hear evidence from the AAIB to learn how far the investigations had proceeded. The witnesses would be examined by himself or his staff and could then be cross examined by counsels on behalf of the organisations that were parties to the proceedings. He anticipated that the first two days would be spent looking at the emergency services before calling the AAIB witnesses. The Attorney General then left and the Chief Constable for the Metropolitan Area, Sir Robert Applegate, was called as the first witness. He was questioned by Janet Crowburn, the leading counsel for the Attorney General. Encouraged by suitable questioning, Sir Robert described how his officers had been alerted by calls from Heathrow saying that the aircraft G-RWAGH was transmitting a hijacking code and that RWA Flight operations had had a message from the aircraft saying that the hijackers wanted the aircraft to be refuelled, some Government held al-Qaeda prisoners to be released and then loaded on to the aircraft. The aircraft would then take-off for somewhere in the Middle East. Apparently the hijackers threatened to blow up the aircraft if the instructions were not complied with. He had been awakened by his people who briefed him on the situation and he had given instructions to find out from RWA if there were any VIPs on the flight. By the time he had arrived at the hijacking control room, RWA had told the office about the Foreign Secretary being on board.

The standard hijacking drill had been implemented and, in spite of the fog, the police. army and special security forces had moved into position awaiting the landing of 798. Just before the aircraft had been due to land they had heard a loud noise, possibly an explosion, and then Heathrow Tower came on the phone saying there had been an accident to the hijacked aircraft which should have landed on runway 27L. 999 calls from householders on the eastern side of the A30 had enabled the exact location of the accident to be pinpointed and the emergency services, which were in position on 27L, immediately drove round to the A30 where the crash had occurred. In fact every credit should be given to the people driving the vehicles since at the time visibility was no more than about 25 yards. The duty officer straightaway formed and manned the Accident Operations Room in accordance with the plan which had been worked out several years before with all the local authorities. Police cars were sent out to close the A30 and the duty officer had the Operations Room staff call the officers and policeman who were on stand-by to report in immediately.

Meanwhile the duty officer at the Heathrow Airport fire station, alerted by the control tower, had sent the crash crews immediately to the site of the disaster and had called in extra fire trucks from Hounslow. Sir Robert explained that there was a disaster plan for aircraft accidents which were in, or close to, the airport and this plan had been put into action straightaway. The Air Accident Investigation Branch had been called and investigators had arrived in about ninety minutes. Ambulances from all the local areas had been asked to come to the scene of the accident the moment the first policeman on the scene had reported seeing survivors walking in a dazed fashion near the accident.

Because the aircraft had been under the control of the hijackers when it crashed, security forces and the army had been needed to check on the survivors as well as the aircraft itself. Luckily these specialists were already available because of the hijack warning. Nevertheless, the rescue operation was made significantly harder because all survivors, badly wounded or not, had to be identified and checked to establish whether any of them were hijackers. It took about 48 hours before it was established that all the hijackers had been killed in the accident.

Another complication was that it had been suspected that there might be at least one bomb in the wreckage and Army Bomb disposal experts were needed at the accident site.

Sir Robert then chronicled the whole history of how the crash had been dealt with. The first move had been to put out all the fires; luckily they had not been very extensive due presumably to the small amount of fuel left in the aircraft. The firemen had then gone into the wreckage to rescue survivors and the ambulances had taken the survivors away. Very fortuitously, no houses had been hit by the aircraft but upward of thirty cars had either been destroyed or involved in the ensuing pile up. Here too the firemen had had to deal with the survivors and get them away in the ambulances. This phase of the operation had taken several hours and was made immeasurably more complicated because it took place in the dark and in dense freezing fog. Large numbers of flood lights with the necessary emergency power supplies had had to be provided and it had been difficult to get the equipment on site because of the poor visibility.

Once all the obvious survivors had been found it was necessary to search for more survivors in the wreckage and to start taking the dead to the nearby mortuaries at Hounslow and Ealing. The number of bodies had been so large that in the end it had been necessary to use four mortuaries. At the request of the AAIB the local army barracks at Windsor was then contacted and plans were made to start searching for accident recorders. In parallel, the police had isolated the whole area to prevent sightseers and looters removing wreckage and possibly important clues to the cause of the accident. The security forces were looking for weapons in the wreckage and it had been impressed on the doctors that all bodies had to be checked carefully for the cause of death. In fact two of the dead were found to have been killed by pistol wounds before the crash and these two bodies had been identified by the security forces.

By dawn on Tuesday the police had had the whole situation completely under control. There was a comprehensive diversionary traffic plan, and arrangements had been made for the local householders to get in and out without going into the prohibited area. The fire crews were still extricating bodies; the crash recorder with all the flight data had been found but the AAIB and the army were continuing to look for the cockpit voice recorder. The coroner had asked that bodies should be identified as soon as possible. A telephone number had been arranged with thirty lines for people to call in and check for information on their relatives and a passenger list had been obtained from Royal World Airlines.

The character of the operation which had been started very quickly on an emergency basis had then gradually changed to a long term procedure. There had been two distinct aspects. First every passenger had had to be accounted for. By dusk the fire crews had reported that, as far as they could tell, all the bodies had been recovered. A check with the passenger list had revealed that there should have been two more bodies or survivors. Sydney had been called to double check on the numbers and all the hospitals with survivors had been asked to check their numbers. As a result of these checks one extra survivor had been discovered at Ealing and it was established that one passenger had not got on to the plane. The second aspect of the operation had been to find all the wreckage. Every piece had had to have its location recorded and then removed to a hangar at the Defence Establishment Research Agency at Farnborough. This latter task had been done by the Army on a long standing arrangement with the AAIB. On Tuesday night the security forces had found the cockpit voice recorder buried in the wreckage.

The search had stopped for the night and resumed the next day, Wednesday. The police felt that they just had to open the road by the end of the day and so the army had been approached for extra soldiers to search for every piece of wreckage. By the evening the AAIB had agreed that everything had been cleared and the road could be reopened. An announcement had been made on the radio that if any wreckage was discovered subsequent to the road reopening then the police should be informed. In fact one or two more pieces were found in the next two or three days.

When Sir Robert had finished chronicling the history of the ground response to the accident Lord Justice Thomas congratulated him and his enormous team for the very professional way the accident had been handled. He asked if Sir Robert felt that the response could have been improved if he had had more resources.

"No my Lord. We had a carefully worked out plan which had been refined as a result of other disasters such as the fire at Kings Cross and the Marchioness on the Thames. This plan had been dovetailed to match the Heathrow aircraft accident procedures and in the event we could do no more.

"I would like to pay tribute to the many, many firemen who risked their lives rescuing the survivors from the very hot wreckage and to the hundreds of people, police, ambulance men, army personnel, who worked for hours at a stretch dealing with this enormous problem. I would also like to pay tribute to the staff at the many hospitals involved and to the general public who co-operated with our plans to enable the rescue and investigation to be carried out so quickly."

Crowburn asked the Chief Constable if he knew the identity and the organisation of the hijackers.

"No, Ma'am. I was informed by the security forces that there had been an anonymous telephone call at about 9.30 that evening claiming that an aircraft would be hijacked and flown to Heathrow. Six high security al-Qaeda prisoners were to be released and put on board the aircraft. This warning had roughly coincided with the alert they had received from the airport. Unfortunately it had not been possible to trace the call. Apparently there had also been another telephone call in the early hours of the morning, allegedly from some outlawed IRA organisation, making it clear that the hijacking was none of their doing."

"Sir Robert, the hijackers apparently threatened to blow up the aircraft. Did you come across any bombs in the wreckage?"

"As I mentioned, we had a team from the Army helping us and apparently there was one badly damaged bag which had some explosive material close by. I don't know the details but the material had not exploded or ignited."

"Sir Robert, were there any weapons discovered during the search of the wreckage?"

"Yes, Ma'am."

"Perhaps you would like to tell us something about these weapons?"

The Chief Constable looked very wary.

"Well Ma,am, I believe there were some weapons discovered by the Army and security experts, but I am not familiar with the details."

There was a pause while Crowburn considered whether to explore the Chief Constable's answer in more detail. She leant down and spoke to one her assistants, hesitated and then indicated that she had finished and it was clear that none of the other counsels were going to ask any questions. It was now lunch time; Sir Robert's evidence had taken well over two hours and the Court adjourned. Mike and I went to a nearby pub to have a sandwich.

"Well Peter that's got the Inquiry on the road. I understand from Tim that Crowburn intends to call the duty police inspector, the duty officer at the British Airports Authority, the duty officer in the Heathrow fire section and the duty Air Traffic Control Officer. Of course the controller would have been the one who pushed the panic button alerting the fire station and indicating where the accident was likely to be. He will be the last witness to be called before the AAIB, since he will describe the air traffic landing procedure."

"What about the explosives expert and the weapons expert for that matter?"

"I think they will leave that until the closed session with security."

"Mike, do you think we need to go back this afternoon?"

"Not really. I think we should be here to-morrow afternoon to hear the air traffic evidence."

"You know Mike, I think they will have to call the approach controller as well as the tower controller because they have got to establish the type of approach the aircraft was doing. They may do it later but it would be a lot tidier if they got all the air traffic evidence over before AAIB."

"I'll mention that to Tim. He may want to have a word with the Attorney General's solicitor to make your suggestion or he may feel that it does not really matter in what order the evidence is taken."

Mike went back to his office but on impulse I decided to go back in to the Inquiry. In fact there was nothing really significant in the evidence but it was necessary for it to be given so that it was clear to the general public that all the emergency services had worked correctly. The Inquiry finished at five o'clock but there was still some more evidence to be given before the air traffic control evidence. I left just before the end and went home.

When I got back I went into the front room and switched on the television to watch the news. The Inquiry was mentioned but at a very low key. I had supper and read some technical magazines, then went to bed and watched the TV. I remembered that John Chester had told me that the relief first officer, Frank Mercer, had not been killed in the accident. Perhaps I should talk to him if he was getting better. Presumably AAIB must be talking to him if he was fit enough. Come to think of it I hadn't spoken to Marcia Hodgson. That was something else I should do. I dropped off to sleep.

***

Next morning I went straight to the Queen Elizabeth Hall at about ten o'clock and sat next to Mike who was already there. I noticed that the seats reserved for the press were filling up. The airport fire officer was giving his evidence.

"He's the last one before the approach controller who will then be followed by the local air traffic controller on duty as you suggested."

We listened to the fire officer and then the approach controller, Harvey Gates, was called. Janet Crowburn was doing the questioning. The controller explained that he had taken the aircraft over from the en-route controller in the Clacton sector and had positioned it for an approach on runway 27L. The pilot of RWA 573 asked if he could use the ILS on 27L for his approach but Gates had explained to him that the ATIS was incorrect and that it was no longer approved for Category 3 approaches and landings and, anyway, the ILS was out of service. The pilot then requested a GESS approach and Gates cleared the aircraft for a GESS approach and to call Heathrow Tower.

Janet Crowburn decided to question Gates.

"Mr. Gates. Why couldn't the aircraft carry out an ILS approach on 27 Left? Surely this is an older and more reliable way to do the automatic landing?"

"Ma'am as I explained, the 27 Left ILS is no longer approved for Category 3 approaches. The latest FM broadcast stations which have been approved for commercial transmissions interfere with the beam and so the Category 3 approval had to be withdrawn."

"I am not sure I understand what you are saying. Are you telling the Court that if government approval had not been given for these broadcast stations, the 27 Left ILS would still be approved for automatic landings?"

"That's my understanding of the situation but, in any event Ma'am, the ILS was out of service. It was not transmitting so RWA 573 could not have used the ILS, even if the pilots had tried."

"Now, the decision by the captain of RWA 573 to use the Galileo European Satellite System to land on 27L. Is that normal?"

"Well the procedure is approved though I can't recall it being used before in Cat 3B conditions. But of course the ILS on 27 Left has only just been decommissioned for Category 3 approaches."

"So in your view Mr. Gates, there was nothing unusual in the RWA 573 saying that they were going to do a GESS approach?"

"It was unusual because, as I said, up to now the 27 Left ILS has been working and has been used. When RWA 573 announced it was going to use the GESS for the approach I checked with the approvals, saw it was permitted, and gave permission from an air traffic viewpoint. It was not my job of course to check if the airline permitted this crew to make this type of approach."

"Thank you very much, Mr. Gates. That is very clear."

There was a pause to see if there was to be any cross examination but all the counsels present seemed to be content. The approach controller stood down and was replaced by the tower controller, Humphrey Brown. Ms Crowburn asked him to tell the story in his own words.

"RWA 573 came on to my frequency when it was at about ten miles finals at 3,000 ft and asked if the GELAS was serviceable. The cloud base was indeterminate and the transmissionmeter at the landing end of 27L was showing close to 20m. I cleared him to land, confirmed the GELAS was serviceable and passed the transmissionmeter settings. Everything looked normal at first. At 800 ft. RWA 573 asked for a wind check and I asked the Met. Office since we only had surface wind in the tower. I then passed the aircraft the wind and there was no reply. I noticed that the aircraft seemed lower than it should have been at one mile. Normally it would have been at about 300 ft. and the height shown was actually below 200ft. I tried to call the aircraft to ask him to check his height but another aircraft came on the frequency and started talking. His transmission prevented mine going out so I could not talk to 573 straightaway. The next thing I knew was that the radar blip for 573 had disappeared. I called the aircraft but there was no reply. The fire crew called and said the aircraft had cashed short of the runway and I pressed the crash button, spoke to the duty fire officer and told him the accident must be somewhere just short of the 27L runway. I told the aircraft on frequency to go around and repeated that the airport was closed. I called approach control and told them that there had been an accident. There was nothing more I could do."

Brown looked very shaken as he finished telling the sequence of events.

"Thank you Mr. Brown for that very clear description. I am afraid there are one or two questions I must ask you for clarification to the Court. First of all transmissionmeter, what does that mean?"

"The transmissionmeter is situated next to the runway and measures the visibility at its location; its readings are shown in front of the tower controller. In fact because visibility in fog is so variable there are normally three transmissionmeters for each runway, one at each end and one in the middle and this was the case for 27 Left. Aircraft landing and take-off minima depend critically on the actual visibility and that is why the readings are shown to the controller so that the controller can pass the information on to the aircraft captains. Of course, in the case of 27 Left the readings were for information only, since the aircraft was permitted to land in zero visibility though had it been zero he would not have been able to taxi without a follow me van."

"Thank you. Now tell the Court about your responsibility for monitoring the height of the aircraft on the approach."

"Well, in fact the duty controller has no responsibility for monitoring the performance of an aircraft on the approach. The reason for that is that the controller does not have the tools. The controller can see from the radar display whether the aircraft is lined up with the runway and an alarm sounds if it is not on centre line, but the alarm gate is set for about 800 yards at two miles and is only really there for aircraft landing in good weather and lining up visually on the wrong runway.

"Vertically, there is no way the controller can monitor the performance unless there is a gross error, since all the controller sees is the height of the aircraft to the nearest ten feet on a relatively small screen.

"However, in the case of 573 the aircraft did appear to me to be well below the correct altitude and so I tried to transmit a warning even though it was not my responsibility. The way the tower radio transmitter works is that it can only transmit if there is no other aircraft transmitting and, unfortunately, another aircraft started to make quite a long transmission which prevented my warning transmission going out. When the aircraft stopped transmitting I told him to standby which he did not do immediately and by the time I could transmit, it was too late, the 573 had gone from the screen."

"Surely it would have been better if you could have transmitted regardless of the other aircraft?"

"Yes it would have been." I noticed that the seats reserved for the press were filling up. "But that is not the way the system works these days. It did in the past."

"Thank you Mr. Brown."

This time there was some cross examination. The counsel for Royal World Airlines got to his feet. He was all sweet reasonableness, searching to be educated.

"Now Mr. Brown. I'm puzzled. Are you telling the Court that in an emergency it is impossible for you to transmit if there is another aircraft transmitting?"

Brown started to look uncomfortable.

"There is an override switch provided to override other transmissions but we never use it except in an emergency."

The Counsel pounced.

"But surely this was an emergency, Mr. Brown?"

I could see the newspaper men scribbling away.

"Not necessarily."

"Are you telling the Court that you could see that the aircraft was below the glide slope but it was not an emergency?"

"Aircraft do not always keep to the glide slope. They vary a bit. It is the crew's job to fly the aircraft, not the tower controller's. Our job is to control the flow of traffic, not to fly the aircraft."

"You do agree, Mr. Brown, that if you had used the override switch there would not have been this terrible accident."

"No, I don't agree. If I had transmitted then, my transmission would have clashed with the aircraft that was transmitting and the chances are that RWA 573 would not have heard anything intelligible."

"But had you operated the override switch the accident might not have happened."

"Who knows? I don't."

The RWA counsel sat down and another counsel who represented the Air Traffic Controller's union stood up.

"Mr. Brown, is it your responsibility to ensure that an aircraft flies an instrument approach correctly?"

"No, not at all."

"Thank you." The Counsel sat down.

There was a consultation between Crowburn and Lord Justice Thomas. It was only 11.30. Things had gone rather faster than anticipated and they must have decided to call Bob Furness before lunch. He was sworn in. Janet Crowburn got to her feet and went through the routine questions. Then she started probing.

"Now Mr. Furness, you are the head of the Air Accident Investigation Branch. Who is your employer?"

Chapter 5

"The Secretary of State for Transport. I report directly to the Department."

"Would you like to tell us what was the cause of the accident to RWA Flight 573, UK aircraft registration G-RWAGH or Golf Hotel as I believe it is colloquially called."

"No, Ma'am. The investigation is still in progress. In fact Martin Foster, one of my senior inspectors was in charge of the investigation until the Secretary of State appointed the Inquiry and so he is in a much better position than I am to brief the Court."

"How is it that you did not take on the responsibility of investigating this tragic accident yourself? This accident is the worst ever to occur to an aircraft on the UK register."

"That is not the way we work at the AAIB. I always appoint a senior inspector in charge and leave it to him or her. I review the progress of all the accident investigations but do not handle any one individually."

"In retrospect don't you think it would have been better to have handled this case yourself?"

"With respect, no I don't. By letting someone else do the initial investigation I am able to review the findings impartially."

"Well, let me come on to another matter. You do agree that there seems to have been a lot of leakage of information in your department to the press?"

"The contents of one channel of the cockpit voice recorder seems to have become public knowledge. I very much regret that and I am doing everything in my power to find out the source of the leak."

"How many people have heard this recording?"

"I'm not really sure."

"You're not sure." Crowburn sounded incredulous. "I would have thought Mr. Furness that with material as sensitive as this you would know exactly how many people had heard the recording."

"Normally I would have known and the number would have been five or six, not more. However, because this was a hijacking we had a lot of security people insisting on listening to the recording."

"But presumably you know all these peoples' names?"

"No I don't. The security people are almost a law unto themselves. I have interviewed personally everybody who might have known about the leak who works for me, but they have all denied giving the information to the press. It would hinder our investigation if we called in the police at this time to try to invoke the Official Secrets Act. A clear cut crime has not been committed. This is a civil accident we are investigating, not a military one. If the transgressor works for me and we find out who it is then he will almost certainly lose his or her job. However, it is my view that the leak did not come from my people."

"That's as maybe Mr. Furness. But there have also been reports purporting to emanate from your team which give the reason for the accident as pilot error."

"I am aware of this and again I have interviewed all my staff individually. The number of people who could have leaked information of this nature is much larger than the number of people who have heard the recording and, in addition, some of the security people could have heard discussions within the building. Having said all that I do not believe that my senior inspector and his people have yet come to any conclusion as to the cause of the accident, so I regard the reports as incorrect as well as very unwelcome."

"Well no doubt the Secretary of State will have a view in this matter. The fact that the recording and other information has been leaked is one of the reasons why this Inquiry has been called and, of course, it has prevented your department from continuing the investigation except under instructions from the assessors."

"I have already said how much I regret the leaks but, once they happened, nothing could be done to mitigate the effect. In addition I am not convinced the leaks came from my staff."

Lord Justice Thomas joined in.

"Ms Crowburn, when is the Court going to find out what is on the recordings?"

"My Lord, may I suggest that we hear the next witness and then perhaps have a recess to discuss this matter. I would respectfully suggest that it may be in the public interest and in the interests of justice, that the recording is only heard in private session and only by the Court and by the very few experts who need to hear it. You may care to consider before the second part of the Inquiry whether the full transcript should be made freely available."

"Very good, Ms Crowburn. Please proceed."

"That is all the questions I have for this witness."

Bob Furness left the witness box. He didn't look a happy man. The clerk said that the Inquiry would reconvene at 2 o'clock. Mike and I left for a nearby pub and had coffee and a sandwich.

"What do you make of all that, Peter?"

"Well, it is the GESS approach which intrigues me. The data transmitted by the GESS has to be augmented by GELAS which is a local transmitter in effect refining the accuracy of the satellite signals from the Galileo European satellites. If the GELAS data is incorrect then an accident could easily result. You will need to call the telecommunication chief from Air Traffic Control and also the people from the GELAS manufacturer to see what checks were done after the crash."

"But if the data was wrong, if the wrong position of the runway had been put in the MMR databases and the flight path was incorrect then wouldn't the pilots see that the aircraft was too low?"

"But how, Mike? As Anne Moncrieff has pointed out, the same deviation goes in front of the pilot as goes to the auto-pilot. What is required is a completely independent check of the flight path. Had the crew been able to watch the 27L ILS deviation down the approach they might have seen they were going low. But it was out of service and anyway Mike, we're running ahead of the game. We haven't heard the recording and learnt the hijack situation."

"What do you make of Bob Furness and the leaks?"

"Well he's right, isn't he? How can he hope to know who did the leaking when so many people knew what was going on. However, I'll tell you this for nothing. I bet the story that AAIB think that the accident was pilot error is probably true."

"You may be right. Let's get back in."

When we got back in the Court had not reconvened and there was a delay of about thirty minutes. Then the Clerk of the Court appeared and announced that instead of calling the next witness the Inquiry would now go into private session for the experts to hear the voice recorder. The Inquiry would probably be back in public session on Thursday morning. The room was to be cleared completely and the solicitors were informed that only technical experts would be allowed to hear the recording, not all the lawyers. Some of the lawyers argued unsuccessfully that they should be allowed to listen but, after a lot of disgruntled murmuring, there were only a few of us who were approved as listeners. The process of clearing and re-entering seemed to take forever. We all had to sign the Official Secrets Act. The only good thing was that we each got a special pass which we were told could be used for subsequent days if necessary. There were only about eight of us plus the Court itself. The Clerk made an announcement.

"As I'm sure you all realise, there are several channels of voice recording on a modern flight data recorder. The recording we are going to play first comes from the main flight deck area microphone. Later, we can hear from the two pilots microphones and the two pilots earphones. The recording we have has been edited so that it only runs when something is happening. We did this to cut down the length of the recording, otherwise it would have gone on for two hours with a lot of blank time when nothing was happening."

I tried to contest this arrangement and asked that we might hear the full unexpurgated recording and I was supported by the other listeners, but we were told that the only recording that was available in London was this particular recording. I decided not to stir things up at this stage but to listen to what was available. However, I asked if there was a transcript available with the times of each transmission and we were promised that we could look at the transcripts later on or on the following day. We all sat at the front of the hall as the recording started to play. The noise was horrendous. We could only just make out the pilots' voices. I remembered what Osborne had written in the Telegraph. Lord Justice Thomas indicated that the recording should be stopped.

"Ms Crowburn. What's the matter with the recording? We can't hear anything."

"My Lord, I'm told by AAIB that the recorder must have been damaged. This is the best quality available. It is just possible to make out the pilots' voices."

"What about the other recordings, Ms Crowburn."

"The earphone recordings seem fine but the pilots' microphones are no better than this recording, My Lord."

"Very well. Let's try again."

The recording was restarted.

"Charles, did you speak with Eva. Was she awake?"

"You bet. She was fine."

"She's a lovely girl. Bursting with energy. Time you settled down."

"We'll see. That was a great evening we had at Maroubra with those two. I like that beach, and Caesars."

"Yes, I could see that. We certainly got through the wine. Well you and the girls did."

"I enjoyed the swim as well"

"Just as well it was warm or you both would have frozen."

"You're a fine one to talk. I'm afraid I didn't get a lot of sleep. Did you have a good time, Harry?"

"Very quiet, thank you."

"That's what they all say."

"Still we got back just in time."

There was a click and then the recording restarted. Presumably there was a length of time with no significant transmissions which had been cut out.

"RWA operations this is Flight 573. We have been hijacked. We have been told to land at Heathrow and then we are going to be given further instructions. If there is any interference with the aircraft after landing then the plane will be blown up with all the passengers."

"573 this is RWA Operations. Your message copied. Your transponder read by Eurocontrol."

Presumably a reference to the hijack code which Harry must have selected.

Chapter 5

"*Operations from 573, the hijackers have asked me to read the following message to be given to the Prime Minister. 'When the aircraft lands the following six prisoners are to be taken from prison and brought to the aircraft.*" A list of six names followed, which I recognised were reputed to be members of al-Qaeda, and the recording continued. "*The prisoners will be loaded on to the aircraft, the aircraft will be refuelled and then the aircraft will take-off for the Middle East. Any delay greater than thirty minutes will result in first, the killing of the Foreign Secretary, and then by the blowing up of the aircraft.*

RWA read Harry's message back.

"*Operations, please advise when refuelling is ready. The hijackers wish to know.*"

"*573, will advise.*"

Another click.

"*Would the Chief Steward come to the flight deck.*" Presumably this was an announcement on the passenger address.

"*Andrew, you are aware we've been hijacked?*"

"*Yes, Captain.*"

"*Good. I want you to carry on the rest of the flight with your cabin staff as normally as possible. I shall make an announcement on the PA.*"

"*Very good, Captain.*"

"*Ladies and Gentleman. I regret to inform you that we have been hijacked. We are carrying on to London as planned, where we shall refuel and then fly to somewhere in the Middle East. We do not know whether anyone will be allowed to disembark in London.*

"*Please obey the instructions from our cabin staff and we will try to make the rest of the flight as normal as possible. I will keep you informed at all times. Thank you.*"

The recording continued with some co-pilot conversations with the various air traffic centres as the aircraft crossed Europe.

"*Harry,*" it was Charles talking, "*Shall I get the latest weather?*"

"*Go ahead.*"

There was a pause. They must have switched the speakers off ready for landing as we could not hear the weather being transmitted by the ATIS, the transmissions were going straight into the headphones.

"*Harry,*" it was Charlie again "*that's real Cat 3B weather. Manchester is clear anyway if we need to divert.*"

There was a click

"*573 from Operations, we've checked your fuel from your ACARS transmission and you are cleared to overfly Frankfurt and land at Heathrow with Manchester as your diversion.*"

The speakers had clearly been switched on again.

"*573 copied.*"

Another click.

"Operations, this is 573. Have you arranged the refuelling?"

"We're still doing that. You are being refuelled by tankers instead of by hydrants on the stands and we are making sure that they have enough fuel for Karachi and that they can get to your parking position on the runway."

"573 understood."

There was a pause.

"RWA Ops This is 573. I have been asked to establish whether the prisoners have been released and are waiting at the airport?"

"573 please stand by. Will advise."

"RWA Ops I have been told to remind you that the hijackers are going to blow up the aircraft if there is any delay to their instructions which I passed to you."

"573 This is RWA Ops Copied."

The recording proceeded with very little other conversation. The aircraft crossed into UK airspace and the aircraft was cleared to descend. Charles called out the descent checks and then the checks for an auto-landing. Air Traffic slowly permitted the aircraft to reduce altitude in stages. Then we heard the weather being broadcast on the VOR. Ceiling indeterminate, visibility 30 metres. Harry was clearly doing the flying and told Charles he was going to do an automatic landing using the ILS.

"Director Royal 573 reaching 4,000."

"Roger Cleared procedural GESS final approach 27 left"

"Royal 573 we'd prefer the ILS"

"Sorry Royal 573 the ATIS is incorrect. The ILS is no longer approved for Cat 3 approaches and is out of service. What are your intentions?"

Harry could be heard speaking to Charles.

"Charles, did you know about the ILS?"

"Yes Harry. This means we won't be able to monitor the approach path on GESS."

"Well that is not a requirement. The GESS is self monitored to death." A pause. *"Charles, you had better set 27L into the MMRs for the GESS."*

"Yes Harry, have just done that."

"OK. Then you can select the Galileo system for the approach."

"Royal 573 Request GESS approach 27 Left."

"You are cleared for GESS approach cleared to descend on the procedure. Maintain heading and call the Tower on 118.5"

"118.5 Royal 573"

Harry was obviously slightly concerned and spoke to Charles again.

"Charles that is permitted, isn't it?"

Chapter 5

"Yes Harry providing the GELAS is OK."

"We've got no warning so it must be OK."

We heard the landing checks being carried out and then they were cleared to the final approach altitude. Harry told Charles to keep an eye on the Navigation Display as he needed to keep his display showing the Primary Flight Display most of the time.

"Tower Royal 573 ten miles 27 Left. Confirm GELAS OK."

"Royal 573 hello. You are clear to land 27 left, wind calm RVR 20, 30,20 GELAS showing OK"

"Roger Royal 573"

Harry said they were now on the glide slope and Charles was calling out the altitude, presumably from the radio altimeter, and the distance to go, presumably from the Navigation Display.

"800 ft. you are showing slightly right, but on glide slope." Sounded like Charles.

"OK, I'm central on the glide slope. You check the approach on your Navigational Display. I'll keep my display in the Primary Flight Display mode. The rate of descent seems rather high. We must have a tail wind." Harry talking. The lack of his Navigational Display was clearly a problem.

"Heathrow Tower RWA 573 please check wind speed".

We heard no reply.

"two miles, 600 ft. on centre line" Charles

"573 from Tower, the wind is calm."

"one mile, 300 ft on centre line" Charles

"200" Radio Altimeter automatic call out

"100" Radio Altimeter automatic call out

"I can't see the loom of the lights yet." Harry

"Still on glide slope" Harry

"On centre line" Charles

"Still can't see the ground" Harry

"50" Radio Altimeter

"30" Radio Altimeter

"There's something wrong with the lights, I'm going around." Harry:

"20" Radio Altimeter

A moment later the background noise seemed to change, presumably as the throttles were opened. We could hear Harry yelling

"Oh my God, we're hitting the road"

"573 you appear to be" Heathrow:

I looked at the Court and the other listeners. We all looked pretty shaken but the effect was mitigated by the noise and the difficulty of making out the words. We listened to the four other recordings but they did not add to the main recording we had heard.

The Clerk of the Court then made a statement.

"Gentlemen, you have all been allowed to listen to the recording to help you in the evidence that you will be giving to the Inquiry. I think you can now all understand why we do not wish the transcript of the recording to be released at the moment. However, the transcript may be introduced as evidence in the second part of the Inquiry. I rely on you all to keep what you have heard to yourselves. To-morrow morning at the Treasury Solicitor's Office in Queen Anne's Chambers you may look at the transcripts of what you have just heard. There will be another private session of this Court in the morning with the security experts. There will probably be another private session in Sydney after we have finished the first part of this Inquiry to find out how these people got on board the aircraft with their weapons. It is very important to do this because, as some of you must have realised, the fact that the hijackers had explosives on board is particularly worrying and we do not wish this fact to become general knowledge, but we must find out how it was done and what the explosive devices were. Good night to you all."

I left and decided I'd better have a brief discussion with Mike and Tim Forrestal. I called Mike and reluctantly we decided we'd better go to an office rather than the nearest pub. We agreed to meet at Tim's offices which were the nearest. He kicked off the discussion the moment we arrived.

"Well what did you hear, Peter?" He looked at me.

"I'm concerned about the recording."

"Why."

"It was almost impossible to hear anything. AAIB said the recorder had been damaged."

There was a long pause while the implication of what I had just said sank in. Mike looked at me.

"What's worrying you?"

"There's no conversation with the hijackers. They said the recorder was damaged. It's probably true. Or were the hijackers genuinely out of range of the microphone?"

"What should we do?"

"Nothing. I can't see how AAIB can blame the pilots when the effect of the hijackers cannot be assessed. My recommendation is that we should challenge the recording when we want to denigrate AAIB. By the way my first impression was how superbly Harry Hodgson, the captain, handled the situation. I believe that may be very important because on the run through of the recording we have just heard, it looks as if the hijacking did not cause the accident. Hodgson seemed right on top of the job and he would therefore have been monitoring the approach. However, he made it clear he was relying on Charles to monitor the Navigation Display. The problem is that the aircraft heights for the distances from the runway which Charles called out at 300ft. and 200 ft. were correct yet we know the aircraft was below the glide slope. If only the ILS indicator had been available for cross checking."

"But Peter," Mike could not contain himself, "they must have been under enormous pressure."

"Yes, you're right. But no-one hearing the recording would say that the hijacking caused the accident. In fact listening to the recording there is absolutely no reason for the accident."

Tim looked at me. "What do you suggest then?"

"Well I want to read the main transcript and I would like to check the recording of the other transcripts."

"Anything else?"

"Yes. Presumably we're going to hear Martin Foster, the AAIB senior inspector, who is dealing with the accident, albeit under instruction from the assessors, before this part of the Inquiry is closed. If this is the only time he is going to give evidence he will need a thorough cross examination." I looked at Tim. "I may need to talk to you after I've read the transcripts to-morrow. How are we going to handle that?"

"Well Peter, I suggest that we review the situation at lunch time to-morrow. You should have read the transcripts by then. When we reconvene at the Inquiry on Friday should we ask about the transcript and the hijackers?"

"No, Tim. I think not for the moment."

"Why not?"

"I think we should wait until the situation becomes clearer."

We broke up and I went straight home and called Mandy who had only just got in.

"How did you get on, Peter?"

"I don't know. Incredibly we couldn't hear the hijackers on the recording, the background noise was so high. We could barely hear the pilots."

"Is that likely?"

"Well we were told that the recorder had been damaged. I'm no expert but I'm suspicious that something is not quite right. I just wondered if we're only being allowed to hear extracts from the recording and not the complete recording."

"That's quite an allegation."

"Yes, I know it is. Perhaps I'm being unfair. However I'm very curious to hear what the AAIB inspector says on Friday."

"Not to-morrow?"

"No. We're reading the transcript to-morrow and don't forget they're having a very private security session."

"You'd better get some sleep. When do we meet again?"

"Why don't you stay at my place this week-end?"

"I'm not comfortable in that house with Diana watching us and I'm not comfortable just being your mistress, enjoyable though it is in some ways."

"Well I don't know what to say. I don't want to lose you."

"That's nice, Peter and I feel the same way about you." There was a pause. "Alright, I'll stay at your place but I'm not sure about anything else."

She rang off. It really was a difficult problem. If only we could find Diana and I could get a divorce on the grounds of desertion.

***

In the morning I bought the Times, Telegraph and FT and studied them on the train. There did not seem to be any leaks of what was said on the voice recorder though the Telegraph was still complaining about the iniquity of having private sessions. Osborne took the opportunity to regurgitate the earlier leak of the recording, mention the bit about the party in Sydney and restate the view of the AAIB that it was just pilot error. I was at Queen Anne's Chambers at 9.30 and went inside after showing my pass. We were all shown into a room where there were transcripts of the recordings. Each one was numbered.

In some ways it was easier to appreciate what had happened on the flight deck by looking at the transcript because there was a time written down for each transmission. However I didn't learn anything new. I met Mike at the pub and he confirmed that John Fairlane had kept 5 o'clock free.

"Well Peter, did you learn anything new?"

"Not on the face of it but I'm still wondering if we're hearing everything."

"We must be. The Court wouldn't allow a miscarriage of justice."

"I hope you're right."

I left Mike when he went back to his office and wandered round the book shops in Charing Cross road. At the appointed time Mike and I met at John Fairlane's chambers and went straight in to his office. John looked at Tim who gave him a debriefing on the last two days' happenings.

"So if I understand you correctly, you think that both the voice recording and the transcript make it seem as if the pilots were monitoring their instruments properly and there is no obvious cause for the accident."

I joined in.

Chapter 5

"From the excerpts on the recording it sounded as if the aircraft was making a perfect approach. What I can't understand is why the Navigation Display ranges from the runway, which the co-pilot called out, did not show that they were at the incorrect height. I would have thought that the heights would have been far too low for the range from the airport and this would have warned both pilots that the aircraft was below the correct glide slope. There could conceivably be shortcomings in the design of the aircraft during a GESS approach or the GESS airfield data could have been wrong. We have to find out if this data was checked and was correct. However, right now we need to judge how much we want to challenge the AAIB inspector to-morrow."

John looked thoughtful.

"What had you in mind?"

"Well I'm puzzled about the recording and transcript. We should have heard more, the hijackers for example. I know the recording was damaged but even so. Will the inspector be recalled when the Inquiry is reconvened?"

"Yes, Peter, I'm sure he will be since the investigation is still going on and he will need to report to the Court. If I am hearing you correctly you are going to do some more investigation as a result of what you have heard. You're not happy with the indicated heights and distances from the runway."

"Yes, there needs to be more investigation. There are some definite avenues which need more exploring and it is going to take time."

"Alright, I'll just play it by ear to-morrow."

Back home I pondered over the situation. Harry had behaved superbly. If there had been something wrong technically on the approach surely he would have noticed it. But if they were on the glide slope at the correct distance from the runway it just did not make sense. Mandy called when she got home and I shared my thoughts with her. She told me that to-morrow was going to be very important and not to come to any conclusion until after Foster had given evidence.

"Are you coming to my office to-morrow?"

"What time do you finish?"

"When you come round, about 5.30; you can wait if I'm not ready."

I retired to bed. I had a lot to do if I was going to earn my money with CrossRisk Insurance.

***

The Inquiry opened at 10 o'clock and it was packed out with the press for some reason. There was an air of expectation in the Inquiry hall.

Martin Foster was called and sworn in. He understandably looked a little nervous.

Janet Crowburn started probing straightaway after the initial identification questions.

"Mr. Foster. You have been in charge of the investigations into the accident to RWA 573?"

"Yes, that's right, until the Public Inquiry was notified. Since then I have been working for the Court."

"Well perhaps you will be kind enough to explain what happened and tell us in your opinion what was the cause of the accident."

"Well Ma'am I have not completed the investigation. The work of my team was delayed when the Inquiry was called."

"We understand that, but you had carried out a lot of work up to that time and I must point out to you that some leaks about the progress of the work have appeared in the press and have suggested you have come to a conclusion."

Foster's face flushed.

"The leaks didn't come from my team."

"You had better tell the Court about the investigation work and your conclusions up to the time the investigation stopped."

Martin started by giving a factual account of the flight from take-off in Sydney to the crash on the A30. He had projected on to a screen in the Inquiry Hall a picture of the flight path of the aircraft as it joined the extended centre line of 27L and the spot where the aircraft hit the ground, half a mile short of the expected touch down point. He said that all the channels of the voice recorder confirmed that the aircraft was carrying out an automatic approach and landing in Category 3B conditions using the GESS. He gave the names of the crew, their experience and their qualifications. He produced the relevant sheet of the technical log at Sydney showing the rectification of the Navigation Display and the Multimode Receiver. He explained that the aircraft was hijacked just less than two hours before landing.

"How do you know that Mr. Foster?"

"Eurocontrol told Heathrow that the aircraft was transmitting the internationally agreed code for hijacking and in addition the Captain told RWA Operations."

"Now then Mr. Foster. You have explained to us in detail the flight progress from Sydney to Heathrow but so far you have not told us what in your opinion went wrong. Before you do that will you tell us if the aircraft was fully serviceable when it started its approach."

"When we were collecting evidence from Royal World Airlines before the Inquiry was called and our work stopped, I had understood from their operations room that RWA 573 had mentioned in one of the routine flight progress reports that the captain's Navigation Display was not working."

Jack Templeman, one of the assessors, chimed in.

"Is that the same one that did not work when the aircraft landed at Sydney?"

"It was a new box that had been fitted by NWIA in Sydney because the previous one did not work."

"Doesn't that suggest that there was something wrong with the aircraft installation and not the displays themselves?"

"Yes sir. Unfortunately our instrumentation was unable to shed any light on this point."

"Mr. Foster, would it matter that the Captain's display did not work?"

"It shouldn't have done, Sir. The Captain still had his Primary Display so he would be able to switch this good display to show the Navigation Display information every so often instead of the normal Primary Flight Display. In addition there was plenty of back up information and the first officer of course had both displays working."

Templeman carried on.

"Would you tell the Court, Mr. Foster, how you know that the Captain could switch displays if the installation was at fault? Might he not have decided that he would not want to risk damaging the good display?"

Foster clearly didn't like that last comment and made no answer.

Janet Crowburn tried to reassume control from the assessor.

"May I carry on, my Lord?"

Lord Justice Thomas nodded.

"Now then Mr. Foster. What in your opinion went wrong?"

There was absolute silence in the room as Martin Foster replied.

"We have analysed the records of the local Distance Measuring Equipment beacon, DME, and it is clear that the aircraft was below the correct approach path for the runway. The aircraft was not using the ILS on the runway in use, 27L, because it was out of service and anyway it was no longer approved for Cat 3B landings. The voice recorder makes it clear, as does the conversation with air traffic control, that the crew elected to use the GESS. This is permissible if the correct selection is made on the flight deck."

Lord Justice Thomas turned to Janet Crowburn.

"Ms Crowburn, are we going to have transcripts of the cockpit voice recorder introduced as evidence?"

"If you think it advisable, my Lord, but if I may suggest, only when the Inquiry reopens."

"Very well Ms Crowburn."

Janet Crowburn returned to her examination.

"Mr. Foster. You say you looked at the local Distance Measuring Equipment readings and it showed that the aircraft was below the glide slope. Where was the beacon? On the airfield?"

"No Ma'am. It was the DME located on the approach to 27 Right."

"Would the crew have been able to see these distances?"

"Yes Ma'am on the Navigation Display."

"Would the crew have been able to do the calculation, in real time, on the approach. Wouldn't they have had to have done a lot of pre-flight preparation to calculate the correct heights for the DME distances.?"

Foster looked very uncertain.

"It could be done."

"Mr. Foster, I put it to you that it would not be possible in the circumstances?"

"I don't agree Ma'am. They should have been able to do it."

"It's standard procedure, then? Would the distances have been displayed."

Foster hesitated.

"I'm not sure Ma'am."

"Well surely you ought to know."

Foster looked stony faced.

"Was there anything wrong in the crew using the GESS?"

"Well, though what they did was permissible, I don't think it was advisable."

I could see that the Royal World Airlines counsel wanted to interrupt but was not allowed to. However, Templeman did not keep quiet.

"That is your personal opinion Mr. Foster. I take it that your view is not supported by Royal World Airlines operations or by the Flight Operations Inspectorate at Gatwick, otherwise the procedure would not have been permitted. Why do you, alone, think the GESS approach is dangerous, because that is what you are implying?"

Foster flushed again.

"Well Sir, I believe that there is altogether too much reliance on software calculations. With ILS there is no doubt where the centre line is, with GESS the centre line is only defined by reference to pre-loaded data in the database and deviations from these virtual centre lines are only obtained from extensive real time computation."

There was a pause and I saw Charles McGuire nodding agreement.

"Mr. Foster" Crowburn interjected "GESS Cat 3 approaches are approved even if you don't think they should be?"

"Yes, Ma'am"

Foster looked uncomfortable and Crowburn indicated that Foster should carry on.

"The captain noticed that they were descending too fast but it must be remembered that the captain may not have had his primary flight display on full time. He may have been switching between the two display formats. The navigation display would have told him the aircraft's position relative to the runway and the primary flight display would have told him the position of the aircraft relative to the glide slope centre line. The crew should have known for example that at two miles from the runway the altimeter reading should have been about 600 ft. The aircraft was clearly well below that altitude. The first officer was calling out the distances and the radio altimeter heights and would be leaving the Captain to concentrate on the vertical deviation. It is my opinion that the crew should have noticed that something was wrong whatever the GESS deviation showed and executed a missed approach."

Janet Crowburn started to ask Foster some questions.

"Now Mr. Foster, did the Captain tell the co-pilot to monitor the navigation display and he would be using the Primary Flight Display mode on the approach?"

"Yes, ma'am."

"Then your statements about what the Captain might have been doing are not appropriate, are they?"

Foster mumbled, losing all credibility. Crowburn went on remorselessly.

"Now, I believe the co-pilot called out the ranges and confirmed the aircraft was on centre line and at the correct height." She looked at her notes. " 'two miles, 600 ft. on centre line' and again 'one mile, 300 ft on centre line' "

Justice Thomas interrupted.

"Ms Crowburn, the recording transcript has not yet been admitted as evidence. Would you rephrase your question?"

"I'm sorry, M'Lord. Were the pilots checking the correct heights for the distance from the runway?"

"Yes ma'am."

"Mr. Foster how do you explain that the information to the pilots was correct and yet the aircraft was far too low. How do you know there was not a fault with the GESS or with the equipment on the aircraft?"

"Well we need to do some more investigation."

"There we agree Mr. Foster. Would you agree with me that at this time there is absolutely no evidence to show that the crew made a mistake."

Foster looked very unhappy and said nothing. Lord Justice Thomas came in.

"Mr. Foster, you must answer the question. Would you agree that at this time there is absolutely no evidence to show that the crew made a mistake?"

"Yes my Lord."

"Then will you please ensure that no further leaks to the press take place from your team."

"There were no leaks from my team, my Lord."

Lord Justice Thomas didn't look too pleased. Crowburn carried on.

"Mr. Foster. Do you have the transcript of the flight deck microphone?"

"Yes, ma'am."

"Will you be offering this transcript as evidence?"

"It is not our normal practice to release the transcript of voice recordings."

"Do I understand that answer to mean that you are not going to?"

"Ma'am, this is a Public Inquiry and we are working for the Court. If the Court wishes to have the transcripts in evidence it will of course be available, but we do not recommend it."

"Why not?"

"These transcripts are best interpreted by experts, Ma'am."

"Mr. Foster, justice must be seen to be done. This matter will be raised again when the Inquiry reopens." Crowburn looked at her notes.

"Were there, in your opinion, any contributory causes to this accident?"

"Well, the crew had been to a party the night before. That would not improve their performance."

The press were listening to every word. The hall was very quiet.

"But surely the crew had been resting on the aircraft for a long time after their first spell of flying and before they took over again for landing?"

"Sleeping in the aircraft is not a very good rest."

Templeman butted in.

"Mr. Foster, that's your opinion again. The rest quarters are fully approved are they not?"

"Yes sir."

Janet Crowburn took over again.

"Mr. Foster, what impact did the hijackers have on the pilots?"

Foster looked taken aback.

"Well Ma,am, it was not possible to hear the hijackers."

"In that case how can you be so certain that the pilots were at fault?"

Foster said nothing but looked very uncomfortable. Janet Crowburn turned to Lord Justice Thomas.

Chapter 5

"My Lord. I think the Court should take note that this witness seems very prejudiced against the pilots because no other explanation has yet been found. It would seem that there needs to be much more detailed investigations of the flight data recorder parameters."

Thomas butted in.

"Thank you, Ms Crowburn. The Court will be giving instructions to the AAIB the moment this part of the Inquiry is finished."

"My apologies, M'Lord. May I respectfully suggest that I release this witness now and that he continues his examination when the Inquiry is reconvened when he can be cross-examined by counsel."

The Court had discussions amongst themselves and then Lord Justice Thomas announced that the Inquiry would be adjourned to a date that would be notified but probably Monday 21st March. Foster left the witness box looking completely destroyed. I wondered how he would fare when the Inquiry re-opened if he hadn't got some definitive explanation of the accident by then. Mind you, I would have a problem as well if I hadn't!

A Flight Too Far

CHAPTER 6

The four of us returned to John's chambers and his secretary produced some coffee.

"Well that's that for the moment. Crowburn demolished Foster but the fact remains we haven't got an explanation of why the pilots did not realise what was happening. We've got a week or two to think of something but it's not going to be easy." John looked at me. "What are you going to do?"

"There are a lot of unexplained things in this accident concerning the electronics which require investigation so they can be eliminated from the suspicious items list. There seems no obvious reason to suspect pilot error but to prevent any claims on CrossRisk we really need a proper explanation of what happened. Harry must have been under enormous pressure. If only the recording had worked properly and we could have heard everything that was happening on the flight deck. Foster must be out of his mind"

"You're not likely to get any help from AAIB are you?" Mike was inquiring and it was a good question which had been exercising me.

"Not from Foster! However Bob is normally very fair. Clearly he won't like my questioning their favoured theory, when they have one. Perhaps Tim you could arrange for me to talk to an assessor if I need to. I'm not sure what the correct procedures are."

"Nor am I but I'm sure all rules would be broken to get at the truth."

I left feeling definitely uncertain of what to do and in due course appeared at Mandy's offices. She appeared looking like a solicitor who had been working hard all day.

"My bag is in the cupboard, Peter. Would you mind?"

We made our normal progress by cab and train, and then cab again in view of the bag, to my house. We were both tired but I had had the forethought to book a table at Simon's for 8 o'clock.

"Peter, my dear, once again I'm going to lie in your bath, Diana or no Diana, and I don't want you helping me. The only massage I need is from the jacuzzi. You can have a shower in the other bathroom and prepare two strong gin and tonics."

That was the nice thing about Mandy. I didn't have to guess what was required. Since we were walking to the restaurant I made the gin and tonics as directed and tested the mix was right. As usual I did not have too long to wait for Mandy despite her long day. She appeared in a dress that was definitely low cut and not too long. We sat down next to one another and she tasted the mix.

"What are you trying to do to me?"

"What are you trying to do to me sitting so close with a dress like that?"

"Perhaps you're right. You can't be trusted." She moved her body away so it wasn't pressed against me but the perfume remained behind. "I've decided we aren't talking shop until to-morrow. What do you think?"

"I have to tell you that for some unaccountable reason I wasn't thinking of shop, as you call it. I was looking at my watch and wondering how much time we had before we had to leave." I rubbed my hand on the inside part of her stocking below the dress. She got up and sat on the chair opposite.

"I think I'd better sit here till we leave. I don't want to spoil my dinner."

She switched the TV on which was a mistake as there was a report on the Inquiry. Roger Tucker was being interviewed.

"Well we're not getting the cockpit voice recorder transcript from AAIB until the Inquiry reconvenes so it's very difficult to come to any conclusion. However quite a few people, so called experts, apart from the AAIB listened to the recording on Wednesday. The senior inspector, Martin Foster, clearly felt that the accident was due to pilot error but the Court counsel made him agree very reluctantly that he had absolutely no justification for doing so. She also formally advised the Court that Foster was prejudiced, which presumably means that the assessors may want him taken off the investigation. Normally, AAIB are very careful not to jump to any unsubstantiated conclusion. In any event I would have expected the presence of hijackers to make the pilots' job much harder during the approach."

Mandy turned the TV off.

"You know, Mandy, listening to that recording reminded me of the Sherlock Holmes story. What was it called? You know the one. 'The strange case of the dog that barked in the night'".

"You mean the dog didn't bark in the night."

"Exactly, you remembered. "

I held her coat as she put it on and we walked to Simon's. I helped her off with her coat and then hugged her before we sat down.

"I liked that, Peter. Perhaps I will stay for the week-end after all."

It was a very pleasant meal and we discussed what theatres and exhibitions we wanted to see in the next few weeks. We walked home and as usual I made the coffee. Mandy came down and we took our drinks through.

"We'd better not turn on the TV or your wretched Inquiry will be on. You can play some soft, amorous music."

Chapter 6

"How about Ravel's Bolero?"

"That's not quite what I had in mind. To much action after a long day. Some Frank Sinatra would be more restful."

I put on the music, turned the lights down and sat next to Mandy.

"Your not wearing very much."

"And you're wearing too much." She helped to put thing right.

We never finished the coffee.

***

We heard the papers arrive but did nothing.

"How wonderful, Peter. The whole week-end ahead and nothing we have to do."

We held each other tight, thinking our own thoughts.

"What were you thinking, Mandy."

"I was thinking, would it be greedy to have two poached eggs and how was I going to persuade you to cook them for me?"

"I was thinking how am I going to avoid having breakfast in bed, with all those crumbs."

"How very prosaic. Anyway the solution is now clear. You get up and cook my eggs and I'll come down in my dressing gown. I may get dressed later, I haven't decided yet."

We carried out Mandy's plan and sat at the kitchen table. I looked at the papers and read about the Inquiry. Osborne said it was clearly pilot error induced by the hijacking. After all, they had clearly said that they only just got back to the hotel on time.

Mandy appeared carrying a fax.

"When did you look at your fax machine last? This must have been here when we got in last night."

"To be honest I rarely look at my fax these days. Everything is email."

"Peter, in the office we still prefer faxes."

"Well not for me. However, I must remember to set up my computer as a fax machine as well so that any occasional faxes are on my printer."

It was from Bill Baker.

> Understand that the Inquiry on Golf Hotel will be adjourned for a few weeks. Can you come out next week for a few days to talk with my 798 training captains on our proposed 798 training course? Would like you to travel Monday if possible. Please call me over week-end at home.
>
> Best regards

I passed the fax over to Mandy.

"Can you spare the time, Peter? Surely you've got to prepare for the Inquiry."

"In a way you're right but I'd like to quiz the engineers over the unserviceabilities of Golf Hotel. I want to be sure that they are not relevant. Going out to NWIA gives me a cheap way of doing it."

Mandy looked at me thoughtfully.

"And you want to check up on the party the night before?"

I grinned at her.

"You can read me altogether too easily. Yes, to be honest I do. Also, I want to eliminate the Navigation Display and the Multimode Receiver from the causes of the accident."

"Well just you be careful. When are you going to ring Bill?

The kitchen clock showed 9.30, it would be 8.30 in the evening in Sydney.

"I'll call him now."

My telephone book was in my brief case. Bill answered straightaway.

"It's Peter Talbert, Bill. Thanks for the invitation and I can manage to travel Monday."

"That's fine. No worries. I took a flier and made a reservation. As RWA own 25% of us I've arranged for you to have a seat in business class on RWA574 leaving at 12 noon getting in 8 o'clock Tuesday night. I've booked you at the downtown Marriott. Please call RWA reservations in London and reconfirm the booking. Look forward to seeing you Wednesday. I'll get Jock Mansfield to collect you from the hotel at 9.30."

RWA found my reservation and I asked for an aisle seat. The tickets would be at the check-in in Terminal 3.

"Peter, I'd better go. You need to get ready."

"No. Don't spoil everything. The flight doesn't leave till midday on Monday so there's no problem. It won't take me long to get organised."

"You've got your mind to pack as well. It's got to be full of 798 avionics and all those good things."

"Mandy, I've been thinking of nothing else since the accident. You know that. In fact talking about it to people who understand and can question my views on the flight deck will be very helpful."

She accepted the force of my arguments but the week-end somehow had lost its relaxed feel. I discovered she had brought

Chapter 6

some work with her and so after a walk along the tow path and a sandwich at the pub, she settled down to read some papers and I got my papers organised for my trip. Then I went upstairs and sorted out my clothes for Sydney's summer heat. We decided not to do shopping but went to a Chinese restaurant and then spent Sunday morning reading the papers. In the afternoon we went for a walk in the rain which was actually rather nice and enabled us to eat crumpets for tea. We both did some more work and then watched the TV for a bit after supper.

***

The alarm went off at 6.15. I got out of bed and went downstairs, put the coffee on and made Mandy some tea. She was already up when I returned with her cup. I went back into the kitchen and prepared breakfast. Mandy appeared shortly ready for work. I took her in my car to the station and held her for a moment.

"I'll miss you, Peter. I'm getting used to having you around."

"Me, too. I'll call you from Sydney, Tuesday morning your time, before I go to bed. Take care."

I watched her walk into the station and drove home. I had a shower and put on the clothes I had put out ready the previous afternoon, blazer, thin trousers, and a sports shirt. I left quite a lot of Mandy's clothes as well as mine for Dora in the clothes basket. I closed my case, put my shaver in the holdall and carried the bags downstairs.

I called Jill and asked where the RWA crews normally stayed in Sydney and she told me it was the Hilton. I called Hilton reservations, made a reservation for a week from Tuesday night and emailed Bill asking him to let Jock Mansfield know that I would be in the Hilton and not the Marriott and would he cancel the hotel. I checked everything, bags, money and passport then I drove to Roehampton Lane and along the A4 to the M4 and Terminal 3 Valet Parking. Mike Mansell could pay for the parking as he was getting my flight for free.

At the check-in desk the girl behind the counter found my ticket. She told me the flight was fairly full but gave me my central aisle seat so I could move around easily. I went through immigration and bought the Times and the FT. I always liked to have my own copies in case the complimentary papers ran out before they reached me. I bought the latest best selling political blockbuster, a VAT and duty free bottle of special Scotch for Bill, and some expensive chocolates for Mary Baker; as usual the prices were no cheaper than the best buys at the local supermarkets but at least I didn't have to carry the bottle from home. I reached the business lounge in plenty of time. However, I had barely sat down when my name was called out on the public address system.

"Mr. Talbert?" I looked at the girl behind the desk and nodded. "Captain Falconer said that you would be very welcome to visit the Flight Deck but you would have to travel in the crew rest area for the whole flight. No-one, except very special first class passengers, is allowed on to the flight deck from the passenger cabin. I need to tell the check-in staff at the gate what you are going to do."

Clearly a snap decision was required. I was looking forward to relaxing all the way to Sydney but clearly this was not going to be possible.

"Please tell the Captain I would be delighted to travel in the crew area."

"Fine. You can go down to the gate now and one of the pilots will meet you and take you on the aircraft."

I made my way along the concourse to the gate. As usual it seemed a very long way, though there were travelators to make it easier. How elderly or infirm people ever got to the gates never ceased to amaze me. Perhaps in future airports there would be special tracks for cars to assist the handicapped.

When I reached the gate I gave my boarding pass to the man who seemed to be in charge.

"Mr. Talbert, Jack Wilson is coming to usher you on board. Suggest you go through to the far end and wait by the Upper Deck entrance."

I went through into the very crowded waiting area and squeezed my way between the rows until I reached the desks and glass doors leading to the walkways into the aircraft. As I got there I saw a First Officer coming through the Upper Deck door.

"Peter Talbert?" I nodded. The pilot spoke to the girl at the desk who checked my ticket and passport and then let me through. She re-opened the Upper Deck door using a keypad.

"Peter, I'm Jack Wilson one of the First Officers on the flight"

We shook hands and went through the glass door and started to climb towards the upper level of the aircraft. We made a turn, finally arriving at the Upper Deck aircraft entrance where a flight attendant was waiting.

"Peter Talbert will be travelling in the Flight Crew area so his seat will be empty."

The flight attendant let me through and we turned left through the Upper Deck. At the end of this section a man got up and virtually barred my way. He seemed to be acting in an official capacity, though not as cabin staff.

"May I see your passport and boarding card, please sir."

Chapter 6

He reminded me of a policeman. I watched him examining my documents. He looked at Jack.

"Do you have authority for Mr., er," he looked at my passport "Talbert to travel with you?"

Jack produced a piece of paper that looked like a computer form print out. The man scrutinized the document and appeared to agree with its contents. He turned towards me.

"Do you mind if I do a thorough search of you and your bag?"

It was clearly a rhetorical question as he immediately went over me with a fine tooth comb. That over, everything in my bag was inspected minutely. Finally he gave me the all clear.

Jack was waiting for me in the next compartment which looked like a First Class Area. The walls of this section were not parallel but gradually narrowed towards the front of the aircraft. At the end of the section we went through heavy curtains into what I recognised as a flight crew area. There appeared to be three bunks on one side and a table on the other with two seats either side. There was a Captain sitting reading a newspaper in one of the seats.

"We've made it. Tom," Jack looked at the Captain sitting down "this is Peter Talbert who will be travelling with us to Sydney."

Tom didn't get up but offered me his hand.

"Hello Peter. Hope you enjoy the flight. I'm Tom Nesbitt the en-route Captain for this trip. What brings you up here instead of relaxing in the back?" He moved slightly. "Come and sit down."

"I'm going out to NWIA to discuss crew training on their new 798s and they organised me on this trip." I paused and turned back to Jack. "What was all that about just now?"

"Peter, that's one of the Flight Marshals that guard the front of the aircraft. We have to have them on all our flights now."

"No wonder I thought he looked like a copper! I suppose it is necessary but what has the world come to?" I paused. "But if there were marshals on the flight that crashed, how did the hijackers get control?"

"That is what we are asking."

"Who employs these marshals? Does the airline?"

"Good question, Peter. Yes, I think we do though no-one seems to talk about it. Presumably we recruit and train them but I suspect they have to be approved by the Government security system. They must have their own scheduling system somewhere, they certainly don't count as crew. They arrive from nowhere but always have the necessary papers, airline tickets etc to get on board and they always seem to sit at the front of the Upper Class. I guess they must be armed in some way but nobody wants to talk about it, or to them for that matter. There's normally two, one on each side."

Tom turned to me.

"Why don't you sit down and make yourself comfortable? Are you hoping to go on the flight deck sometime?"

"Yes, I would like that. I'm hoping Captain Falconer will let me sit in the jump seat going in to Sydney."

"Well he's pretty busy now getting everything organised for departure. You can discuss it with him when we take over. Incidentally, if you want to come up when I'm flying you will be very welcome." He looked at me. "If you are going out to talk to NWIA about crew training you must be an expert on this airplane?"

I told Tom a bit about myself and what I was trying to do to earn a living. I decided there was no need for him, or anyone else for that matter, to know that I was being retained by Mike Mansell and CrossRisk Insurance.

The plane started to shake in a very characteristic manner which meant that the passengers were being loaded. In a surprisingly short time considering the hundreds of people going on board, I could hear the doors being closed and the aircraft being pushed back. The engines started and we were soon on our way to Sydney; I still found the whole concept of flying to the other side of the world non-stop absolutely amazing but perhaps it was because I had not yet actually done it.

Tom and Jack went to lie down on their bunks while I settled down and started reading the FT. Jim had written an article on the accident following the Inquiry and as usual had excelled himself. He said that the auto-pilot was flying the aircraft and all was set up for a landing using the Galileo European Satellite System. The cause of the accident was not yet known though AAIB seemed to be favouring the pilots making a mistake. He could not understand this at all since Hodgson had been checking that the aircraft was on the glide slope at the correct range. It was going to be very interesting to read the recording transcript when the Inquiry reopened and see the influence of the hijackers on the crew during the final part of the approach. If the hijackers had been talking to the captain during the last critical minutes of the approach it would have been a contributing factor, preventing the captain concentrating on monitoring the automatic pilot. The puzzling thing Jim pointed out was that the crew thought the aircraft was flying correctly down the flight path whereas it clearly was not. The loss of height could have occurred at the last moment but in fact the crew had noticed a slightly faster rate of descent than usual earlier on. Meanwhile he understood that the regulatory authorities, both the EASA and the FAA, together with Independant were reviewing the new system concepts that had been introduced in the 798, to make sure that nothing had been missed in the design.

Chapter 6

One of the cabin attendants came forward and asked me what I wanted to eat. I chose roast beef which looked great on the menu. He brought it to me on a tray and left me to get on with it. This suited me very well since I had no desire to eat and drink myself silly all the way to Australia. In fact the beef was very good and it justified the description on the menu,

The Chief Steward appeared to take my tray away.

"You are in luck. The VIP cabin is empty. You can sleep on one of the full length beds if you like."

"That's fantastic. I've got some work to do in Sydney so a good sleep will be a bonus." I looked a him. "Where do the marshals sleep?"

The steward look uncomfortable. Clearly it was bad form to mention the marshals. He leant forward and lowered his voice.

"They just put their seats back. They go back a long way. I think they take it in turns to sleep."

He rushed away not wanting to discuss the matter further but came back almost immediately and said that it was OK for me to go on to the flight deck. We went forward and he entered some numbers on a key pad by the entrance door to the flight deck. He then looked into a small camera which I had not noticed on the cabin wall. There was a click and he pushed open the door.

We went in, he introduced me to the Captain and then left. As he closed the door there was a very loud clunking noise which presumably was the door locking again.

"Peter Talbert? Didn't you give us a lecture on managing the systems, human factors and the pilot/computer interface on our training course?" I nodded. "Dick Falconer is my name and this is Fred Longshaw." He introduced me to the First Officer. "Sit down in the jump seat so that you can see what is going on."

I eased myself in to sit on the centre seat behind and midway between the pilots.

"Yes, I have been giving lectures to the 798 courses but my contract is nearly finished. As you know I specialise in the relationship between the human being and the computers on the flight deck --- Managing the Systems."

"Have you been up on a 798 flight deck before?"

"No. I've done quite a bit in the RWA simulators and also in Seattle. But however good the simulation and the visuals, the real thing is something different. It smells different for a start and there is much more activity behind the seats." I added wryly "And it's easier to get on to the flight deck."

Dick nodded but didn't actually smile.

"It's a cross we have to bear these days I'm afraid." He rapidly changed the subject. "What are you doing going to Sydney, if I may ask."

"No problem. Bill Baker the NWIA chief training pilot has asked me to advise on their training course for the 798s they are getting and perhaps give some lectures. I'm going to suggest that a Video might be a good idea so that it can be used on every course."

"What do you think about the accident to Golf Hotel, Peter?"

"Terrible, and seemingly inexplicable. Did you read about the Inquiry in the papers today? What do you people think?"

"Well, Peter, we were all pretty shaken. The frightening thing is that accidents can normally be explained very quickly but this one seems different. I think most of us thought that a hijacking was impossible. I still believe that the highjacking must be the primary cause but I know there is a view that it may only have been a contributory factor. The sooner we find the true explanation the better."

I looked down out of the side window. "Are we coming up to Mongolia?"

"How did you know? You can't know the area."

"I selected the map on the passenger video screen you've got in the flight deck area. The map is really very good and RWA does overlay latitude and longitude on the maps in the magazine."

"Yes, I must say even when I'm only deadheading I like to know where we are. By the way here's our actual position." He pointed to a spot on his radio navigation chart and then adjusted the map on the Navigation Display in front of him so that I could see we were looking at the same thing. It was just as well we had something to look at inside the aircraft, below all we could see was cloud. Not worth getting a real map out of the electronic library.

Silence descended for a few minutes. We were probably all thinking about Golf Hotel.

"Dick, how good is the navigation? This is the first time that RWA has had the Galileo European Satellite System as well as the triple Inertial Solid State Reference System. Does the Flight Management System integrate the GESS properly with the IRS?"

"Yes, it works very well. After an hour or so the GPS position calculated from the satellites is much better than the aircraft based Inertial Reference Systems positions and the Flight Management System takes this into account. At the end of the flight there may be Inertial System errors of 20 miles but of course the GESS does not degrade at all. It really is superb."

"Do you ever use the US GPS as well for navigation?"

"We can do but we have to select it on the FMS. The default is the European GESS system. As you probably are well aware, the GPS output is sent to the Flight Management Computer but is not averaged with GESS; we can select GPS instead of GESS but we never do unless the GESS goes wrong. Same thing applies to the Russian GLOSNASS, we can select it but I can't imagine ever doing so. The European system is so much more advanced and the integrity and self checking is so good than the earlier GPS and GLOSNASS systems are just not needed except perhaps if the GESS fails. Anyway we only have one receiver for the GPS and GLOSNASS systems while we have three for GESS which increases it's accuracy and reliability."

"Yes, it should be more accurate, Dick, but remember the accuracy also depends on the total system so that, conceivably, all three receivers could be producing the same wrong information. Luckily things have improved enormously recently now that the INMARSAT geostationary satellites are sending signals to improve the Galileo satellites accuracy."

"We don't use these corrections for our routine navigation do we?"

"Yes, now you do. The ability to correct depends on the modification state of the GESS receivers. It's silly really because the corrections which are being transmitted are not needed for en route navigation and are not good enough for runway approaches. However, individual satellite malfunctions are reported in the data as well which is very important."

"But Peter the FAA allows US carriers to make Category 1 approaches worldwide down to 200 ft. using GPS augmented with corrections from their so called Wide Area Augmentation System, WAAS."

"I know but they shouldn't in my opinion. A much more accurate local correction system is needed for airfield operation, certainly for bad weather approaches below 200ft., and even then some local correction systems are not good enough at certain locations. In fact I think there are local correction systems both at Heathrow and Paris but the US carriers aren't allowed to make GPS approaches at either place because the Local Area Augmentation System needs considerable improvement. Apparently the faults are only temporary since FAA say that the approaches were working correctly. In my view FAA really ought to order the LAAS transmitters to be switched off temporarily but politically the US don't want their system to be seen to be inferior to the European system and they are trying very hard to fix the problems. RWA are probably very sensible to prevent the use of GPS on any approach now that GESS is available with the accuracy enhanced by the GELAS when Cat 3 landings are required."

"Nevertheless Peter, I'm glad that RWA did agree to have the GPS as a back-up to GESS since, though there is no doubt that for normal navigation GESS is superb, in fact we did have a problem with GESS some months ago and were very pleased to be able to use GPS for navigation."

There was a strident buzzing noise and Dick looked at a small screen to his left where I could see the face of the Chief Steward. Dick pressed a button on top of the screen and the steward came in with some coffee. It occurred to me that there must be some secret code so that the Captain would know if the person trying to get on to the flight deck was being threatened. Though it would be a brave person to use the code if he or she had a pistol or knife in their back.

In spite of having control wheels instead of side stick controllers, the view of the instruments and controls was superb. The navigation displays showed the aircraft moving steadily along the airway and the flight management display showed the expected arrival time at Kingsford Smith Airport.

"Did you notice, Peter, that at the moment we are using the 4D method of control; the automatic throttles are controlling the speed so that we will arrive at Sydney exactly at the flight plan time. It won't last of course as we shall have to alter our altitude in a moment or change our mach number more likely."

The autopilot was flying the aircraft and the model aeroplane on the display was sitting inside the flight plan predicted time box ; the four throttles moved very slightly to adjust the airspeed to keep the aircraft there. I could see that the Flight Management System, FMS, was navigating the aircraft laterally and vertically and, for the moment, was also controlling the speed. This ideal situation clearly would not last as the crew needed continually to alter their flight plan, both in height and laterally, to meet the required air traffic clearances. The problem was compounded by the desire to choose the optimum flight levels for the weight of the aircraft, to vary cleared altitude because of turbulence or weather and, on occasions, to change level to avoid an aircraft ahead flying at a lower speed.

It occurred to me that the pilots' jobs on the flight deck had changed enormously through the years as the number of crew required to fly an aircraft on long haul flights had changed. The old flight engineers tasks were now automated in the aircraft systems. The radio operators tasks were done automatically in many ways thanks to satellite communication with automatic position reporting and, of course, the navigators tasks were done by the Flight Management System. As a percentage of flight time, the pilots spent very little time actually flying the aircraft. From a safety viewpoint the problem was going to be the need for the crew to recognize and deal with emergencies correctly; this was the challenge not only for the pilots but also for the aircraft designers and the organizations certificating the aircraft. This situation was always the one I was discussing with airlines when they were bringing their new aircraft into service.

As I drank my coffee, Fred drew my attention to a traffic advisory on the Traffic and Conflict Alerting System display, TCAS. An aircraft was ahead of us going our way but two thousand feet below. We were slowly overtaking it. It was an Airbus A330 of Cathay Pacific on its way to Hong Kong. Fred started talking to the Cathay crew which was something I always recommended to keep the crews interested.

"Peter, we are getting towards the end of our shift and the other crew will be taking over. Would you like to come back again later? If you like you can spend the last hour with us descending into Sydney for landing."

I leapt at the opportunity. "Yes please Dick. It would be very interesting. I'll get out of your way now and perhaps you could send a message back when you are ready for me."

I left the jump seat and returned to my seat in the crew compartment. I tried to put myself into neutral, reading my book for a bit. Tom and Jack got up, freshened themselves up and after the now normal security procedure at the flight deck door, went onto the flight deck. A few minutes later Dick and Fred appeared from the flight deck, had a quick meal off a tray and went to lie down. The stewardess appeared and asked if I was ready to lie down in the VIP Cabin. I agreed rapidly and settled down to sleep. In fact I managed to get about five hours so that when I woke up we only had three hours to go. We were 300 miles east of Darwin over the Gulf of Carpentaria. I went back into the crew compartment where Tom and Jack were having breakfast. It looked good and Tom arranged for a stewardess to bring me the same as he was having. I was only just finishing eating when she came back again and said it would be OK if I went back on to the flight deck. I packed up all my belongings so that would not waste any time when I returned after landing. The stewardess obviously knew the magic number on the flight deck door and we went in. It was dark by now and there were lots of lights from the ground 47,000 ft below.

"Good morning Peter. Where are we then?"

"26° S 145° E Dick, if the front of the aircraft is in the same place as the monitor in the crew compartment."

Dick looked at his Flight Management System display and selected present position.

"Quite right, Peter. We're on schedule and will be letting down fairly soon. The weather's good at Kingsford-Smith, 10 miles visibility, no cloud, 15 knots from the south and a temperature of 28°C if you can believe that."

Dick got clearance to descend and wound the knob on the glare shield in front of him to the new cleared altitude of flight level 190. He then initiated the descent to 19,000 ft. and the throttles closed. The Flight Management System took the aircraft steadily along and down the standard instrument approach, Dick gradually lowering the setting of the altitude controller as he received clearances from the ground.

"I think we won't interfere to-day. We will let the autopilot do the landing." He selected the GESS vertical position on the glare shield landing aid controller. "Oh, sorry. We can't. I see they haven't repaired the Galileo European Local Augmentation System yet. It failed a day or so ago. We will just have to use the ILS." Dick turned the approach selector one click anti-clockwise which selected ILS on the controller and he checked the correct identification.

We could see the lights of Sydney below and then the runway lights gradually emerged from the surrounding illumination as the aircraft got closer. Dick and Fred carried out the landing checks and Fred selected the landing gear down as we subsided on to the glide slope. The four throttles went back until the approach speed had been reached and then opened slightly to maintain the speed. The runway lights got closer and closer and slowly moved apart so that we could see the runway centre line markings. The radio altimeter called out the heights as the aircraft descended and at about 30 ft. the throttles closed, the stick came back and the aircraft touched down quite firmly. The aircraft pitched down, the nose wheels touched the ground and after a few moments Dick disconnected the autopilot and applied the brakes. It was a perfect landing. I looked at my watch, it was on schedule at 2000.

Dick taxied the aircraft clear of the runway and then followed instructions to reach gate C45.

"Thanks so much, Dick, for letting me watch that. It was great. Where are you staying?"

"At the Hilton until Tuesday unless the plan changes."

"I'm at the Hilton as well so I'll probably see you. Thanks again." I went back to flight deck area just before the aircraft came to a halt. We all had to wait until the passengers had left and then we filed out slowly from the top deck, the flight crew and the cabin attendants. It seemed miles to customs and immigration but at least we did not have to queue like all the passengers. On the other hand the flight crew line was not insignificant once we were joined by the lower deck cabin staff. There were a lot of passengers to be looked after. The immigration department had clearly done a marvellous job preparing for these large aircraft but however fast they were and however many officials there were, there always seemed to be long queues.

I said goodbye to the crew and became a civilian again. My bag, marked with its business class sticker, appeared quite quickly on the carousel and I walked through the customs line without being stopped. I rang the Hilton courtesy phone.

"Just go to the hotel pick-up point and there is a coach every fifteen minutes. See you soon," the voice at the other end said. I followed instructions and realised for the first time as I left the air conditioned terminal how hot it still was at 9 o'clock at night. The coach appeared and I was at the Hilton in about 40 minutes.

When I checked in they told me there was a message from Matt Thompson. I took the elevator to the sixth floor and went to 617. It was like any other hotel room but it did have a magnificent view over the harbour. I unpacked my things and had a shower to freshen up.

I called Matt first but there was no reply and I left a message. Then I tried Mandy. Again there was no reply. She had obviously decided that sailing and the yacht club was the thing to do for the week-end and, unreasonably, I decided not to leave a message on her answering machine.

I lay down on the bed and thought about Golf Hotel. Why didn't the crew realise they were below the glide slope? Why was the voice recording so noisy? Did the hijackers prevent the crew noticing some warning clue? There had to be an explanation. Richard's dying words weren't much help and the fact that NWIA had changed a display and a Multimode Receiver before departure didn't help either. Matt calling me might turn out to be a bit of luck because then I might have the chance to investigate the maintenance without seeming too inquisitive.

***

When I woke up Sydney still had its heat wave. It was going to be a magnificent day. At the pool reception, the girl gave me a towel. I put my wrap and towel on one of the loungers and went to the deep end to dive in. The pool was quite busy bearing in mind it was only 6.30 in the morning. The swimmers were mostly people like myself getting some exercise before the start of the day.

The water was deliciously warm and there was no smell of chlorine which ruins so many hotel pools and spoils the pleasure in swimming. After ten lengths of the pool I felt quite tired, perhaps not surprisingly since it was quite a long pool. I dried myself sufficiently to avoid dripping in the elevator and wandered back to my room. There did not seem to be much activity in the other rooms judging by the newspapers still lying on the floor outside the doors.

After a shower and wearing my lightweight slacks and shirt I went down to the breakfast room. Dick Falconer was having breakfast with a lady who turned out to be his wife. I went over and he introduced me to Jill.

"Were you on our flight? Dick never mentioned it."

"Yes. I was in the flight crew area."

"How did you like the flight?"

"It was fine but awfully long. Still its nice not to have to stop on the way. That was my first non-stop flight."

"Did you sleep?"

"Quite well really when Dick was not showing me the flight deck. They let me sleep in the VIP compartment."

Dick invited me to join them for breakfast. They had only just ordered and the waiter laid a place in front of me. I ordered coffee, grapefruit and scrambled eggs.

"What are you doing to-day, Peter?" Dick asked.

"Jock Mansfield is collecting me and we're going over to start work on their training course. What about you."

"I'm taking Jill over to Randwick where our daughter and her family live. Jill's staying over for a week or so until I come out again."

The room was slowly filling up. Fred Longshaw was with Jack Wilson.

"Do the flight crew normally stay here, Dick? I see Fred over there."

"Yes pretty well. We rent the rooms all the time and our Operations Office at the airport keeps the hotel informed, tells them when they need to change the sheets, etc."

"Where do the cabin crew stay?"

"Normally at the Oakford Executive Apartments and the Winyard Travel Lodge Plaza. You know the attendants make up a coach-load there are so many. Its a full time job for one person in the office sorting out the accommodation."

Luckily Dick refrained from asking me why I wanted to know. I would not have wanted to tell him that I was checking up on Golf Hotel's crew. After breakfast I excused myself and went upstairs and got my papers ready in my holdall. At the news stand I bought the Sydney Herald. The London papers on sale must have been the ones we brought out with us though I noticed the Mail was printed locally. The main news in the Herald was the cricket and whether the West Indies could score enough runs in their first innings to save the follow on. I searched for some news about Golf Hotel and was disconcerted to read that we had brought two bodies back to Australia for burial on yesterday's flight. However, some of the other bodies could not be brought back because of difficulties with positive identification.

Chapter 6

There was no technical news about the possible cause of the accident nor, I was glad to see, was there any more news about the cockpit voice recorder and the party in Sydney.

I considered what should be my next move and how to find out what Golf Hotel's crew had been up to. I didn't know how long the crew had been staying in the hotel before they left for England and I didn't fancy asking at reception. Anyway they might not have known. Asking RWA's flight operations at the airport would be a possibility but that would alert them and it might get back to John. I decided that I would try talking to the barman in the main bar at the lobby level at about 5.30 that evening before it got too crowded. Barmen always seemed to know what was going on.

Jock Mansfield came into the lobby at 9.30 prompt. That was one of the nice things about the airline business, everybody was on time or slightly early. We introduced ourselves and I got into Jock's Honda. We set course for the airport.

"When did you finish your course in Seattle, Jock?"

"On Friday night. We got in here 6 o'clock Sunday morning. It's quite a long flight 16 hours. Not as long as from England but long enough."

"How was the course?"

"It certainly is a fantastic aircraft. They seemed to have thought of everything. Mind you the systems are quite complicated, especially if anything goes wrong."

"Well I suppose that's why we're meeting to-day. We all feel there's a problem in this area. How to keep the crews alert and ready to deal with any emergency."

We threaded our way through the traffic and arrived at the NWIA training block. Jock parked his car and we went into reception. The girl took my photograph with a Polaroid she had hidden under the desk and gave me an 'unaccompanied' pass valid until Thursday.

"It is magnetised so you will be able to get in and out of this building but it won't work everywhere in NWIA."

We went up to Bill's office which was quite palatial. His secretary took us in.

"Great to see you Peter. Let me get Jack Phillips the other Captain and Frank Trotter who actually runs the Ground School here.

"Lorna" Bill shouted to his secretary "Ask Jack Phillips and Frank Trotter to come up."

"And please bring some coffee in." he added.

We sat down at a working desk and the coffee appeared. Bill waited for Jack and Frank to settle down before we started.

"I've got Peter to come out here now that you two are back from Seattle because I believe we need to think more carefully than usual about training our crews for the 798. The accident to Golf Hotel shows how difficult it is to prevent accidents. The sooner the investigators find out the cause the better. I suppose we all hope it will be the hijackers fault but it's beginning to look as if they were not the direct cause.

"Anyway, my concern is that we must have a training course that covers all our flight operations. The really long flights require two full crews and we have to ensure that the duty crew is ready and rested as they take-over the flight deck. All the systems including the navigation and flight controls are fully automatic, not only for normal flight but also when things start malfunctioning. The challenge for us is to devise a training program that enables the crew to deal with emergencies and situations which are not expected. I've heard Peter lecture on these issues both here and in London. Managing the Systems he calls it, and the phrase he uses which I like very much is 'we must prepare for the emergencies that the designers have not thought of'. This is what I want you four to think about in the next two days. Show me a training plan which faces up to the problem."

We talked a bit more and then the four of us went into a small conference room that had been booked for us. Jock produced the Independant training course and started discussing the strengths and weaknesses of the course. We gradually started to plan the NWIA training course.

"Is your aircraft going to be the same standard as Royal World Airlines, Jock?"

"No. We are going to match United and American exactly on the flight deck. I understand that RWA have a slightly different way of using the satellite positioning systems?"

"Yes, that's quite right. Your aircraft will have the capability of doing all three types of instrument approach ILS, GPS and GESS while RWA can only use ILS and GESS. You've got both a Local Area Augmentation System and a Galileo European Local Augmentation System at Sydney I believe?"

"Yes, but I don't think either system is too reliable at the moment. We don't have much occasion to make blind landings out here and our ILS works fine. NWIA has not fitted any of its aircraft with satellite systems yet, the 798 will be our first. We like the idea of satellite approaches because they will work anywhere, even GPS now that the Defense Department has stopped playing around with the accuracy."

"Well I'll arrange my talks to cover your installation."

We broke for lunch and went to the canteen. We carried on through the afternoon making good progress. I raised the subject of making a

Chapter 6

video which could be used for later courses and Jock agreed to get the NWIA expert over. Jock took me back to the hotel and he volunteered to pick me up again in the morning. Apart from the video we reckoned we would be through by the end of Friday.

I collected my key, left my things in my room and went down in the elevator as planned and sat at the bar. I ordered a gin and slimline tonic. The barman was dark, short and was called Mario, he sounded Italian. We chatted for a bit.

"Are you with Royal World Airlines?"

"No. I am working with NWIA" I didn't mind telling him since he was sure to find out. "That was a terrible accident to the 798."

"Yes. The crew had been staying here for several days before they left. We knew them very well because they always stayed here. You know Royal World Airlines put all their flight crew up here. It was a shame. Captain Hodgson was such a nice guy."

"Did you know Charles Tumbrill as well then.?"

"Oh yes. He was much younger than Hodgson and always out for a party. In fact I saw them both on the Saturday night. Tumbrill appeared with a couple of girls and they were drinking at that table over there. It was quite early, about this time. He called for the bill and I heard him say that they had better be going to Maroubra as their reservation was for eight o'clock."

"Saturday night? But they left for the flight early Monday morning. Did you see them Sunday?"

"No I didn't. But they normally go to bed early when they are flying the next day. Not like some of them when they arrive."

"How do you mean?"

Mario went away again but returned after a bit.

"Can I get you a drink?"

"Not really when I'm working but if I may I'll put a large beer on your tab to have later."

"Fine. what did you mean about the crews not going to bed when they arrive from England?"

"You seem very interested. You a newspaperman or something."

"No. I told you I'm working with NWIA but I used to fly myself with Britannia."

"Britannia stay here as well." He gave me another drink.

"I was telling you, on Saturday night Tumbrill and Hodgson went off to the beach. On Sunday night I did not see the other crew but very early on the Monday morning I saw two flight crew who had just come in from England checking in to the hotel with their bags. They were wearing slacks and short sleeved shirts so they must have got changed somewhere."

"Would you recognise either of the girls that were here on Saturday night?"

He looked hard at me. I was clearly showing too much interest. However he carried on.

"Oh yes. We see quite a lot of one of them. I think she works in the Royal World Airlines operations office. I haven't seen her since the accident."

"Is she Australian."

"No she sounds like a real Pom to me, like you. She is a brunette, smashing legs, good boobs, very nearly as tall as you. Don't know her name."

"Thanks a lot, Mario. I must be off now." I gave him a $10 note besides signing a generous tip on the bill.

I was glad to get upstairs and lie down on the bed even though it was only 8 o'clock. I had had to drink three strong gin and tonics to get what I needed from Mario. The phone rang.

"Mr. Talbert?" I admitted to the operator that that was my name.

"I have a call for you."

Before I could prepare myself I heard Mandy.

"Peter, are you there?"

"Yes my darling. I'm safe and sound in bed."

"In bed! What time is it?"

"Well I've just drunk three double gin and tonics and bed seemed a good idea. I'm just resting."

"I take my eyes off you and you go on to the bottle. Are you alone" she said suspiciously.

"No my dearest Mandy. I mean yes I am alone."

"You just said you weren't."

"Look. Your not cross examining me in court."

"All I am trying to establish is what time it is in Sydney and whether you are by yourself."

"It is 8 o'clock in the evening and yes, I am alone."

"The sooner they bring in TV phones the better. However I believe you …"

"Of course."

"as far as I can see you." she finished.

"That's not very friendly."

"I'm not sure I'm feeling friendly. I'm feeling cross, lonely and I miss you" she said suddenly changing her tone of voice.

"Would it be trite to say I miss you too?"

"I am afraid it would be in your condition – as some of my clients would say – 'slightly pissed'."

Chapter 6

"That's not a very ladylike thing for a young girl to say. I'll go along with 'slightly the worse for wear'."

"I don't feel ladylike and it was my clients talking. I'd better not tell you what I feel like, not that you could help in your condition."

"I only had three doubles and it was all in the course of research. I was chatting up the barman."

Mandy suddenly became serious. "How did you get on?"

"Rather well apart from the side effects. The party the Telegraph mentioned seems to have been the night before the night before the flight if you know what I mean. The barman knew one of the girls, she works for RWA in operations. I guess all the crews know her as well, though not I trust in the biblical sense."

Mandy ignored my comment.

"That's good news. Anything else?"

"Not really. The crew that flew the plane in had a party after they got in but that is not going to help as far as I can see."

"Are you going to talk to the girl."

"Yes, if I can find her. I'll have a go to-morrow if I can but it looks as if I shall be working flat out for the next two days. I've also got to see the maintenance people. I'm booked for a Sunday morning departure which gets in late Sunday night but Sunday seems a long way away at the moment."

"Alright. Take care. Don't get into trouble and call me soon. All my love." She rang off and I suddenly felt lonely and sober. I got up and had a shower.

I thought about what Mario had said. Clearly Charles and Harry had had a beach party on Saturday night. Nothing wrong in that from a flight operations viewpoint though it might cause problems socially. Let's hope the pilots had been referring to the Saturday night party on the recording. Marcia Hodgson might still be unhappy but from my point of view it was good news. However it occurred to me that it might be interesting to find the girl and talk over not only what had happened on Saturday night but if she knew anything about Sunday night. She probably knew the crew if she was in operations. How was I going to meet the girl?

I remembered I had not spoken to Matt. I called him and this time he answered.

"Matt, I don't think we've met. This is Peter Talbert. You left a message for me to ring you and I wanted to talk to you anyway. How can I help you?"

"Hi, Peter. I wanted to meet with you and chat over Golf Hotel. What are you doing to-morrow?"

"Well Bill has mapped out a pretty full program for me and it's his party."

"I understand that. Why don't I come over to your place at about 6.30 to-morrow evening and we'll go out for a meal?"

"Sounds good to me. If we don't make contact before I'll see you then. How will I recognise you?"

"I'll be wearing a red shirt and trousers, I'm 6 ft. tall and some people say I'm thin."

"OK. See you to-morrow."

It was now 9 o'clock. I was not too hungry but I decided I had better have something before I went to bed. I put some clothes on, took my book and went down to the coffee shop. I had a bowl of clam chowder, Australian style, some water followed by strong decaffeinated coffee. I retired to bed and slept through until it started to get light at about 6 o'clock. I managed my swim and breakfast next to the pool before Jock came and collected me. I asked Jock if he could take me to RWA Operations at lunch time.

"Yes, that's no problem. I've got the video man coming after lunch at 2 o'clock. I'll drop you off at Ops and you can go into the main airport for lunch if you want to. I'll pick you up at 1.45 from RWA Ops"

We did a good morning's work and I was in Ops at noon. There were several girls at the desk and I asked to speak to the duty officer. The girl I spoke to said that Ted Richmond was the man I needed and he would be back very shortly. I was wondering how to proceed when the girl, Barbara on her badge, made it simple for me.

"What are you people making of the accident?" She sounded as if she had been born in Sydney.

"We are appalled. Everybody is very shaken and very puzzled. Harry was a fine man and I knew him well."

"We knew them all of course. They were in and out of here all the time. We couldn't believe it. I think Liz was the most upset as she had got to know Harry quite well."

Ted Richmond appeared and introduced himself. I followed him into his office. I explained that I was working with NWIA and asked about getting back on Sunday. He looked at his computer and checked on the RWA allocated tickets.

"You have a firm booking for Sunday, that's fine."

"Could you tell me the Captain's name so I can contact him in the hotel?"

Ted consulted his machine again.

"Bill Wentworth. He came in last night."

"Thanks. Ted, may I talk about the accident?"

He smiled.

"Sure, go ahead. I guessed there had to be another reason for your coming here."

168

Chapter 6

"I'm a friend of Harry's wife, Marcia. She's very upset and she asked me to talk to one of your staff who both she and Harry knew well. Apparently Harry saw her just before the flight. Is her name Liz or something like that?"

"Oh you mean Liz Ward. I'm afraid she took Harry's death very badly. I told her to take a week of her annual holiday but she's started working again now. I got her moved into reservations downtown so she'd get away from the crews."

"Marcia couldn't find her address. Do you think you could let me have it so I can call on her?"

"Sure." He looked at his computer yet again and then printed out Liz Ward's address and telephone number.

"Thanks. I'll get out of your way."

I felt a bit guilty lying to Ted in order to get the information about the girl but I did not want to stir up any particular interest. Fortunately he did not behave as if anything I said was particularly unusual. I wandered over to the terminal, bought yesterday's Times and FT and had a tuna sandwich in one of the many eating places. The accident was no longer the main topic of news and I guessed the next bit of media interest would be when the AAIB preliminary report came out.

Jock picked me up and took me back to the training block. We had a discussion with the Video expert and decided that when I came out again to give a talk to the first course I would also make a video which could be used for subsequent courses. I made a mental note to discuss the financial side of this plan with Bill Baker.

We settled down again to finish the training plan and I spoke to Bill to arrange to see him the following afternoon. Jock took me back to the Hilton. Matt arrived on time and he took me to the Polynesian restaurant Trader Vic's, which seem to be attached to all of the Hiltons bordering the Pacific.

He passed me the drinks menu which had at least one hundred and one ways of serving rum steeped in fruit juice.

"What are you having?"

"If you don't mind I'll stick to Scotch and water."

"That's fine by me. Two Scotch and bring the water" he said turning to the waiter who was dressed to match the Polynesian theme. If he felt we should be having rum he didn't show it.

"Well Peter what have you being doing?"

"Preparing the pilot training courses. Bill has kindly asked me to help. The 798 is a challenge for the flight crews. How about the engineering of the aircraft?"

"Typical Independant. Very well thought out and conservative in approach. My people are used to the Independant approach and we like all their aircraft. Let's hope the 798 will be as easy to maintain as our other aircraft. We've already got most of our spares and of course we're getting a lot of experience looking after the RWA aircraft. It seems very reliable."

"Matt, I had better explain. I have been retained by one of RWA's insurers to try to find out exactly what happened to Golf Hotel. They don't want to leave it completely to AAIB. Do you mind if I ask you some questions?"

"Not a bit. But surely the accident was due to the hijackers?"

"Well we've just been listening to the voice recorder and reading the transcript of the flight deck microphone at the Public Inquiry and it's not obvious why the hijackers caused the accident though they must have been a distraction to the crew during the approach. I want to be certain that the maintenance your people did had nothing to do with the accident."

"Good. Well I did wonder what your interest was. Go ahead and I'll see if I can help."

"This aircraft that crashed. Was the failure of the Navigation Display unusual in any way?"

"Not as far as we were concerned. However, after the crew had filled in the tech. log, my avionics expert on the night shift functioned the unit and it worked perfectly. As you know NWIA policy is not to allow a 'ground tested and found serviceable' entry in the log so we actually changed the unit. We functioned the new unit on the aircraft and then we did an all night function on the unit we had removed. It worked perfectly and so we've placed the unit back in stores as a spare."

"Well as I am sure you know, Matt, the new display failed again shortly after take-off so it looks as if the aircraft installation was at fault rather than the display itself. Had the aircraft not crashed, there would have been an opportunity to find out what the matter really was."

"So I understand. Anyway I don't think the display had anything to do with the crash, do you?"

"I just don't know. It may have contributed to the accident. Who knows? The whole thing looks like a complete mystery. Tell me about the GESS fault?"

"Well as you know, to ensure the correct integrity for automatic landings the 798 has a triplex system with three Multimode Receivers. Now the satellite landing systems are very different from ILS in that, in order to get a glide slope deviation signal to drive the auto-pilot, each MMR has to calculate the deviation from a computed synthetic glide slope. You can see it's much more complicated than with ILS, where you can tell whether you are on centre line by just looking at the signal. The calculation of course relies completely on the installed software and the accuracy of the database in the Multimode Receiver.

Chapter 6

"On Golf Hotel the crew reported that when they selected GESS on the approach, one of the Multimode Receivers was giving a false reading. The engineer on the night shift decided it was a hardware fault and changed one of the Multimode Receivers. The engineer then did a full check and pronounced the aircraft serviceable."

"Well that sounds fine. Tell me, have the AAIB been on to you again?"

"No, it's surprisingly quiet. I would have thought that they would have flown somebody out to see the tech. log pages at the very least. We did what they asked and faxed them copies."

Our conversation drifted away from the accident and Golf Hotel and we talked about more general matters. The meal when it came was superb but not heavy and I did not feel that I had over indulged when we had finished.

Matt took me back to the hotel and I called Mandy's office and was told she was in court. I said I would try again on Friday. I slept well, waking up to another perfect day. I had my 7 o'clock swim. While I was dressing before going down to breakfast my phone rang.

"Peter. This is Bill Wentworth of RWA. I am taking you back to England on Sunday. How about having breakfast together?"

"Fine by me. See you by the news stand in ten minutes. I've got to make a phone call and then I'll come down."

I looked at the local directory and it gave the main police headquarters' number at Paramatta. They answered straightaway and, at my request, the connected me to the homicide department.

"I'm visiting from England. I wondered whether you had any more news on the body that was found in the Hyatt car park."

"What's it to you? What did you say your name was?" The voice was surly and didn't sound too helpful."

"My name is Talbert and I'm working on the aircraft accident at London Airport. I understand that the person should have been on the plane..."

I didn't get any further.

"I don't know where your getting your information from, Mr. Tarbuck, but this matter is still under investigation. I suggest you get on with the technical investigation and leave police matters to the police."

I was left looking at a dead phone. Sounded as if the Sydney police was operating a D-Notice regime as well. Maybe they were sensitive that the hijackers had got on to the aircraft.

Bill was waiting when I got to the shop. He was about my height, 40 years old and looked very fit. We went over to the coffee shop but stayed inside rather going to the pool.

Bill came to the point straightaway.

"I wanted to meet you Peter. I know about your interest in the flight deck and navigation and I was looking forward to talking with you on the flight back on Sunday. However, out of the blue John Chester called me at flight operations before I left while I was picking up the flight plan. He said that he did not want you to go on the flight deck again. I thought I would tell you now rather than embarrass you on the flight."

I felt absolutely amazed and I suppose my face showed it.

"You look surprised."

"To be honest Bill, I am. I have known John for years and we have worked together at GAPAN and at RWA. I would have thought if he had a problem he would have had the courtesy to phone me."

"You know I think John is very worried about the crash" Bill remarked.

"Of course, but so are we all. John called me on the morning after the accident and we met for lunch but since then he seems to have got worried about something else and he is keeping it to himself. I must say I do appreciate your being so straightforward about this. It's very kind."

"Forget it. What are you doing to-day?"

"Well I'm having a day off. How about you?"

"So am I. I was thinking of going over to the Opera House for a conducted tour. Care to join me?"

I accepted with pleasure and we had a splendid morning looking at the extraordinary architecture and being shown all over the enormous complex with it's two theatres and many side rooms. We had lunch in one of the many restaurants in Circular Quay and then I went over to the airport to see Bill Baker. We agreed a deal over the video and I took my farewell. His secretary took me over to the terminal and I picked up a rental car and drove back to the Hilton to get changed. I got my map out and made sure where Liz Ward lived before setting out. I felt rather flat. I had taken a job halfway across the world when I really couldn't spare the time in order to try to investigate the crash of the 798. I had achieved precisely nothing and yet somehow I didn't believe that Harry Hodgson had made a mistake. He had handled the hijacking magnificently, he hadn't been rattled, there was something else in the equation that nobody had found.

CHAPTER 7

I steered the car into the right area and found that the address was a small bungalow set in a myriad of bungalows. There were some lights in the rooms. I parked the car and walked up the path. A Siamese cat was sitting on the doorstep. I pressed the bell and I could hear a buzzer somewhere at the back. I heard noises and I could see through the opaque glass door someone looking through the spy hole. The door opened slightly on a chain.

"Yes?" came a female voice from inside.

"Miss Ward, I'm out from England working with NWIA" As usual I kept to the truth as much as possible since that way I didn't have to remember what story I had told. "I was a friend of Harry Hodgson. They told me in the RWA office that you knew him. I hope you don't mind but I got them to give me your address. I don't believe what they said in the press about a party the night before the flight. I wanted to find out the truth and if possible help his family."

There was a long pause and finally I heard the chain coming off the door which opened revealing a tall brunette, mid twenties possibly, longish hair, slim and alarmingly attractive. I could not decide whether this was due to her very short shorts and skimpy top or due to her superior look which seemed to say 'I know what you men want but don't hold your breath.' She eyed me carefully, looking me up and down. I noticed the whites of her eyes were red and it looked as if she had been crying.

"Come on in. What did you say your name was?"

"I didn't but it's Peter Talbert. I'm a specialist in electronics and the aircraft flight deck."

"Mine's Elizabeth but everybody calls me Liz."

When I entered the house I thought she might have been Australian but her accent was very English. She showed me to the living room in the back of the house which overlooked a very small garden and the other bungalows. It was very warm inside and the patio door was open. I sat on the settee. There were bits of clothing in the making, half sewn, in various parts of the room.

"Would you like a drink?"

I could have used a beer but the time didn't seem right for alcohol. I didn't want to miss anything and I was clearly going to have to concentrate and not start thinking of other things.

"A coke or something soft if you have one."

"You're sure? There's most things available."

"No, really. Coke would be just fine."

The room was quite ordinary and fairly tidy. There were some recent English newspapers lying around as well as the Sydney Herald.

She returned with two cokes in long glasses stuffed with ice. She put them down and sat opposite me on a chair and looked at me enquiringly, waiting for me to begin.

"You know that somebody leaked the cockpit voice recorder conversation to the press just after the accident? Everybody's assuming that the crew had been out partying the night before and consequently they might have made a mistake when landing. I don't happen to believe that and I'm trying to find out what really happened."

"I thought the accident was due to hijacking."

"We all hoped that, but now that some of us have heard the voice recorder and read the transcripts it's difficult to see that the hijackers directly caused the accident. So people are looking around again for another reason."

"Why did you come to me?"

"Well I spoke to the barman in the Hilton and from what he told me it appeared that Harry and Charles Tumbrill the first officer had gone out on Saturday with two ladies and he thought one of them worked for RWA operations in Sydney. So it was not very difficult to find you and here I am. Obviously, I want to find out how Harry and Charles spent Sunday night, hopefully in their own beds before the flight. What happened on Saturday is not important from my point of view."

There was a long silence.

"Harry was a fine person. He was a good friend. I miss him. And I've lost my room mate. I know life has to go on but at the moment things don't look too good."

"Your room mate? I'm afraid I don't understand."

"Are you on the level, Peter? You're not a reporter or a detective or something."

"No, I'm not a reporter or a detective or a something. However, I am dedicated to trying to save the crews' name. I don't believe that it was pilot error, pure and simple. I want to get at the truth and find out what really happened."

"Well that's fine by me. I'll try and tell you the story as best I can. I'm afraid I'm not in very good shape."

Luckily I knew what she meant and I kept very quiet.

"As you know I worked in the RWA operations office and obviously I got to know all the crews. It doesn't need a lot of imagination to guess that a lot of them tried to take me out and make passes. The married men were normally the worst. To cut a long story short about six months ago Charles met my room mate Eva by chance, when she was visiting me in the office and persuaded her to go out to dinner. Eva was a NWIA trainee

174

cabin attendant based in Sydney and was training on the 798. Eva said OK providing I could come along as well." She paused and swallowed before she carried on.

"We agreed a time and Charles found the bungalow as you did. Harry was with him. We went out to a down town restaurant and had a good evening. Charles was smitten with Eva and she liked him a lot. Eva was about my age, maybe a little younger and like me she had known quite a few men. We enjoyed life." I noticed she used the past tense.

"Harry was different. He was happily married, teenage children of his own and he did not start chasing me all round the room, if you know what I mean." I nodded. I knew what she meant.

"After this first meeting we started meeting regularly whenever they came out. Harry and Charles often flew together but sometimes they came out at different times. Well, that Saturday they flew out together and this heat wave had already started. Eva suggested we went out to the beach and have a meal at one of the many restaurants. We drove round to the Hilton, had a drink, went out to Maroubra beach and ate at Caesars. It was marvellous out there and Charles could hardly keep his hands off Eva. By some strange chance NWIA had arranged for Eva and one or two other girls to travel on the very 798 which Harry and Charles were flying back to England on the Monday, in order to get some flight experience. The girls had not flown outside Australia before." She paused again, I think uncertain whether to carry on.

She leant forward and held both my hands.

"You are a straight guy? You're not going to tell this story round the world?"

The way she looked at that particular moment I would have done anything for her.

"I promise you this story will go no further unless you want it to."

She carried on holding my hands, leaning very close to me as if to make sure. I couldn't decide if she knew the effect she was having on me.

"For once there was no surf. The heat was getting to Eva and Charles in more ways than one and Eva, I think it was, suggested we should go swimming and the two of them rushed off down the beach. The moon was overcast and we could not see them. I asked Harry if he wanted to go swimming and he said yes. We went down on the beach and we took our clothes off and swam naked in the warm water. It was magnificent. Harry and I stood opposite each other with the water up to our necks. I held his hand and we walked back out of the water. I could see he was aroused. I told him it was OK by me but he suddenly turned away and went back to his clothes and sat down. We lay down a few feet apart drying off and then we got dressed.

I liked and admired Harry but we'd never had sex together. If he'd wanted to that night it would have been OK by me." She stopped, let go of my hands and stood up.

"Well that's about it. We went back to the restaurant and after a bit Charles and Eva came back looking as if they had had cream. Charles drove us home but both he and Harry seemed a bit impatient and were looking at their watches. I think they had a breakfast appointment. I never saw Harry or Charles again." She all but burst into tears and went out of the room. She returned a few minutes later holding a handkerchief.

"I'm sorry." She used the handkerchief again. "I know Harry was in on the Sunday night because he left a message on our answering machine and I called him back in the Hilton at 8 o'clock. He was in his room and he told me he was going to bed."

She came back from the past.

"Would you like another drink or something to eat?"

I looked at my watch. "When did you eat last? Why don't I take you somewhere for a meal? It's the least I can do." She looked undecided so I tried again. "Come on, Liz. When did you last have a proper meal?"

She hesitated.

"I've only been grazing for the last week or so. I just haven't felt like eating."

Suddenly she smiled. "OK. You're on. Why don't we go to the same beach restaurant that we went to on that Saturday? It's a nice place. You'd enjoy it. Have a real drink." Before I could answer she disappeared. I could hear a shower going in the distance. I went into the kitchen, looked in the fridge. There was an open bottle of wine. I found some glasses and poured out the wine. Liz returned wearing a T-shirt and a very short skirt. She wasn't wearing a bra and her nipples showed though clearly. I gave her a glass of wine and we drank. We were very quiet. Golf Hotel was certainly having an effect on both our lives.

She locked up the house and we drove out to Maroubra beach. We barely spoke a word except when she told me the roads to take. I parked the car at Caesars but Liz suddenly changed her mind.

"Let's go to Frank's Bar over there." She pointed. "They have music and I need cheering up. Besides Eva and I were at Frank's the following night."

I didn't argue. I reversed out of the parking lot and drove to Frank's. I helped her out and we sat outside under a new moon in the tropical heat. I ordered some food and wine. There was no wind and surprisingly no surf.

"Let's dance." She dragged me unprotesting to the small floor on the sand. I held her close but apparently not close enough. She pulled me closer. The music was slow. She smelt fresh and seemed to melt round

176

me. The music stopped which was perhaps just as well and we went back to our table. Our wine was waiting for us. Not that I needed it. I was intoxicated already.

"You know, there is something else I haven't told you, Peter." Thankfully I forced myself back to Golf Hotel. I felt rather guilty thinking of anything else. I was prepared to stay very close to Liz to hear the rest of the story. I listened gratefully, watching her every move as we enjoyed our meal.

"Eva and I slept most of the Sunday. We had agreed two weeks earlier in flight operations, on the spur of the moment, to go out with a Captain and a first officer from an incoming 798 flight the moment they landed. They had confirmed the arrangement by phone on Thursday. Eva agreed before she knew that she had to report at 6.30 on the Monday morning. I tried everything but I could not persuade her to cancel the evening.

"The pilots turned up straight from the airport and changed at our place. They telephoned NWIA maintenance about some navigation problem they had forgotten to report. We came straight here at about midnight, danced, had a meal and probably too many drinks. It was the reverse of the previous night. Tony Giles, the first officer was my date, and he was all over me. Eva was thinking of Charles and being faithful and anyway Robbie Robson, the Captain, was not proving to be much fun. I think she hoped that Charles would propose when they got to England."

She stopped her story, grabbed me and took me back to the dance floor. This time she held me very close indeed and rubbed her body against my thighs. She whispered. "It was just like this on Sunday night. Tony and I went for a swim, shall we?" She looked me in the eye. "There's more to tell but I'll tell it my way."

We went down the beach. I felt events were happening that I couldn't control. The new moon was setting and it was getting dark. We sat down on the sand and she knelt in front of me, her breasts showing through her top.

"I undid Tony's trousers like this to relieve the pressure." She held me very gently. I took her T-shirt off and kissed her breasts. She rubbed her hands all over my body. She seemed to be talking in the past.

"I got up. We undressed and went for a swim. It was just like the night with Harry except that Tony did not go away as we walked out of the water."

She got up, took her skirt off and went into the water. I stood up, stepped over my trousers and followed her. I was determined not to miss the end of the story. We pressed against one another in the water. It was idyllic. We walked slowly back up the beach and we lay down together on the sand as the water dried off. Liz reached in to her bag and took out a condom which she rolled very gently down my erection as she squeezed my hand between her legs. She climbed on top of me and I helped her wriggle until I was firmly inside her. I held her tight and forgot about Mandy.

***

We lay on the sand afterwards, next to one another, side by side, very close. I held her in my arms and she started to cry. I tried to comfort her.

"It's alright. My life's in such a mess. And I think you're sweet." She paused then whispered next to my ear.

"I must tell you the rest of the story. I think it might be important. Tony and I returned to Frank's bar. Eva and Robbie were talking. We ordered a drink. Tony started to discuss something that had happened on the flight that apparently should not have done. I can't remember what exactly. Robbie said something to the effect that he was going to call the chief pilot in England the moment he got back to the hotel. They started muttering about not filling in the technical log. We left soon after, so that Eva could get two or three hours sleep. Robbie called England collect from my house when they dropped us off but I went to bed and did not listen. That's all I remember, I'm afraid. Is that what you wanted, Peter?"

"Yes, my dear. That's exactly what I wanted."

I held her close. I realised I would have to change all my plans. I needed to call Matt in the morning and find out what had really happened that night when the crew were working on the aircraft. There was now no point in going back to England on Sunday. I dropped off to sleep still holding Liz very close. She woke me. It was still dark but we could just see that dawn was breaking. She started kissing me very tenderly. I didn't think I had it in me but she clearly did, and she was right.

We went back to the car slowly. She gripped my hand very closely and I helped her up the beach. I drove her home and as we approached she kissed me again very quickly and leapt out as we stopped. I watched her open her front door and go in.

I got back to the hotel at about 6.30, got my key and went up to my room. I rang RWA reservations and delayed my flight. I had a shower and sorted out my clothes for the laundry so that I would get them back in the evening. I told the hotel I would not be leaving until Tuesday.

As I rested on the bed and planned my day I worried about Liz and felt in some way responsible. She had been a marvellous help to me in finding out what had taken place. I didn't feel I had taken advantage of her since she clearly wanted me to be with her. Unless she was a great actress she had enjoyed the evening as much as I did. However, I felt she needed help and a secure relationship but I didn't think I could be the person.

I tried to get Liz out of my mind and rang Matt in the office. It was Saturday but there was an emergency number and I asked the engineer on duty to get Matt to call me. He called me back almost immediately and I explained I needed to talk to him urgently about the accident. He agreed to see me straightaway in his office. I still had the car and drove to maintenance at the airport.

"Matt. Was the display change and changing the MMR the only maintenance carried out on Golf Hotel?"

"As far as I know. Why do you ask?"

"I have reason to believe that something else happened that was not recorded on the tech. log. Any chance of your checking with the night shift?"

"Peter, that's a pretty serious thing to say. Can you prove it?"

"No I can't Matt. But I would be prepared to bet money."

"OK. Give me moment and I'll find out who the foreman was."

Matt started telephoning and apparently located the man he wanted. He also checked on some of the other people on that shift.

"We've had some luck. The night shift on the Sunday night are now working days and Tip Brewster the foreman is coming up to see me."

Brewster came in. He was a large red headed man and wearing the supervisor's uniform.

"Brewster. This is Peter Talbert from England. He is helping the insurers of Golf Hotel and he says he has heard that your shift did more than routine servicing, changing the display and reprogramming the Multimode Receiver the night before it left for the last time."

"Matt, that's absolute rubbish." He glared at me in a very unfriendly manner.

"Brewster, think very carefully. If there was anything, don't be afraid to tell me."

"Matt, cross my heart and hope to die. There was nothing that you don't know about."

"OK. I'll believe you. Thanks for coming." Brewster glared at me again and went out.

Matt looked at me and I looked at him. There was nothing to be said. However I did have one last idea.

"Matt. May I talk to the person who tested the new display on the aircraft and changed the Multimode Receiver?"

"Yes. I can arrange that. Would you like to talk to him without my being present. If there is anything going on that shouldn't be, you'll be more likely to find out."

I looked at him gratefully.

"Yes Matt, I would."

"Well I thought you might want to talk to the guy. His name is Lance Stephens and luckily to-day he is in the avionics test house. I'll ask him to meet you in the empty office over the corridor. And Peter?"

"Yes?"

"Let me know how you get on."

I went into the empty office and there was knock on the door. A young lad appeared, about 22 years old, slight with large spectacles. We introduced ourselves. I told him I was interested in Golf Hotel. He appeared slightly uneasy.

"Lance. I gather you checked the display and it worked OK."

"Yes. That's right."

"How about the display that you took out?"

Lance relaxed a little and started to warm to his task. He was obviously a very keen and able engineer.

"Well we gave it a very long and thorough test. It seemed absolutely fine. I left it running all the following day and it was still working perfectly the next night."

"What about the Multimode Receiver?"

"As you know they reported one was wrong and I could reproduce the fault using the GESS test set which made it easier. It was clear that one of the MMRs was definitely faulty so I changed the box. I then functioned the complete system on GESS and it worked fine."

"Now then Lance. Think carefully. Did you do any other tests on Golf Hotel?"

Lance looked most unhappy.

"Is this conversation private and off the record?"

"I'll do a deal with you. I only want to know the truth. I won't tell Matt or anyone else for that matter unless it is absolutely necessary. I need to know the truth in case it's important. We must do all we can so that this type of accident will never happen again."

Lance hesitated.

"Lance. I know something went on but I don't know exactly what. It may not be important but I can only judge that when I know the truth."

"OK Mr. Talbert. I'll trust you. I checked the GPS system. Apparently the crew forgot to enter that they had a faulty GPS in the tech. log and only remembered when they got into the hotel. They phoned engineering and reported the fault. Brewster was nowhere to be seen. I don't think he had come in. Jack James got the call. He told me to check the GPS and if it was faulty to fit a new box. The GPS did not work properly so I got a new item out of stores and fitted it. The set worked fine."

"What happened then?"

"I wanted to sign the tech. log but Brewster still had not turned up and Jack and I agreed to forget about the whole thing and forget about the tech. log."

"What did you do with the faulty set."

"The box was manufactured by Honeywell and so we gave the set to the local rep. who said he would sent it back to Phoenix in the States to have it repaired."

"Do you have a lot of trouble with the avionics equipment on the 798."

"No, not at all. We keep an analysis of the faults and rectifications. Would you like to see it?"

"Very much. Is that possible."

"No problem." Lance went over to the computer at the end of the room and signed on. He selected what he wanted from the menu and seemed satisfied. He went outside to the printer in the office area and returned holding a piece of paper.

"Here are a list of faults on the RWA 798s at Sydney in the last two months."

I looked at the sheet.

"Lance did you notice that Golf Hotel had a GPS fault two weeks earlier. Did you change the box?"

"No. Let me see who was on duty that night."

He went back to the machine and after some time went out to the printer, returning with some more sheets.

"Here are copies of the maintenance pages for that repair on Golf Hotel. Jack Lawrence did the repair but he has left us now and gone to work for United in the States. Personnel may be able to help you. I've also given you a copy of the tech. log pages for the Sunday night. Obviously I can't give you a copy for the GPS rectification that I did as we did not use the tech. log."

"Lance. I've got an idea. Does your system track material issued from stores? Could you let me have copies of the boxes issued on the first night when Jack Lawrence was on duty and the Sunday night when you were on?"

"Yes, I can get you copies of those sheets."

Lance returned yet again to the machine and finally returned from the printer with copies of the equipment issued from stores. I put all the papers together and put them in a plastic folder.

"One final point. What would have happened to the unit that was taken out by Jack Lawrence? Can you find out?"

"Well it might be in stores awaiting repair but more likely it would have gone to the Honeywell rep. Paperwork should have been raised for both the boxes. Let me think about it and I'll let you know."

"Lance. Thanks very much for all of that. I don't know whether what you have just told me is significant as far as the accident is concerned. Probably not. However it might be. If I need anything more I'll let you know. Here's my card if you get anything. How can I contact you?"

Lance gave me his contact address.

"One other thing Lance. Did you do a 798 course at Independant?"

"No. NWIA only send their shift supervisors like Brewster to Seattle. The rest of us do our courses at United at Denver. I think they do that because it's cheaper."

"Well United clearly gave you some very good training."

I wandered back to Matt's office but he was not there, neither was his secretary because it was Saturday. I left a note on Matt's desk. Could he get his secretary on Monday to ask Personnel to let her have the forwarding address in the States, where I understood he now works, of a Jack Lawrence, who used to work in Brewster's shift. If they came up with anything would she would send me an email.

I used Matt's phone. It was afternoon in Seattle on Friday. I called Roger O'Kane at Independant. Roger had given me the original avionics design briefing on the 798 flight deck. He was in his office.

"Roger. It's Peter Talbert. I need help. Remember you briefed me on the 798 avionics some time ago. I need some details. I'm going to be in Seattle on Sunday on my way home from Australia. Can you manage to see me?"

"Peter. It's good to hear from you. Isn't Seattle rather a long way home?"

He paused. Knowing him, I knew he was giving me a hard time. He was smart enough not to ask me what I wanted.

"OK. How about Monday morning? You know my office number. Call me when you get in Sunday. Do you want me to make a hotel reservation?"

"No thanks. I am not sure of my flight yet. I'll get the airline to do it. Thanks so much. See you soon."

I logged on to the computer on the secretary's desk. The Seattle flights left daily at 10 am so that they arrived in Seattle at 8 am the same day having crossed the international date line. I called NWIA reservations and booked a flight for the following day, Sunday. I would be in Seattle on Sunday morning. I requested the Red Lion Hotel at Bellevue and a rental car. The man in reservations booked me on the British Airways flight Monday night Seattle/London. I would pick the ticket up at the check-in desk. I remembered to get a message to valet parking at

Chapter 7

Heathrow letting them know my revised arrival time in London. There was not much else I could do. I called RWA and told them I did not know when I would be going back to UK. I drove back to the hotel and told the desk I would be leaving in the morning, then I went up to my room.

I lay on my bed and reviewed the situation. Golf Hotel had had a new GPS set fitted and it worked. That bit sounded alright. But why had the 798 Captain called England? And who had he called? Presumably John Chester and presumably John Chester didn't want me to know. I was glad I had decided to visit Roger O'Kane to understand the installation in more detail.

The phone rang. It was Matt.

"How did you get on with Lance?"

"Do you really want to know?"

"Not unless you think I should."

"Matt. I will tell you something you should do. Find out what time Brewster came on duty on that Sunday night. Does he have to sign in?"

"Yes. Of course he does."

"Well you need to do some careful checking on your systems to make certain there are no loopholes. I'm off to Seattle to-morrow. If anything develops relating to Golf Hotel and I need to do some more investigation, I'll call you. If you find out anything let me know. However do me a favour."

"What do you want?"

"Don't chase Lance for the moment or we may lose him and the chance to get to the truth."

"OK. Not unless the Brewster trail leads that way. Have a good time in Seattle."

I decided to call Liz. The phone rang for a long long time before she picked it up.

"Liz. It's Peter here."

"I thought you were going home to-day."

"I was until I heard your story. It was very important, thank you. Liz, are you alright?"

"Yes Peter. I'm OK."

"You don't sound too sure. Look, I know its none of my business but do you have a family in England?"

"Why do you ask?"

"Well I'm concerned for you. I feel you need support. Especially now that Eva is no longer there. Can't you get someone else in?"

"Peter you're sweet. Don't worry. I'll manage."

"Liz. Come round and have dinner with me to-night. Make it early because I'm off to Seattle in the morning. We can eat in the restaurant or the coffee shop. Which ever you want and you can be home by 9.30. The information you gave me last night was very important and I'd like to see if I can help you in return."

"Peter. You did help me. You made me think about what I've been doing."

"Good, there's more to life than what we did, marvellous though it was. Come on. Come and talk to me and wear plenty of clothes so I can concentrate, if you know what I mean."

She laughed.

"OK. You're on. Meet me at the front of the hotel at 6.30 and take me to the Nikko restaurant on the top floor."

I gulped. She had chosen one of the best restaurants in Sydney. I hoped Mike would think it worth while. I went for another swim and had a sandwich by the pool. I kept looking at my watch waiting for Mike and Mandy to wake up in England. I went back to my room and at 6.15 I called Mandy in Bournemouth. A sleepy voice answered. "Hello"

"This is room service with your wake-up call."

"Well drop dead and call me in the office on Monday."

I looked at the silent phone. I called Mike at home.

"Good Morning. Did I wake you up."

"Yes Peter you did. However never mind. What's new."

"Good news or bad news?"

"Bad"

"You are going to have to pay for me to come home via Seattle."

"And the good."

"I believe I am making some progress but I need to understand the 798 navigation system better, hence Seattle."

"Well I'm glad you're making some progress. Despite what Crowburn said to Foster, Osborne is still saying that AAIB think it's pilot error."

"Alright Mike. I know how you feel and I do have some ideas but it is going to take time. I'll keep in touch and call you from Seattle. I'll be there Sunday morning and I'll contact you on Monday. Bye for now."

I decided that if we were going to eat on the top floor of the Nikko I needed a tie. I showered, put on my smartest clothes and went down to the lobby. I watched through the swing doors as it was still very hot outside. A fairly elderly Honda appeared amidst the BMWs, Mercedes and rental cars. I barely recognised the driver. Liz was wearing a very smart lightweight blue jacket and skirt and dark glasses. It occurred to me that she probably did not want to be recognised which was why we were going out and not eating in the Hilton. I got in the car and she drove round to the Nikko. She managed to find a parking slot near the entrance; good luck like that never happened to me. I helped her out and she held my arm as I escorted her into the hotel, past the bell captain and his many helpers, to the elevator. I noticed that despite her disguise both the women and the men in the lobby eyed Liz very carefully.

While we were waiting, a free lance photographer, who seem to frequent hotel lobbies everywhere, asked if we would like a picture. I looked at Liz who did not refuse. I said alright if it was a polaroid. He took our picture. I paid him $10 and he gave us the photo. It was rather good and Liz looked very elegant in her blue suit. I put the photo in my pocket. We went back to the elevators.

We were alone in our elevator.

"I'm no good at giving compliments but you look magnificent, Liz, in that outfit. Where did you get it?"

She looked at me seriously.

"Thank you. Real compliments are so nice. I made it."

"Really? I had no idea. You are very talented. Where did you learn that skill?"

"From my foster mother. She was an ace."

She leaned forward and kissed me very quickly.

When we reached the top I gave my name and we were shown to our table overlooking the harbour. It really was a splendid sight. Liz clearly liked the ambiance and the waiter asked us if we wanted a drink. Liz asked for a Pimms which made the waiter blink and I chose my normal whisky and water. The waiter returned as I knew he would to query the Pimms but I got it completely wrong.

"Did Madam want No 1, gin based, or No 3, brandy based."

Liz grinned, noticing my surprise.

"Madam would like gin based." she announced.

"You thought they wouldn't have Pimms, didn't you Peter." I nodded shamefacedly.

"Well what have you been doing to-day, Liz?"

"Resting. Catching up with my sleep. How about you?"

"Trying to find out what really went on when they were servicing Golf Hotel on the Sunday night. Then I booked a flight to Seattle and generally reorganised my life."

"Do you think you know why the aircraft crashed?"

"No, not yet. I'm just trying to eliminate all the reasons I can. This thing you told me about, it's sounds irregular but that's about all." I thought for a moment and looked at Liz. "Anyway, I didn't ask you out to-night to talk about the crash. I wanted to know what you are going to do with your life."

"Don't you like what I am doing at the moment?" She asked looking at me.

I couldn't decide how to respond and decided the safest thing was to ignore her remark. Luckily the drinks, nuts and the menu arrived. We studied the large choice. Liz chose jumbo shrimps and a tournedos, medium rare. I managed to find my favorite whitebait on the menu and then followed Liz with the meat. I asked for side salads and looked at the wine list. I chose a good Chardonnay and a Burgundy, both Australian.

"We can't drink two bottles, Peter."

"Well you can take the bottles home."

I became serious.

"Liz, you need a plan. Are you going to have a career with Royal World Airlines? How long are you staying out here? Do you have any qualifications?"

"What a lot of questions, Peter. Alright, I know you are only trying to be kind but I have to work this thing out by myself. I did consider going back to England and staying with RWA but there are two problems. Firstly, I have no qualifications and the second is that I don't think I could stand the climate."

"How old are you?"

"Twenty five on a good day."

"Well, can't you try to get a qualification, either sponsored or supported by RWA?"

"Maybe, but the weather is so marvellous here. I'd much prefer a job in Australia."

"You could be right. I just feel you need to stop and think what is happening to you. Take a holiday in the UK. See your family. Discuss it with them."

"I only have a sister, she is married and lives in Christchurch, England. We were orphans, our parents died in a car crash when we were small. As I told you we were brought up by elderly foster parents who both died about two years ago, one after the other."

"Well go and see your sister. And I'll tell you something else. I'm no expert but if you can make clothes like that suit you're wearing you may be wasting your time with RWA. Think about it."

Our food arrived and we became more relaxed as we drank the wine. It was a good meal, in a superb location. We drank our coffee and then went down to the lobby.

"Liz, I'm going to walk back to the hotel. It's not far and it will do me good."

"When am I going to see you again?"

"Somewhere soon. Perhaps in England. Here's my card. Make sure you keep in touch. If you move or come back to England I'd like to know."

We went out to the car and I held her for a long time in my arms as we said good-bye. We kissed and her eyes were very full as we separated.

"Peter, look after yourself. You're a nice guy."

Chapter 7

She got into her car and drove away without looking back. I walked back to the hotel feeling rather sad, lonely and inadequate. I went up to my room and there was a message to call Mandy. I got through to her flat but she wasn't there again. I left a message on her answering machine telling her my plans were changed and that I was off to Seattle in the morning. I put my things together ready, I needed to leave the hotel no later than 8 o'clock.

***

I called Mandy at home from the embarkation lounge.

"Sorry I was so rude when you called on Saturday morning. Where are you, Peter? I got some message you were going to Seattle instead of coming home."

"I'm just about to get on the NWIA flight to Seattle. I need to understand the navigation electronics better on the 798. There was some work done on the aircraft before it left and I don't understand if it matters or not. I'm off to see Roger O'Kane."

"When do you come home?"

"I don't know. It depends on Roger but I might get away Monday night. I'm booked on the BA flight Monday night arriving Tuesday midday. I'll call you from Seattle. Must fly."

I just had time to call Jim Akers.

"Where have you been Peter? I thought you had disappeared."

I explained that NWIA had done some servicing that was not written in the log but that he must keep this to himself for the moment as the significance was not known. I told him I was off to Seattle.

"Well you ought to find time to talk to Michael Noble. He is a friend of mine and the local editor of Aviation Week. Get him to tell you what is the word in Seattle. Call me if you ever get back to England. The rumour is that AAIB say that the accident is a clear cut case of pilot error and the pilots not monitoring the instruments. The story is coming from Chuck Osborne again."

"So I understand from Mike Mansell. See you soon."

The flight from Sydney was long and uneventful. The aircraft was a Boeing 747-400 and as usual the flight was full. The passengers in the business cabin seemed very varied but in the back of the airplane there seemed to be not only the regulation large number of Japanese tourists but also a lot of Chinese tourists as well. No wonder the long distance airlines needed so many of the large new aircraft.

I watched the CNN news on my video and then decided I had better write down my Sydney expenses for Mike Mansell before I forgot them. From experience I knew it had to be done fairly quickly after the expenses were incurred or I would miss some out even though I tried to keep all my bills and credit card vouchers. A lot of my expenses in this case were covered by NWIA but my car hire and entertaining Liz had to be laid at Mike's door. When I had finished this chore I started to read my book. However, my neighbour was a Seattle restaurateur who was returning from Australia having been round all the vineyards choosing wines. We spent a lot of time discussing the merits and demerits of Australian wines compared with US wines and he kept on reminding me of the excellence of Washington wines. He gave me his card and I promised to visit his restaurant in Seattle. In fact it was in Bellevue and I thought I might really give it a try since he seemed a real expert in his trade.

We settled down for the night and I managed to get about five hours sleep. We reset our watches and put them back a day. I found it difficult to be convinced that after I had been on the plane nearly sixteen hours and had left Sunday morning that it was still Sunday morning in Seattle, early Monday morning in Sydney and Sunday evening in England. All very confusing when trying to decide when to telephone someone on the other side of the world.

There decidedly wasn't a heat wave in Seattle. It was cloudy and raining and the temperature was 5°C. Just like home. I got through customs quite quickly but I had to stand in line at the Avis counter for about 10 minutes before I got a car. I crossed the bridge into the car park, found the car and managed to get onto US405. The Boeing and Independant Sunday shifts were already at work so it didn't take too long to get by Renton and across US90 up to Bellevue. I exited as Bellevue came into sight and found my way into the hotel parking lot, checked in and went up to my room. I called Roger at his home and we agreed to meet in his office at Renton at 10 o'clock to give him time to sort himself out on a Monday morning. Mandy was at home getting ready to go to bed.

"I'm in the Red Lion at Bellevue. How's things?"

"Presumably you know the Sunday Telegraph says the 798 accident was pilot error. The other papers seem to be copying the Telegraph."

"So I understand. I'm off to see Roger in the morning. I'll call you to-morrow."

"Well I'll spoil you. You can phone me before you go to bed and wake me up to get me to the office on time."

I rang Michael Noble. He was in and I explained that I was a friend of Jim Akers. He suggested we had dinner together in Kirkland where he lived, that evening. He would let me know the name of the restaurant and the time. There did not seem to be any point in ringing anyone else in England until I had spoken to Roger. I sorted my clothes out and had a shower. I didn't feel like sleeping so I went down to the car and drove over to the Olympic National Park west of Seattle. I went by ferry from

Chapter 7

Edmonds and then on the Hood floating bridge. It was a lovely drive on the peninsula and I drove down the west bank of the Hood Canal to Skokomish. I had a sandwich at one of the few places open in the winter and then drove home via Bremerton.

When I got back there was a message to call Michael Noble. He had booked a table at the Le Provencal for 6.30, quite early, but it suited me as I was short of sleep. I drove up to Kirkland the back way. It was misty and all the deciduous trees were bare. The Seattle winter was not unpleasant and seemed very refreshing after the oppressive Sydney heat. I managed to find the restaurant. Noble was already at the table which was just as well as we had not met. He was quite short 5 ft. 4 ins. but very wiry. We introduced ourselves. The waiter appeared and we ordered two Kirs.

"I've known Jim for a long time. He's a very sound journalist and I like the way he gets technical help if he needs it. Sending you out here to do an article on the 798 technically was a good idea. Why did you come back again?"

"Oh I'm involved in trying to find out the cause of the accident to the 798 and I need to be sure I understand all the technical issues if I can. I'm seeing Roger O'Kane to-morrow to probe a little more deeply than last time."

"From what I'm hearing from London the AAIB still seem to be favouring pilot error. I also understand that the second part of the Public Inquiry is going to start quite soon."

"I hope not, there's still a lot of work that we need to do. I agree that AAIB or rather the Senior Inspector seem to favour pilot error but he has absolutely no reason for it, as far as I can see. The counsel virtually told the Court he was a hostile witness. I must say I think it is scandalous the way the press seems to know what AAIB are thinking. To my knowledge that has never happened before."

The menu appeared and we concentrated on choosing our meal. I chose salade niçoise and sole meuniere, Michael went for paté maison and a tournedos. We chose an Idaho Chardonnay and a half bottle of a Californian burgundy.

"What is going to happen next then in your judgement, Peter?"

"Well as you said the Inquiry is going to start again very soon. All too soon as far as I'm concerned."

"Are those likely to be found to blame able to represented?"

"Yes. They can have counsels and all the normal paraphernalia of a court. By the way I forgot to say that the Lord Chancellor has appointed two technical experts, assessors, to help Lord Justice Thomas. The actual case is controlled by the Attorney General and presented by the Treasury Solicitor."

"It sounds a very high powered proceeding."

"Yes it definitely is. In order to hear the recording and read the transcript of the voice recorder we had to sign the Official Secrets Act. I think we'll be sent to the Tower of London at the very least if we say more than has been said at the Inquiry. You see the whole investigation is overlaid with the hijacking and the security aspects surrounding it. By the time I get back I imagine that the dates will be firming up, assuming the coroner's inquest is finished, though I expect Lord Justice Thomas wants to make certain the assessors feel reasonably certain of the cause before starting. AAIB expertise will still be crucial in this matter in my opinion."

"Well Peter, Independant will be there in force and brief the best counsels in the UK if I'm any judge of the matter. I have been talking not only to the President of the Independant Transport Aircraft Company, Bob Parnell, but also to the CEO and they are understandably very concerned. The passenger litigation following the Inquiry will be horrendous and the sums of money will run into many billions. Not only that, if Independant is found to blame then future sales of the 798 vis a vis the new Airbus A380 will be affected. There is a lot at stake."

"You're right. Of course, Independant are not the only people who are very worried. Royal World Airlines are clearly in the firing line and GE will need to be represented, though they will probably be in the clear. Then the pilots' association representing the families will be there and possibly some electronic manufacturers. The Inquiry could go on for some time depending on whether the cause is obvious or whether it is contentious."

"Peter, in reality whoever is to blame, an insurance company will pay."

"You're right, Michael. That's why CrossRisk Insurance have retained me as a consultant to try to ensure that the pilots are not held to blame. If they are then CrossRisk is liable."

Our meal arrived which silenced our conversation for a bit. The room was reasonably full and quite noisy which I liked. There was no view from the restaurant so the food and the conversation was important.

"When are you going back? If you hurry you can get the plane to-night."

"Thanks for the kind thought but I haven't seen Roger yet and I slept last night on an aircraft and to-night my sleep is going to be in a bed. I'm booked on the RWA flight to-morrow night. That will get me back on Tuesday morning."

"What did you do to-day?"

"I got some fresh air and tried to think things through. There is something we are all missing in this accident and I am determined to find out what really happened. Meantime I'm eliminating everything I can."

Chapter 7

"Sounds good. Give me your card and if anything happens over here I'll let you know. Perhaps you could do the same for me. A bit of advance warning is always nice."

We finished our meal and I got back to the hotel at about 9.30. My room overlooked US405 and the traffic seemed to be streaming both ways without a break. Luckily I could not hear it. I turned the TV on in time to see the end of Larry King Live but Larry King was not doing it and his replacement did not seem as good. I got the TV guide out but there were so many channels I could not decide what to watch and anyway none of it seemed particularly interesting. I couldn't very well call Mandy before 10.30 so I watched the Public Broadcast Service which had an old BBC series on. At 10.30 prompt I was on the phone.

"This is your wake up call."

"How nice. I was expecting it and have been dozing. How are things with you?"

"Well I had a super drive in the National Park and a nice meal with the Aviation Week man here. I'm looking forward to seeing Roger tomorrow."

"Do you want me to meet you on Tuesday?"

"No thanks. It's a nice idea but my car is at the airport so I'll have to drive home. I'll be shot so I'll probably go early to bed on Tuesday night and be human on Wednesday."

"Give me a call when you get in. All my love."

I went to bed but woke up at 5.30 and the traffic was still pounding up and back along 405. I managed to get some more sleep and then lay in bed making a mental list of things that needed pursuing. Who was the supervisor at NWIA the first time the GPS set was changed in Sydney? Maybe he could tell me what they did that night. I must chase Lance to find out where the spare units were. Was the airfield position on the MMR database correct data? If that was wrong the accident could be explained straightaway. I needed to find out how Frank Mercer was and if he could tell me anything. I realised that I still had not worked out what Richard Trentham was trying to tell me before he died. What could he have possibly seen? Who did the stand-by Captain of Golf Hotel on the inbound flight to Sydney talk to in England and what did he say? Come to think of it who was leaking information from the AAIB to the papers and why? I had an idea about the voice recorder leak and I needed to investigate that when I got back. I really ought to talk to Marcia Hodgson but what would I say?

There was no hurry since I had allowed Roger time to sort his office work out before I went to see him. After breakfast in the coffee shop I checked out and drove down to the Independant engineering parking lot at Renton and went into the lobby. The girl was the same one that was there when I was last out but she did not recognise me. I filled in the visitor's pass and she rang Roger. I sat down to wait.

Roger was very quick and he led me to a small meeting room near his office. He was about fifty years of age and a real expert in his field. He was employed by central engineering so that he was not on one specific Independant type but had the experience of them all. He was fairly senior in the Independant engineering hierarchy but I could never fathom how that worked.

"Well what's the problem?"

"Well Roger the problem is the crash of the 798 Golf Hotel. As I told you, I'm a consultant to one of RWA's insurance companies, CrossRisk, and it will cost them a bomb if the accident is due to pilot error. However, as far as I'm concerned I don't mind if it is pilot error or not. I just want to find out what really happened. I am dead scared that AAIB, encouraged by Independant, will take the easy way out and go for pilot error.

"I don't know if you have heard yet, Roger, but the Secretary of State called a Public Inquiry, probably because of the hijacking, the leaks from the AAIB and the seriousness of the accident. It's never been done before. The Inquiry has had its first session and it's now been adjourned."

"Yes we did hear and we think that it's a good idea. At least everything will be out in the open. Your AAIB investigations are very thorough but they're so secretive you have to wonder what's not being put in the report. Over here with the NTSB we are much more open as you know."

I did know. The United States National Transportation Safety Board was a very powerful institution with a lot of power over the FAA and the regulators. It was my view that we needed something like the NTSB in Europe to keep the European Aviation Safety Agency under control."

Roger went on.

"Anyway, first of all let me reassure you that Independant always wants to get at the truth and would not support pilot error as a get out to bad engineering. In fact as you well know, most of the time if a pilot makes a mistake flying a commercial airliner it is generally the airplane designer who has made a poor judgement designing the flight deck/pilot interface or the man/machine interface as the media love to call it. The challenge for us is to make sure that the very complicated electronic computing on the aircraft can be understood by the pilots and can be easily controlled in the event of a malfunction. Of course, the problem is made immeasurably more difficult by having to cater for the wide range of pilot ability covering all our customers.

"Now then considering Golf Hotel, as you might expect we have been helping AAIB in the UK in determining what might have happened to cause the accident. You already know that the analysis of the DME distances on the recorder showed quite clearly that the aircraft was below the glide slope and yet the crew did not show any concern, presumably because they were looking at the deviation computed by the MMR based on the GESS positions."

I interrupted.

"Surely, they wouldn't have been able to see the DME distances if they were making a satellite approach?"

"Yes they could. The DME distances would have been displayed on a stand-by instrument together with the ILS on the left of the centre instrument panel." He continued. "Mind you to be fair, unless the beacon was lined up with the runway ahead of them the distances would have been unusable in real time."

"I agree with you completely, Roger. It's alright for us, sitting down in our office or lab to calculate what the true height should have been. Virtually impossible in the aircraft, even without someone holding a pistol to your head."

Roger carried on.

"AAIB have not managed yet to analyse the GESS deviation. They seem to think that the pilots were to blame and that the problem might have been compounded by the failure of the Navigation Display. At Independant we feel sure that the hijacking must have been a significant contributory cause. At the Inquiry private session, when I know you were present, our man hearing the recording concluded that the only explanation was the hijackers prevented the crew monitoring the instruments properly. However, he couldn't understand why the Captain didn't notice something and, of course, he was very disappointed that the recording was of such poor quality. We are not really comfortable with the pilots having made a mistake but realistically we can't think of any other explanation."

Roger's words took a little time to sink in. If he knew about the recording and that there were no hijackers on it, it wouldn't be long before it leaked out. However, perhaps Roger was right. Even though the GESS glide slope deviation looked OK, perhaps there was something that Harry should have noticed. Of course the hijackers interfering didn't give Harry much of a chance.

"Thanks Roger for bringing me up to date. I wondered if you could explain to me the difference between the Royal World Airlines navigation fit and the US carriers."

"Be glad to. As I suspect you know, the Independant 798 used a relatively new type of electronics box called the Multimode receiver, MMR. The concept of this box, agreed between the world's major airlines, aircraft manufacturers and avionics manufacturers was that an airline, when it ordered the aircraft from the manufacturer, could choose which approach aids it wanted to be able to use. The choices were from ILS, GPS or GESS. Nobody wanted to use GLOSNASS. The airline could have all three approach aids or just one. Whatever the chosen aids, the output of the MMR went to the auto-pilot to control the aircraft down the glide slope to landing. With this design concept, we did not have to redesign the electronics every time a new airline ordered something different. OK so far?"

I nodded. Roger paused to let me catch up with my note taking, though in reality he wasn't telling me anything new.

"There were three launch customers for the aircraft. The two US carriers, American and United, wanted their new aircraft to have the capability of making approaches and carrying out automatic landings using either ILS, GPS or GESS, though of course it was necessary to have local receivers, GELAS or LAAS to verify the accuracy of the satellite signals. In fact, as you know US carriers are not as keen about automatic landings as European airlines but nevertheless they recognised that they might need the capability. RWA, as the other launch customer, wanted to have automatic landing as standard from day one, using ILS or GESS. They were not prepared to have GPS at all because it was a military system and could conceivably be downgraded or switched off at any time by the Department of Defense, notwithstanding that currently they are not doing so. They insisted that the capability was physically prevented, something that the MMR concept had not anticipated.

"We tried very hard to persuade RWA to have the same system as the other launch customers so that when the GPS system became useable, all they would have to do, without any wiring change, would be to replace the GPS box with a box containing three receivers instead of one. RWA refused and despite the MMR concept we had to make a change.

"The 798 uses three identical channels to achieve the required safety integrity on the approach and so in fact there are three Multimode Receivers sending steering information to the three channels of the auto-pilot and to the display. Consequently, the only way we could achieve what RWA wanted was to put a special selector switch in for RWA which prohibited the use of GPS. We were able to do this without changing any of the wiring which was important for all the launch customers, to avoid special modifications forcing the costs up."

"Well that seems straightforward enough."

"We thought so and so at first did the European Aviation Safety Agency who were certificating the aircraft themselves and not merely validating the FAA type certificate. However, apparently there was some young engineer in the EASA who did not like our modification and though she was only an observer she tried very hard to stop the EASA agreeing to what we had done. I don't know who it was. All I know, I had to write a special review of the modification and let the EASA team leader have it."

"Roger. Do you have a copy of the report? It could be very useful."

"Sure. Anything else?"

"Yes. I've met the engineer you referred to."

"You're joking. How did you manage that?"

"She called me. Though she didn't say so in so many words, I think she thinks the accident is due to the Independant design and it's all the fault of the EASA who did not listen to her."

"Why on earth would she think that?"

I explained Anne Moncrieff's concerns about the switch modification, the software certification standard and the lack of independent display of monitoring information to the pilot. Roger didn't look too pleased by the time I had finished. He looked at his watch.

"How about some lunch before Independant and Boeing fill all the eating places?"

"Is the diner still going?"

"You bet. Let's go."

I told the girl at the Independant lobby desk I would be coming back and kept my pass. Roger drove us over to the diner and we sat down just in time. I noticed a few minutes later a long line had developed of people waiting to sit down which confirmed our correct choice of restaurant. Roger was interested in my flight on the 798. Amazingly the nearest he had got to the 798 was the simulator at Renton. I gave him my view that it was an awfully long flight but that if you really needed to go to the other side of the world quickly it was probably worth it. Like me he was interested in the challenge of keeping the crew ready for the unexpected, since the electronics tried to do everything, normal and failure modes.

I asked him about his prospects in Independant and he felt that he would not get much higher. The top jobs were filled by up and coming youngsters who had been spotted early by the firm and given the necessary training. He was not complaining since, as an electronic engineer, he had had a fascinating life. He used to work for Boeing and had seen the digital technology develop from the 757/767 through the 777. He joined Independant when it was formed and was the ideal person to design the avionic architecture of the 798. He represented the firm on international committees, like the Society of Automotive Engineers S7 flight deck committee, of which I was a member, and the standards committee of the Airlines. At international meetings he exchanged views with his old colleagues at Boeing, Airbus technicians and the regulating authorities of FAA and EASA. He knew instinctively what would be acceptable to the regulators.

After lunch we went back to Roger's office and discussed the 798 electronic displays.

"Golf Hotel must have had something wrong with the display installation, Roger. The crew reported a failure on landing at Sydney but though NWIA could find nothing wrong with the unit they put in a new one. After take-off the display failed again on the captain's side. NWIA did a very long check in their shops of the unit they removed but it was perfect. I wonder if AAIB have found the unit in the wreckage and if it's operable. Have you heard anything?"

"Not a thing. I can't believe a display failure could have anything to do with the crash."

"What about monitoring the approach. It would have helped there, wouldn't it?"

"Not really, Peter. The key glide slope deviation information is on the Primary Flight Display. What is so difficult to understand is why the crew did not spot that the aircraft was way below the correct runway vertical approach path. Surely it has to be the hijackers interfering with the crew?"

"Well Roger, Harry did check that he was on the glide slope and at the correct distances which Charles, the co-pilot called out to him. It's weird. I only wish we could have heard what the hijackers were doing and saying to the pilots. I can't believe they weren't saying anything." I paused for a moment deciding how much to tell Roger. "By the way there was something else. Did you know that there was a faulty Multimode Receiver when they landed at Sydney and the engineer changed the box. The engineer then checked the system out and all was well. I don't know whether this fault was significant but it is a remarkable coincidence."

"Yes, I had heard. Strange that the fault was on the MMR."

We carried on discussing the problem for a bit and then I made my farewell armed with some more drawings and detailed descriptions of the 798 electronics. Roger said he would send on the report justifying the RWA approach to the switching modification which they had written for the EASA. I managed to get out on to 405 and back to the hotel before Independant and Boeing employees filled the highway and then set course for Seatac airport. It was too early for the flight but the executive lounge was as good a place as any to wait, anyway I wanted a meal before going on to the plane. That way I was ready to go to sleep when I got on the aircraft. I did not favour being kept awake by the time wasting and counter productive practice so beloved by many airlines of serving drinks and a meal so that by the time the service was all over it was just about time for breakfast and the landing.

The flight appeared to be on time looking at the arrival time at San Francisco. Unless the aircraft had picked up some defects on the way

Chapter 7

from London there should not be a problem. I did some work and, in fact, the flight did come in on schedule and nine hours later we landed at Heathrow at 2 in the afternoon. I managed to get about five hours sleep which was not too bad and had had some orange juice and coffee before landing. It did not take long going through immigration and I waited in the customs hall for the flight to be allocated a carousel. It was my lucky day. My bag was one of the first to appear. I grabbed it and wheeled my luggage through the green lane. I rang valet parking to give them the news. When I got outside I saw Mandy which was a real delight.

"What are you doing here? I am so pleased to see you. This is a marvellous surprise. You should be working. What will your clients say? Any news about the accident?"

"For once in your life just stop talking and kiss me."

We embraced and I think she was as pleased as I was.

"I decided that I might just as well come and meet you. I fixed my diary, caught the tube and here I am."

"You've got no clothes."

"Some people are never satisfied. Anyway Dora should have done my washing."

"Well it's made my day."

We went out to the valet parking hut and I settled up for the car. It took a bit longer than usual as I'd left from Terminal 3 and arrived back at Terminal 5. We were home in 40 minutes. Mandy held my hand when I wasn't using it to drive, occasionally running her fingers round my palm which I found distinctly exciting and didn't improve my road holding.

A Flight Too Far

CHAPTER 8

I woke up in the middle of the night. Mandy was sleeping peacefully and I tried not to disturb her. How was I going to get hold of the two pilots who went out with Liz and Eva on the Sunday night? It was going to be difficult if John Chester thought I was interfering. In the morning Mandy left for the office and we agreed to talk when I'd sorted myself out. I decided to risk calling Jill Stanton. My luck was in because John was doing a trip in a 767 to Cyprus to keep current.

"Jill? I am trying to find someone called John Robson, everybody calls him Robbie. He was a Guild member and they appear to have lost his address. Do you think you can help?"

"Yes I'm sure I can. I'll call you back as soon as I can."

Carol was my next call, really to assuage my guilt.

"Peter, I have taken your advice. We are all going skiing on Friday for a week. The children are very excited as they haven't been before. When are you coming round to see us?"

It was very difficult to refuse. She wanted to hear how I had got on in Sydney and Seattle. I said I might be able to manage to-morrow night. I'd let her know.

I decided that, after what I'd just said to Jill, I had better check the Guild directory but all was well. There was no John Robson or Tony Giles for that matter in the listing. However, there was a Frank Mercer. I could speak to him assuming he was getting better after the accident.

Jill called me back and gave me John Robson's number. I called the number and a lady's voice answered. John would be available this evening. I decided not to give my name in case John Chester had been talking to him. I tried Frank Mercer and again a lady answered.

"I'm a member of the Guild and I wondered how Frank was doing."

"He's on the mend thank you but he won't be out of hospital for another week."

"That's great news. My name is Peter Talbert. I give lectures on the 798 to RWA pilots on the flight deck/pilot interface. I'm involved in finding out the truth of what happened. Frank and I have probably met. We're both Guild members. If he feels like it, I'd welcome the chance to talk to him. I'm not very happy with what I've been reading in the press." I gave the lady my telephone number and rang off.

Mike Mansell came on the line.

"Good. You're back. Things are hotting up. I understand that there is a presentation at Farnborough by the AAIB this afternoon. Can you go to that?"

"I expect so but why have a presentation? Particularly as the investigation is now out of AAIB's direct control. I'll call Jim."

"I understand that the coroner is about finished for the moment and that AAIB are very well advanced sorting out the cause of the accident. It won't be too long before they reconvene the Inquiry. How are you getting on?"

"Mike. I told you this was not going to be easy. I am making some progress but I need time. The Inquiry seems to be proceeding at a most unusual pace, indeed unseemly haste bearing in mind that we are dealing with the legal profession where more time means more money. I have to tell you that the way things are looking at the moment you ought to assume that there will be some element of pilot error in the Court's findings. Can't you try and delay the proceedings?"

"I'm afraid not. For once the Government is proceeding full speed ahead. They want to demonstrate that when something like this happens they can act very quickly and effectively. I agree with you that at the moment we cannot refute pilot error, if that is what AAIB are going to say, even though they don't have evidence. We are really relying on you to get us out of this mess."

"Well do your best to get a delay. I need to follow some leads, if only to eliminate them. I'll call you in the next day or so, the moment I have some news."

"By the way, Peter, I meant to ask you. Did you try and talk to the Sydney police about the body in the Hyatt Car Park?"

"Yes, Mike, I did try and talk to the Police and got a flea in my ear, which actually makes me more suspicious."

I rang off and called Jim who agreed to take me to the AAIB presentation if I was at the FT by 12 o'clock. He asked me how I was getting on but I put him off until we met. I didn't have a lot of time. I got ready, put on my raincoat and walked to the station. It was cold and there were frequent gusts of rain. It would have been quicker by car but I would never have been able to park the car at the FT so I suffered the rain. I read the Times on the train. There was nothing really new about the accident and the papers were reverting to their normal diet of politics, sex and money, the order being dictated by the readership of the paper. At Waterloo I decided to try to get a taxi but, as an insurance policy, I started to go towards the footbridge to cross the river. I was in luck and flagged down a cab and so got to the FT office with about ten minutes to spare.

Jim arrived and the car, an old but smart Jaguar was waiting outside. I took off my coat and we got into the back and I thought how great it must be to work for a large company. Jim must have read my mind.

"Don't think I normally travel in this luxury. I had to attend an editorial meeting this morning and I have to be back this evening with the story of this afternoon's meeting ready to roll. I plan to dictate the story on the way home in the car and I have got my secretary standing by to edit it straight into the system. If I had had to drive myself I would have run out of time."

"Well whatever the reason, Jim, it is great to travel in style."

We were quiet for a few minutes as the car started to thread its way onto the Victoria Embankment.

"Any fresh ideas yet, Peter? I imagine that after the first part of the Inquiry AAIB, in the person of Foster, will have to be a lot more careful talking about pilot error."

"I hope so. Presumably they will have a new inspector in charge of the accident investigation by then. The problem at the Inquiry when it is reconvened is that the assessors will find it very hard to go against the considered advice of the AAIB, assuming with Forster replaced they still think it's pilot error. Maybe we shall hear a bit more this afternoon but despite hearing the recording and reading the transcript of the cockpit voice recorder there don't seem to be any obvious clues. I'm puzzled why AAIB are giving us this briefing. They cannot and must not say anything that will prejudice the Inquiry.

"Of course one factor in the accident, Jim, is the weather. I hope at the Inquiry AAIB give us a proper briefing on what the crew heard and the wind and weather at the time of the accident. The rules state that when an accident occurs there has to be an immediate check. Why didn't the crew know something was not right before they hit the ground? There must have been something terribly wrong. Surely it couldn't have been just simple pilot error. The hijacking has got to be relevant."

Jim did not reply. There was nothing to be said. We crawled along Cheyne Walk, left the river and finally got on to the Great West Road. We finally got by the Hogarth roundabout, crossed the South Circular Road and got onto the M3. The rain belted down for about ten minutes. We reached the Farnborough Defence Establishment Research Agency main gates in plenty of time. It had stopped raining for the moment. We got out of the car and went in to reception to get our passes and a pass for our car. The man behind the desk checked our identity very carefully before giving us our badges which had been printed in advance. He showed our driver on the map where the meeting was being held. In fact I realised that we were not going to the AAIB complex on the other side of the airfield but instead we were going into part of the Defence Establishment Research Agency.

We got back into the car and slowly drove round the perimeter track. It was like driving through a ghost town. There was no activity on the airfield and on the far side, at the back of the DERA, they were building a large housing estate. We followed the special signs to the AAIB visitors' car park. There were quite a few cars in the car park already and people were streaming into a building which was next to an old hangar.

We went with the other visitors along some corridors and finally reached the conference room. Jim obviously knew a lot of the other journalists. He introduced me to Jane Franklin of the Times; from her writings I knew she was a very professional lady and I was surprised to see that she could not have been more than 30 years old. I could see Roger Tucker of Flight and we nodded to one another. I recognised Spud Mulligan, the European Editor of Aviation Week though I had never met him.

We sat down near the front and waited for Bob Furness to appear. He arrived spot on 2.30 looking very grim with two other people. Jim nudged me. He had seen what I had seen. Bob had arrived with Chuck Osborne and Martin Foster.

"Bob's probably tried to find out Chuck's source" he whispered.

"I can't believe Martin Foster is still in charge" I whispered back.

It was difficult to believe that Furness had not taken Foster off the job; surely the Court would have insisted. Martin was wearing flying overalls for some reason and sat down also at the front, but nowhere near Osborne, who did not look too happy.

Bob climbed onto the dais and looked around the room before starting.

"Good afternoon, Ladies and Gentleman. As you know the Secretary of State called for a Public Inquiry into the accident to RWA 573, G-RWAGH. The last such inquiry was after the Trident landing accident many years ago. This Inquiry has meant that my department stopped investigating the accident on its own behalf some time ago and is now working for the Court of the Inquiry and, in particular, for the Assessors. At their suggestion, in these days of almost complete openness, we are showing you in very general terms what we have been doing to establish the cause of the accident.

"I hope you find this briefing helpful. We cannot of course say anything substantive in view of the Inquiry. It is just to give you a background understanding of our capability and responsibilities. Our work is really detective work and, like a lot of detective work, it tends to be long and tedious since of course, like detective work, we are looking at the most minute clues."

He paused as someone's telephone started to ring.

"Please would you all switch off your telephones and pagers and all other hi tech devices. You will have plenty of time to report to your papers when I have finished."

He waited while everybody complied with his request.

Chapter 8

"The accident to the 798 is the worst air transport accident we have ever had in the United Kingdom and it is absolutely vital that we find the true cause. Air Transport is so safe that the few accidents that occur are always due to some unexpected cause and I am sure that this will be no different. Every likely cause has been allowed for in the design of a new aircraft so we always have to look for the unexpected.

"Our modus operandi here is always to appoint a senior inspector to be in charge of each accident and for this one, as you know from the Inquiry, I appointed Martin Foster. Since he has done most of the work he is our main line of communication to the Assessors."

Martin Foster got up so that we could all see him. He looked uncomfortable.

"Martin would normally be responsible for producing the report. Of course, as I have indicated, the rules are now different for the investigation and reporting of this terrible disaster because we are having a Public Inquiry and we are merely assisting the Commissioner, Lord Justice Thomas, and the assessors. Martin here has already started to present evidence at the Inquiry and will carry on when the Inquiry is reconvened.

"As you know a meeting such as this is very unusual since it is normal practice to brief the press at the time the accident report is issued. In this case we have a very undesirable development in that the conversation on the cockpit voice recorder has been leaked to the press. This is the first time that this has ever happened and, as you must realise, the leak will be causing untold grief to the families concerned.

"So far we have been unable to find the source of the leak and the Daily Telegraph is not co-operating with us, which I deplore." Bob looked straight at Osborne with obvious dislike.

"All I want to say at this time is that the conversations reported in the press do not give a true flavour of the actual dialogue and, anyway, there were more channels of information on the voice recorder than the one that has been leaked and published by the press. You have to realise that all this speculation as a result of the leak just does not help my team in any way. It takes the team all their time to get the complete information dump from the recordings including the voice recorder channels. I am sure you understand that they have no time to explain every move they are making and how they are getting on, to you the media.

"As I have said, in view of the Public Inquiry it is entirely inappropriate to make any comments on what may have happened. However, it is clear that when the pilots realised there was something wrong it was too late to overshoot and make a missed approach. Our job is to find out why they did not realise they were below the true 3° glide slope to the runway touchdown point.

"Our investigation is divided into several stages. We have to analyse the outputs from both crash recorders, we have to try to assemble the wreckage in a hangar in case that gives us some causal clues and we have to inspect all the maintenance and licensing records of the aircraft and the crews. This work involves not only the aircraft recorders but also the air traffic voice and radar recorders and the recordings which the airlines make. It is a huge task which has to be done in a very short time scale.

"In fact we have now analysed nearly all the hundreds of channels in the aircraft recorders and are getting a good idea of what was working on the aircraft. You will appreciate that this is a very demanding task since some of the traces can only be decoded with the help of the trace calibrations. When we do know all the parameters that we need, we have to try to get simulator runs which match the traces so that we can ascertain the aircraft's true flight path.

"It will probably take us a few more days before we know for sure the exact path the aircraft took down the approach and what the crew saw. This information may be crucial in determining what happened. We anticipate having all this ready for the Inquiry.

"There is a story in the press that the crew made a mistake. I have no idea from where this story originated. There are reports that the information is coming from the AAIB and I absolutely refute this. Clearly, the Inquiry has to find out the cause of the accident and whether it was indeed pilot error. If it was pilot error then the Inquiry needs to know if there were any contributory causes like the hijacking. It is now all up to the Inquiry to determine all the reasons for the accident. The problem is that if the true cause of the accident is not discovered, it may not be possible to prevent a similar accident from happening again."

There was dead silence in the room. Press men are not very sympathetic because, apart from anything else, they are being chased all the time for stories by their editors. However, I did feel that perhaps Bob had made his audience just think for a moment about what a very responsible task AAIB had and ask themselves whether the way they were reporting the story was really helping the vital task of finding the cause of the accident.

"I propose now that we go into the hangar and then in about 45 minutes we can reassemble here and I am prepared to try to answer some questions but only in very general terms."

We all got up and filed out into the corridor. We were shown into the neighbouring hangar.

The hangar was full of crumpled pieces of aircraft and the large bits had been laid out in the shape of an aircraft. The AAIB had done a magnificent job in a short time assembling the wreckage. We were not able to get very close to the 'aircraft' because a rope barrier had been erected but we could get an idea of what the investigators were trying to achieve. I looked round the hangar and could see a pile of pieces, each piece numbered, in a separate area.

I went up to Martin Foster.

"Martin, what are all the pieces over there?"

"They are the parts we have not yet managed to identify and locate in the 'aircraft' we are building. Independant have given us a lot of help but it takes time to sort it out.

"I see you're with the FT." he said reading my name tag. "Your paper is very responsible in its reporting."

"Can I look at the parts in the corner?"

"Yes if we go quickly. I don't want everyone to come over."

He lifted the rope barrier and we went over to the parts. It was going to be a nightmare to find out where all the parts went. Besides metal structure, there were electronic boxes and the insides of electronic boxes. I could see cards with electronic chips lying on the floor and discrete chips on special tables. Presumably the reference numbers on the chips would enable the parts to be identified but not much seemed to be happening.

"If you look out of the window over there you can see the parts which the army has brought in and which we have not had time to arrange."

I thanked Martin and we went back to the others. Jim came over to me.

"What were you looking at?"

"I wanted to see how they were setting about dealing with the smaller stuff and in particular if they were going to sort out the avionics, you know the electronic computers. I suppose they will in time but from what I saw it's not going to be quick. They don't seem to be looking at the components at all."

We started wandering back into the conference room and sat down. Bob Furness came back in and Martin Foster went back to his seat in the front row.

"Well I hope you have got some idea of the enormity of the task. This job will take a very long time, particularly if we have to become interested in the smaller pieces of wreckage.

"Do you have any questions that I can answer?"

Roger Tucker of Flight stood up.

"How do you know that the Captain had selected GESS for an automatic landing."

"We know what the Captain said he had selected. We don't yet know what was actually selected but we hope to know once we have completely decoded the recordings and no doubt this subject will come up at the Inquiry."

"Was the GESS flight checked after the accident?"

"No. There is no need with GESS to carry out flight checking as we have to do with ILS. We can tell whether the GESS is serviceable by the monitors and the equipment was functioning perfectly. I think that is enough on that matter as I do not want to prejudice anything that is going to be investigated at the Inquiry."

"Next please."

"Did the aircraft have enough fuel? It had come all the way from Sydney." This from Jane Franklin.

"We have every reason to believe that there was enough fuel for an approach, a missed approach and a diversion to Manchester. Again this matter will be raised at the Inquiry."

"Were all the engines under power when the aircraft crashed?" asked Jim.

"We are analysing the engine parts but, from what we know now, all the engines had more than descent power when the impact took place, presumably because the crew had just initiated a missed approach. Again this is a matter for the Inquiry."

There were a few more questions and then Bob summed up.

"We have not finished this investigation and we are doing all we can to support the assessors. You will of course have the opportunity to hear the evidence at that time.

"Let me remind you once again that it is not unusual for there to be remarks on cockpit voice recorders that are not relevant to the accident. Please remember the families of the bereaved.

"Good afternoon."

Bob and Martin Foster left the room. We slowly filed out and ran to our cars in the rain. Our driver was waiting and we stopped at the gate to give in our passes.

"Peter, can we drop you off on the way home.? We must be going somewhere near where you live."

"Thanks very much. If you go round the M25 and get on the A3 you will only have to make a very small detour to drop me off."

As we drove back Jim started dictating into a machine he had in his pocket. His article seemed to be stressing the fact that the cause of the accident was not known for sure but that the AAIB had inferred that in a few days they would have reached a conclusion which they could present at the Inquiry. Jim mentioned that Furness had strongly refuted the idea that pilot error was necessarily the cause of the accident. However, the impression had been gained from AAIB leaks that the most likely explanation was that the pilots made a mistake and did not realise they were below the correct glide slope. Significantly, no mention had been made of the hijacking as a cause of the accident.

"Is there any special point that you feel should be mentioned?" Jim asked me.

"Not really. I'm amazed Bob has not moved Martin from the Inquiry, particularly as I'm convinced that they are not seeing eye to eye in this matter. I think Bob is much less sure than his inspector. Presumably it will be Foster that gives most of the evidence at the Inquiry, not Bob. There is just one point which needs watching. You heard at the Inquiry that AAIB are having trouble finding the GESS instrumentation and finding out what Harry had actually selected From what was said to-day and what Chuck has written I'm beginning to suspect that AAIB are still not out of the wood in this area. That's between you and me, Jim. For the moment just keep an eye on what is being said."

Jim carried on dictating and as we approached the Kingston-by-Pass I showed the driver how to get to my house. I got out quickly, thanked Jim and saw them leave. Jim had a lot of work to do before he was finished that night.

When I got in I decided to try John Robson again. A man's voice answered.

"Robson here."

"Captain Robson my name is Peter Talbert. We may have met. I give some lectures on 798 courses relating to the flight deck and the pilot interface, concentrating on managing the systems."

"Yes, Peter. I have heard your talks. They are very good if I may say so and I enjoyed them very much. How can I help you? You had better call me Robbie, everybody else does." He didn't sound very helpful even though he used the right words.

"Robbie, I believe you were the second crew on the London-Sydney leg on the flight before Golf Hotel crashed. Was there anything unusual you noticed about the aircraft.?"

"No, everything was quite normal."

"Robbie, are you quite sure? This accident is the subject of a Public Inquiry now you know, and it will not be possible to keep things that happened to yourself."

"You heard what I said." He sounded unhappy and uncertain.

"Robbie I think I know how difficult your position is. I should tell you, if you don't know already, that I was out with NWIA last week. I am not going to press you any more now but I believe you should think very carefully about your position. It may be a lot easier to tell me what really happened before the Inquiry, than have it dragged out under cross examination."

"Are you threatening me?"

"No, Robbie, really I'm not. I just want you to realise that keeping things quiet between friends is no good in this situation. Have you got something to write with? I'll give you my number and you can contact me if you change your mind. Think it over. I'm around off and on. You can leave a message on my answering machine if necessary." I gave him my number and left him to stew overnight. I was pretty confident he would call me to-morrow. What I was not sure about was whether he would call John Chester.

I called Mandy at Bournemouth.

"What's new Peter? I know you've been busy. According to the Evening Standard AAIB had an open day. Did you go?"

"Yes I did, but really the visit was a waste of time because the Commissioner is now in charge of the investigation and not the AAIB, though the AAIB work will be crucial under instruction from the assessors. Not surprisingly the AAIB were even more tight lipped than usual. I did get the feeling however that there was not unanimity in their ranks, specifically between the inspector in charge, Martin Foster, and Bob Furness. It's peculiar Bob has not taken Martin off the job."

"Perhaps because Martin was in the middle of giving evidence. Anyway, they had better get their act together before the Inquiry starts again or they will be in trouble."

"By the way, I have managed to speak to the second Captain on the flight into Sydney. He wasn't about to tell me the time of day but I think he was getting worried when I rang off. My guess is that he'll call me to-morrow but I'm not sure if he'll call John Chester first."

"Yes he will, Peter. He will wish to clear his yard arm with John, saying he has no alternative. And let's face it, he hasn't. If he doesn't tell you what happened now it will be dragged out of him at the Inquiry. It probably will be anyway to corroborate your theory, assuming you will have got one by then."

"Touché. I still have not worked out exactly what happened though I have a glimmer of an idea."

"Well, when are we meeting next? I've kept to-morrow evening free from washing and doing my hair."

"I'm sorry I can't manage to-morrow. I half promised to go and see Carol before she takes the family skiing. How about Friday?"

"I'll have to think about it. I think I'm watching TV for the rest of the week. Keep in touch." She was gone. I definitely had the impression she didn't like my talking to Carol in spite of the fact that all I was doing was trying to help get Carol's life started again. Rationally she knew I was doing the right thing but Mandy clearly didn't like it.

The phone rang. It was John Chester.

"Peter. I don't like the way you are pressurising my pilots and asking them questions. The AAIB are investigating the accident to Golf Hotel and we must leave it to them. I know you are working on behalf of the insurance company but it is after all one of our insurance companies and I must ask you to stop interfering."

"John, I think I must tell you that I have made quite a lot of progress in investigating this accident. I suspect that when we met for lunch the day after the accident you did not tell me everything you knew. The problem for all of us now is that we are not dealing with an AAIB investigation. We are now in the middle of a Public Inquiry and it just will not be possible to hold things back. Let me say to you what I said to Robbie Robson, you need to consider your own position in this matter."

There was a pause as my message sank in. When he replied his tone was quite different.

"Peter. I could lose my job over this."

I tried to sound sympathetic.

"John. I don't know yet what Robbie Robson told you over the phone from Sydney but it is no use blaming yourself unnecessarily. You can't be clairvoyant. What he said to you and what you said to him may have been perfectly reasonable at the time. My suggestion to you is the same as the suggestion I made to Robbie. Sleep on it and give me a call if you want to tell me what happened. All I would say, John, is that it is much better that we know now before the Inquiry, it may save you being called as a witness." I rang off.

I looked at my watch. It was not too late.

"Carol, sorry I'm so late ringing you back. To-morrow night is fine. I'm looking forward to it. What time shall I come round?"

"Peter why don't we go out? My mother can baby sit and it will be a relief to get away. I'll make a reservation at a nice restaurant near here, OK?"

I was not at all sure this was what I wanted but I felt trapped.

"Fine, Carol. I'll be round at seven." Mandy must have scented trouble.

I was glad to turn the lights out and go up to bed. Telephone calls can be quite exhausting. I suddenly realised that I had not really eaten anything all day but it seemed too late to start now.

***

A postman arrived with a special delivery. It was the report Roger O'Kane had promised me on the justification for the avionics architecture on the 798. I scanned through it. My judgement was that Anne Moncrieff would have seen it off in two minutes flat. In spite of my great respect for

Roger, the report certainly didn't seem very convincing on a first look. But then he was supporting the party line; even if he had doubts he couldn't voice them.

I decided to call Matt to see what he had discovered. His secretary put me straight through.

"Matt. How did you get on with Brewster?"

"Peter. Thanks for tipping me off. Brewster had been coming in late, quite frequently, and getting someone else to sign on for him. It should have been impossible but as so often happens, someone had worked out how to beat the system and Brewster took advantage. I've had to demote him and get the software firm who put the system in to plug the leak."

"Do you know, Matt, if Brewster was the foreman the first time they changed the GPS on Golf Hotel"

"I knew you would ask me that. Yes he was, which makes it difficult to find out what happened that night because there is no continuity. Brewster just does not know what Lawrence did and I am not sure he would tell me anyway. We have a contact address for Lawrence, do you want to call him or shall we do it?"

"I might as well, to save your time in having to talk to him and then call me. Give me the number."

I made a note but I realised I would not be able to try to talk to Lawrence until the afternoon.

"Peter. How did you make out in Seattle?"

"Well I'm not sure I made much progress. I still can't think of any alternative explanation to the AAIB story which says the pilots are to blame, though in my opinion the hijacking must feature in some way. Luckily the Public Inquiry has put a brake on the AAIB, which may give me time to find the true answer."

"OK. Well good luck. and keep in touch."

He rang off and I went in to the kitchen to make myself some coffee. I scanned the paper and was about to ring up Mike Mansell when John Chester came on the line.

"I've been thinking. You're quite right. I should have been quite open with you from the beginning but I was hoping that the whole thing could be hushed up. Clearly with the advent of the Inquiry, and now that you have found out that Robbie called me from Sydney, there is no way anything can be kept quiet. I suggest you come round to my office this afternoon. I'll have Robbie here and we can talk about it."

"I think I can manage that. If you don't hear from me I'll be round about 4 o'clock. Is that time OK?"

"Yes. That will be fine."

I called Mike to hear how things were going.

"How are you making out, Peter."

Chapter 8

"Not as well as I would like. However, I am seeing John Chester this afternoon to find out the conversation that he had with the alternate crew inbound to Sydney. It's obviously very important I find out what it was all about but I don't suppose it will change much. John had hoped to hush it up but he had no alternative once he realised that I knew about the conversation. There is also a contact I am following up in the USA. Possibly by to-morrow I may have eliminated another red herring."

"Well, we'll have to have a meeting with John Fairlane our counsel fairly soon to get ready for the Inquiry. Let's try and fix a date to-morrow, OK?"

I put the phone down and immediately Robbie Robson came on the line.

"I gather you've spoken with John Chester, Peter. There's one thing I want to mention. Presumably you know how we spent the evening when we arrived in Sydney. Must John and everyone else know that we went out? You can imagine what my wife would say if she found out."

"I don't know. All I'm interested in is knowing what happened on the flight, what you did and what you said to whom. If you come completely clean with me it is possible that you may not be called as a witness in the Inquiry. Obviously if you are called, everything may come out. What have you said to John about the evening?"

"I just said that Tony and I were drinking in the bar when we remembered that we had a GPS snag."

"Alright but be careful. Have you spoken with Tony Giles yet?"

"Not yet. He is in Hong Kong or somewhere and I shall have to wait until he gets back and then I shall be away."

"You've got a problem. I won't raise the matter of how you spent the evening but I must be frank with you. I wouldn't bet that it will not come out. See you later."

Robbie was obviously a worried man. It was impossible to advise him what to do for the best.

I decided I had better try and make my peace with Mandy, even though I had done nothing wrong arranging to have dinner with Carol. Still I did not want to lose Mandy. In my experience building an enduring relationship needed a lot of hard work, not that I had been particularly successful up to now with anyone else. Mandy's secretary asked who was calling and then said she was unavailable. That could mean anything but probably meant she did not want to speak with me. I had better try her at home in the evening but that was going to be difficult if I was out with Carol. I would try her from the car. I looked at my watch. and saw that it was nearly lunch time. I had no food in the house so I dashed round to the local store and got milk, bread, fruit and some cold meat. I made a sandwich and decided to call the contact number that Matt had given me for Jack Lawrence. I checked with my US area code program on my computer and saw that the code was in the Chicago area so that with any luck Lawrence would still be at home. I called the number but there was no reply. I made a note to call later on when I got home from Carol's.

I finished my lunch and got ready to go to the airport. There wouldn't be time to get home before I went on to Carol's but that would not matter as I was wearing a suit to see John Chester. I arrived in reasonable time, unusually managed to find room in the visitors' parking area and got myself a pass in reception. Jill Stanton came down to collect me and took me up in the elevator to the office. There was someone in the outer office I did not recognise but who I surmised was probably Robbie Robson. He introduced himself and we waited without saying much until John Chester had finished a telephone conversation he was having. Eventually he buzzed his secretary and Jill showed us in. John got up and invited us to sit down at his office table. Jill reappeared with some tea and biscuits which helped to soften the atmosphere.

"Well Peter, how shall we start?"

"John let me put my cards on the table and then you must decide what you want to say. The day following the accident you called me and we had lunch. At the time I felt there was something you weren't telling me but that was clearly up to you. I wondered at the time whether Jack Chiltern had warned you not to disclose anything to me or whether there was a security problem with the hijackers. Anyway, be that as it may I left with a question mark about what I was missing.

"I then phoned Bill Baker in Sydney to check on the maintenance that had been carried out on Golf Hotel and discovered that the navigational display had been changed and that there had been a fault on one of the Multimode Receivers when GESS was selected. Luckily, as a result of my conversation with Bill, he invited me out to Sydney to do some work so that I was able to speak to the engineer who did the jobs and he told me that he could find nothing wrong with the display that was removed. The Multimode Receiver was more of a challenge but he reckoned that the fault was in the satellite section of the box and he changed the box. The system checked out OK."

I stopped. They were giving me their full attention. Robbie Robson was now looking distinctly nervous. I carried on.

"I pressed the engineer and asked him if he carried out any further work on the aircraft and he told me that some time after the aircraft had landed he received a call from one of the pilots saying that there was a fault on the GPS which had not been entered in the maintenance manual. Apparently he found the fault, changed the GPS set and functioned the system satisfactorily. However, I managed to discover that there had been a conversation between a pilot and someone senior in the UK and it did

212

not take me too long to work out that Robbie must have spoken to you John. I believe the conversation could have an important bearing on what happened subsequently and that is why I am so keen to hear the truth in this matter."

I stopped and looked first at John and then at Robbie. It was John Chester who spoke first.

"Peter, how did you find out about the conversation?"

"John, that's not relevant to the problem in hand and I do not propose to disclose my source." Robbie tried to look impassive but I could see he was less tense. He decided to join in.

"Let me tell you what happened on the flight. Somewhere over Singapore we got a GPS warning but when we checked the GPS position on the Flight Management System everything seemed to be alright at first. However, the warning persisted and Tony started checking the maintenance pages on the Flight Management System. He discovered that there was a warning coming from the No. 2 GPS receiver. We could not understand this since we only had one GPS receiver. We watched the performance of the navigation system very closely for the rest of our watch and everything seemed fine. In fact just before the other crew took over the fault disappeared and we thought nothing more about it.

"We went to our bunks for a rest and then after we had landed Tony and I went out to a bar in Sydney for a drink. We discussed the matter and decided that we had better snag the GPS, which we did by phoning maintenance, and I called John to tell him what had happened."

John Chester interrupted.

"I told Robbie that I would deal with the matter when Golf Hotel got back and said that I was glad he had snagged the GPS. You can imagine how I felt when I heard that Golf Hotel had crashed. I was sure then, and I am just as sure now, that the GPS fault had nothing to do with the accident but nevertheless I wished that I had asked Robbie to get the matter investigated more fully.

"I was going to tell you all about it, Peter, but somehow I felt it would be better not to disclose the matter to you since it was not important"

I sympathised with John in thinking that the GPS fault was not important since, like him, for the life of me I could not see how it could be a contributory cause of the accident. However, he really should not have tried to keep things quiet but should have told the AAIB. I decided however not to dismiss the GPS as being irrelevant but to go home and think it through. I would probably need to talk to Roger O'Kane to find out how it was possible to get a No. 2 GPS fault when there was only one GPS receiver on the aircraft.

"I wish you had told me this story straightaway John. It would have saved me so much time in Sydney and I might have got some details from the engineer. Even if you're right about the fault not being important it certainly requires more investigation."

The meeting broke up and I set course for Carol's house. I arrived about 6.45 and Carol's mother opened the door. She seemed quite active and I wondered if looking after the children was actually helping her. Apparently Carol was upstairs getting changed. Tristram was watching the television and Wendy was doing some homework. Presumably Tristram had done his but thankfully it was none of my business.

Carol appeared looking very smart wearing a blouse and skirt.

"Help yourself to a drink. What would you like?"

I chose my normal Scotch and water. Carol had a gin and tonic. Her mother joined us and had a glass of white wine.

"I've booked a table at the Running Stag. It's not too fancy but they look after you quite well."

Carol's mother asked me how I was getting on with my investigations into the cause of the accident.

"I'm making some progress eliminating all the things that didn't cause the accident. In fact you have just reminded me that I need to call an expert friend of mine in Seattle. Carol, may I make a call before we go out?"

Carol nodded and I carried on.

"The Public Inquiry has actually taken over from the Air Accident Investigation Branch in finding out the cause of the accident. You probably read the papers saying that the AAIB think it was pilot error. I think the assessors who will be responsible for advising the Commissioner, Lord Justice Thomas, will need convincing, but are unlikely to go against the specialist opinion from the AAIB."

"When is the Inquiry going to reconvene?"

"I am not sure exactly but it can't be long now that the identification part of the inquest is nearly over. The problem here is that the AAIB normally goes on as fast as it can in parallel with the inquest but now that the Inquiry has started, the AAIB staff can only work as instructed by the assessors."

"What's your idea of what happened?" Carol's mother was not going to be deflected.

"Despite what has been said I can't think the pilots made a mistake. I'm still hoping something happened which resulted in them being misled completely."

I looked at my watch.

"What time did you say you had booked the table? 8 o'clock? Excuse me if I make my call now so as not to be late."

214

Chapter 8

I went into the dining room and punched in Roger O'Kane's direct number on my mobile. Roger answered straightaway.

"Thanks very much for your report to the EASA on the avionic architecture. I've only just skimmed through it. From my earlier conversation with Anne Moncrieff, Roger, I don't think your report would convince her but I'll show it to her if I may. Anyway, don't let's waste our time over that. I need your help again. I've discovered that on Golf Hotel's flight into Sydney before the fatal flight, the crew got a GPS warning. Everything seemed to be working normally but when they investigated the Flight Management System maintenance pages they found that there was a warning of incorrect operation from No. 2 GPS, which seems impossible. Is there any possibility of a No. 2 warning from the RWA GPS?"

"My immediate reaction is 'no chance'. Would you like me to check with Honeywell?"

"Yes, that would be a good idea. However I believe that I may have a very simple explanation. I need to check it out but I have had an idea. How about if NWIA installed the wrong GPS into the aircraft? I think they may have installed a NWIA GPS spare box which is of course fitted with three GPS cards. There could be a No.2 warning then if No.2 GPS had actually failed."

"But Peter, how on earth could Golf Hotel have the wrong GPS box?"

"Well what you don't know, because I didn't think at first it was too important, was that Golf Hotel had a GPS failure going into Sydney a few days earlier and that the GPS was changed overnight by the NWIA maintenance crew. I am trying to speak to the engineer who did the work but he has left NWIA and now works in the States."

"Well if the wrong box was fitted it wouldn't matter, the navigation wouldn't be affected. The MMRs don't care where the signal is coming from. What the MMRs do care about is if there is a GPS invalid signal when a GPS receiver card fails. That's why Golf Hotel got the warning."

"Even if the GPS is not selected?"

"Yes. The MMR has to monitor all the time to ensure the pilot knows in advance which systems he can't use."

"OK Roger, that's fine. However, would you please check with Honeywell anyway that there is no other way the warning could come from a GPS box just fitted with one GPS card. We may need your evidence at the Inquiry." I thought for a moment before carrying on.

"However, just because the wrong GPS box was fitted, it doesn't explain the accident. I still think that it is a remarkable coincidence that one of the Multimode Receivers was changed just before the accident which was of course on a GESS approach. If you have any ideas, Roger, please contact me straightaway. I must stop now and try to talk to the engineer in the States who changed the GPS box the first time. Bye."

I dialled Lawrence in the States. There was still no reply and I wondered whether I would have to wait until the week-end. I went back to Carol in the living room.

"How did you get on with the phoning, Peter? No, tell me later. We'd better be going if we are not going to be late for our table."

She said good night to the children and told them not to be late going to bed.

"Don't wait up Mother, though we're not going to be late."

I said goodbye to her Mother and we went out to my car and drove to the restaurant. As Carol had indicated, the Running Stag was not going to produce a gastronomic experience. On the other hand it was clean and the staff seemed very friendly. I ordered a gin and tonic for Carol and a Scotch for myself. We studied the menu.

"It's great to get away for an hour or two from the children and mother. I feel devastated without Richard and somehow I never seem to have time to think things through during the day. At night I just lie down and wonder what I should do. Anyway, thanks very much for the idea of going skiing. At least that gives us all something to look forward to."

"What are you going to do now? You can't just give up. You're still a young woman, very attractive and lots of energy. You've got a language degree, you worked for Britannia as a trainee manager and you should be mapping out a career. It seems to me that you could be getting another qualification like business studies or learning about computers. Have you approached any airlines for a job? Britannia? Or you could start doing some translating for some agencies. With the Common Market being such a large part of our economy, there must be opportunities for you."

I finished my harangue apologetically. Thinking about it later I realised that I was very keen to get Carol started doing something constructive which did not involve her asking me what to do next. She was very understandably grief stricken at the moment but nature would reassert itself and it was difficult to ignore the fact that she was very attractive. The bra she was wearing accentuated the curve of her breasts and she was using a very special perfume. In other circumstances I might be getting myself into some difficulty. Conveniently, the waiter came over to take our order.

"What are you having, meat or fish. Do you feel like sharing a chateaubriand?"

"Sounds good to me. What about a starter?"

"I'll have the avocado, thank you."

I turned to the waiter who had been taking notes.

"And I'll have the soup. We'll have a half bottle of the house red."

Chapter 8

The waiter disappeared and Carol resumed our conversation.

"I had been thinking about starting my career again but it is not easy to find a system which enables the children to go to school and for me to go to work."

"Well that's really why I wondered whether translating was a possibility. It is a drudge but these days it can be done from home, using a computer for rapid response. But as I said you probably would need some instruction in using the latest technology unless of course you are already adept in these matters."

"No I'm not. I use a computer of course for routine correspondence but not professionally and I know nothing about the latest computer systems."

"Well it is probably worth getting some instruction on how to send data, files, letters etc. using Broadband. It is not difficult at all and you can use the skill for accessing all sorts of databases, yellow pages, Google, internet etc. However, having said all that, I can't help feeling you should be trying the airlines for work rather than translation. If I may say so you are capable of more than just doing translation."

The first course arrived and we stopped the discussion for a moment.

"Where are you going skiing?"

"Meribel, in the French Alps. The children haven't done any skiing at all and they can go on the nursery slopes. We can meet for lunch and then they go back afterwards. We are staying in a chalet. We get breakfast and an evening meal provided. It is a super arrangement."

"I hope you have got full insurance cover."

"Yes thank you. Breaking a leg is the last thing any of us need but if it happens at least we will be insured." She paused.

"By the way. You never really told my mother this evening what you actually think happened."

"Well I don't think it was just pure pilot error whatever the AAIB inspector may say. Hijacking must be relevant. But proving that is not easy. Let's hope the assessors have an open mind. Have you heard anything more from Cathay?"

"Yes, thank goodness. I told you I've had one cheque and they have promised the other in about two weeks. Not that I know what to do with the money."

"I hope they are as quick as they say they are going to be. In my experience it all seems to take a long time. Anyway when it does come I suggest you put it into a building society initially and then perhaps you should place some in a fund that tracks the Financial Times index. It won't make your fortune but you should be able to keep the purchasing power of the money. What about the house?"

"The mortgage was covered by an insurance policy on Richard's life so that will be paid off."

"Well, at least, it doesn't sound as if you are going to be destitute. You had better be careful or someone will marry you for your money."

She looked at me and I wished I had not said that. I poured out some more wine for Carol and water for myself. Two whiskies and a small glass of red wine were all I dared drink and stay within limits. Even that was probably too much.

We finished the meal and I took her home. She asked me in but I decided that it was probably better not to. Especially if her mother had gone to bed. I helped her out of the car and took her to the front door. I kissed her on the cheek and she came close so I had to hold her in my arms for a moment.

"Thanks so much Peter. You are such a help and strength."

She opened the door and went in. I felt relieved. I didn't mind giving help but I did not want anything else. I drove home and got back about 11.30. I tried Lawrence again but got no reply. There was a message to call Mike but it was too late and I went to bed.

***

Mandy called at 8.15 prompt. I was in the shower. I got to the telephone, dripping wet, holding a towel, in time to hear her asking the answering machine where had I been last night.

"Good Morning, Mandy. Its lovely to hear from you."

"Don't 'good morning Mandy' me. I called you last night at 11 o'clock and you were not back. I am just beginning to be suspicious about the way you are consoling Carol."

"Now Mandy, my love, you have no reason to be suspicious. I spent all the evening trying to persuade Carol to get a job and start her life again. She's still young, very attractive, full of energy, a degree in languages, she ought to be starting a new life."

"You told her all that? You are an innocent abroad. I can see that I will have to accompany you to future meetings to make sure she gets legal advice as well as career guidance."

"We said goodbye on the door step at about 10.30. I must have got home just after you called. Why didn't you leave a message?"

"I need a TV phone."

"You might see more than an innocent young woman should if you had a TV phone right now. I was in the shower when the phone started and I haven't any clothes on. I'm freezing."

"In that case I'm not interested. If you had a TV phone you would see me in the office drinking my second cup of coffee. We can't all lie in bed all day."

"Stop giving me a hard time, darling. When do I see you next?"

"Well, if you tried really hard to persuade me I might agree to come round to-night. I won't have to work in the morning."

"You're on. Are we eating in or out?"

"Haven't you learnt yet I don't make those kinds of decisions? However, I will give you a clue. Though I am only a solicitor I will need to be briefed on how you are getting on and that will need a lot of concentration from both of us."

The phone went dead. I returned to the shower and tried again but the phone rang again. This time it was Mike.

"Sorry to ring you so early but I wanted you to know we have an appointment with John Fairlane at 2 o'clock in his chambers. Can you make it? The Inquiry is expected to reconvene on Monday week. He has a brief from our solicitors but quite frankly I doubt that will do. You will have to give him a lot more information. OK?"

"Yes, that will be fine. I'll hang up now if you will call me straight back and leave the address on the answering machine, I can't remember where it is. You are the second person to call me when I was in the shower and I don't have a dry piece of paper."

"Fine. Must dash to the office. We are having a Board Meeting at 11 o'clock and I need to get ready. Everybody is very fearful about the Inquiry."

I went back to the shower again and this time managed to finish, shave and get dressed. I had been considering for some time whether to call AAIB to inspect the avionic wreckage. I decided that I might as well have a go. I copied Fairlane's address which Mike had left on the answer phone and called Bob Furness.

"Bob, this is Peter Talbert. You know I freelance for the FT on aviation matters. You may not know that I am also retained by CrossRisk Insurance in connection with the Golf Hotel accident. Is it possible for me to look at the wreckage? I am curious about some of the avionic boxes."

"Well I would normally say 'no chance' for the very good reason that we would be in the middle of getting our AAIB report out. In addition I would want to know exactly what you were looking for and why. However, in view of the Inquiry I am not sure what rules apply. I tell you what, we're having to work week-ends on this job. Come down at lunch time to my office to-morrow. We can have a sandwich and then go over to the DERA hangar and look at the reconstruction."

I agreed quickly and then called Mike.

"Sorry to disturb you before your meeting. Thanks for the information about Fairlane. Just for my diary what is the timing on the Inquiry?"

"Well the inquest will be wrapped up a week to-morrow as far as identification is concerned and then it will be adjourned."

"Surely they haven't managed to identify all the bodies already.?"

"Well you're right. But they have done most of them. Of course they will be investigating the unidentified ones during the adjournment. Meanwhile the Inquiry re-opens the following Monday in the Queen Elizabeth Hall. Martin Foster will continue his evidence and be called to explain the details of the accident and give his opinion on the cause of the crash. What happens after that may depend on us, or more specifically you, and what you have been able to come up with. My guess is that Foster's evidence and cross examination will certainly take the whole of the first day by the time he's been cross questioned. Then there'll be a lot of expert witnesses called by AAIB and by the interested parties, like you for example."

"Fine. I just wanted to get a feel on the time-table and to discover how much time I have to try to find some sort of an explanation. See you this afternoon just before two at Lincoln's Inn."

I called Mandy but she was not available. I was clearly going to be late home from John Fairlane. Luckily, I had already given her a key and told her the alarm code so I asked her secretary to tell her to go straight to my house.

I decided to ring Lawrence before I left to see Fairlane hoping he would still be at home and this time I got an answer from a deep, man's voice.

"I am trying to contact Jack Lawrence. I'm calling from England."

"Who wants him?" was the very churlish and suspicious reply.

"My name is Talbert, Peter Talbert. I've just returned from Sydney and I understand that you used to work for NWIA."'

"What about it?"

"You did a particular piece of maintenance on a 798 and I am trying to check on something that you did."

"I did lots of maintenance on the 798 when I was with NWIA. I can't possibly remember any details. Anyway I'm far too busy working for United now."

"Look, if I send you the maintenance page relating to the work would that help."

"What's it worth? My time costs money."

"If you give me your fax number and email address I will send you a copy of the page. I will call you again this time to-morrow night, if that suits you, and, if you would answer a few questions, I will send you $400."

"OK. You've got a deal." He gave me his fax number and email details. The moment he rang off I wrote a covering note and faxed him my note and the maintenance page. I sent him an email as well to try to be certain he got the sheet. I rushed off to the station.

A Flight Too Far

CHAPTER 9

I walked to Lincoln's Inn and was there a few minutes early but so was Mike and we were shown in to John Fairlane's chambers. He welcomed us in. Tim was already there.

"Well the Inquiry reconvenes Monday week with Martin Foster still in the witness box. Before we discuss what he might say and what we need to do, Peter, what do we believe happened?"

"Well we know that Golf Hotel did a GESS approach. All perfectly kosher. I'm not happy that the GELAS was checked properly for correct functioning after the accident for this approach. You realise that if the correction data was wrong, then all three channels would be wrong in the aircraft."

"But wouldn't the crew notice they were not on the correct flight path?"

"They might not. You see once the aircraft is on the GESS approach, the centre line references for the display is the GESS itself. The pilots can only see if something is wrong if they have an independent reference like the ILS centre line but of course that won't be shown on the Displays. Actually the ILS is displayed on the centre instrument panel as a back-up but of course, in this case, the ILS was not working."

"That doesn't sound too good, Peter. Surely the EASA should not have certificated that system?"

"That's what Ms Moncrieff told them when the 798 was certificated and they wouldn't listen to her. You need to call her as a witness, John but you'll also need an acknowledged expert as well."

"Won't you be the ideal witness?"

"Yes, I expect you're right."

I carried on.

"The remarkable thing about Golf Hotel is that the co-pilot called out the heights and distances which confirmed to Harry that he was on the glide slope centre line and yet the aircraft was far too low."

"Well did you learn anything in Sydney that might explain the situation?"

"There is something but it seems irrelevant. When the aircraft flew into Sydney it had another fault which was not put in the technical log. The Global Positioning System had an intermittent fault which should not have happened on an RWA aircraft. To cut a long story short I believe that the wrong GPS box was fitted in Sydney, the box that was fitted had three receiver cards instead of one."

"Would that matter, Peter?"

"That is the really critical question and I'm not yet in a position to answer it. Hopefully, I will be able to by the time I go on to the witness stand."

"How do you know this?"

"Well, I found one of the girls mentioned on the recording. I also discovered that the other girl, Eva, was on the aircraft and was killed. In addition, the party referred to on the voice recording took place the night before the night before take-off. The girl actually phoned Hodgson in his hotel the night before the flight. That same night the two girls did go out but with two of the incoming aircraft crew and the girl told me about a telephone call the Captain made to NWIA maintenance and another call to the UK. Once I had these clues, I was able to sort out what had happened."

"Well you've certainly done a superb detective job. Won't we need some witnesses?"

"Well John, it all depends on what line you are going to take. I think you will need the chief ATC ground installation engineer for Heathrow, the firm that makes the GELAS transmitter, Microspot who provide the database for their MMRs and possibly the SRG airport safety regulator who is based at Gatwick. Those four will sow doubt on the GESS. With regard to the wrong GPS box you'll need the maintenance from NWIA but he may not want to come. You also should try to find out from FAA the problem with the local LAAS augmentation."

"We'll also want the girl who told you about the party and the telephone calls."

"Why, John? You can call the Captain, John Robson, who flew the aircraft to Sydney and snagged the box. You can also call John Chester if you want to confirm he knew the snag."

"I know. But I want to be able to show that Hodgson was in his room the night before take-off and not partying on the beach."

I looked unconvinced and John realised that I wasn't about to agree but he decided not to argue.

"Well I'll think about the whole thing and then we can discuss it some more. Tim, for the preliminary hearing you had better assume that the NWIA engineer will be present, possibly the girl, John Robson, Peter here and John Chester. Peter will have to tell you how to contact all of these people."

John indicated that the meeting was over and we got up to go. As the others left John called me back and shut the door.

"Look Peter. This girl could be important. Why don't you want her called?"

"She's had a hard time losing her room mate and her friend, Harry Hodgson. Having to come to England and be exposed to all the glare of publicity as a good time girl would be terrible for her. Anyway, we don't know yet our favoured cause for the accident. I want you to win the case without calling her. If you can't, you had better let me know in good time." I paused. "Look we're going to have to talk again before the Inquiry."

"Yes, we certainly are."

We shook hands and I left to go home. It had been a long day and I remembered that it was not over yet. It was 6.30 and Mandy was coming round if she wasn't there already and I realised I was looking forward to talking to her and hearing all her news. I saw her as I got off the train.

"Carry your bag, Miss?"

"How do you know I'm not married? Anyway I'm not tipping you."

"Don't worry. I'm doing it for love."

"That's what I'm afraid of."

But judging from the way she kissed me she didn't seem too scared. We were both tired and I got a cab. She unpacked upstairs when we got home and we celebrated with Kir Royale made with some sparkling wine.

"How did you get on to-day?"

"Well I finally managed to get through to the man who worked on Golf Hotel and changed the GPS set at Sydney two weeks before the accident. I've sent him the details and I need to talk to him again. Apart from that I spent the whole afternoon with Fairlane trying to get him up to speed."

"What line is he going to take?"

"I don't really know. Anyway enough of my problems, what have you been doing to-day?"

"Do you really want to hear about divorce, conveyancing, wills, indecent exposure, you name it, I've got it."

"Sounds fascinating but not to-night."

"Why don't we have another drink and get smashed?"

I looked at her.

"Good Lord, your glass must be leaking. Anyway if you drink too quickly you won't be able to stand up."

"I don't want to. It's you that has to do the standing!"

"Ms. Arrowsmith, I think your clients are leading you astray."

I poured out two more drinks and took the telephone off the hook.

"You do realise I won't be able to resist temptation."

"I should hope not. We've got the whole week-end in front of us."

I looked at her.

"Ah. There's something I haven't told you. Do you want to know now or later."

"Definitely later. Turn the lights down and come here."

Mandy clearly didn't always like the conventional. I didn't really mind but it occurred to me later that perhaps a bed was more comfortable. I rolled over.

"You're leaving me. Why can't you lie still afterwards?"

"My bit of carpet is not fully sprung."

"You're always complaining. Alright you can call the Chinese takeaway for Nos 3, 10, 34, 46, 47 and 48."

"How on earth did you remember the numbers?"

"I didn't but they're the numbers I used on my lottery ticket this week. I expect I've won by now and we can live in Paradise."

"I'm certain you won't be in Paradise after you've eaten all those numbers from our local Chinese. And you'll be overweight."

I got up and rang the take-away.

"Please may I have Nos 3, 10, 34, 46, 47 and 48." I paused. "Well we like a lot of chop suey."

Mandy rushed over to disconnect the phone but discovered I was holding the hook down.

"You bastard. Pass me the menu."

"Not when you haven't any clothes on."

"Stop making rules. I'll have sweet and sour chicken, spring roll and special rice. And if you go and collect it like that, I'll have another case of indecent exposure on my books."

We gradually sorted ourselves out and I brought the food back. I called Lawrence while Mandy dealt with the meal.

"Did you get my fax?"

"No but I got the email. I do remember the incident now. The GPS was reported as not working and I was able to confirm the fault. I got a spare from our stores and tested the box for giving correct inputs to the Flight Management System. There was not a lot of time as we had great difficulty finding a spare."

"Jack. Did the spare come from the RWA pool or from the NWIA pool?"

"I've no idea. Is there any difference?"

I decided to ignore his question since nothing would be gained by answering it.

"Did you do anything else Jack besides test the GPS for navigation?"

"No, nothing."

"That's fine. I'll mail you a cheque you will be able to cash in dollars. Let me have your mailing address."

I copied the information down and joined Mandy in the front room.

"Well the guy who changed the first GPS set at Sydney did not know that there was any difference between the RWA and the NWIA GPS boxes. Clearly they must have put in a NWIA box but that's conjecture.

226

It's the only way they could have got a No.2 GPS warning in flight. I must try and prove it somehow though I don't quite see how it can be relevant. Perhaps I'm missing something."

"You were going to tell me something about this week-end before I interrupted you."

"You didn't interrupt me, you seduced me. Stop hitting me. What I was going to tell you was that I've got to go down to AAIB at Farnborough to-morrow lunch time and probably for the afternoon, Bob has agreed I can rake over the avionic boxes."

"Look, in that case I think I'll go back to my flat to-morrow and do all the chores, if you don't mind."

"And if I do mind?"

"In that case I think I'll go back to my flat to-morrow and do all the chores."

"Good, well that's settled. Seriously though, it's a pity but you do understand? I've just got to talk to Bob and count the boxes."

We ate our Chinese, watched the television and went to bed, still in the spare room. Even though Mandy was concerned about our not finding Diana, she was clearly taking a broad view. In the morning we had a leisurely breakfast and I took Mandy to the station to save carrying her bag. We embraced and I watched her disappear into the station.

When I got back I spent the next hour or so catching up with my mail and making a list of the avionic boxes to be checked in the DERA hangar. Then I got the car out and drove to Bob's Office in Aldershot. At reception the girl on duty called upstairs and Bob came down himself to lead me up to his office. He poured some coffee from the percolator in the outer office into two mugs and put it on the table in his office before we sat down.

"Peter. Let's put our cards on the table. I've been talking to John Chester and he let slip that you have been flying round the world investigating this accident. Have you found out anything? I expect you are sore that the papers are saying that AAIB are convinced that the pilots made a mistake. Let me assure you that I personally am by no means convinced that they made a mistake and I am absolutely furious that such a statement got into the newspapers. I will not demean your intelligence by pretending that Martin Foster does not believe it was pilot error but he absolutely refutes any suggestion that he was responsible for the leak, or for the original leak of the transcript of the cockpit voice recorder."

"Bob, are you happy with the performance of the flight deck microphone on the recording? The recording seemed rather abbreviated."

He looked at me, trying to choose his words.

"Well it was either damaged in the crash or the microphone wasn't working properly. I favour the latter explanation. I promise you that you heard everything there was to hear on the recording."

"Thank you, that's exactly what I wanted to know." I changed the subject. "Bob, it's quite true that I have been to Sydney and spoken to NWIA and also to Independant to check on certain design features. There's some new information which is probably quite irrelevant and quite frankly I don't understand. I would like to know how many of the avionic boxes you managed to recover, to check how they are identified and to see what part numbers they have. I'm also interested in how you are handling the avionic parts that came from boxes that were smashed. If you come round with me you can see exactly what I'm looking for and what I'm looking at. As Martin Foster is still effectively on the witness stand and in view of what I have read in the press, it no longer seems the right course of action for me to talk to him. If I am on to something significant I will need to convince the assessors."

Bob suggested we went over to the old Queen's Hotel for a sandwich before going to the DERA. We took both our cars to save my having to return back to Bob's office. Over lunch it became pretty clear that Bob had a problem with Martin. There seemed no point in giving him my opinion, which was that he allowed his inspectors too much control when they were investigating an accident. Bob needed to monitor the accident investigations much more closely himself.

We went down the road to the main gate and drove over to the DERA hangar. It was open with one or two of Bob's people moving wreckage and cataloguing the parts. The scene had changed even in the day or so since I had been there. A lot more of the electronic boxes had been put on staging and a lot of the boxes had been labelled. I asked Bob if I could start looking around.

"Fine by me. Are you looking for anything in particular?"

"Well for a start I want to check that the avionic boxes in the aircraft are the correct ones. Presumably your people are checking all the time with Independant and getting them to identify all the pieces of equipment."

"Oh yes. We have their people helping us but very often even though we can recognise the box, the part number will not be identifiable."

I produced a list of the important avionic boxes and showed them to Bob.

"It's going to take a long time to go through this list. If you would like to give me a copy of it I could get Martin or some one to mark up what we have found."

Chapter 9

"OK, thanks a lot. If I write my email address and fax on the list, could you send the marked up list to me? Meantime can I look at some of the electronic scrap that you have not been able to place?"

"Fine. I'll leave you to it. Call me if you think there is anything I ought to know. I'll send you the list, hopefully to-morrow. We should have it all on a database. The only problem might be identifying a box from the description you have given it since it may not be the same as Independant's description."

Bob went off to my intense relief and I started to look at the boxes. Luckily I had printed out two other copies of my list and I got one out of my briefcase. The boxes that had been identified had been marked on their cases by the AAIB and I marked my list accordingly. I could only find one Multimode Receiver and that was heavily impacted. I could not find the GPS box. All six displays were there but they were all smashed. Both the Flight Management computers had been found and miraculously they looked as if they might work, hardly a mark on them.

I wandered over to the pile of electronic scrap and I noticed that curiously no attempt had been made by AAIB to identify where the components came from. At that moment I noticed Martin Foster had arrived not looking at all pleased.

"Peter, I don't know why Bob let you in here. You may be retained by CrossRisk Insurance but you should not be in here. Everything here is confidential."

I felt like saying 'You mean like the voice recordings and the opinions of the AAIB inspectors', but decided that scoring points would achieve nothing.

"Martin, I don't buy that. You are appointed by the Department of Transport and on Monday week you will have to make your findings known to the Inquiry. It will then be for the Court, not you and your team, to decide what happened, of course as advised by you. However, almost certainly I shall be giving evidence at the Inquiry and I have a right to look at the wreckage. If you don't agree we shall make a submission to the assessors so that I am permitted to examine everything."

Martin flushed and looked very annoyed but said nothing. I started to examine all the scrap very closely.

"Oh we've looked at all that. There's nothing useful there."

"In that case you won't mind if I look, will you?"

I put my marked up list away and took out my notepad. Martin Foster soon got bored and went away. I systematically noted all the component numbers of the very large scale integrated circuits which were clearly custom made for firms like Honeywell, Collins, GEC, Thales, Microspot and Smiths Industries. My plan would be to send the numbers to these firms to see if they could identify the parts and the boxes they came from.

Beside the component scrap there were numerous switches which had become detached from the flight deck panels but again AAIB did not seem to be bothering to refit the switches to the panels they had propped in place in the aircraft reconstruction. I looked at all the parts very carefully. My guess was that Martin was convinced the accident was due to pilot error and since the Inquiry had been called he had stopped a lot of the work. Presumably the Inquiry would be adjourned if the assessors and the Commissioner needed more information.

It took me about three hours to finish my listings and by that time the AAIB staff were ready to leave. I made my farewells, drove home and spent the evening putting all the information into my computer, producing lists to send to the avionic firms, ringing my contacts in the United States firms to get the right names, email addresses and fax numbers, and finally sending the lists to the US firms and the UK product and technical directors. By the time all that was done it was 11.30. It was just as well Mandy hadn't stayed.

On Monday morning I phoned Lance at NWIA but he was still working on the night maintenance shift and was not available. I got transferred to Matt who was still in the office.

"Matt, you know the Inquiry will be starting the week after next. I believe CrossRisk Insurance will be asking Lance to come over and give evidence. We're not saying that the wrong GPS caused the accident but it will show that AAIB just have not done their job properly. Do you have any problems with that?"

"Yes Peter, I did know about the Inquiry and to be frank we are all very nervous about it. Clearly we don't like the idea of everybody knowing that someone in NWIA did some irregular maintenance on Golf Hotel without signing the technical log. More importantly, we are bound to be found liable for negligence if the accident is due in some way to our poor maintenance. The sums of money involved are mind boggling. We're insured of course but that's irrelevant. It will reflect badly on NWIA and also on me as the ultimate supervisor. Having said all of that it is my view, and my MD supports me, that it is important to find out the real cause of the accident so I'm not going to try to block Lance travelling to London. Incidentally, we don't believe for a moment it can be due to the wrong GPS box. By the way have you spoken to Lance yet?"

"No I haven't. I've tried but he is working nights. I was going to try later."

"Well as you know, Lance is a very good lad and very sharp. He received the request from CrossRisk this morning and his supervisor called me from home. Apparently he is very nervous about the whole thing and the need to give evidence. You had better treat him very gently or he may bolt."

"Matt, thanks for the advice. Do you think you could arrange to reassure him and get him to call me when he comes in this evening?"

"I'll do my best. Keep in touch if you discover anything else."

I put the receiver down and immediately the phone rang. It was Product Support at GEC. They had looked at the list of components I had sent them and had recognised a few of the parts. They were going to send me a marked up copy of the list. I called Smiths Industries and spoke to their Product Support. They also had looked at the list but did not recognise any of their parts. I would not get anything from the USA until the afternoon or evening.

I went through my mail and opened a letter from American Airlines. They had accepted my quotation and wanted me to start as soon as possible. Would I please call them to make the arrangements. I looked at my watch. Only 11.30, far too early to call Dallas.

My printer started to eject paper. I looked at the first sheet. It was a fax from Bob Furness returning my list with all the boxes that had been found. I looked at the list when it finally arrived. AAIB had done a good job finding well over half the boxes I had listed but the GPS box had not been found. It was good of Bob to return my list so promptly. I guessed Martin Foster could not have been pleased. My assessment was that Bob, mindful of the Inquiry coming up, did not want to have an argument in public that he knew he would lose.

My phone rang. It was Lance. He did not sound too happy.

"Lance. Did you manage to find out what happened to the two GPS boxes that came off Golf Hotel?"

"Yes Mr. Talbert. The second set was functioned by the Honeywell people locally and they found nothing wrong. The set is back in our stores. The first set was apparently not to the same standard as the NWIA GPS boxes and the Honeywell man has it in his repair shop until he hears from his office in Phoenix."

"Ask him to fax or email me the box type and serial number, please Lance. Did you check the reference and serial numbers of the set you took out of Golf Hotel?"

"Yes. It was a NWIA box and the Honeywell man told me that it should not have been fitted to the RWA aircraft."

"Lance. Doesn't that mean that the set on Golf Hotel was also a NWIA box?"

"Yes, unfortunately it does. It never occurred to me that there was something wrong. I checked that the spare I fitted was exactly the same reference as the one I took out."

Lance sounded even unhappier than he had at the beginning.

"Don't worry Lance. You weren't to know. I gather from Matt you have agreed to take a trip to England and come to the Inquiry?"

"Yes I am but I'm not looking forward to it."

"All you've got to do is to say what you did. Look, is there anything I can do to help you? When are you coming over?"

"I don't know yet. It's a week or so away. NWIA are going to meet me and arrange my hotel."

"That's fine. Lance, if anything changes in your plans please let me know." Lance said he would and I hung up.

I had some soup and cheese for lunch with some coffee then I called American in Dallas and spoke to Tom Gardner who had written to me approving my quote. I introduced myself.

"Peter. We know all about you because we have a training captain, Jake Rodgers, on the SAE S7 Flight Deck Committee. To be truthful we got Jake to talk to the RWA man in connection with our requirement and your quote. I gather you are fully involved in the 798 accident inquiry. I won't ask you what you think happened."

"I don't know how you know that, Tom. I don't give evidence for a week or so and my involvement is not meant to be general knowledge."

"You know as well as I do it's impossible to keep anything secret in our business. Anyway I guess you're going to tell me you can't start straightaway until the Inquiry is over."

"Yes you're right. Is that OK? When do you get your 798s?"

"Not for six months and then at quite a slow rate. We'll be very happy to wait. Make sure you sort it all out before you come. Bye."

No sooner had I put the phone down than it rang again. It was Honeywell. They had got my list and had worked through it. There were a few LSI chips that they recognised as being their proprietary design and there were a lot more chips that were generally available. They were going to email me immediately saying which of the LSI chips were theirs and from which box they had come. I rang off. Honeywell was as good as their word and the email came through almost immediately.

I looked through it but unfortunately the list was not much help. There was a chip from the Traffic Collision and Avoidance System, some chips from radio receivers and one chip used on their GPS card. No wonder that AAIB had not found the GPS box, it must have got smashed if Honeywell recognised one of their custom LSI chips. I was disappointed that there were not two GPS chips but in fact I had all the evidence I needed about the GPS boxes and the number of GPS cards from the evidence of Lawrence and Lance. However, none of it seemed relevant since the RWA aircraft did not do GPS approaches. There seemed no way that the wrong GPS box could cause the aircraft to crash on the approach. Perhaps I needed to get some more advice. The most likely cause of the accident just had to be the fact that the aircraft had been flying a GESS approach and some wrong data had been fed into the Multimode Receivers like an incorrect airfield position. Alternatively, I supposed that the pilots might have been distracted by the hijackers and not spotted they were too low. Of course there could have been some other reason which I had missed completely.

Mike Mansell called.

"Peter, John Fairlane called. He says that he really ought to have the Australian girl available even if in the end she is not called. What do you think?"

"Well I'm not keen and I am sure she won't be. Leave it with me to think over. Can I speak to John direct?"

Mike gave me John's number but before calling I decided for better or for worse I had better discuss the matter with Mandy. She was busy with a client. I asked that she call me back. I got out the central London yellow pages and looked up 'Dressmakers' followed by 'Dress, blouse and skirt mfrs.' There were columns of entries. I decided I had better go up to Town and chat up some of the big stores in the morning.

Mandy came on the line.

"Darling, you remember that girl I told you about in Australia, Liz, who told what really happened out there?"

"Yes I do. Go on." She had suddenly gone quiet.

"Well John Fairlane wants her to come over to England for the Inquiry. I know she won't be keen and quite frankly I don't think she will contribute much providing Robbie Robson is going to give evidence.

"I am going to call John Fairlane back to discuss it but I thought of a reason why she might agree to come. You see, what I didn't tell you because we were interrupted when I was debriefing myself to you, as you might say..."

"I hope that is a figure of speech."

I ignored her.

"What I didn't tell you was that the girl, Liz, had a flair for dressmaking as far as I could judge."

"How do you know that, Mr. Talbert."

"Well your Honour, I took her out to dinner as a thank you for giving me all the information and she turned up in a really smart outfit which I thought must have been incredibly expensive. She told me she had designed and made it herself."

"Did you check any of her other clothes?"

"Good point. No. Two reasons. Firstly, I wasn't sure you would like that and anyway there was no need since when I met her in her house there were a lot of half finished clothes lying around, under construction you might say. The other reason was that I didn't have the opportunity as I left the following morning."

"Peter, I believe the second reason. I have to tell you that I would need convincing on the first."

"Mandy, what was going through my mind was that if she came over here with some samples, would it be possible to arrange for her to visit some of the good designers?"

"Possibly, but I am not sure I can help you."

"Well I thought I might go and chat up the buyer in Harrods and possibly one or two other stores to-morrow to see if they have any suggestions."

"Yes, that seems a good idea. If the worst came to the worst she could visit the big designers on spec. and just knock on their doors. If the stuff really is any good she should be able to get a job, though the routine work is not very well paid I believe."

"Alright, I'll have a go to-morrow but meantime I'll talk to John. Bye."

I called John Fairlane in his office.

"Peter, you've obviously heard I really do feel that the girl in Australia should be available for the Inquiry. As I told you, we need to establish that the Captain was in his room the night before they left. What about it?"

"Well John, I've thought about it and I might be able to persuade her to come for an entirely different reason. Would you like me to call her?"

"Yes please. Mike will have to pay all her expenses but it is a very small insurance premium to pay when one considers the likely size of the claims."

"I will telephone her. But John. Please don't call her unless you have to. The papers will be on to her like a shot because they will realise the sort of life that she was leading at the time. She is very attractive and inevitably if you call her some people are going to get hurt, especially Mrs. Hodgson and the Robsons."

"OK Peter. But I cannot promise. The stakes are enormous."

I put the phone down feeling very worried for Liz and for the damage she would inevitably cause. I wanted to call her straightaway but she would be asleep. I decided to call her at 9.30pm when she would probably be having breakfast. I started work on my American contract and apart from supper worked through until it was time to call Liz.

She answered the phone immediately.

"Liz, it's Peter. Remember?"

"Yes Peter. I'm not likely to forget you in a hurry."

"Hope I didn't wake you up."

Chapter 9

"No. I'm a reformed character. I go to work on time in downtown Sydney and go to bed early. I'm having breakfast before I go to the office. How can I help you?"

"Liz. There is a Public Inquiry into the accident to Golf Hotel and the insurance company who are retaining me, may want to call you as a witness."

"But Peter, how can I help? I don't know anything."

"Well you can explain that the reference about an evening out on the voice recorder was not the night before the flight but the night before that. I know its irrelevant because they had plenty of time to sleep in the aircraft but nevertheless John Fairlane the counsel may want to make that clear. More importantly, our counsel wants you to make it known that Harry was actually in his room the night before the flight getting some rest.

"The other issue is of course the extra maintenance that was carried out that night before the last flight. You can testify about the conversations between the pilots and NWIA and Robson's call to someone in England."

I paused waiting for Liz to say something. There was a deathly hush.

"Now Liz I've been thinking. Don't give me an answer now. I have some unfinished business with NWIA and I plan to travel out on Wednesday, to be with you Thursday night. The Inquiry does not reconvene until Tuesday so I won't have to leave until Sunday. In fact if you agree to come you can come back with me if you'd like to. I'll work Friday and we can spend some time together Saturday. I have an idea which may appeal to you about getting a job in England. What do you say?"

"Peter I really would like to see you again. I'm not sure about giving evidence. Wouldn't the papers make me out to be a good time girl? Anyway it would hurt Mrs. Hodgson and the Robsons if the story came out. You had better come out anyway if you've got work to do and we can talk it over. You can sleep here if you like. I haven't got another room mate yet. Tell you what. I'll meet you off the aircraft."

"Liz. That's a sweet offer but I am not going to accept. First of all we don't get in until quite late and you have to be working in the morning. Secondly I don't think I should sleep at your place. I don't want to be accused in the Inquiry of tampering with a witness."

"That sounds very interesting."

"No it doesn't. By the way, have you got some clothes that you have made, readily available to bring to England?"

"Probably, but I have not agreed to come to England. I will need a lot of persuading. See you Thursday night. Bye, Peter." She was gone before I could remind her that she was not going to see me until Saturday.

I went up to bed wondering what I had let myself in for.

In the morning I phoned Mandy at 8 o'clock in her office and told her what I was doing. She didn't sound best pleased but agreed that, all in all, it was the best thing to do.

"Won't you be very tired when you get back and the Inquiry coming?"

"Possibly, but the Inquiry does not start until the Tuesday and remember the flight is a long one so I should get some sleep and we land in time to go to bed. I'll get a good night's sleep when we get in and anyway I won't be giving evidence before Wednesday."

Mandy still sounded doubtful.

"I suppose it will be alright. However, if you learn anything you will need to brief your counsel. He won't want to get a surprise right at the last moment. When do I see you again?"

"Well you can come round to-night or the Sunday night of my return."

"No, my darling. I don't think so. If you are flying off to-morrow you need to get ready for the trip. Similarly on the Sunday night when you get back you are going to need some sleep. Let's make it the Monday." I agreed reluctantly and Mandy got on with her work.

I called Bill Baker at home. He was just leaving for the office. I asked him if it was OK to make the video on Friday and he said he would check and let me know by email. I called Mike at home and told him what I was planning. I also told him that I had had an idea and I needed to talk to Lance.

"Well Peter you had better go. I assume that NWIA will pay for the travel and the video. I'll pay the extra for first class travel or you won't be fit for anything either in Sydney or back here for the Inquiry."

"Thanks Mike. I hope I can make it worth CrossRisk's while. However, if I persuade the girl to come back with me I think the best solution would be for us both to travel business class."

"Whatever, Peter. I know I can trust you completely in these matters."

"Fine. Would you send an advance of £10,000 for expenses. You owe me a lot already and I'll have the girl's tickets to pay for. I'll send you some more expense claims when I get back." Mike agreed and I rang off.

I called RWA reservations and booked myself out on Wednesday on the 798 non-stop and booked myself back on the Sunday business class. I paid with my Amex Card which only just covered the ticket. I then made a reservation for Liz to travel back with me in business class and said I would pay for the ticket in Sydney on the Saturday.

Chapter 9

I called Hilton reservations and booked in for the three nights. I made one final call to Lance who still sounded very unhappy.

"Hello Mr. Talbert. How can I help you. You only just caught me, I'm working days now."

"That's a bit of luck. I'm arriving Sydney this Thursday to do a job for NWIA. Can we meet Friday evening?"

"I suppose so. Where do you suggest?"

"I've no idea Lance. Do you know a quiet place for dinner?"

"Where are you staying?"

"I'm at the Hilton. Meet me in the lobby at 6 o'clock and we can take it from there."

"Fine by me. See you Friday."

Dora was doing her normal Tuesday magic and ironing some clothes.

"My paper says the Inquiry starts next Tuesday. Are you going to be there?"

I reassured her that I would indeed be there and would probably have to give evidence. She was clearly impressed and would undoubtedly tell the Fox and Hounds. I promised to let her know when I knew the actual day so she could read the evening paper.

I had dressed to go into London and left straightaway to try to get the best out of the buyer before Harrods filled up. I was in the store at 9.30 and went up to the dress department. I looked around for suits like the one that Liz had worn at the Nikko and inspected the labels. A lady who had been watching me came over and asked if she could help.

"I'm looking for the buyer in charge of this department."

"Please wait and I'll see if she is free."

The lady disappeared and reappeared with a lady of about 40 years of age, very smartly dressed, slight and with brown hair.

"How can I help you?"

I decided that the truth was the easiest to remember.

"When I was in Australia a few days ago I met a lady who was wearing a really smart blue lightweight suit. It was so striking that I asked her where she got it because I was fairly sure she couldn't afford that sort of expensive outfit and she told me that she had designed and made it herself. She's coming over to England next week and I was so impressed with her talent that I've suggested to her that she brings some of her work with her to show to someone with a view to getting a job as a designer. I was looking at the labels on the clothes you were selling and I was going to try to make some appointments for her at the various manufacturers."

I showed her the picture of us both, taken in the lobby of Nikko's with Liz wearing the blue suit.

"Well you could certainly try that." She peered at the photo very closely and got a magnifying glass out. "That suit does look very good. I tell you what, I'll give you my card and she could come and see me. When might this be?"

"I expect it will be next Monday or Tuesday if that is alright. You really are very kind."

"No problem. You never know what can happen. It is one of the things that makes my job interesting."

I thanked her again and made my way out of the store using the stairs, that way I knew where I was going. Big stores always made me nervous as it was never immediately obvious how to get out quickly in an emergency nor, in my opinion, was it obvious where the nearest elevator or escalator was located. I had written down a few of the names from the labels and it occurred to me that Liz could make a few phone calls as well if she wanted to. I noticed that I was assuming all the time that Liz was going to come. I hoped I was right. It clearly was by no means a certainty.

I walked slowly down and went out into the cold street. It was blowing quite hard which always made walking in London so awkward as the wind varied the whole time, depending on the location and size of the buildings. There was no hurry and I carried on down Knightsbridge, under Hyde Park Corner and along Piccadilly until I reached Green Park. I caught the underground to Waterloo and went home.

Dora was still there and seemed in good spirits. Her daughter seemed to be doing well at school despite a lot of unsupervised homework. The Fox and Hounds debating club was clearly flourishing. I told Dora about my trip to Australia and told her that I would be back in time to give evidence at the Inquiry. I found it very difficult to escape into my office. I finalised my script for the NWIA training video which took most of the afternoon and printed off two copies and made two spare discs as well.

I went upstairs to pack. As usual it was always difficult to decide what to take when going from winter at one end to summer at the other. I decided to leave my coat in the car but take a pullover which I could use in the plane. I would check one bag to keep down the weight of my old Lark carry-on bag. As I was only going for three nights I did not need much but of course I was going to have to spend two more days travelling in the aircraft. I called Mandy at home before I went to bed to reassure her that all was well. I told her about my visit to Harrods.

"Where's Liz Ward going to stay if she comes over?"

"I don't know, Mandy. I'm not having her here."

"Too right you're not. Can't she stay in a hotel? Doesn't she have any contacts in London?"

"I just don't know. It will be soon enough to find out if she decides to come."

"Well she can't stay here. There might be a conflict of interests in more ways than one."

Chapter 9

I decided to ignore her remark.

"We have to face the fact that if she does give evidence I'm afraid it will be inevitable that the newspapers will be after her and try to get her life story. What is needed is a secure anonymous apartment in London. I think I'll get Mike on to the job since it is CrossRisk who want her to give evidence and they can pick up the tab."

"That seems a good idea. By the way is it alright if I go to your place to get some of my clothes? I think I must have left a dress I need."

"Of course. Why do you need the dress so urgently? What am I missing?"

"Trust me. Nothing you need concern your sweet head about." She changed the subject. "Are you staying at the Hilton again?"

"Yes. I'll call you Friday morning your time when I get in. Bye, my darling."

I decided to call Mike though it was getting quite late. I explained the problem of Liz's accommodation.

"I'll call you from Sydney the moment I have news but you need to be getting a place organised in principle now. I am convinced the media are going to be a pain. The girl's no fool and she has already mentioned the problem to me. I need to be able to reassure her."

"OK Peter. I'll do what I can and send you an email which you will get when you arrive at the Hilton."

I finally got to bed and managed to sleep well. I set the alarm and left the house at about 08.45. I used valet parking again at Terminal 3 and let the man in the office know my return flight and scheduled arrival time.

I checked in at the first class desk, collected my tickets, confirmed I had the seat I wanted and went through bag inspection and immigration. I found some magazines I had not read and also a thick novel off the shelves. I made my way to the first class lounge, got some black coffee and read the Financial Times. The flight was called but there was no rush for those of us lucky enough to be on he lower deck at the front of the aircraft. Just when I was getting nervous, we were finally called and made our way down the hall to the gate. A hostess showed me to my seat and took my blazer. I went into the toilet and put on some thin old slacks and my pullover and settled down for the flight. I had managed to get one of the single seats near the front of the cabin which saved me the need of talking to a next door neighbour.

We took off on time and I switched on my passenger entertainment system to watch the BBC news. There was nothing of special interest and I switched the screen off. I was tempted to use the phone and thought of calling Mandy but there was nothing I could add to our last conversation. The steward took my order for drinks and I chose a tomato juice. I decided to read the paper and have the meal, whatever it was called, before doing any work. The food in first class was superb but I found it went on a bit. I managed to restrict myself to soup, fruit and cheese but it took a lot of will power. By the time I had finished my second cup of coffee three hours had gone by and I had finished looking at both the Times and the FT. I was very relieved when the hostess cleared everything away. On balance I preferred the faster business class service but I knew that the real benefit would come later. It was already dark outside.

I got out my work and finalised my plans for American using my small portable computer. I stopped and got my book out and read for a couple of hours. The aircraft Captain came round, I guessed he must be just about to go off watch.

"Haven't I seen you before somewhere?" were his opening words. We soon established that he had attended some of my lectures during crew training. I gave him my card and he looked at it very carefully. I could see the penny drop.

"Wait a minute. Aren't you the guy who is investigating the accident to Golf Hotel? The Inquiry starts next week, doesn't it?"

"Yes you're right, I am involved to some extent. I'm just fitting in a job for NWIA before the Inquiry."

"It really was a horrendous accident and we were particularly sad about the loss of our crews. The hijackers have a lot to answer for. As it happens my wife and I knew Harry and his wife very well. She is heartbroken and of course was very upset about the leaked voice recorder transcript. It is so unfair. She has no redress at all. She also feels that the story going about that it was Harry's fault is untrue and completely unsubstantiated."

"You are quite right. However I'm hopeful that at the Inquiry some light will be thrown on what actually happened. By the way, could you let me have Marcia's number? For some reason it is not listed on the Guild database. I think I would like to go and see her."

"Of course I can. Why don't you come up to the flight deck? I've got the number up there."

"I didn't know that was allowed." I paused as I remembered my previous flight. "Is it OK then if you're First Class?"

"Only if the Captain says OK. But you'll have to have a very stringent examination by a guard before you will be allowed into the VIP cabin and the flight deck area."

"Well that's great. Perhaps I could come up for the last two hours and watch the landing. Is that alright?

"You bet. It will be a real pleasure. I won't ask you what you think really happened to Golf Hotel though, as you can imagine, we all want to know."

240

Chapter 9

"Thanks. To be honest it still isn't clear what happened. Actually another trip on the flight deck will be really useful before the Inquiry."

The captain went off and we were offered more food. I decided to have only a very small taste of whatever it was, since I had established over many years flying that it was vital to get one's stomach synchronised with the destination country as quickly as possible. What I would need to do would be to eat towards the end of the flight just before going up on to the flight deck. I stretched my legs and walked to the back of the aircraft. The flight was fairly full and most of the passengers seemed comatose after their meal. I went back to the front, got out my book and after a bit I started to doze. I called one of the cabin attendants who sorted out my bed, arranged the pillows, sheets and blankets. I lay down, put my eye shades on and felt myself dropping off. This was what first class was all about.

I woke up and looked it my watch. We had been flying for about ten hours and had reached Lanzhou, about 500 miles west south west of Peking. It was already light and I calculated that it was 10 a.m. in Sydney. I asked if I could have something to eat. Most of the other passengers were asleep and they were not planning to serve breakfast for some time. There was a stewardess who had come on duty and she offered to boil me two eggs, always a tricky operation when the cabin altitude was 8,000 ft and the water boiled at 92°C. However she did a super job and I really enjoyed my breakfast.

I tried to do some more work, not too successfully and then got out the magazines I had bought at the airport. The flight dragged on and I had some more breakfast when breakfast was served to the other passengers, then dozed a bit. The time seemed to stand still. I looked at the map in the cabin and checked our position when we had three hours to go. We were just coasting in, a hundred miles or so east of Darwin.

I was in the middle of tidying up my things when the stewardess came down with a message that it would be OK for me to go up to the flight deck. I made my way up the stairs and was met by a marshal. He was obviously very unhappy that I should go on to the flight deck. The Chief Steward appeared and convinced him that it would be OK. He checked my ticket carefully. Then we all went through to the flight crew area where the marshal gave me a very through search. The Chief Steward operated the keypad and we were let in. Justin Lockyer, I had discovered the Captain's name, looked over his shoulder and beckoned me to sit down. The en-route first officer was on the jump seat but he got up when he saw me.

Everything seemed to be normal. We were flying at 45,000 ft. and .86 mach number. There was no cloud below us and we could see the inhospitable ground beneath. The sun was only just above the horizon in the west.

"What a super evening. What's the weather like in Sydney?

"It's still hot but it has cooled a bit. There are some fires left in New South Wales but luckily this time Sydney seems to be in the clear. We should be landing spot on time."

"What sort of approach are you going to do?"

"Well they've got the GELAS running at last so I thought we might try an auto-land. Suit you?"

"Very much so. I want to watch your procedures again if you don't mind."

The flight proceeded normally and we got our descent clearance about 45 minutes out. Though there seemed to be a lot of traffic, air traffic control fed us into the traffic pattern without asking us to hold. Justin selected the runway to be used on the MMR controller and put the approach selector switch in the vertical GESS position. The MMR positioned the aircraft for capturing the GESS centre line and the first officer lowered the landing gear as the aircraft captured the synthetic GESS glide slope. The navigation display showed the aircraft on the runway centre line and it seemed to be exactly on the glide slope. I glanced at the ILS indicator on the left centre instrument panel and was reassured when I saw that both needles were central so that we were on the ILS runway centre line and on the ILS glide slope. Not surprisingly, because of standardised crew drills, the altitude call outs from the first officer and the radio altimeter were exactly the same as the 573 recording. It was slightly unnerving. At 30 ft. the throttles started to close and we did a perfect landing on the correct spot. The nosewheel touched the runway and at about 80 knots Justin disconnected the auto-pilot and applied the brakes.

I thanked Justin and the crew and went back to my seat as we taxied in. I was first off the aircraft and got through immigration in record time. My bag, with a first class sticker, was already waiting for me on the carousel and I was through the customs door about twenty minutes after touch down. I decided I liked travelling first class.

As I came through the door I saw Liz waiting for me. She was wearing a very lightweight, semi-transparent mid length coat with a blouse and shorts underneath. She had a magnificent tan and I was sure it was not confined to the parts I could see. With her long legs she looked terrific and I guessed that most models would not mind looking as she did. She came up to me and I tried to kiss her on the cheek but got her lips instead. I tried to make sure it was a perfunctory embrace but it was not easy.

Chapter 9

"I thought we'd agreed that you were not going to meet me, Miss Ward."

"No, Peter. You suggested that it was not necessary but I wanted to see you anyway. There are very few really nice men in my life."

"Thank you for that but you are a working girl and I don't want you to be late for work in the morning."

"That's very thoughtful of you but I can look after myself, thank you Mr. Talbert."

We went over to the Avis desk to pick up a car. There was a line from the previous flight. As we chatted I realised that her coat was not just to stop her getting too cold in the air conditioned airport. Her blouse was almost translucent and I was sure I could see her nipples thrusting through the material. I hoped she was going to keep wearing her coat on the way home.

"Liz. Did you make the stuff you're wearing yourself?"

"Yes of course."

"It's a magnificent outfit but why don't you make bras as well?"

"Well they're a lot of hard work and I don't feel I really need them all the time. What do you think?"

"Now look, Miss Ward. We've got to sort something out. I really enjoyed that night on the beach. It was fantastic and I'll never forget it. But we've got to be sensible. You need to find a career and stop going out every night. I'm no expert but I feel you have a real talent for making clothes. I want you to show some samples of what you can do to some firms in England."

Liz thought about that, but there appeared to be something else on her mind.

"Peter. Do you have a girl friend?"

"You know I do. She's a lawyer and we are, what's the phrase, going steady."

"Well I think she's very lucky."

I made no comment. I signed the necessary papers and collected the car.

"You had better go home now, Liz. It was lovely of you to meet me but I think we both have got to get ready to work in the morning. Why don't you come to the hotel for breakfast on Saturday at 9 a.m. but please, for my sake, wear a bra. I'm only human. As Oscar Wilde said, 'I can resist anything except temptation.'"

Liz grinned.

We went outside and it was still hot even though it was 9 o'clock at night. Still it was better than my last visit. I escorted Liz to her car which was near the front of the airport and she took her coat off and put it in the back of the car before saying goodbye. I kissed her good night but this time I got the tongue as well as the full lips. I could feel myself hardening against her. How I broke off I don't know. Liz certainly didn't help. I helped her into the driving seat and shut the door. I watched her go and then went to the Avis park to pick up my car.

I drove to the Hilton and checked in. There was a message from Mike saying that he had got an apartment organised for Liz in Chelsea Cloisters. I took my keys and went up to my room. It was still only 9.30 and I felt quite hungry. I had a shower, changed and went down for a snack in the coffee shop. Justin and the other Captain were already there and I joined them. I did not stay long and went up to bed and slept until 6 o'clock in the morning which wasn't bad in the circumstances.

I got up and went down for a swim. The sky was still absolutely clear and the pool water felt almost tepid. There was a light breeze for a change. I did ten lengths of the large pool and went up to my room to get dressed, then went down to breakfast without my lightweight jacket. I was finished by 7.30 and collected my papers and jacket from my room. I went to the parking lot, drove to NWIA at the airport and arrived at Bill Baker's office at the same time as he did.

"It's great to see you, Peter. You are looking very well. I can't believe you've just flown in from England. How was the flight?"

"Marvellous thank you. It takes a long time but it really is the way to travel. CrossRisk arranged for me to be upgraded to first class so I was able to eat and sleep as I wanted, which makes all the difference if you want to work the next day."

He looked at me.

"I reckon you have got other things to do beside make the video." I nodded. "When do you have to give evidence at the Inquiry? Do you know yet what really happened?"

"I think I may be giving evidence in the middle of next week, Bill, but you can never be sure when the legal profession are calling the shots. As to what caused the accident, I think we're all still groping for an explanation, apart from AAIB who, according to the papers, have made their mind up that it's pilot error. That's one of the reasons I'm out here. I want to eliminate some theories and persuade some witnesses we need to come to England."

"Well the best of luck. The video man should be here in a moment and then I'll leave you to his tender mercies."

The video expert arrived and we went down to a room he had set up for the filming. He had a mountain of lights and recording equipment which was quite beyond me but he also had some computer gear and a document scanner. He checked on what diagrams I had to go with the talk.

244

Chapter 9

"What I suggest is that we scan your talk on to my special computer and then I've got some software here that will run your talk on a screen placed behind the cameras. What I would like you to do is to indicate when the diagrams are coming so that I can patch them into the tape."

We fed my talk through the scanner's document feeder and then I altered the narrative to match the diagrams. We had a trial run to make sure that I was able to talk to the cameras as the speech scrolled through. It took a bit of practice to be able to look convincing and read at the same time but I got used to it. Luckily, I knew what was coming and only had to do relatively small segments between the diagrams. However, it all took time. The video operator was an expert and knew what he wanted. By lunch time we had done twenty five minutes of the video and we went to the airport terminal for a sandwich. The operator had a beer but I stuck to coca-cola. I found time to go over to the NWIA ticket desk to take a gamble and buy Liz's ticket with my Mastercard.

We went back after lunch and gradually put the rest of my talk on to tape. The whole thing, not counting the diagrams, actually took one hour fifty minutes. I felt fairly confident that by the time the video operator had put the whole thing together it would look quite professional. The operator worked under sub-contract to NWIA and I asked him if I could have copies when he had finished. He pointed out that NWIA had the copyright so that I would have to negotiate with them. I called Bill and asked him about having copies.

"Well Peter. I would like to say OK but I will need to take advice. Of course the NWIA logo will be all over it so in some ways it will be a very good advertisement. I'll see if I can arrange a good deal for you. You can certainly have one copy for yourself but I'd rather you did not use it to show anyone else until I've sorted out the contractual position internally."

That seemed very fair to me and I drove back to the Hilton. I had decided before I left England that I needed to keep my cash flow under control so when I got up to my room I started to write up my expenses before I forgot. I planned to mail the completed sheet with the other sheet for my last visit back to Bill the moment I got back. I reflected that I also needed to get my expenses submitted to Mike pretty quickly or my bank manager would be after me.

I had a quick shower and went down to the lobby to meet Lance. He arrived on time wearing a shirt and tie but no jacket, hardly surprising considering the weather.

"What would you like to do Lance? Why don't we have a drink here and then decide."

We went to the bar and sat down. The waiter came over and I ordered a whisky and water, Lance ordered a Fosters.

"Lance, I needed to talk to you because I want you to be ready when you come over to England. I don't want to spring any surprises on you."

Lance looked nervous.

"What do you mean, Mr. Talbert?"

"You had better call me Peter, Lance."

I carried on.

"Well on that fateful night before the accident to Golf Hotel you sorted out the navigation display and the Multimode Receiver with the faulty GPS. Those entries are in the log. It may well be that the cause of the accident will prove to be due to carrying out a GESS approach and clearly people will investigate that very closely. However, we need to make sure that there is not some other reason, or even fault, which could have caused the accident. Let me put this to you straight Lance. When you changed the GPS box did you do anything else?"

Lance looked slightly uncomfortable.

"Lance, you took out the GPS, checked the part number and fitted a spare from NWIA with the identical part number, right?" Lance nodded. "As luck would have it you were trained by United, not by Independant, and you did not realise that there were two different standards of boxes. What happened then, Lance?"

"I told you, Peter. I functioned the GPS and it worked fine. There was no supervisor and so I made no entry in the log."

"Is that it, Lance? Are you sure? Did you work on any other equipment? Find anything else wrong?"

"That's it, Peter, I just made sure everything worked."

"OK. That's fine." I looked at him. "Lance one of the reasons I came to Australia now was that I wanted to talk to you before the Inquiry. You need to describe to the Court, when you are asked the question about changing the GPS, exactly what you told me. Your supervisor should have been present and remember he had been trained in Seattle. He knew the difference between the 798 aircraft and the two standards of GPS box. Be quite straightforward about it. John Fairlane is the counsel who will be asking you the questions and he is a very reasonable man. He will ask you where you were trained and whether the RWA equipment standard was ever explained to you. There is really no reason for you to be upset. You will obviously be a bit nervous but then so will I."

"But you didn't do anything wrong."

"But neither did you, Lance, within your own knowledge base. You changed a box on an aircraft for an identical part and functioned it, right?"

Lance nodded, dubiously. We stopped at that point and I asked Lance again where he would like to eat. We decided that the coffee shop in the hotel would be fine and we went in and had our meal. He cheered up a bit during the evening but, understandably he felt very concerned.

246

Chapter 9

"Do I have to come to England, Peter?"

"No you don't, but if you don't people may not believe the story of the wrong GPS being fitted. Lawrence won't come and give evidence and of course one can't really blame him since he was trained with United as well. Of course having the wrong GPS is not really important, is it Lance, since the RWA 798s can't use GPS except in a navigation mode?"

Lance nodded uncertainly. We finished our meal and I walked with Lance to the lobby and out to his car.

"When are you coming over?"

"Matt has booked me to travel on Monday. He has made all the arrangements in London as well."

"Well here's my card again. Give me a call when you get in or leave a message on my answering machine if I am out. We will need to keep in touch so that you will know when you will be called."

We shook hands and he drove off. I had hoped that talking to Lance would throw more light on the situation but I had got nowhere. I was not looking forward to giving evidence at the Inquiry. True I had made some progress but I had not come up with a solution. Pilot error for reasons unknown did look a real possibility.

I went to bed and slept soundly until 6.30. In the morning I had my usual swim and watched the news. I went down to the lobby at 8.45 to meet Liz. She arrived just before 9 o'clock looking very relaxed in a thin top and a 'not too short' skirt. I managed to kiss her on the cheek and noticed with some relief that she appeared to be wearing a bra.

"Let's have breakfast outside, Peter."

We went out to the verandah overlooking the pool. It was very pleasant, not too hot but we sat under an umbrella to keep out of the sun. We ordered breakfast, mine quite light, Liz's fairly substantial.

"It's not like this in England, Liz. You had better bring some warm clothes. I hope you have some."

"Peter, I have not yet agreed to come to England. I'm going to take a lot of persuading. Why don't we just have breakfast and not talk of unpleasant things for a moment. We can talk about the Inquiry later."

Liz changed the subject abruptly.

"What are we going to do for the rest of the day? It's far too good to stay here."

"What do you suggest?"

"Let's go sailing. We can arrange a bare boat charter for the day near here."

I did not have much alternative but to agree since I was going to have to persuade Liz to travel to England and she was not about to give in easily.

"I'll need to buy a shirt."

"You can do that in the shops downstairs. Go up and get changed and I'll buy you something suitable. Meet you in the lobby."

I did what I was told but felt a bit guilty taking a day off, even if it was in a good cause, trying to make Liz go to England. I put a few things and my bathing costume in my Lark bag and went downstairs. Liz reappeared in a few minutes with a rather nice shirt.

"How much do I owe you?"

"$80"

"Australian, I hope."

She nodded and I paid her right away. It cost more than my regular shirts but that's because I rarely bought expensive clothes.

"Let's go in my car. I've got my things there."

We went over to her car and she drove to the marina where the chartering was taking place. The weather seemed almost too perfect. Just a light breeze and forecast to remain sunny. We went into the office and I convinced them that I could manage and paid a deposit. They obviously knew Liz so they didn't need much convincing. Anyway perhaps she was on commission.

"Don't go outside the Heads." the man said as I left.

Liz went to the trunk of the car and reappeared with a bag and a cold box.

"What's all this? You had it all planned."

"Well I knew I would need a lot of convincing. What's the phrase 'those that play together, stay together.'"

I hoped she was teasing me but I wasn't sure.

"Liz we're not going to stay together. You're a super girl and I think you're fantastic but our relationship would not work, long term."

"Alright Peter. Don't take the bait quite so quickly."

We reached the boat, a 24 footer, and put our kit on board. Liz disappeared below and reappeared wearing a bikini, leaving very little to the imagination. Her brown skin protected her from the sun. I put on my trunks and the shirt Liz had bought. I stood next to her, my white skin against her tan looked very incongruous.

"That's settled it, Liz. I don't believe in mixed relationships."

I could have bit my tongue off for even suggesting that there was a possibility of a relationship. Liz had clearly not missed the significance of what I said.

"I've got nothing against it. We'd soon be able to match the colours, if we tried hard."

We cast off and had an idyllic sail. Liz obviously knew the cruising area very well and we sailed across gently to the other side of the great harbour where we anchored off an island for lunch. I went down below and opened the windows to allow the breeze through the cabin and keep it cool.

"Take your shirt off and feel the warmth of the sun. Here I'll rub some oil on your back. Its a real blocker, just what you need."

The way Liz rubbed oil on my back was an experience, probably accentuated by the fact that she did not confine herself to my back.

"Will you put some on my back, my darling? Try and keep the oil off the strap if you can."

She passed me the oil and turned round. I tentatively rubbed some oil on her brown smooth skin.

"You can do better than that, Peter." She undid her bikini top and took it off.

"Does that make it easier? Don't be nervous. I won't eat you."

"It's not being eaten that I am nervous about, Liz."

She turned round and faced me and grasped the first finger of my left hand.

Her breasts were full and almost the same colour as her body.

"I really don't understand you, Peter. Most men I know would be trying to make love to me by now."

"I know, Liz. But I am trying not be most men. You are a superb woman but I am not sure that satisfying my carnal desires as the saying goes is really very sensible in the long term."

"Well you know best, but I don't think your body is agreeing with you." She reached down and gently stroked the front of my bathing shorts. I should have moved away. She leant forward and we kissed. Suddenly she stopped.

"Let's take our time. There's all day ahead. Why don't we sunbathe? There's just about room for both of us on the coach top. You had better put some more oil on."

I decided to swim over the side first. I found some plastic steps which fitted over the stern. The water was clear and not too cold, judging by my big toe. It looked superb but just as I was about to dive in Liz yelled at me.

"Stop, Peter, you can't do that."

"Why on earth not. It's ideal."

"Hasn't anyone told you about the sharks? You should only swim where you are protected. I'm not saying you wouldn't be alright here but you mustn't take the risk. We don't want you to leave bits behind here when you go home."

I looked around but couldn't see any sharks. Reluctantly I gave up the idea of swimming and lay down on the boat next to Liz. We had to lay our towels on the top to prevent the coach top burning us. It was not too easy to find room because of the numerous fairleads and jamming cleats but it was worth the effort. The weather was fantastic, with the breeze keeping us cool. Predictably Liz eased her bikini bottoms off to make sure that she browned all over. I decided I had better try to talk to her about coming to England.

"Not now Peter. Let's talk later when we are both fully relaxed."

We lay a bit longer and then Liz suddenly sat up.

"I'm hungry for food. Let's have lunch."

She got up, put her bikini back on and went down below. She brought up the lunch box. I noticed that she had moved the two long cushions on the bunks and put them together on the floor of the cabin.

The sandwiches were delicious. I think she had bought them from a take-away. Shrimp, tuna and ham. There was also a bottle of white wine, not the greatest I noticed but, looking at the label, perhaps the strongest. We sat next to each other in the sun and England seemed a long way away. When we had finished Liz collected all the things and put them back in the box.

Liz took her bikini top off again and I stroked her breasts. There was one part of me that indicated we definitely were not going to relax.

"Let's digest our lunch down below, my darling, we don't want to be run in by the coastguard. Topless sun bathing is permitted but not much more."

We went below. Liz was right. There was no hurry. We lay down for a bit. We just had room to kneel to get our costumes off. I realised that England was not at that moment at the top of my priorities.

Nature took its course and we lay next to one another in the warm breeze blowing through the cabin. I lay on my back. Liz lay on her side next to me.

"My darling, you do see. I could never live in England again. This place has everything."

"Liz, for you that may be true but not for me. "

We both said nothing for a moment then to my surprise Liz opened the subject of the Inquiry.

"Peter, my love. I'm all sorts of things but I'm not a complete idiot. If I'm called to give evidence the newspapers will say I'm a hooker and hound me night and day. My life won't be worth living."

"But Liz, there is no-one who knows what went on except you. Poor Eva and Charles are no longer with us. There are only two bits of evidence that matter from your viewpoint. My recommendation is that you say you went along to dinner because Eva asked you to go with her which in some ways is quite true. It will be clear when you explain that the dinner was on the Saturday night and not the Sunday night. The counsel will ask you to confirm that on the Sunday you called the hotel to thank Harry for the meal and that he was in his room.

Chapter 9

"With regard to the second night, again you went along with Eva and you must then explain about the telephone calls. I am going to make sure as far as I can that there is no cross examination since it would not be relevant.

"In fact I am going to try to ensure that you are not called at all but I cannot promise."

Liz was not convinced but did not turn me down flat.

"Where are you going to be if I come to London?"

"I'll be around. I've arranged for you to stay in an apartment in Chelsea Cloisters which is quite convenient. My suggestion is that you should travel back with me leaving to-morrow morning. We will get in late in the evening. I'll arrange for someone to meet us and take you to your apartment but I'll have to go straight home to prepare for the Inquiry the following morning. Do you know anyone in England?"

"I know a few acquaintances from RWA and my sister."

"Well give her a call and plan to go and visit her the following week-end. Look on the bright side. You probably won't have to give evidence and you are getting a free trip to England all expenses paid and I include in that a very generous daily rate.

"In addition I believe even more than ever that you have a real skill as a clothes designer. I have spoken to the buyer at Harrods, showed her that photo of the two of us with that blue suit you were wearing and she is prepared to look at some of the clothes you have made and give an opinion. By the way you didn't answer my question. Do you have any warm clothes?"

"Not really."

"Well I've an idea. On the Monday afternoon we'll go to Harrods together and you can buy some clothes. Wear something really gorgeous that you've made and try and keep warm on the way. Have you got a reasonably thick coat?" Liz nodded.

"After you've bought something we'll talk to the buyer, you can show her some of your work and see what she says. How does that sound?"

"That bit sounds alright though I am not sure your girl friend will like you buying clothes for me."

"Don't worry. Mike is going to pay for them. If I can prove this accident is not pilot error I will have saved his firm a fortune. Buying you a warm suit is the least he can do. Anyway, if you're going to appear in court you will need to have something to wear."

"You've convinced me about the suit but not about coming to England. Anyway my boss would be most unhappy for me not to turn up on Monday and be away, probably for the best part of two weeks."

"Haven't you mentioned it to him."

"Certainly not. He'd probably fire me."

Liz had given me a problem and I was not sure what to do for the best. I decided that I could talk to the duty officer in the evening when I got in. I sensed the wind freshening and I hastily found my trunks and put them on. There was a storm cloud heading our way and in no time flat the wind was gusting 30 knots. Luckily the anchor was quite heavy but I felt uncomfortable because the wind was on shore.

"Don't worry its only a shower, Peter."

"I do worry. I'm going to reef the main just in case."

I pulled down two slabs and made sure everything was set. I started the outboard and waited to watch events. Liz appeared with a sweatshirt on top of her bikini. The storm looked quite extensive but the wind had slackened slightly.

"Liz I'll pull the main up, make sure the sheet is free. Then go ahead slowly until we're over the anchor and I'll pull it up. Open up fully and then I'll come back and get the boat sailing."

All went well but before I had got back to the stern after getting up the anchor Liz had got the boat sailing on the port tack and had unfurled the jib just enough so we did not heel over too much.

"You've done this before."

"Once or twice, darling. You are not the only person in the world who can sail."

We tacked backwards and forwards slowly across the harbour keeping away from the Heads and the deep water. Luckily the wind was from the South West so there was not too much swell coming in. As we made the marina the wind dropped and the heavens opened, rain falling like buckets. We tied up absolutely wet through, not that it mattered in that climate.

We waited in the cabin for about half an hour until the rain stopped and then we went into the office and I collected my deposit.

"We needed that rain. I only wish it was still raining. Did you have a good day?"

"Superb thank you. Everything is working OK"

We went back to the car and Liz suggested we went back to her place. I demurred and after some discussion she reluctantly agreed to drive me back to the hotel.

"Are you coming in for a drink?"

She was sulking.

"No, thank you. The least you could do after our lunch is to come back home with me and see I'm alright."

"I've told you before. You're very much alright but we must be sensible."

"I don't see why."

Chapter 9

"Liz, life is more than making love. We all need to have a plan. You said yourself that Australia was for you and I've told you, England is for me with all its shortcomings."

I changed the subject.

"My dear. Go home and pack your best clothes. Here are your tickets for England. Your seat is next to mine in business class. The flight leaves as you well know at 9.30 to-morrow morning. I'll see you in the business class lounge."

"I'll think about it. I am not sure that I'm going to come. Anyway I haven't told my boss."

"Don't worry about that. I am going to do that now and you can call your office on Monday morning when we land Sunday night."

Liz looked very doubtful. Then she pulled herself together.

"Sorry to spoil everything, darling. It's been a marvellous day. Nothing can take that away from us."

She grinned and gave me a non-fraternal kiss and I watched her drive away

I collected my key and went up to my room. In spite of everything it was still only 6 o'clock. I called NWIA main exchange and got transferred to the duty officer. I explained the situation about Liz, the Inquiry and her travelling to England.

"She's likely to be away for about ten days depending on the Court. You know you can never tell when witnesses are actually going to be called. I'll get her to call her boss at about 9 o'clock on Monday morning. Could you make sure you have explained the situation to him first thing?"

"OK. I'll double bank by sending him an e-mail which he'll read when he comes in on Monday."

There was nothing more I could do. I had a snack in the coffee shop, watched some TV and went to bed. I got up at six, swam, had a light breakfast and checked out. As I drove to the airport I suddenly realised I had not rung Mandy. I looked at my watch, it was only 9 o'clock on Sunday night. I decided I had better try and put things right. I checked the car in with Avis, saw that I was in a wifi area, got out my pocket pc and called Mandy using skype. She answered straightaway.

"Have all the phones been down? I've been watching the news. As you hadn't called I thought there must have been an earthquake."

I ignored the sarcasm

"No, darling. All is well. I'm at the airport, just about to check in."

"Well I have to tell you, Peter, that I'm very curious about what you have been doing. I normally get better service. I hope the service didn't go elsewhere."

"You're clients are teaching you some rude remarks."

She ignored my comment.

"Well how did everything go?"

"Fine. I did the video. I didn't get anywhere with the NWIA engineer. He said all he did was to change the GPS box but, as we know, that is irrelevant on the RWA 798."

"How did you get on with the girl?"

"I think I've persuaded her to come to England but I just don't know. She's nowhere to be seen at the moment, I'm afraid. Look I'll call you from the lounge if you don't think it's too late."

"No, you do that."

I went to the check in desk but there was still no sign of Liz. I waited as long as I dared and then I checked in. I went straight through immigration to the business class lounge but Liz was nowhere to be seen. I called Mandy as they were calling the flight.

"No luck I'm afraid. She's not here. Took fright. I'm sure John will be able to manage without her. Must fly."

I went to the gate and on to the aircraft. The stewardess showed me to my seat. Liz was already there.

She smiled a warm greeting, very smug.

"Well I do work for RWA. Why should I queue with the common herd?"

CHAPTER 10

Liz and I arrived on time at 9.30 in the evening and it was still Sunday. It was a long, long flight against the wind, twenty two hours. We slept a lot of the time. We did not talk much. She was tired and very nervous and I did all I could to reassure her. The problem with the flight was that it was daylight nearly all the way because of the time change. I told Liz to stop fiddling with her watch and put it back eleven hours straightaway so that she had some chance of synchronising her stomach and sleep pattern with the UK. Not surprisingly, it was difficult to sleep even though all the blinds were lowered after about ten hours into the flight.

I took advantage of the latest satellite technology and called Mike and Mandy from my mobile. I did wonder how much I would be charged for the call but comforted myself that Mike was going to have to pay. Mike said he would meet us. I told Mandy I would call her when I woke up.

It was a fine clear night but the temperature was -5°C when we landed. Liz had managed to find an old raincoat which did not look too bad and would help to keep her warm. She had put on a very heavy pullover before we got out of the aircraft. We were soon through immigration and customs and I was delighted to see Mike there, especially as Liz had taken me at my word and brought two bags, both full of clothes, most of them not wearable in an English winter. I could see that Mike kept on looking at Liz when he thought she wasn't noticing.

"What sort of flight did you have?" came the inevitable remark and we soon sorted that out. Mike agreed to take Liz to Chelsea Cloisters and settle her in her apartment.

"Do you need anything to eat, Liz?"

"Never again, thank you Mike. We've been eating all the way. I shall have to alter all my clothes when I get back to Sydney."

"Which reminds me Mike. Liz will need some UK clothes. Have you got a float for her? It's unreasonable to expect her to come all this way into a climate that does not exist in Australia and buy clothes she is unlikely ever to need again."

"I agree and I do have a float. Liz do you have a UK bank account?"

"I'm afraid not but I bank with the Australian & New Zealand Bank and they've a branch in London."

"Alright, I'll give you £1,000 in cash and I'll get my secretary to come to your apartment to-morrow morning at 10 o'clock to give you a cheque to pay in to your account. I'd appreciate some record of what you've spent sometime to keep our records straight. You can fax or email it to me when you get back to Sydney."

Liz nodded and I broke in.

"Mike, when are we going to see Fairlane?"

"9.30 in his office, OK?" I nodded. "Liz, if you need help, go through Mike's office. If you need me they will know where I am. To-morrow you need to get yourself some clothes. Mike's secretary can advise you where to go. Selfridges might be a good place to start. If I don't hear from you I will be at your place at 2 o'clock and I'll take you to Harrods to see the buyer. Mike will look after you now. Please Liz, don't forget to call your boss the moment you get to the apartment."

I gave her a perfunctory kiss but she squeezed my hand hard on the side that Mike couldn't see. I watched them go, Mike wheeling her baggage. I went to valet parking and drove home. I went upstairs, set the alarm, unpacked my clothes, made a pile of dirty washing and went to bed.

I woke early and called Mandy, she was just getting up.

"I'm home, my darling. Mike was there and took Liz to her apartment."

"Good. I have to say that I am curious to see Liz. Could she join us for dinner to-night?"

I was not too keen on this line of talk.

"Not unless we eat near Chelsea Cloisters. She hasn't got any wheels."

"Well that's OK by me and then we can go home to your place."

"Fine. I'll call her sometime to-day and try and fix it. I'm taking her to see the Harrods buyer this afternoon. I'll take the car and leave it at the Chelsea Cloisters car park. She shouldn't be short of things to wear, she brought two large bags of clothes with her."

"You had better keep moving, Peter. Aren't you going to see your counsel sometime?"

"You're right again. Call you later."

I got dressed. The weather had not got any warmer overnight. Liz must be hating it. I switched on the TV and the forecaster had put snow showers all over the map. I got rid of the car at Chelsea Cloisters and arrived at Fairlane's chambers just before 09.30 and for once Mike was not there but he arrived a few minutes later.

"How did you get on with Liz?"

"Oh fine. She's a nice girl and not unattractive."

"You noticed? I thought confirmed bachelors did not notice these things."

Mike ignored me.

Chapter 10

"I've managed to arrange the money and instruct my secretary before I left the office. That's why I am a few minutes late.

"By the way there's two thing I haven't told you, Peter. First of all your Lance Stephens has chickened out and won't be coming to give evidence."

"That's not good news. His evidence would have confirmed my story on changing the GPS set. I've got paperwork if it's needed but it's not the same thing."

"The other thing is that the NWIA insurers are in a real panic. They've obviously been warned by NWIA that there may be a problem and I suppose it could bankrupt the firm if they have not made all necessary arrangements. The insurer is a UK firm, Pacific Aerospace Insurance plc, PAI, and they clearly want the fault to be pilot error, so CrossRisk Insurance, and that includes you, are not the flavour of the month with those boys. NWIA and Pacific Aerospace have applied, and it has been agreed, that they can be a party to the proceedings. It looks like an insurers' benefit since both ourselves and Hull Claims insurance are present as well as PAI. To be honest, Peter, that's the trouble with holding this sort of an Inquiry instead of leaving it to the AAIB. Everybody wants to be represented to defend their corner."

"How did my name come on the screen?"

"That's easy. Once they became a party to the proceedings they would see the witnesses who are scheduled to be called and who were 'promoting' the witnesses They will know that we are only calling you because we are refuting that pilot error is in any way responsible for the accident."

"Well Mike I have to say it makes me feel very uncomfortable."

John called us in to his room. He had his copious notes in front of him.

"Well Peter, what's new since we met?"

"Just to recap on where we finished last, it was my view that it was a pity that the transcript did not have any conversation with the hijackers. We need to discuss that with AAIB and ask them how they can come to any conclusion without knowing what the hiackers were doing. Mike was going to organise the BAA, ATC and SRG witnesses. When I was in Sydney I thought I had persuaded the NWIA mechanic to come over to give evidence on the work he did, but Mike tells me he has changed his mind. However as you wanted, the girl who can say that the so called party was not the night before the flight, travelled with me yesterday and is now in London. She doesn't want to be called as a witness and I don't think she is needed.

"Now since we met last I have established that a few flights before the fateful flight, a NWIA maintenance engineer changed the GPS box in

Golf Hotel but he put the NWIA three receiver card box into the aircraft instead of the single GPS card. His supervisor, who knew that the NWIA box was different from the RWA box was not on duty, even though his time sheet showed he was. The engineer who changed the box now works in the USA but he told me the story over the phone and we have paperwork showing the issue of a 'wrong' GPS box and the technical log showing it was fitted to Golf Hotel."

"But Peter, that's good detective work but would it matter?"

"I don't think so but I have to eliminate everything. Let me carry on. On the fateful night before the last flight the same supervisor was still not present. A different engineer changed the GPS set, a good engineer this time. Unfortunately he too, being trained by United and not Independant, did not know there were two standards of GPS boxes but he did check that the set he put in was the same part number as the set he took out. He functioned the set which worked correctly. The fact that he checked the part number for the GPS shows quite clearly that the wrong GPS was fitted some flights earlier by NWIA but let me stress, John, as I did last time we met, that bad GPS maintenance by NWIA ought not to be a factor in the accident since the RWA 798s cannot fly a GPS approach."

"Peter, the story of the NWIA bad maintenance may not be significant technically but it is important, since it shows very clearly that Foster of AAIB did not do his job thoroughly because, unlike you, he did not investigate things properly. Unfortunately, we still haven't managed to find an alternative solution that explains what happened and therefore we will not be able to convince the Court it wasn't pilot error. You are going to have to be very eloquent to persuade everybody that hijackers on the flight deck would have prevented the pilots monitoring properly."

"Yes, John, but the point is that the normal monitoring apparently would have showed nothing wrong. Now I'm fairly certain that when you question the GESS experts you're going to find that the GELAS transmitter was not checked after the accident. The ATC man will say he didn't ask for it to be checked because it was not required and I suspect the SRG man will say the integrity of the system is such that it's not necessary to check it. My view is that the data should have been checked. The other very important point is to try to establish whether the runway details for 27 Left that were fed into the MMR boxes were correct. If the data was wrong then an accident would be very likely. It seems to me you're going to have to do something akin to your normal lawyers' trick 'I wasn't there, I didn't do it, but if I was, and if I did, I'm sorry.' Certainly the hijackers must have prevented the pilots from concentrating and the GESS was almost certainly wrong."

"Alright Peter, if that's the best we can do, so be it."

I called Liz in her flat from John's chambers.

Chapter 10

"How did you manage this morning?"

"Well, my darling, Mike's secretary came round and we went to my bank and put Mike's cheque in. I took a taxi to Selfridges and bought some warm trousers and a pullover. I took another taxi home. I don't feel equal yet for the London public transport system."

"Do you feel equal to coming out to dinner with Mandy and me to-night? We'd go to a place near you."

"That sounds fun, darling."

"Have you bought any food yet?"

"Just a little and I saw a small restaurant where I planned to eat if you stood me up, my love."

"Liz, to-night I think it would be helpful if you called me Peter, and not darling."

"OK, my love. I mean Peter. But it is not going to be easy, darling Peter."

"Stop giving me a hard time Liz. You know exactly what I mean. I'll pick you up at two this afternoon. Have your clothes bag ready. I'll order a cab to take us there."

Dinner to-night was going to be tricky. I had a brainwave and called Mike who had got back to the Office.

"Mike, what are you doing to-night? How about making up a foursome with Mandy and Liz? I'm going to book a table at Chez Augustine in the Kings Road for 8 o'clock."

Mike was delighted and he agreed that he would walk Liz to the restaurant. I said that we would meet him there. I called Mandy feeling a lot easier. I had come to the obvious conclusion that a threesome with Mandy and Liz had all the makings of an irrecoverable disaster. Even with four there would need to be no nodding off.

I called Mandy's office. I waited a few minutes and was put through.

"Chez Augustine's at 8 o'clock, darling. Mike, Liz, you and me. I'll be at your office at 7 o'clock and we can take it from there. My car's in position at Chelsea Cloisters so it should work out very well."

"I don't remember our including Mike in."

"I don't remember we included him out. He's a super chap and he seems to like Liz. He will make certain there are no awkward gaps in the conversation."

"How do you know I don't want awkward gaps in the conversation?"

There was no answer to that so I didn't give one.

"See you to-night, darling."

"Don't bet on it, Peter."

She hung up, but I judged only to keep me on my toes. I caught a taxi to Chelsea Cloisters. I was a bit early for the Harrods trip and, feeling slightly hungry, I went to the restaurant close-by.

"Great minds. I was hungry, Peter, and didn't have any food in the apartment. You haven't got very much."

"I'm planning on having just this lunch and dinner to-day and that's enough for me."

"No wonder you are so thin and gorgeous, my own sweet darling."

I was just beginning to know when she was teasing me. I ate my baguette and drank my coffee. Liz tucked in to her bacon, lettuce and tomato sandwich. She seemed to be able to tuck the food away without any effect on her figure which didn't seem fair. I went back with her to her apartment and waited while she sorted herself out. She was wearing what I guessed was the pullover and trousers she had bought at Selfridges. She looked great, but then most things looked great on her. I helped her on with her raincoat which rather spoilt the effect but kept the cold out.

"Where are your gloves?"

"I forgot to buy a pair. It was on my list but they didn't make the cut."

"Well we're taking a taxi so you should be alright but it's quite cold out and going to snow."

I carried Liz's bag and she locked up. We went to the front and a taxi was waiting. The traffic was heavy but we got to Harrods quite quickly. We went upstairs to the department I was at before and Liz started to look for a suit. I could see that this was going to take some time and I sat down to read the paper. I saw the buyer coming over.

"Hello again, Mr. Talbert. I think I recognise the young lady over there buying a suit from the photograph you showed me."

"Yes. Living in Sydney she had no need for a suit to wear in our English weather."

"She is a very striking person. She could be model if she wanted to. That suit she found looks very good on her."

Liz came over and I introduced her to the buyer.

"That's a lovely suit for you, Miss Ward."

"Yes. I like it. In fact I'm going to buy it."

"Why don't you put on something you've made, my dear, and let me see it?"

Liz disappeared into the changing room and reappeared with a mid length dress which fitted her to perfection. I could see the buyer was impressed. She went up to Liz and looked at the finish of the garment and the stitching.

"That's lovely. Have you anything else you want to show me. Have you a suit."

"Liz, how about the suit you wore in Nikkos?"

Liz reappeared a few minutes later looking very elegant.

Chapter 10

"Thank you my dear. I suggest you get dressed and bring the clothes to my office at the back when you have paid for the new suit."

Liz did all the paperwork and I carried the bag into the buyer's office. The buyer opened the bag and looked at all the clothes, pulling them out one by one and then laying them down in a pile. She and Liz then repacked the case.

"Miss Ward."

"Liz."

"Well then, Liz. Mr. Talbert here was quite right. You are a very accomplished designer and also you are very good at making the clothes, not the same thing at all as you well know. However, there are probably quite a few things for you to learn to simplify turning design into production. I know that one firm we buy from is looking for a designer and I will give you the owner's details. Of course we buy from many firms and you have seen all the different labels. Would you like contacts at some of these firms."

"Yes, please. The more names the better really. I know I have a lot to learn but I feel I was well taught when I was growing up. I should have quite a bit of time while I'm over here on this visit to try my luck."

The buyer wrote the information down and we took our leave. Liz was profuse with her thanks. We stopped on the ground floor, Liz bought some gloves and then we caught a cab back to Liz's apartment in Chelsea Cloisters. I was glad to be relieved of all the clothes. In truth I had thought that there were more than was needed but in the event I was very impressed by the way the buyer had looked at them all.

"That seemed to go well, what do you think, Liz?"

"The buyer was very nice. And you were quite right, Peter. Though I knew I could make clothes, I never really believed I could make money out of it."

"Well you haven't yet. You need to make appointments to start visiting all these people. Be very careful they don't try to take advantage of you, particularly the men. Don't agree to anything on the spot. Let your bye-word be 'I'll think about it and call you back.' The good ones will understand and the others you don't need.

"Now what I need to do next is to find out when you might be called, so you can plan your appointments. Nothing will happen until after I have given evidence and that won't be until Wednesday at the earliest. I'll try and find out some more and let you know to-night. The next two days are clear anyway.

"About to-night. I'll go round to pick up Mandy. Mike will be round to pick you up at about 7.30. The plan is for you both to walk to the restaurant, its only about half a mile but you'll need your gloves by the look of the weather. You've probably got time for a few telephone calls."

A Flight Too Far

I kissed Liz good-bye, on the cheek, and went to Mandy's offices to wait. She was getting changed when I arrived and appeared looking like a young lady being taken out to dinner and not an aspiring solicitor with large spectacles. She was wearing quite a long dress and was carrying a warm camel coat and gloves. There had been some snow flurries during the day but, certainly in London, nothing had settled.

"Hello, my darling. You look superb."

"Thank you. You may kiss me."

I obliged and started to do a thorough job.

"That's quite enough, thank you. You are cutting my face to ribbons with your beard and getting me a bad name at the same time."

"Hardly, you must be the only solicitor in the building."

"Well you're wrong actually. Anyway, what sort of a day have you had?"

"I went to John Fairlane and briefed him on the situation."

"Is that all? No wonder you look so relaxed. Why don't you go into the men's room and freshen up?"

"You anticipate my every desire."

"Not if I can help it."

I had a shave with the electric razor I always carried in my brief case and threw some water on my face.

"Now that looks a lot better. Let me test if you've done a good job."

I started to oblige.

"Stop. You've passed the test. We don't both want to be wearing make-up. Let's see if we can find a cab."

I carried my brief case and Mandy's overnight bag downstairs and we went out into Fleet Street and flagged a cab down.

"Peter, I'm puzzled. I thought you had been working in Sydney. How do you explain your sunburn?"

"Well I didn't work all the time. I took the opportunity to sunbathe."

"So I see. Are you telling me, if I was brave enough to look, that your body is tanned as well?

"Not much. I covered it with sun blocking oil."

"How very sensible. How did you manage your back?"

"I didn't. I had to be careful."

Not for the first time I thought Mandy should have been a barrister. I changed the subject as best I could.

"What sort of day did you have, darling?"

"As usual a bit of everything except GE business which I am glad to say my boss is dealing with. When are you going to be performing?"

"Probably Wednesday morning, I'm not sure yet.

"Let me know. I want to be there."

Chapter 10

We reached Chez Augustine just as a heavy snow shower descended on us. We rushed inside and checked our coats. Mike and Liz had not arrived. We went to our table and we both had a Kir Royale to celebrate my return. About five minutes later the other two arrived. They both had snow in their hair and Liz was full of excitement since she had not seen snow for many years. She was still wearing her rather ancient raincoat but when she took it off and gave it to Mike to have it checked we could all see that she was wearing a lovely long skirt and a low cut silk blouse which showed her figure and her sun tanned skin off to perfection. I could see Mandy appreciating the situation and framing a few questions for later. I made the introductions. Mike held Liz's chair as she sat down. I signalled for two more Kir Royales.

"This is a super place, Peter. I love French food."

Mandy cut in. "Miss Ward, that's a lovely outfit you are wearing. Did you make it yourself?"

"Please call me Liz. Thank you. Yes I did. The skirt was not too difficult but the blouse seemed to take for ever both in the cutting and the stitching. There was quite a lot of waste."

"Well it was clearly worth the effort. Very eye catching."

Liz grinned. I was not sure I liked the inference in the last remark. Mike rushed in.

"Liz showed me some of the clothes she brought with her. They look fantastic to me."

"Liz, did you have any luck following up any of the contacts the buyer gave you?"

"Yes, Peter, I called three or four of the big firms and have got two appointments for to-morrow."

The Kir Royales arrived and we toasted Liz's future as a dress designer.

"I think you are all being rather too appreciative of my skills and not sufficiently critical. The chances of being accepted as a designer must be very slim."

We all studied the menu. Liz announced she'd like Beef Wellington but it needed two people. Mike, who was clearly rather taken with Liz, agreed to have Beef Wellington as well. Mandy went for a tournedos and, as usual, I chose grilled sole on the bone. We all decided to have soup as a starter, presumably because it was cold outside. I chose a Pouilly Fumé to start the meal. I let Mike choose the red wine as it was not my speciality, he chose the house Bordeaux.

I was glad to notice that the atmosphere became more relaxed as the wine was consumed. I only had a half glass of white and a half glass of red as I had to drive back to Kingston and, perhaps more importantly, I needed a clear head to survive the meal.

Mandy started questioning Liz.

"How long have you been out in Australia, Liz?"

"About eight years. I went out on holiday and got various jobs but I've been working with Royal World Airlines for about five years, firstly in their operations office at the airport and now downtown in the ticket office. I like the job, the people, the climate, the sport and the chance of free travel. To be honest, I'm nervous of being offered a tempting job in England, I think I would miss Australia terribly. Have you ever been to Australia, Miss Arrowsmith?"

"Mandy, please. No, but I would like to."

"Get Peter to bring you. I'm sure you will both need a holiday when this Inquiry is over."

"I'm not sure I would want to go with Peter. It might be more fun to go by myself."

"You could be right there. Men can be a bit restrictive."

"Do you have a family over here, Liz?"

"Only a sister, Mandy. Our parents died when we were young and we were brought up by foster parents who died two and three years ago. It was my foster mother who taught me to cut and sew dresses."

"Well she certainly did a good job."

There was a pause as we ate our food and Mandy carried on.

"Do you sail at all? If you don't mind my saying so you look as if you spend every day sailing in Sydney Harbour."

"Not quite, but I do sail a little, not seriously."

"Peter will have to do a lot more sunbathing before he matches your colour, Liz."

I held my breath in case Liz had assumed that I had mentioned the sailing. I need not have worried. Liz was clearly a skilled campaigner.

"Peter tells me that you are an expert sailor, Mandy."

"Well I do a bit at week-ends but by the time I get home during the week it is too dark, too cold and too late to sail in the evenings."

"Well we have the advantage there. I can go sailing or swimming in the evenings during the summer and usually in the winter as well, no trouble at all.

"Mike, have you been to Australia?"

"Yes Liz, several times, but all I have ever done is to work and investigate insurance claims. I need someone like you to show me round before I am too old."

"OK. You've got yourself a deal. I'll give you my telephone number and next time you come you can call me."

Mike almost simpered. He had Liz just where she wanted him. Mandy, not to be diverted, resumed her cross examination.

Chapter 10

"Where did you take Peter to keep him amused, Liz, when he wasn't working?"

"You've got that the wrong way round, Mandy. After I told Peter about the RWA crews he was kind enough to take me to the restaurant at Nikko's as a thank you. It was so nice of him. That's when he noticed the suit I was wearing." Liz smiled sweetly at me.

Mandy agreed straightaway.

"Yes, he can be nice sometimes when he is saying thank you or when he wants something."

Mandy also smiled sweetly at me. I was not sure I liked their combined benedictions. I hastily plied them both with more wine. Mike, I decided, had had enough if he was seeing Liz back to her flat.

Mandy carried on, innocence herself. I hoped I looked impassive.

"Liz, how did Peter manage to persuade you to come to England?"

"To tell you the truth I didn't want to come. Of course the thought of getting a professional opinion on my clothes was tempting. However, if I have to give evidence I am afraid that the newspapers will get the impression that I am a good time girl, living on the beach. It just happened that my room mate liked going out and needed a companion on those two nights. Did Peter tell you she was killed in the accident? It's really terrible. I miss her. She was a real friend."

Mandy was stopped for a moment and we carried on with our meal. Liz as the youngster of our party had crème brulée as a dessert. The rest of us went straight to coffee.

"Mike, do you think I will have to give evidence?"

"I don't know Liz. A lot will depend on Peter and whether the Court believes his explanation. I promise I will try to prevent John Fairlane calling you if I can but I think you're right. The papers will try to make the most of the conversation on the recording and look for any parties on the beach."

We did not spend too long when we had finished as we were all working in the morning, even Liz. We put our coats and gloves on. It had stopped snowing but there was some snow on the road. We walked back to Chelsea Cloisters and Mandy and I said goodnight to Liz, Mandy shaking hands and I gave Liz a very light kiss on the cheek. We went to the car, I let Mandy in and walked round, took my coat off, put it into the back seat, and got in.

As we drove back to my house I tried to make light conversation. Mandy was very quiet and uncommunicative. I decided that least said, soonest mended. I parked the car, let Mandy in and then put the car in the garage. Mandy was boiling the kettle, clearly making a cup of tea before going to bed.

"We've both got a busy day in the morning, good night Peter." She headed upstairs with her bag.

"Wait a minute, Mandy. What's got into you? We've just had a nice evening and you are all het up."

"It may have been nice for you Peter but I suspect that you have not debriefed me fully about what went on in Australia on both your visits. Miss Ward is the sort of girl you would fall for in a big way if she fluttered her eyelids at you and everybody in the restaurant could not help noticing that she is, as some of my clients would say, well stacked."

"Liz is a nice girl Mandy. Don't give me a hard time just because you're jealous."

"Jealous? What have I got to be jealous of? That settles it. Good night."

She was off and I went to bed hoping that time would be the great healer but resolved to help time on its way by keeping Liz and Mandy as far apart as possible.

In the morning we went through our normal routine, I took the tea into Mandy's room but this time it seemed to me that Mandy had not pulled the sheet up quite as high as she sometimes did. Perhaps I was reading too much into little clues.

We had a subdued breakfast, I read the business section and she read the main paper. We put our coats and gloves on, it was still very cold, and walked to the station. I carried my brief case but Mandy carried her overnight bag as well as her briefcase. She refused to let me carry it. I clearly had misread the portents. We walked together to Waterloo. I went to Mike's office as it was still a bit early for the Inquiry and Mandy went to her office after offering a small section of her cheek to be kissed.

Mike arrived shortly after I did and we went up to his room. The telephone rang. Mike answered the phone.

"Hello Liz. How are you to-day?"

Liz seemed to be going on a bit.

"Yes he is. Hold on a moment."

Mike passed me the phone.

"Peter, thank you so much for last night. It was lovely. I really enjoyed myself. Mandy is so nice. She is very lucky and so are you."

I managed to restrain myself from all the comments that came flooding into my brain.

"Yes it was nice. Mike obviously got you home."

Mike looked uncomfortable.

"Yes. He took me to the night club by the apartments for a brandy before he left."

Chapter 10

"You young things. I don't know how you do it. Liz, good luck to-day. Remember don't say yes straightaway to the first offer of a job. You need to shop around."

"I have no intention of saying yes straightaway to anything. Is Mandy staying with you this evening?"

"None of your business, Miss Ward."

"That means yes. Did I upset her."

"I can't possibly discuss the matter any further."

"You mean Mike is still listening. Well don't answer but if Mandy is in a huff you could come round to see me and discuss the matter, I'm free."

"Let me know how you get on to-day, Liz. Mike and I must go to the Inquiry."

Mike was looking at me and I hoped I did not look as flushed as he did. We went to the Inquiry. We were there at 09.45 and I noticed that the seats reserved for the press were filling up. The Court appeared promptly at 10 o'clock. Lord Justice Thomas made an opening statement.

"May I remind you that the Inquiry was adjourned when Mr. Martin Foster, a senior inspector of the AAIB who has been working on the investigation, was giving evidence. Mr. Foster will now carry on giving evidence."

Martin Foster was reminded that he was giving evidence on oath. Janet Crowburn started the questioning.

"Mr. Foster, when you were giving evidence before the Inquiry was adjourned you told us that the chances were that the accident was caused by the pilots not monitoring their instruments and displays properly and therefore not noticing that the aircraft was below the glide slope. I warned you that your case seemed very weak. Is it still your view that the pilots made a mistake?"

"Yes Ma'am, it still looks like pilot error."

"What extra work have you now done to confirm your opinion that pilot error was the cause of the accident?"

"Well we have now analysed all the data in the recorders and all the systems in the aircraft appeared to be working correctly at the time of the crash."

"Have you established the position of the approach selector switch?"

"No Ma'am, for some reason the switch position wasn't shown on the instrumentation."

"Well then, have you now analysed the GESS deviations."

"No Ma'am, the traces of the Multimode receiver output were not working nor could we get the output to the auto-pilot and pilots' navigation displays."

"But you have analysed the output of the ILS?"

"No Ma'am. We could not do that because it was not working. As I mentioned before, we were able to analyze the distance outputs of the DME beacon situated on the extended centre line of 27 Right and it was quite clear that the aircraft was too low."

Janet Crowburn looked at her notes.

"We are all aware that the aircraft was too low. What I asked you before was whether it would be easy and a normal thing for the crew to use the DME to check on the aircraft's position relative to the runway and the correct glide slope?"

Foster started to go red in the face. He hesitated.

"I put it to you, Mr. Foster, that what you were able to do in a laboratory was not possible when doing a blind landing unless special preparation had been made."

Foster started to mumble. "Speak up please, Mr. Foster."

"It could have been done." He sounded very unsure.

"Mr. Foster how would they know they were below the correct glide slope?"

"It must have been obvious when they looked at their displays even if their GESS deviations were zero."

"Why Mr. Foster? Does not the Navigation Display show exactly the same deviation as the autopilot sees."

Foster squirmed.

"Yes."

"Mr. Foster, have you brought the transcripts of the voice recorder?"

"Yes ma'am."

"May I have them, please?"

She gave the transcript to the Clerk of the Court and then produced her own copy.

"Now Mr. Foster, last time we met I asked you from the transcript, did the Captain tell the co-pilot to monitor the navigation display and he would be using the Primary Flight Display mode on the approach and you agreed?"

"Yes, ma'am."

"Mr. Foster is it true from the transcript that the co-pilot called out the ranges and confirmed the aircraft was on centre line and the heights were consistent with being on the glide slope?"

"Yes ma'am."

"So why do you say that the pilots made a mistake?"

"Well the first officer must have been distracted by the hijackers. It is just not possible for the heights which he called out to have been correct."

Chapter 10

"Mr. Foster I asked you before and I must ask you again, how do you know there was not a fault with the GESS or with the equipment on the aircraft?"

Foster was speechless. Lord Justice Thomas came in.

"Mr. Foster, you must answer the question. How do you know there was not a fault with the GESS or with the equipment on the aircraft which misled the crew?"

"Well Sir. The DME showed the aircraft was low and all the traces we have looked at show the aircraft systems were all working perfectly."

"But you were not able to look at the GESS deviations on the flight data recorder?"

"No, Sir."

"And the pilots could not use the DME distances?"

"Yes they could."

"But you agree that to use the distances to calculate the correct height at the final part of the approach would have been impossible for the pilots?"

Foster half nodded in spite of himself.

"In that case perhaps there is more to be discovered."

"I still believe the pilots made a mistake."

"But you have no evidence, Mr. Foster. You are wasting the Court's time."

Janet Crowburn wanted to release Foster for cross examination by the other counsels but Charles McGuire, the second assessor and software professor, indicated he wanted to ask some questions.

"Mr. Foster, would you like to explain to the Court very briefly the way the GESS functions. I am not clear about the function of the GELAS."

"Yes, Sir. The GESS receives signals from the Galileo European satellites and there is software in the Multimode receiver which calculates the vertical deviation of the aircraft from a computed glide slope centre line and horizontal deviation from a computed runway centre line. It can only do this providing there is valid output from the GELAS ensuring that the satellite signals are accurate."

"Now Mr. Foster, as you said earlier, it is true to say that the whole safety of the aircraft on the approach depends on the calculation. The crew can never see the aircraft's true glide slope deviation. They only see the computed deviation that is sent to the auto-pilot. Do you think that's a good idea?"

"That's not for me to say Sir. That is a certification matter."

"But you would agree that the standard of the software is important?"

"Yes, Sir."

"Mr. Foster what is the software certification standard in the Multimode receiver?"

"I don't know Sir. That is decided by the certification authorities. In this case EASA."

"Did you ask the question?"

"No Sir."

"Perhaps you should have done, Mr. Foster" McGuire paused, disgust all over his face. "Well Mr. Foster, let's consider something else. Presumably the GESS system would only have worked correctly if the position of the runway, direction and height had been entered correctly into the database of the MultiMode receivers?"

"Yes, Sir."

"Mr. Foster, did you check with Microspot that the airfield information that was loaded for 27 Left was correct?"

"No Sir."

"Did you check the information on the MMR database chips?"

"No, Sir."

"Why not, Mr. Foster?"

"Well Sir, the boxes were all damaged."

"But surely the information is stored on the database memory chip. You could have checked one of chips?"

Foster shifted uneasily.

"We only found one of the database chips."

"And was the information correct?"

"I don't know. We have not checked it yet."

"Mr. Foster, I suggest that job should be on top of your priority list when you leave the witness box. It is an absolutely vital piece of information." McGuire looked at his notes and carried on.

"Mr. Foster did you check immediately after the accident whether the positional information being transmitted by the GELAS to the aircraft had been checked and was correct?"

"No Sir."

"Don't you think you should have done?"

"No Sir. The GELAS transmitter is self monitored."

"But the data being transmitted might have been wrong? There would have been no warning of that, would there?"

Foster looked in trouble. He mumbled.

"Most unlikely."

"But surely it should have been checked?"

Foster seemed speechless. McGuire shrugged his shoulders in disgust. Janet Crowburn indicated that the witness could be cross-examined. John Fairlane got to his feet.

Chapter 10

"Now then, was there anything unusual about the voice recording, the one which covered the whole flight deck area?"

"The quality was not very good."

"Can you be more specific?"

"Well it was only just possible to hear the pilots' voices."

"Wouldn't you have expected to have heard the hijackers' voices?"

"If the quality had been good, yes Sir."

"Is the transcript you have given the Court the full transcript? Have you edited this transcript?"

"No Sir."

"Mr. Foster, would you agree that if the hijackers had been talking to the pilots while they were making the approach it would have been very difficult for them to concentrate?"

"It might have distracted them a little but they should have noticed something was wrong."

"Don't you think it must have been very disturbing for Captain Hodgson to have to fly the aircraft and react to the hijacker?"

"The auto-pilot was flying the aircraft."

"But surely your point is that the pilots should have been monitoring the performance of the aircraft?"

"The hijacking wouldn't have made any difference."

"That's your opinion?"

"Yes Sir,"

"Even if there was no Navigation Display?"

Foster said nothing but looked very unsure of himself.

"Please answer my question."

"Well certainly it would have been much harder to monitor if there was no display."

"Mr. Foster, have you ever done a real Cat 3B landing in a modern jet aircraft?"

"No Sir."

"Mr. Foster, have you ever been hijacked and been responsible for 500 passengers."

"No Sir."

"In that case Mr. Foster, the Court will be able to judge how much importance should be attached to your opinions." He paused. "Mr. Foster, has it occurred to you that there might have been something wrong with the transmitted GELAS information?"

"Yes Sir. I checked that the monitoring did not raise an alarm."

"Is that good enough? Shouldn't there have been a flight check? Shouldn't you have checked the navigational data being sent to the aircraft as Professor McGuire has suggested? Why didn't you check the MMR database chip?"

"That is outside my area of expertise Sir."

"But Mr. Foster, you are the Senior Inspector for this Investigation. You could have seen that it was done." There was a pause. "And you have not been able to make the instrumentation work on the GESS."

"That's probably a coincidence."

"Don't you think it a rather remarkable coincidence in the circumstances? Shouldn't you have investigated the lack of instrumentation more carefully?"

"No, Sir."

"Mr. Foster, do you think you have done everything you reasonably could have done to look for possible avionic malfunctions?"

"Yes Sir."

"Well no doubt the Court will judge that."

John looked at his notes.

"Now Mr. Foster, would you explain to us what investigations you or your team carried out in Sydney to find out the serviceability of the aircraft before departure?"

"We asked NWIA what work had been carried out overnight after the aircraft had landed at 8 o'clock the previous evening. As I have explained NWIA changed a Multimode receiver and the captain's Navigation Display."

"Was any other non-routine maintenance work carried out?"

"Not according to NWIA."

"Did you send anyone out to NWIA to check?"

"No Sir."

"Would you be surprised to learn that the Global Positioning System had been changed overnight?"

"Very. There was no entry in the technical log."

"Did you speak to the foreman of the night shift?"

"No Sir."

"I have a witness, a Mr. Peter Talbert, who will show that some significant maintenance was carried out that night which was not entered in the log."

"I find that very hard to believe, Sir, without seeing some paperwork. Anyway the GPS is irrelevant to this accident."

"Oh Mr. Foster, I promise you will see some paperwork. The witness seems to have done all the investigation that should have been done by your team. As to whether the GPS is relevant or not, it might be said that you and your team have taken the easy option of saying 'pilot error' without considering the effect of hijacking, without checking whether the GESS was working correctly and without checking whether the correct functioning of the GPS was important."

Chapter 10

Foster was perspiring and thinking hard at the same time, wondering what was coming next.

"Now then about this party and the voice recorder transcript which was reported in the Telegraph. Mr. Foster, do you know how the Daily Telegraph got hold of the transcript?"

Foster went very red and seemed unsure of himself.

"No Sir."

"Are you sure?"

"Yes, Sir."

"Let me remind you that you are under oath. Do you know how the Daily Telegraph got hold of the transcript?"

Foster looked panic stricken.

"No sir."

"Was the transcript that appeared in the Daily Telegraph accurate."

"I didn't check."

"Mr. Foster, are you saying you didn't read the reports in the Telegraph?"

"I just glanced at them."

"Well then Mr. Foster, what were the exact words on the voice recorder?"

"I can't remember."

"Then let me refresh your memory from the transcript.

Hodgson	Charles, did you speak with Eva. Was she awake?
Tumbrill	You bet. She's fine.
Hodgson	She's a lovely girl. Bursting with energy. Time you settled down.
Tumbrill	We'll see. That was a great evening we had at Maroubra with those two. I like that beach, and Caesars.
Hodgson	Yes, I could see that. We certainly got through the wine. Well you and the girls did.
Tumbrill	I enjoyed the swim as well.
Hodgson	Just as well it was warm or you both would have frozen.
Tumbrill	You're a fine one to talk. I'm afraid I didn't get a lot of sleep. Did you have a good time, Harry?
Hodgson	Very quiet, thank you.
Tumbrill	That's what they all say.
Hodgson	Still we got back just in time.

"Now then Mr. Foster what did you infer from that?"

"The pilots had been out on a party with two girls the night before."

"I see. If you thought the party would affect the crew's performance why did you not check what actually happened?"

"Well sir. It is obvious what happened."

"It may be to you Mr. Foster but in fact if you thought it might have had a bearing on the flight don't you think you should have investigated the situation more closely?"

Foster clearly knew he was in deep trouble.

"I suggest to you Mr. Foster that you jumped to a conclusion on the reason for the crash and that you did not investigate what actually happened at all. Mr. Foster, I believe that you have been incredibly slack in the whole of this investigation and your opinion as to the cause cannot be relied on."

"That is not true Sir."

"Well Mr. Foster, we shall be telling the Court in due course what we believe really happened. The Court can then make its mind up how good a job you did."

Foster was clearly very shaken. The counsels for RWA and the British Airline Pilots Association then also re-examined Foster and Foster blustered his way through trying to make the case for pilot error on the approach. The last counsel re-examining Foster was Hull Claims insurance who understandably tried to encourage Foster to rebuild his credibility since Hull Claims had no desire to pay for the whole loss and the claims from the dependants of those killed in the accident. However, Foster was too shattered to be much help to Hull Claims. He left the witness stand looking very worried indeed.

Crowburn then called an AAIB electronics expert who spoke about the instrumentation and when cross-examined by Fairlane agreed that it was surprising that the GESS instrumentation on the recorder did not work but had no ideas why not. Asked about the data on the single MMR database chip, he explained that it might not be possible to extract the necessary data from the chip; they were currently getting the help of Microspot who made the MMR box.

More witnesses gave evidence of the crews licensing and recent flight checks. Lord Justice Thomas decided that it was a good time to break for lunch. Mike and I went to a local pub we knew. Jim Akers had obviously been following us because he arrived about fifteen seconds later. He started questioning me.

"Peter, what do you make of all that. Crowburn and Fairlane have destroyed Foster. I would have thought that no-one would still believe pilot error as the primary cause. McGuire didn't help Foster either."

Chapter 10

For once I decided to keep my mouth shut. All Jim wanted was a story and for all I knew I might be on the witness stand myself later in the afternoon. I just nodded my head. I needed to be careful. We ate our sandwiches without discussing the case too much and returned to the Inquiry. To my surprise I suddenly saw Roger O'Kane being sworn in to give evidence. The Court had clearly decided that it was necessary for them to understand how the automatic landing system worked and how all the flow of information took place. Roger gave a very good account of the system and explained how Royal World Airlines could select either ILS or GESS. I noticed that he did not explain how the other 798s were arranged, nor was he asked. I sent a note to John Fairlane suggesting that he did not expose the differences between the aircraft until I got on the stand.

Roger's evidence took a long time as it was very complicated to anybody new to the various concepts. Only McGuire and to a lesser extent Templeman seemed to understand fully. But of course that was why they were there. The Court adjourned when Roger had finished.

I went up to Roger as we filed out.

"Sorry I did not let you know I was coming, Peter. It all happened rather suddenly, I only got in this morning. I understand you're giving evidence to-morrow?"

"Yes, Roger. I'm rather nervous. I hope I do as well as you. What are you doing this evening?"

"Nothing much. Got any ideas?"

"Why don't we go for a meal somewhere? Mike, care to join us?" I introduced them to one another.

"Sure. Where shall we go."

"Let's go to Langans in Stratton Street. It's not too elaborate or expensive and reasonably quick. Let me check. Mike have you got your phone with you?"

I made the reservation and we agreed to meet Roger at 7.45. Mike and I went back to his office. We picked up an Evening Standard on the way. 'INVESTIGATOR CRITICISED BY COURT' blared the headline. It mentioned that Foster had been asked twice whether he knew how Osborne got hold of the transcript. We agreed that Martin Foster had been roasted by the paper. Mike turned to me.

"Peter, what are you going to say to-morrow? I know Foster has been discredited but things don't look cast iron for us by a long chalk."

I didn't answer the question as I was thinking of Roger's evidence.

"Mike, can I use a computer? I need to send a message to Matt."

"He'll be asleep now."

"I know but I'll back it up with a text message."

I went to the machine Mike pointed at and sent Matt an email and texted him to check his email as soon as he could. Listening to Roger's evidence I had finally realised what must have happened.

"Did you send the message OK, Peter"

"Yes. I've had an idea. The problem with this accident is that nobody wants to say what they actually did." I thought a moment. "If the worst comes to the worst and I'm wrong I do have some ideas to help denigrate the 'pilot error' even more and, of course, I've got some paperwork to prove the GPS change, but I'm not sure that will be good enough."

I broke away and called Liz.

"How did you get on to-day?"

"I got offered two jobs, quite well paid actually. I am seeing another firm and the small specialist firm to-morrow. Any news about my being a witness?"

"Not yet. To-morrow is the critical day. I'll call you this time to-morrow."

"Are you coming round this evening?"

"Not to-night I'm afraid Liz. I'm with Mike getting ready for my evidence to-morrow."

"That's a shame. I was looking forward to seeing you."

"Sorry, Liz. When are you seeing your sister?"

"This week-end. I'm travelling Friday night, back Sunday."

"Well call me if you need me. Otherwise I'll call you to-morrow."

I could see Mike had been listening to our conversation but he said nothing. We reviewed the plan for to-morrow and felt that we were as well prepared as we could be. I called Mandy but she wasn't at home. I told her answer phone that I would be giving evidence to-morrow and hopefully would see her at the Inquiry. Mike and I left for Langans.

We arrived before Roger and ordered ourselves some drinks. Roger arrived about ten minutes later.

"Sorted it all out, Peter?"

"Not exactly. However, I think I may know what probably happened. I'm waiting to hear from NWIA, hopefully to-morrow morning, our time. If I draw a blank, there is not much to go on except hijacker interference and the GPS being faulty. Whatever the primary cause of the accident, it looks as if it could have been avoided if only the pilots could have seen where they were relative to the correct glide slope. On any 798, whether you select ILS, GESS or GPS the pilot can only see the same signals that are going into the auto-pilot. I'm not sure that's a very sound design, if I may say so, Roger."

"Well Peter, I understand what you're saying but it would be extremely difficult to do what you are in effect asking for, that is an entirely independent monitor by the pilots of the aircraft's position on the approach. The ILS is shown as a stand-by as you know."

"Well that's not much use when, as in this case, the ILS was not working."

Roger decided to ignore my remark.

"The Independant solution which we adopted was to make absolutely sure that our system was immaculate and, after looking at it very carefully, the FAA and the EASA accepted our submissions. You remember Peter, I sent you a copy of our extra report on the subject we wrote specifically for the EASA after that new certification engineer said she was unhappy with the system."

"Yes I did get the report but remember I wasn't convinced. However you look at it, something seems to have gone wrong. Perhaps you'll have to look at the system again. Anyway, my immediate problem is to convince the Court that it was not pilot error despite what the AAIB may say and that the Court will have to look for another solution. The professor just loves the software in the Multimode receiver so he won't take much convincing."

"Yes he seems to. It's probably not relevant but I guess the software categorisation by the EASA is going to get some stick."

"You could be right, Roger."

"You know Peter, Foster may have a point. Accepting that the glide slope deviation was central, the Navigation Display should have been showing them as being too low for the distance. Surely they should have spotted something was wrong?"

"But Harry didn't have a display and the first officer distance and height check sounded quite normal. Harry checked the deviation was central as Charles called out the ranges. Anyway to ensure that the display matches the approach aid when GESS or GPS is being used you people make the display agree with the navigation from the approach aid. How would he know something was wrong?"

We gave up and stopped discussing the accident and went on to other things. We broke up at about 11.15 and I walked home from the station. I saw blue police lights flashing as I got close to the house and realised to my horror that it was my house. I went up to one of the policemen who was talking to John Marchant, my neighbor. John introduced me. The policeman took me to the other policeman who seemed to be in charge.

"Central station phoned us about 45 minutes ago. We came straight round. Your front dining room window seems to have been the only entry point. Your next door neighbour here was down as a keyholder so we got him to let us in and cancel the alarm. We've had a look in but nothing much seems to have been touched. Would you like to have a quick look round?"

A Flight Too Far

I went in and looked round the front room. The TV recorder and my silver tray were missing. I wandered into my study/dining room. All the papers in my vertical trays seemed to have gone. Nothing else seemed to have been touched. I called out to the police officer.

I explained what was missing to the policemen.

"Just a straightforward hit and run, Sir. Happens all the time. I guess the burglar could only have been in your house about one minute. He was lucky the neighbours did not catch him though nowadays people are afraid to interfere in case they are knifed or taken to court by the burglar. It's a strange world."

"Sergeant, have you taken any fingerprints?"

"No, Sir."

"Well I think you should. I know the evidence suggests robbery but I've just realised it may not be as simple as that. I am due to give evidence at a big aircraft accident Inquiry to-morrow and all my key papers have been stolen. I think I know a possible suspect so if there are any prints I could suggest a name."

"We don't normally bother too much for this sort of robbery, Sir. It would cost an awful lot of time and money if we took prints every time we had a case like this."

"Well Sergeant I don't want to be difficult but if you don't take prints I shall make a complaint, because this case to-morrow is very important. Perhaps you remember the accident, an aircraft landing in fog just after the Christmas holidays. Hundreds of people killed and injured."

"Of course I remember the accident. We were called in to help control the traffic. I read about the Inquiry this evening in the Standard. The accident investigator got rather a hard time didn't he? Alright Sir, let me call my Inspector and get permission."

He wandered outside and took out his phone. He was back in two minutes.

"Yes, Sir. That's fine, we'll have the fingerprints man round in half an hour. I'll leave you now if I may. There's not much more I can do. I'm on duty all night. If there are prints I'll let you know and you had better tell me who you suspect. Meanwhile try not to touch anything." He added as an afterthought "I think we've found your TV recorder outside on the grass with your silver tray. You may be right about the robbery motive, Sir. Perhaps you had better give me the name of the person you think might have broken in."

I gave him Martin Foster's name. I explained the background as briefly as I could and told him to contact me through Mike to-morrow if necessary or ring the Inquiry Hall.

The finger print man duly arrived. He took my prints and then he went into the dining room and living room.

Chapter 10

"I've found some good prints in the living room. Your cleaner must do a good job as there are very few prints. I also found some prints on the window catch. I'll be on my way."

The fingerprint man left me and I found a large piece of cardboard in the garage which I cut and fitted to the broken window.

If it was Martin he must have been desperate. In fact if it was Martin he had been incredibly lucky to be able to get the papers and even luckier because I had no immediate copies. It was entirely my own fault which always made matters worse. I supposed I could get some replacements but it would take time since most would have to come from Australia. It occurred to me that I could get some from Anne Moncrieff. But the whole thing made me look so inefficient. There was nothing else for it, I called Matt in Australia and was lucky enough to catch him. I explained my predicament.

"Well I'll try to fax you and send you copies of the technical logs for the two nights in question in the next day or so. I am just going into a meeting with my MD and I am going to run out of time. I will also send you copies of the stores issuing certificates for the two GPS sets, the Navigation Display and the Multi mode Receiver. I got your email yesterday and I shall be talking to Lance but goodness knows when. If anything comes out of it I will contact you."

"Matt, I really need all the paperwork for the Inquiry. And I need you to talk to Lance very urgently. Can you email the info as well? And text me."

"I'll do what I can."

Feeling very depressed I got to bed at about 1.30 and managed to sleep until 6.30. I called Mandy who I knew would be getting up.

"Hello Mandy. I'm in trouble."

For once Mandy didn't make the obvious retort. She must have sensed I was really in difficulty.

"What's happened, darling."

"I was robbed last night. I think it must be Foster. The only things that have gone are all the papers on my desk which I need for to-day."

Mandy was super. She didn't say 'I told you so.' She was straight to the point.

"You're right. Sounds like Martin Foster though surely he did not believe he would really gain anything. Poor chap, he must be desperate."

"That's what I told the sergeant. They found some prints. What am I going to do?"

"You are going to get dressed as quickly as you can and meet me for breakfast at that café opposite the Inquiry hall. Don't worry darling. I may be able to help you."

A Flight Too Far

CHAPTER 11

It was all very well for Mandy to tell me not to worry but I was panic stricken. Before leaving I copied down the number of my local odd job man so I could get the glass repaired as quickly as possible. I didn't think he would thank me if I called him at 6.45. I took my briefcase with me but I was woefully short of papers.

I got to the cafe at 8.30 a.m. and found Mandy already there reading the paper with a coffee in front of her, looking very smart, relaxed and without a care in the world.

"I don't believe it. How long have you been here? I can't believe you could have been so quick. You look magnificent."

She looked pleased.

"Well I managed to save time getting ready at home by not having breakfast. I was able to catch the earlier train. Have you read the papers?"

"Not properly. To be honest I'm too worried about losing the papers I need for the Court. I did notice they seem to have given Foster a roasting. The Secretary of State will have to make some changes at the AAIB I should think when all this is over."

"Well settle down. You've got a long day ahead of you and you must have something to eat."

She beckoned the waiter over and we both ordered orange juice, scrambled egg, toast, marmalade and coffee, not that I felt like anything to eat. While we were waiting she opened her brief case and gave me a large envelope. I opened it and saw all the papers that had been stolen. I was speechless.

"You are a miracle worker. How did you get these? Did you steal them?"

"Peter, don't be stupid. You must be worried. Look again."

I did and noticed that the papers Mandy had given to me were copies, not the rather creased documents that had been in my tray on the desk.

"How did you get these copies, Mandy?"

"All very simple, my dear. When I went round to your house to collect my dress I decided the time had come to make copies of your papers which you seemed to like spreading, like confetti, all over your study. You know I didn't like the way you kept them in that stacked set of baskets on your desk. I took the papers to that place on the corner near the station, made two sets of copies, put one back in your tray, put the other set in my bag and then put the originals in our office safe."

She looked very smug.

"I could kiss you."

"Well you'll have to wait a moment while I conduct an investigation. Where were you last night? I called, ready perhaps to offer you a hope that sometime I might be ready to forgive you and you were out. I tried your mobile but there was no reply. I don't have to tell you where I thought you might be. I rang Mike to get Liz's number but he wasn't in the office or at home."

It was my turn to look smug.

"Serve you right. We wouldn't have answered anyway. We were having an orgy" Mandy started to rise. "All three of us. We went to Langans. Roger O'Kane the Independant man who had just given evidence, Mike and I. If you'd called me later you could have spoken to the policeman investigating the robbery and my next door neighbour as well as me."

"Alright then, you may kiss me."

I did as instructed.

"Do you think I should have the originals?"

"I'm having them sent over this morning."

"You seem to have thought of everything."

Mandy beamed. Our breakfast arrived and we glanced at the papers again.

"I see you're giving evidence to-day according to the FT."

"Trust Jim to get a plug in as well as a good story."

"Possibly. I almost feel sorry for Foster. He must have some real problem if it was him."

"Well, I suppose we'd better be getting over the road. At least we don't have to queue for seats. Look at that line over there. It must be more popular than that latest Lloyd Webber musical."

"That's only because the seats are free."

After we crossed the road Mandy stopped.

"Peter. I am sorry I'm being so touchy. I love being with you and everything. But I am nervous about the Diana situation. It could ruin our lives and, as for Liz," She smiled up at me "I'm suspicious as hell and probably jealous."

She gave me an apologetic kiss.

"Have a nice day, my darling."

We signed in and separated after agreeing to meet outside for lunch. I waited outside as the hall filled up. The press were there in force. Chuck came up to me and I pitched in to him.

"You know Chuck you have almost certainly ruined a man's career tempting him with money."

Chuck flushed.

"You've got that wrong. He was desperate to get some money."

Chapter 11

I turned away, my suspicions confirmed. Spot on time my name was called. It was quite a sight, very different from the previous days. Every seat was taken and the press benches seemed overflowing. I went to the witness box and was sworn in. John Fairlane got to his feet. Everyone was looking our way.

John got me to explain to the Court my background, my electronic engineering degree, my years as a pilot with Britannia. He got me to relate my subsequent specialisation on the interface between the flight crew and the modern computer controlled flight deck, with all the very sophisticated electronic displays integrating the enormous amount of information that the pilot had to assimilate.

"Mr. Talbert you are an expert in your field? You are on the Society of Automotive Engineers S7 Flight Deck Committee?"

"In that very narrow area of expertise I suppose I am well known in the industry."

"Come on, Mr. Talbert. Airlines round the world get you to help with crew training. You are respected as an expert."

"If you say so."

John got me to explain how I got involved with Golf Hotel. The call from John Chester, the call from an old friend whose husband was fatally injured, the call from Mike Mansell asking me to help establish the cause of the accident.

"Mr. Talbert, I think you need to make your position absolutely plain. Mr. Mansell asked you to help because his firm was at risk financially if the cause of the accident was found to be pilot error. What did you say to him?"

"I told him that I would be pleased to help with the investigation but I was only interested in finding out the truth, pilot error or no pilot error. However, I felt that the hijacking had almost certainly been the most likely cause of the accident either directly, or indirectly by having caused the pilots to make a mistake."

"Mr. Talbert. You've heard the voice recorder and have read the transcript? Have you any comments?"

"Yes Sir. I believe that AAIB have written down what was on the recording that they have. However, I believe the recording they have is not the genuine recording. In my judgement certain parts of the original recording have been removed in making the AAIB recording, presumably for security purposes and, of course, this makes it difficult to assess the real cause of the accident."

There was complete silence and then a buzz went round the room. I looked at Lord Justice Thomas. If it was possible for a Judge to look uncertain, he looked uncertain. It occurred to me that John must have been a bit surprised but he was the supreme professional.

"Mr. Talbert, have you thought through what you are saying? This is a very serious allegation."

"Certainly, Sir."

"Why do you make this allegation?"

"Well Sir, I noticed that the Prime Minister in his original broadcast on the morning after the tragedy referred to two passengers being killed. None of that information was on the AAIB transcript. The next thing I noticed was that the Secretary of State also referred to 'two hijackers being on the flight deck'. The Government clearly knew more than the AAIB. And there was another thing I noticed."

"Go on, Mr. Talbert."

"The Chief Steward could be heard acknowledging that there had been a hijack. I wondered why, if his voice could be heard, nobody else's could."

"Mr. Talbert, all this seems a rather wild accusation. What do you suggest happened?"

"Well Sir, as you know the crash recorder with all the flight parameters was found very quickly but I was surprised that the cockpit voice recorder took so long to be found so…"

That was as far as I got. Lord Justice Thomas spoke to the Clerk of the Court who immediately announced that the Inquiry was adjourned for an hour. The room was to be cleared. Fairlane was told to meet the judge in his chambers. I was told to wait. The place was in an uproar and in the confusion I went over to Mike. Mandy came over with a worried look.

"Peter, you've really done it this time. You are the complete limit. You'll be sent to the Tower. I can't believe what you're implying actually happened. The Government couldn't have been that stupid."

"Well, the security people had plenty of time to hear the recording and doctor it and remember, it was the security people who 'found' the voice recorder the following night." I pondered for a moment. "You know it has been said that Governments seem to have a sublime belief in their own infallibility. I suppose they feel that what they do must be right by definition and, anyway, they believe that maintaining security gives them complete cover to do anything they like."

John Fairlane came over.

"I shall be disbarred. Thomas said I should have warned him."

"What did you say?"

"'How could I, my Lord? I had no idea what he was going to say.'"

"Did he believe you?"

"I'm not sure. You've put him in a real fix."

"Why?"

"My guess is that he was given a full copy of the transcript but he was told not to use it because of the security implications, unless he felt

284

that AAIB really needed the recording to get the right solution. Now he's caught with egg on his face."

Mike could not contain himself.

"He's got egg on his face? Think about the Government."

All of a sudden the Inquiry was reconvened and everybody trooped back. The press seats were full to bursting. Lord Justice Thomas made a statement.

"The Court has received a transcript which purports to be the unexpurgated version of the voice recorder flight deck microphone recording. The Inquiry will go in to private session to establish the authenticity of this transcript and to establish why there was a difference between the original recording available to the AAIB and this latest transcript. However to try to save time, the AAIB and expert witnesses will be able to read the new transcript. Will Counsel please advise the Clerk of the Court if they believe they have witnesses that need to read the full transcript."

It took an hour before the private proceedings to read the transcript started; presumably copies had to be made and Lord Justice Thomas must have been considering how he was going to explain the arrival of the new transcript. There were just a few of us present, Furness, Foster, myself, Roger O'Kane and John Chester plus our respective counsels. John Fairlane got up and made a submission

"Mr. Talbert advises me that for the Court to get a true appreciation of the pressures which the crew were under it is necessary to actually hear the recording and not read the transcript."

The judge turned to Janet Crowburn.

"I agree with Mr. Talbert, my Lord."

"Very well. I had rather anticipated this request. I understand that if you are prepared to listen from a loudspeaker rather than headphones we can start in a few minutes. I am told that the recording is like the earlier recording that AAIB produced, it skips the parts where there is no talking. If you want to hear the full two hour recording then I suggest we adjourn until after lunch and go to the Treasury Solicitors Offices where they can arrange a room with the necessary number of headphones for the experts."

Fairlane looked to me and I suggested to John that we heard the abbreviated recording now and then decide what to do. Lord Justice Thomas agreed and we settled down to hear the recording. There was a steady whine behind all the conversation which gave no doubt as to the realism of the recording. The quality was very clear.

"Charles, did you speak with Eva. Was she awake?"

"You bet. She was fine."

"She's a lovely girl. Bursting with energy. Time you settled down."

"We'll see. That was a great evening we had at Maroubra with those two. I like that beach, and Caesars."

"Yes, I could see that. We certainly got through the wine. Well you and the girls did."

"I enjoyed the swim as well."

"Just as well it was warm or you both would have frozen."

"You're a fine one to talk. I'm afraid I didn't get a lot of sleep. Did you have a good time, Harry?"

"Very quiet, thank you."

"That's what they all say."

"Still, we got back just in time."

Air Traffic came in with a call for RWA 573 which Charles answered. There was no further reference to the girls. I heard Harry asking Dick if he was OK; presumably Dick Tremlett the off-duty Captain was watching from the jump seat. We then heard the noise of the crew door being operated.

"Captain. May I come in for a moment."

There was a thump and a new voice was heard.

"Captain, if you want to keep alive you will do exactly as I say. I have a special small pistol here and I will not hesitate to use it if you do not do exactly as I say. My colleague over there has his pistol next to the neck of your other pilot. We have two more people at the back of the flight deck here with your spare pilots and the Minister. We also have two more people preventing access from the rest of the aircraft. We have shut the door so no-one can now get in.

"You will announce to the passengers that the aircraft has been hijacked but that we are going to land as planned at Heathrow. No-one will be hurt if everyone carries on normally."

"What is your name, Sir?" I recognised Harry's voice, very calm.

"What does that matter?"

"It will be easier for me to talk to you if I know how you wish to be addressed."

"Call me Ahmed. Get on with the announcement, Captain."

We could just hear Harry make the announcement talking into his microphone.

"Now Captain, you are to tell Air Traffic that the aircraft has been taken over and that, after landing, you are to stop on the runway and be refuelled for Karachi. Wait, Captain. You will say that if the aircraft is not allowed to proceed after landing at Heathrow then passengers will be killed starting with the Foreign Secretary. If there is any delay greater than thirty minutes the aircraft will be blown up."

"Ahmed, we are out of range of London Air Traffic. I will have to call our airline operations."

286

Chapter 11

"Very well, Captain. You may do that."

We heard Harry passing this information to RWA Operations.

"Captain, you will call them now and ask them to arrange not only refuelling to Karachi but the necessary turn around facilities. No-one is to come on board the aircraft unless I have authorized it. In addition here is a message you are to read out and which they must repeat back to you, word for word."

"RWA Ops, this is 573."

"Go ahead, 573."

"As you are aware we have been hijacked. Please arrange for the aircraft to be turned around and refuelled for Karachi. No-one is to come on board the aircraft unless authorized. Assume the same passenger and freight load as we have inbound. I am to advise you that if the aircraft is not allowed to take-off after landing at Heathrow then passengers will be killed starting with the Foreign Secretary of State. If there is any delay greater than thirty minutes the aircraft will be blown up."

"Copied 573."

"I have been told to read out the following message. Please copy it down and read it back, word for word."

"Go ahead, 573"

"Operations from 573, the hijackers have asked me to read the following message to be given to the Prime Minister. 'When the aircraft lands the following six prisoners are to be taken from prison and brought to the aircraft." The list of the six al-Qaeda names followed. *"The prisoners will be loaded on to the aircraft at the front Upper Deck entrance, the aircraft will be refuelled and then the aircraft will take-off for Karachi. Any delay greater than thirty minutes will result in first, the killing of the Foreign Secretary, and then by the blowing up of the aircraft."*

RWA read Harry's message back.

"Captain, tell them to let you know when the fuel is ready. Also when the prisoners will be at the aircraft."

"Operations, please advise when refuelling is ready. The hijackers wish to know. Also when the prisoners will be at the aircraft."

"573, will advise."

"Ahmed. We have hundreds of people on this plane. They will know some thing is wrong. I must reassure them if they are not to panic. The cabin staff must look after them. I need to talk to my chief steward before I talk to the passengers."

"Captain, is this a trick?"

"Ahmed. I am in no position to trick you. I want to give instructions to prevent the passengers getting out of control. May I ask for the Chief Steward to come here?"

"Very well."

"Would the Chief Steward come to the flight deck."

Presumably this was an announcement on the passenger address.

"Captain Hodgson?"

"Andrew, you are aware we've been hijacked?"

"Yes Captain. There appears to be two dead men in the front upper cabin who may have been the security guards for the Secretary of State. I think they've been shot in the head but the bullet wounds are very peculiar."

"Don't touch the bodies but cover them with blankets. Can you move the passengers that are next to them?"

"Luckily they were on the front row with the Foreign Secretary who is now in the flight deck rest area. The rest of the passengers are in the rows behind."

"Good. I want you to carry on the rest of the flight with your cabin staff as normally as possible. I shall make an announcement on the PA."

"Very good, Captain."

"Ladies and Gentleman. This is Captain Hodgson speaking. As I announced earlier, I regret to inform you that we have been hijacked. We shall refuel and then fly to Karachi. We do not know whether anyone will be allowed to disembark in London.

"Please obey the instructions from our cabin staff and we will try to make the rest of the flight as normal as possible. I will keep you informed at all times. Thank you."

"Harry," it was Charles talking, *"Shall I get the latest weather?"*

"Go ahead."

There was a pause. They must have switched the speakers off as we could not hear the weather being transmitted by the ATIS, the transmissions were going straight into the headphones.

"Harry," it was Charles again *"that's real Cat 3B weather. Manchester is clear anyway if we need to divert."*

"Captain, why can't I hear the ground talking to us?"

"Ahmed we are not allowed to use loudspeakers when landing."

"Captain, turn them back on immediately or I will fire."

That seemed rather an idle threat to me but clearly Harry hadn't argued.

"573 from Operations, we've checked your fuel from your ACARS transmission and you are cleared to overfly Frankfurt and land at Heathrow with Manchester as your diversion."

"573 copied."

"Captain."

"Yes Ahmed."

"Is the weather alright for landing in London?"

Chapter 11

"Yes Ahmed. The weather is foggy but we carry blind landing equipment."

"Is that safe?"

"Completely."

"Is the fuel ready?"

"Operations, this is 573. Have you arranged the refuelling?"

"We're still doing that. You are being refuelled by tankers instead of by hydrants on the stands and we are making sure that they have enough fuel for Karachi and that they can get to your parking position on the runway."

"573 understood."

"Captain, what are they doing?"

"Ahmed, they have to refuel the aircraft from tankers if we are to remain on the runway."

"Captain, are the prisoners ready at the airport?"

"RWA Ops This is 573. I have been asked to establish whether the prisoners have been released and are waiting at the airport?"

"573 please stand by. Will advise."

"Captain, remind the ground that we shall blow the aircraft up if there are any delays to our instructions."

"RWA Ops I have been told to remind you that the hijackers are going to blow up the aircraft if there is any delay to their instructions which I passed to you."

"573 This is RWA Ops Copied."

There was no answer so presumably the answer was satisfactory to the hijackers. The flight proceeded with very little other conversation. The aircraft crossed into UK airspace and was cleared to descend. Charles called out the descent checks and then the checks for an auto-landing. Air Traffic slowly permitted the aircraft to reduce altitude in stages. Then we heard the weather being broadcast on the VOR. Ceiling indeterminate, visibility 30 metres.

"Director Royal 573 reaching 4,000."

"Roger Cleared procedural GESS final approach 27 left"

"Royal 573 we'd prefer the ILS"

"Sorry Royal 573 the ATIS is incorrect. The ILS is no longer approved for Cat 3B approaches and is out of service. What are your intentions?"

Harry could be heard speaking to Charles.

"Charles, did you know about the ILS?"

"Yes Harry. This means we won't be able to monitor the approach path on GESS."

"Well that is not a requirement. The GESS is self monitored to death." A pause. *"Charles, you had better set 27L into the MMRs for the GESS."*

"Yes Harry, have just done that."

"OK. Then you can select the Galileo system for the approach."

"Royal 573 Request GESS approach 27 Left."

"You are cleared for GESS approach cleared to descend on the procedure. Maintain heading and call the Tower on 118.5"

"118.5 Royal 573"

Harry was obviously slightly concerned and spoke to Charles again.

"Charles that is permitted, isn't it?"

"Yes Harry providing the GELAS is OK."

"We've got no warning so it must be OK."

We heard the landing checks being carried out and then they were cleared to the final approach altitude. Harry told Charles to keep an eye on the Navigation Display as he needed to keep his display showing the Primary Flight Display most of the time.

"Tower Royal 573 ten miles 27 Left. Confirm GELAS OK."

"Royal 573 hello. You are clear to land 27 left, wind calm RVR 20, 30,20 GELAS showing OK"

"Roger Royal 573"

Harry said they were now on the glide slope and Charles was calling out the altitude from the radio altimeter, and the distance to go, presumably from the Navigation Display.

Ahmed   *"Captain, I can't see the ground. Is this a trick."*

Harry   *"Ahmed, shut up. I told you its very foggy. You'll kill us all if you don't stop talking."*

Charles *"800 ft. you are showing slightly right, but on glide slope."*

Harry: *"OK, I'm central on the glide slope. You check the approach on your Navigational Display. I'll keep my display in the Primary Flight Display mode. The rate of descent seems rather high. We must have a tail wind."*

Harry was clearly missing his Navigational display.

Harry: *"Heathrow Tower RWA 573 please check wind speed".*

We heard no reply.

Charles: *"two miles, 600 ft. on centre line"*

Tower *"573 from Tower, the wind is calm."*

Ahmed: *"Captain what's happening. I can't see the ground."*

He sounded worried

Harry: *"Ahmed, use your pistol or be quiet."*

Charles: *"one mile, 300 ft on centre line"*

Radio Altimeter   *"200"*

Radio Altimeter   *"100"*

Chapter 11

Harry:	*"I can't see the loom of the lights yet"*
Harry	*"Still on glide slope"*
Charles	*"On centre line"*
Ahmed:	*"What's happening."*
Harry:	*"For Christ's sake shut up"*
Harry	*"Still can't see the ground"*
Ahmed:	*"Captain, tell me what's going on."*
Ahmed:	*"Stop at once."*
Radio Altimeter	*"50"*
Radio Altimeter	*"30"*

Harry: *"there's something wrong with the lights, I'm going around."*

Radio Altimeter   *"20"*

A moment later with this clear recording the engines could be heard increasing power. Harry's yells were horrifying.

Harry:	*"Oh my God, we're hitting the road"*
Heathrow:	*"573 you appear to be"*

The recording stopped and I looked around. Everybody looked very shaken. Nobody said anything for a bit. I whispered to John that he needed to recall Furness and ask for his opinion of carrying out an approach with such interference from the hijackers. I also told him that I personally didn't think we needed to listen to the full two hour recording at the moment, but we should keep that as a possibility. However, we certainly needed the transcript with time added. The Counsels had a conference with the Court. It was decided that the Inquiry would remain in private session to discuss the authenticity of the new transcript and reconvene after lunch in open session when I would continue to give my evidence. However the full transcript would not be given out but the interruptions below 800 ft. would be added to the existing transcript. I couldn't be bothered to argue since I was pretty sure the media would sort it all out and force the rest of the recordings from the Secretary of State.

I could not believe the time. I got up and made my way to the door but I could see the press making a beeline for me. John Fairlane pulled me back and indicated I should follow him

"You'd better not appear at the front or you will get submerged by the media. Let's see if we can find another way out."

We escaped by a side door. Mandy had been watching and found us outside a few seconds later.

"How did you find us?"

"Peter, I work round here."

We set course away from the building. I had left my coat with Mike so I was freezing. Mandy had brought her coat with her. John made his excuses and disappeared. We took a taxi to Covent Garden and disappeared into one of the many small cafes.

Mandy looked at me.

"You've got yourself a problem, Peter, the way you've carried on. You're going to be front page news for the next day or so and the media will be after you. They'll want you to appear on TV. You had better make your mind up what you want to do."

"You know I don't like the media. They twist every word to get a story."

"Well you had better come home with me to-night. We can use the same escape route and then go to the station."

"Sounds a great idea."

"Now don't get any ideas. It will be a house of convenience, not of ill repute."

"Anything you say, Ms Arrowsmith. Please excuse me, I've just remembered I must organise a replacement window."

I called my building man and asked him to organise a replacement double glazing unit as quickly as possible. He had been listening to the one o'clock news.

"Are you the Mr. Talbert they are all talking about?"

"Yes I am, but don't tell anyone."

My mobile phone vibrated. There was a text message from Matt.

'Peter, you were quite right. I spoke to Lance and he told me the whole story. Sending fax and email to Mike. Good Luck.'

We had left Mike in the Inquiry hall, presumably he must have gone to his office. I called him.

"Peter, I've got an email with some attachments from Matt. Do you need them?"

"Mike, have you looked at them? I needed them weeks ago."

The first editions of the Evening Standard were out with 'COURT HAD TRUE CRASH RECORDING' on front page and the article describing how I had proved the AAIB recording had been rigged, presumably by Government Security experts, and that Lord Justice Thomas had the real recording all the time. We had a quick sandwich and caught a cab back to the Inquiry. Luckily we had timed it well as the Court was due to start again and the media were all inside. Mike was waiting with John Fairlane.

"Peter, these extra papers from NWIA. Are they good news? Can you manage without a recess?"

"I think so John. If I get into difficulties then you had better explain the short notice to the Court and get one."

The Court reconvened and Lord Justice Thomas announced that the Court had decided that the new recording and transcript from the voice recorder was authentic. John Fairlane then reminded me I was still under oath.

"Mr. Talbert, you have now heard the full recording. How does it differ from the AAIB transcript?"

"The conversations with the hijackers are quite clear. The main hijacker was interrupting the crew all the way down the approach."

"In your opinion would it be possible for the crew to carry out an approach in the freezing fog with that level of interruption."

"Not safely. It would be impossible to monitor everything, particularly with only one Navigation Display."

"Now then Mr. Talbert, the crew were carrying out a GESS approach. Do you have any comments?"

"The GELAS data being transmitted to the crew should have been checked immediately after the crash. Also the runway data should have been checked in the MMR databases. However, neither of those omissions was the reason for the crash."

There was a complete silence in the hall and then an air of expectancy from the press rows.

"Mr. Talbert, that's an extraordinary statement. Do you think you know the explanation for this terrible accident? Wasn't the distraction from the hijackers the explanation?"

"In my opinion the distraction made the crash inevitable but it was not the primary cause."

"Would you please tell us what you believe caused the accident? Please start at the beginning of your investigations."

"Well Sir, I was never happy from the moment I heard the edited recording. Captain Hodgson said he was on the glide slope when his co-pilot was reading out the ranges from his Navigation Display. They matched up perfectly."

"Matched up?"

"Very roughly the aircraft loses 300 ft. per mile on a standard 3° glide slope. So when the co-pilot called one mile range the aircraft should have been at 300 ft. and we know that it wasn't from the evidence of the air traffic controller. Clearly the range on the navigation display was wrong. AAIB seemed to have accepted that the GESS calculated glide slope was wrong but failed to realise that the Navigation Display range was incorrect as well. Consequently, the pilots were misled. The challenge was to find why the electronics were wrong."

"How did you manage to do that, Mr. Talbert."

"Well I suspected that the problem was caused, like most accidents, by a combination of faults. With the help of an avionics expert who gave me some supporting documents, I had already identified a design feature which was undesirable. The expert gave me some papers which explain the point." I gave the material which Anne Moncrieff had given me to one of the Court's officials.

"Are you going to tell us what you both felt was undesirable?"

"In a moment Sir. My problem at the time was to find what else had gone wrong."

I explained how I rang Bill Baker to find out what maintenance had been carried out by NWIA on Golf Hotel and how Bill had offered me a training job which I accepted straightaway. Going to Australia gave me an opportunity to make some investigations myself, since I did not believe the reports that came out in the press about the pilots having been to a party the night before the flight. I told how I found out that Tumbrill had been friendly with a girl and how I had managed to find out the girl's room mate. I skated over my investigations as delicately as I could, telling the Court how horrified I was when I discovered that Tumbrill's girl friend had been killed in the accident. John explored this in detail.

"Mr. Talbert, let me understand this situation. Tumbrill's girl friend, a trainee stewardess, was actually on the fatal flight? Her name was 'Eva'?"

"Yes, sir. That's quite right."

"So the quote about 'did you speak with Eva' in the recorder transcript could have meant that Captain Hodgson was asking if Tumbrill had gone in to the back of the aircraft and spoken to his girl friend?"

I could feel the hall listening to my every word.

"Yes, that is exactly what I believe it did mean. As a result of my conversation with Miss Ward, Eva's room mate, it was clear that the four of them had gone out to dinner two evenings before the fateful flight. In fact I discovered that Miss Ward had spoken to Captain Hodgson to thank him for the dinner the night following, that is the night before the flight, and spoke to him in his room at 8 o'clock."

"You must have read the papers and know the interpretation put on that snatch of conversation. Do you have any comments?"

"Only that the conversation was clearly misunderstood and shows the danger of letting transcripts of voice recordings get in to the public domain."

"Mr. Talbert did you learn anything else from Miss Ward."

"Miss Ward worked in Royal World Airlines flight Operations department at Sydney so she met all the flight crews. She told me that on the night following the dinner with Hodgson and Tumbrill, Eva and she had a long standing arrangement to go out to dinner with the back-up crew which had just brought Golf Hotel to Sydney. Miss Ward had wanted to cancel the dinner but apparently Eva felt it would be rude to cancel at such short notice. The crew arrived and immediately called NWIA maintenance about some problem with the Global Positioning

System and the Captain called a senior pilot in England to describe the fault."

There was a murmur in the audience. I could see that this information was being copied at length by the press.

"Can you tell us what was the nature of the fault that caused a conversation with Royal World Airlines headquarters?"

"Well, Sir, may I first expand on what the Independant electronics witness said yesterday. He explained the avionic architecture of the Royal World Airlines 798. What he did not explain was the fact that the RWA 798 design is different from all other 798s because it has a different GPS box."

Again I could see the press writing away. I went on to explain the concept of GPS and how it could be used as a landing aid under some circumstances with all 798s except the Royal World Airlines 798s and that for this to be possible there had to be three GPS cards within the GPS box and not just one. I explained that to use the system as a landing aid there had to be a local system, LAAS, at each airport if Cat 3 approaches were to be carried out. I then told how I contacted Captain Robson to find out exactly what was the fault they had on Golf Hotel and who he telephoned.

"The fault was that there was a warning of failure of the No. 2 GPS card and of course, as I have just explained, the RWA aircraft only has one GPS card. His story in fact did not completely surprise me because I had already spoken to the mechanic in NWIA who had changed the GPS on Golf Hotel that night. He had done a straight swap of GPS boxes checking that the part number of the box he put in was the same as the part number of the one he took out. However I had noticed that a week or so earlier Golf Hotel had had a previous GPS fault and the GPS box had been changed by a less meticulous mechanic. The box taken out was a RWA GPS box with a single GPS card, the box the mechanic put in was an NWIA GPS box with three GPS cards."

There was a buzz of excitement. Lord Justice Thomas came in.

"Mr. Talbert this is all very interesting but we are talking about a GESS approach aren't we? NWIA may have fitted the wrong GPS box but what has this got to do with the accident?"

"You are quite right, my Lord, but irregular maintenance in the system we are looking at cannot be ignored. We now know that the NWIA engineer who fitted the box the night before the aircraft took off did a very thorough check of the system. It was true he had fitted the wrong box but he had not been trained on the Royal World Airlines avionic fit, he just swapped identical boxes. However, being a first class mechanic he did the full check on the new box he had fitted and he discovered that it was not possible to carry out a GPS approach as laid down in the maintenance manual for the NWIA aircraft. He noticed that the approach selector switch on the RWA aircraft wouldn't select GPS but only ILS and GESS. So he got another three position switch out of the NWIA stores, fitted it, and everything then checked out correctly with the NWIA maintenance manual."

Templeman broke in.

"Mr. Talbert, that's all very interesting but why would it cause the accident?"

"Well Sir, the RWA aircraft approach selector switch is wired so that only ILS or GESS can be selected. All other 798s have a three position switch to permit ILS, GESS or GPS to be selected for landing. The vertical and right hand position of the switch selects GESS for the RWA aircraft. For all other aircraft the vertical position selects GPS and the right hand position GESS. What no-one had anticipated was that this change could be done during routine maintenance."

John Fairlane took over again.

"Mr. Talbert, you have explained to us what you believe happened the night before the last flight. Would you now go on and explain the accident?"

"Well Sir, everything happened exactly as has been described by Mr. Foster but, when Captain Hodgson selected a GESS approach, he was in reality selecting a GPS approach. Unfortunately, although there is a Local Area Augmentation System installed for Heathrow to correct the GPS inaccuracies, at the moment the LAAS does not work well enough to ensure an automatic landing and so Cat 3 approaches using GPS are not permitted for the US carriers using the airport. Because of the incorrect switch, Golf Hotel instead of doing a GESS approach on 27 Left actually made a GPS approach and crashed because the accuracy of the GPS system was not good enough."

Again there was a buzz around the room. The press were working overtime.

"Mr. Talbert, surely the crew should have noticed that they were below the glide slope?"

"No Sir, with respect that's not so. You may remember that I referred earlier to an unsatisfactory design feature. On all 798s the pilots only see the signal that is being used to drive the auto-pilot. If the pilots have ILS selected then they see the ILS deviation. If they have GPS selected, as in this case, they would see the deviation as calculated by the Multimode Receivers using the GPS position which, at London, we know is not accurate enough. The aircraft does have an ILS indicator as a back-up but, of course, in this case the ILS was out of service. I support Mme Moncrieff in her criticism of the 798 certification by EASA. I believe that aircraft that carry as many passengers as the 798 should be certificated to a higher standard than aircraft with fewer passengers. The whole safety standard of these very larger aircraft needs reviewing, not only in design but also in operation.

"In my opinion the pilots flew centrally down a GPS calculated glide slope which was hopelessly inaccurate and took them straight into the ground. The pilots had no independent view of the aircraft's vertical position relative to the runway.

"In the case of GESS, as Mr. Foster of the AAIB tried to explain, the Navigation Display would show fairly accurate distance from the runway touchdown point. In the case of a GPS approach the information would not be accurate because the LAAS was not accurate enough. On the recorder transcript we can see that they were checking the range and were checking not only that they were on the glide slope but that they were at the right height for the distance being displayed. At 100 ft. Captain Hodgson said that the aircraft was on the glide slope. No crew could do more."

I could see that my point had got home to the press but McGuire couldn't restrain himself any longer.

"Mr. Talbert you claim to be an expert. I have to say it all sounds very fanciful. Don't you think it is far more likely that there was something wrong with the GESS software or database and the hijackers prevented the pilots realising what was happening."

"Well Sir, it could be. Of course proper checks need to be carried out as soon as possible to find out if the GELAS transmitter was transmitting the correct navigational information to enable a GESS to be carried out and also whether the runway 27 Left information was correct in the database. However, I found it very interesting that Mr. Foster yesterday said that they couldn't get information from the GESS recordings. I believe Sir, that this was because the instrumentation could only work if the aircraft was fitted with the correct equipment and the correct approach selector switch. It is very probable that the instrumentation would not work with the wrong approach switch fitted."

I could see that I had scored a point. Certainly the press thought so but McGuire persevered.

"Have you any paperwork at all to support your theory?"

"Yes Sir. I have the technical log page for the first GPS swap. I also have the NWIA spares issuing slip for that night showing that the GPS fitted was not an RWA GPS but a NWIA GPS. There is of course no maintenance page for the critical night but I have two spares issuing slips, one for the GPS showing it was a NWIA spare and I now have just received one from NWIA confirming the wrong approach selector switch was fitted.

"Captain Robson will be able to confirm the fact that there was a No. 2 GPS fault and Mr. Roger O'Kane will be able to confirm that the aircraft would work as I have described with the equipment that NWIA fitted. Presumably it will be possible at some stage to take evidence from the NWIA mechanic who fitted the wrong switch. Unfortunately he is not here to-day. In addition it might be useful to confirm with Mr. O'Kane that the GESS recorder information would not have worked on Golf Hotel with the wrong GPS box and approach switch fitted."

McGuire seemed satisfied and John Fairland got ready to resume the questioning. I looked at him.

"There is one other thing."

John looked at me suspiciously.

"Yes Mr. Talbert?"

"I found this rotary switch in a pile of discarded scrap in the Farnborough hangar."

"Shouldn't you have given it to the AAIB team?"

"Yes Sir, I should, but they were regarding this switch as scrap and I was afraid it might not get fully investigated. It's very battered with wires hanging off it as you can see. Luckily I found a stores reference number on it but I have not had time to ask Independant to check it out. I believe this switch may be the approach selector switch, and that this switch is not used in the RWA fleet."

Lord Justice Thomas came in.

"Mr. Talbert your evidence is remarkable and almost incredible. Can you sum up for us how you believe this accident was possible?"

"Yes My Lord, I will try. Because aviation is so safe, accidents these days are always a collection of unexpected occurrences, all happening at the same time. In my opinion this accident happened firstly because the mechanics had only received training on their own airline's equipment, secondly because it was possible to change the aircraft modification standard during routine maintenance and thirdly because the pilots were receiving the same information as the auto-pilot. Had the GPS system been accurate when used with the LAAS system at Heathrow of course all would have been well, even though GPS was being used, but unfortunately it wasn't. The crew thought everything was alright because they could see they were on the centre line on the Navigation Display and the glide slope deviation was zero but it was a synthetic glide slope and it was not accurate enough using GPS as the sensor because of the innaccurate system. As with most accidents these days, it only happened because there were a chapter of earlier mistakes and, possibly, a deficiency in the certification requirements."

John came back in.

Chapter 11

"One final question Mr. Talbert. In your opinion were the crew to blame in any way for what happened to flight RWA 573."

"No Sir. Any chance they might have had of seeing something was wrong was almost certainly ruined by the presence of the hijackers."

"Thank you."

John Fairlane sat down. Janet Crowburn got up.

"Mr. Talbert. You've told us an extraordinary tale. If the accident happened as you say, how do you explain that the AAIB did not discover it? Don't you think it more likely that the AAIB would find the true cause rather than you yourself, acting alone?"

"Ma'am I would prefer not to comment on what the AAIB did or didn't do. I did think when I started that the most likely cause was pilot error but I was fortunate in my investigations and I did not have any pre-conceived notions."

"Thank you for your very clear evidence on this very complicated subject, Mr. Talbert. I have often noticed that people like yourself who claim to be fortunate often work very hard indeed to achieve their good fortune. If there are no further questions you may step down."

I left the box and went over to sit next to Mike. Anne Moncrieff took my place and was sworn in. John got her to explain what happened during the EASA certification of the 798 and to confirm that the papers I had given the Court were the relevant ones in her disagreements with the EASA.

"Summing up then Ms Moncrieff, you felt that it was wrong to have the three GPS cards in one box. You felt it was wrong not to have the Multimode receiver software classified at the highest safety level. You felt it was wrong that the flight crew did not have an independent display of the glide slope centre line on the approach. Finally you disliked the whole concept of the RWA special modification. Have you changed your mind at all since you wrote your letter to the chief certification engineer?"

"No, Sir. Unfortunately I believe that I have been proved right. If I may say so Mr. Talbert has done an excellent job finding the truth."

McGuire asked a few questions but Moncrieff dealt with them all very easily. Roger O'Kane was recalled, sworn in and questioned by Janet Crowburn.

"Mr. O'Kane, did you hear the evidence which has just been given by Mr. Talbert?"

Roger nodded.

"With your detailed knowledge of the avionics on the 798, could the accident have happened as Mr. Talbert suggests?"

"Well Ma'am I cannot comment on what happened when the aircraft was flying but if a three card GPS was fitted to a RWA 798 and the wrong approach selector switch also fitted to the same aircraft then the aircraft would be identical to all other 798s and could carry out an approach using GPS as the sensor."

"What about Mr. Talbert's statements about what the crew would see? If the GPS was inaccurate would the crew know that the aircraft was not on the ideal glide slope?"

"Ma'am, the pilots look at what the auto-pilot sees. If the calculation is wrong, then the pilots will not know. However my company took every step to ensure that the design met every known safety standard and the FAA and EASA agreed."

"But you had not allowed for the faulty maintenance as described by Mr. Talbert?"

"There is a limit to what can be allowed for. Safety is all a matter of probability."

McGuire chipped in.

"Mr. O'Kane, it is not just faulty maintenance, is it? The aircraft was carrying out a GPS approach the way any other 798 aircraft would do. The problem surely is that GPS is not good enough for Cat 3 approaches and there has be an independent method for the crew to check what is happening to the aircraft relative to the runway."

"Well Sir, I cannot possibly comment on whether Cat 3 GPS approaches are possible. My understanding is that with a Local Area Augmentation System it should be possible, but I am not an expert."

"Agreed Mr. O'Kane but maybe the way the system is implemented in your aircraft needs examination. Perhaps the FAA and EASA need to take a good look at what the pilot can see."

Roger didn't have to respond because Crowburn got to her feet again.

"Mr. O'Kane one final question. Would the GESS instrumentation on the recorder have worked on Golf Hotel with the wrong equipment fitted?"

"No Ma'am."

"Thank you, Mr. O'Kane."

Lord Justice Thomas called Crowburn and Fairlane up to the bench. There was a long discussion and the counsels returned to their seats. Lord Justice Thomas said that the Court would be adjourned until Monday with a possibility that there would be a further adjournment after that. More evidence was required from Australia as well as from the UK.

John came over to Mike and myself.

"Foster has disappeared. The police have found what looks like a suicide note and a confession. The prints on the note matched the prints found in your house. The police have just told Crowburn and the Judge. Apparently Foster did some betting and got overdrawn. He saw an opportunity to get some money by leaking information to Osborne. On an impulse last night he went to your place to talk to you, saw you were out, and broke in. The police are looking for him now. The Court is adjourned so that the assessors can talk to Furness and decide what to do. They obviously want some statement from the NWIA engineer and that will take time to organise. They will want Robson and Chester to testify and also they will want some more evidence from Roger O'Kane to confirm your analysis and examine the switch. By the way you were sailing very close to the wind, pinching that switch."

"John, you are bound to know who said 'He either fears his fate too much or his deserts are small, that puts it not unto the touch to win or lose it all.'?"

He smiled at me.

"That was Montrose just before his execution. You were lucky, you got away with it. By the way you will be pleased to know that the Court agrees with my view that there is no point in calling Miss Ward since she can contribute nothing more and there is a danger of some counsels going on a fishing expedition.

"In my view now, the chances of CrossRisk Insurance being named as a party to any action claim must be very small."

"That's good John, but the dependents will need to get recompense from someone. The statutory minimum from RWA will be quite inadequate unfortunately."

John paused and Mike took over.

"Well NWIA are a target for claims, RWA another target perhaps for not ensuring that NWIA was properly trained but I think they might wriggle out of that. However the support contract between NWIA and RWA says that RWA must hold NWIA harmless for any servicing errors. I think one of the most interesting parties to be named might be the European Aviation Safety Agency. It is not normal for a regulating authority to be sued but some lawyers might take a view that they should never have certificated the aircraft with that avionic installation. Certainly that would be my view."

Mandy had come over and heard most of the conversation.

"But would they get any money out of the EASA? Dos it really have an independent legal existence? The EC should never have made the validation of certificates of airworthiness mandatory by member states."

"Well who can the dependents claim from? How about the EC?"

"Possibly if they can't claim from EASA, the airline and NWIA."

"Mike, what about Independant?"

"Well Peter, Independant are bound to be named because they are the aircraft design authority and clearly there is room for improvement on all aircraft. The quickest and best thing for the dependents, but not the lawyers, would be for RWA, NWIA, and Independant to agree their various percentages of any claim and make an offer to the dependents, but I am afraid it never works out that way.

"Anyway that's enough talk. I think we ought to celebrate. I'll buy you all dinner to-night. John, can your wife join us?"

John said he would find out. He had a flat in the Barbican they used during the week. He left to check. Mike turned to me.

"By the time we've finished dinner the press will have put their papers to bed so they won't be so persistent. However Peter I advise you to keep away from your house. By to-morrow evening everything should be forgotten. I'll tell you what we'll do. I will book two rooms for Mandy and you in the Savoy and we can all eat there. Is that alright?"

I looked at Mandy who nodded.

"Just as well I keep some clothes in the office. What time shall I meet you there?"

We agreed 8 o'clock in the bar lounge area. We chose the back route again to get out of the building but this time there was a photographer who caught Mandy and I leaving. Luckily there were no reporters. I went with Mike to his office where John joined us.

"Have you seen the latest Standards?"

The first Standard had the front two pages full of the accident. They had found an old picture of me from the Guild which made me look very young. 'EXPERTS PROVED WRONG'. There were detailed explanations of how the accident happened. The later Standard had a headline 'TALBERT TELLS THE TALE' with the front page devoted to Foster's disappearance. The accident explanation had been transferred to Page 2.

I called Liz and told her the good news. She had seen the first edition Standard but did not know about the adjournment and her being excused. She had not had such a good day as yesterday and was feeling a bit down. I tried to cheer her up without much success. She was fed up with the weather.

"When do I see you next?"

"Well not until after the week-end. When do you go and see your sister?"

"Friday evening still, back Sunday evening."

"The Court is meant to be starting again on Monday but as far as I know I need not be there. I'll come and have breakfast with you on Monday, OK?"

"Fine, see you then."

I felt a bit mean but there was not much I could do. I left Mike's office and went round to Mandy's. I called Jim Akers at the FT. He had been looking everywhere for me. He offered me a good fee for an exclusive on my accident investigation. We agreed I would do it in the

Chapter 11

morning for the Week-End FT. He checked on one or two points for the article he was producing for the morning.

I decided to ring Frank Mercer. Catherine, his wife answered.

"I'm so glad you phoned. Frank has been listening to the news. He is still in bed but getting better rapidly, thank goodness. I'll take the phone into him. I know he's dying to talk to you."

There was a pause and Frank came on the phone. He sounded a bit weak.

"Peter, thank you for phoning. I've just heard the news. Well done."

"Frank, I though you must be in a very bad way and not able to talk because I was expecting to hear your story plastered all over the front pages. Have you been interviewed? What happened on the Flight Deck."

"Peter, would you believe I don't know? I was in the back of the Upper Class talking to a friend of mine when the two Marshals went into the VIP Area, there was a couple of thumps and then four passengers went forward into the VIP Area. Two of them reappeared carrying guns and threatened us all as Harry announced the hijacking over the PA system."

"None of this appeared in the media, Frank."

"I know. I shouldn't have told you I suppose but you seem to know everything that happened. Some sinister guys came round, flashed their badges, said they were Government Security and told me not to tell anyone the story I've just told you. Official Secrets Act etc."

We talked for a bit more and then I said I would come round and see him when things quietened down. I thought about what Frank had said. He had had a very lucky escape. So it was the Marshals who had the weapons. That would explain a lot. They could get them on board. It suddenly dawned on me that the dead man in Sydney was probably a bona fide Marshal and the other was probably 'bent'. No wonder security wanted it all hushed up.

Mandy finished tidying up her desk getting ready for the morning. No day off for her. I told her about the Marshals and Frank Mercer as we went round to the Savoy and checked in. Mike had done us proud. Our rooms were next to one another overlooking the river. The lad carrying our bags looked sideways at me when he realised that I didn't have one. Mandy told me she would need some time to get ready. I went down to the Strand and bought a few necessities and then went back to my room. I was just in time to hear a knocking on the adjoining door and opened it to discover Mandy in a slip.

"I thought I heard you. You can zip my dress up and then go and shower and shave."

I hesitated for a moment. I felt I was being dragged back in to the past when Diana and I were together. I pulled myself together and kissed the back of Mandy's neck as she pulled her dress on which slowed things down. Then I pulled the zip up as requested. I left her to finish getting ready. I joined Mike, John and John's wife, Liz, in the bar area. Mike had already ordered a bottle of champagne. We opened it and were well into our second glass when Mandy found us. She was looking very elegant and, of course, without her spectacles.

"You might have waited for me."

Mike gave her a drink and ordered two more bottles. She sat next to me. We drank to our success. Mike cleared his throat and looked slightly embarassed.

"I hope you don't mind but I've asked two more people to join us. Roger O'Kane and Liz Ward."

I looked at Mandy who said nothing. I smiled reassuringly at Mike.

"That's nice Mike. They are both on their own in Town. I think it was a splendid idea. I don't know why I didn't think of it myself."

I looked at Mike who was pleased and at Mandy who looked liked the Sphinx as she hit me under the table, unnecessarily hard I thought.

Roger arrived and was introduced to Mandy and Liz Fairhall. Mike looked at his watch. We were running a bit late. Then I saw Liz being shown to our table. She had obviously disposed of her raincoat and gloves, put her hair up and was wearing a fantastic dress which seemed moulded to her figure. Everybody in the room watched her progress to the table. She seemed not to notice, I supposed she was used to it. Mike welcomed her.

"Liz you look stunning. Who don't you know here?"

She was introduced to Roger, John and John's wife, who looked at Liz all over, though whether with appreciation it was hard to judge. Mike gave Liz a drink and was going to suggest we went to our table when the head waiter brought the menus over. We all relaxed in our seats again.

Liz Fairlane looked across.

"Miss Ward, I understand from Mike here that you design and make your own clothes. That dress you have on. Surely you did not make that yourself? It is wonderful if I may say so. Mind you with your figure you have an advantage over me, but not Mandy of course" she added hastily.

"Yes I did make it. My problem over here is that my clothes were not made for this climate. Unless the rooms are warm I freeze and come out in goose pimple which spoils the effect."

"Why don't you get a job, Liz, if I may call you that. Please call me Liz, Liz, if that doesn't confuse every body." She grinned. "If I tried to buy a dress like that it would cost a fortune and John would go mad even though he is quite a successful QC."

"Liz, I'm going to. It was Peter here who really gave me the courage to go for it though I had been wondering about it for some time."

304

Chapter 11

She smiled unreservedly at me and then more guardedly at Mandy.

"I've had some offers in the last day or two and I'm going back home on Monday to think about it."

"Can't you stay?"

"Not really. I've got a house to think about and to be quite honest, I'm worried if I could ever live in the European climate."

We ordered our meal and the conversation broadened, savouring today's Inquiry and then going further afield. We went in to the River Room. Liz Fairhall sat on Mike's right and Liz on his left. Luckily Mike put Roger next to Liz and I sat next to Roger with Mandy on my left. John completed the table. Roger and I tacitly agreed not to talk electronics; anyway he was a bit down after the questioning from McGuire. Mike was a good host and the dinner went very well with the background of the activity on the Thames. The meal took quite a time and we did not finish until 11.30.

We all thanked Mike for a super evening.

"You must all thank Peter. He made it possible. Without him I have no doubt my firm would be bankrupt."

I felt pleased but embarrassed. Mandy squeezed my hand and then did her favorite trick of running her finger round my palm while I tried to make sensible conversation. We all agreed to call each other as necessary in the morning. Mandy and I went to the lobby with Mike and Liz. I kissed Liz goodnight, quickly, and we watched Mike and Liz in to a taxi. We turned and got our keys from the desk. Mandy ordered a wake-up call at 7.15 with the FT, Times, Telegraph, Guardian, Independent, The Sun, Mirror, Mail and Express. She must have thought there was going to be something interesting in the papers. We went up in the elevator.

"You having a lie in to-morrow then?"

"I hope so."

She leant forward and kissed me as the doors opened to reveal some guests waiting to go down. Mandy appeared not to notice.

I escorted her to her room and kissed her good-night on the cheek. She responded suitably and disappeared. I went into my room, locked it with the bolt and opened the adjoining door to find Mandy waiting.

"I wanted to say good night properly."

"Well now you can say good-night improperly."

I was tempted to ask what her clients would say but I felt I knew the answer. We decided to sleep in Mandy's room so as not to miss the wake-up call. As I was dropping off to sleep worn out by the day's exertions, Mandy switched on the TV and started to watch Sky News. I could hear my name being mentioned and Mandy kept prodding me to sit up and watch. The always informed air correspondents were being grilled and had some nice things to say. Then they had a review of the following days papers except it was so late it was the morning's papers. My name and picture appeared to be on every front page and the EASA and the AAIB got rather a roasting. Jim Akers of course pointed out the difficulties that now existed with the EASA issuing the type certificate instead of a National Regulatory Authority, half implying it would never have happened if the CAA had done the certification He also made the point that presumably the Judge had had the full transcript from day one, but covered by a Public Immunity Certificate signed at least by the Secretary of State for Transport, for one.

"Mandy, can I go to sleep now, my darling?"

"It seems such a shame to sleep when we are in the Savoy."

"Well what else is there left to do at two in the morning?"

"I wonder about you sometimes."

It was still dark when Mandy got up in the morning, put her dressing gown on and brought in the papers. She took her dressing gown off, stood by the bed and held the papers.

"Which would you prefer?"

"I'll start with the FT please."

"You've made the wrong choice and you know it. However you're right. I must get to the office."

She disappeared in to the bathroom and I glanced at the papers. They were all full of the Inquiry and were very complimentary about the part I had played. As usual Jim Akers' report was by far the best. He even mentioned the switch I had taken from the DERA hangar, saying it was the only way to convince the AAIB they had got it wrong.

"You had better get back in to your room while I get dressed. Take all the papers with you and keep them for posterity."

I obliged but in fact I did not stay in bed but decided to get up.

"Darling, shall I ring down for coffee or shall we have something downstairs?"

"We don't sleep in the Savoy every night. Let's have a quick breakfast downstairs."

Mandy packed her bag and we both packed our briefcases. I felt rather tired with very little sleep and a bit dishevelled. I had put my trousers in the trouser press but there was not much more I could do. Mandy on the other hand seemed ready for anything. We went down and had a continental breakfast in style. We felt spoilt. Mandy had picked up some complimentary papers, I had put ours in my briefcase so it was almost bursting.

"I must say, my dearest, that they have done you proud. If you don't watch it you could become a celebrity."

"Not me. The papers will soon forget."

Chapter 11

"Maybe but the Inquiry opens again on Monday. If you show your face it will be photographed. Talking of that have you looked at the Telegraph?"

She passed it to me. There was a picture of me and a smart looking Mandy coming out of the Inquiry hall.

"That will be bad for your business Mandy. The senior partners won't like it. You had better rush to the office and collect the Telegraphs."

"No point. The photograph has been syndicated to the other papers. Here it is again in the Mail. Anyway my firm won't mind. They will just be jealous, especially the ladies."

"I see that Foster has still not been found. What a mess. Anyway when do I see you next?"

"That's up to you, my darling. How about coming to my place for the week-end. You know how I feel about ghosts and your house."

"Sounds good. Shall we catch the 6.30? I'll meet you at the platform entrance."

It was still very cold. We put on our coats and walked towards Fleet Street. I turned right across the bridge to Waterloo and Mandy carried on to her office. I was home by 10 o'clock. Dora was in and full of the Inquiry and the pictures of me and Mandy.

"You look a lovely couple. And you're famous. The phone has never stopped ringing."

"I hope you told them Dora that I had gone to Australia."

"No I didn't" she said indignantly. "I said I was expecting you home shortly and I was quite right. By the way, did you know they found a body in the river by Tower Bridge. They think it might be your Accident man."

The phone went again. It was a bit of luck Dora taking all the calls since it had stopped to some extent my answering machine from being clogged up. As I picked up the phone I noticed that there were ten messages on the machine and a lot more in Dora's writing. It was the BBC asking me to take part in Panorama on Monday night. The lady calling could hear I was reluctant and offered me a good fee. I refused saying the Inquiry was still on and I felt it would be improper to take part. That was clearly a concept the lady could not understand. We agreed to differ. She was obviously not going to be popular with her producer for failing in her mission.

I started work on the article for Jim Akers. The phone kept on ringing with media people and I kept on with the same reply. Then Liz came on the line.

"How did you get on with Mike?"

"Never you mind. Is breakfast still on for Monday?"

"I though you were going back on Monday?"

"I was but it is now Tuesday and I have another appointment on Monday afternoon I want to keep. What time suits you?"

If Mandy was true to form she would be catching an early train. We agreed 8.45 and I said I hoped she had a good week-end with her sister. I returned to my article, struggling with the phone. Then Carol came on the line.

"You were magnificent. I was in the Hall."

"Carol, why didn't you tell me? You must have queued for hours. I could have got you in."

"It was not too bad. I got someone in to take the children to school and was there at 8 o'clock"

"You make me feel rotten. Anyway I hope you enjoyed it. How are you getting on?"

Apparently things had improved with the children after the skiing and Carol was doing some translating and looking for other jobs. She confided in me that an old friend of Dick's had called and taken her out. I got the impression there might eventually be something in it. I asked her to keep in touch.

I played the answerphone back while I was eating a sandwich I had bought at Prêt a Manger on the way home. They were mostly from the same people who had called me during the morning which was a relief. I rang my builder and he told me he should have a window by Tuesday. I went back and finished the article and put it in the e-mail to Jim at the FT. I packed for the week-end and then called Jim.

"Peter, that's absolutely fine. Just what I wanted. I like your point about a higher safety standard being required for these large aircraft carrying so many passengers. We'll put it over your name if that's OK."

"Well just check with your legal people on my behalf that I can write that article bearing in mind that I was a witness and I suppose I could be recalled. I've refused to talk to the media."

I did my expenses for Mike and NWIA. I was going to be broke if I didn't watch it. There was a special delivery. I opened the envelope and found a very large cheque indeed from Mike and a note 'Just to keep you going. Final settlement later. Thanks for everything.' He must have moved like lightning to get that approved by his firm. I called American and we agreed provisionally I would be with them Monday week.

Bob Furness called.

"Peter this is a pretty mess. I shall be lucky if I keep my job. I just wanted to congratulate you on the magnificent job you did. I feel very ashamed of our poor efforts."

"Bob, you were let down by Martin. By the way, is it true they've found him?"

"I think so."

"Poor chap. I almost feel sorry for him. Has he got a family?"

"Yes, Peter, I'm afraid so. It really is an awful situation."

"Bob, I'm sure you don't need my advice but I think you should plan for the future. You've got lots of very good people in your team but these accident investigations can be terribly harrowing. They do need close supervision."

"You're right. That's where I went wrong."

"Bob anyway thanks so much for calling me. I do appreciate it."

I decided I had better call Marcia Hodgson. I introduced myself and said how sorry I was about Harry.

"Mr. Talbert, thank you so much for everything you have done. My life is completely upside down as you can imagine but my children are marvellous. I knew Harry would not make a mistake like that and it was cruel of the AAIB. As for the recording it was disgraceful to start all that story for a straightforward dinner party. You were simply splendid."

I muttered a few platitudes and wished her the very best for the future. There was nothing more I could say.

There was a funny call from the Department of Transport later on. It was from a senior civil servant in the organisation. He tried to wrap it up but I detected that he was sounding me out to see if I would be interested in joining the AAIB. I stopped him in his tracks.

"There is a very capable chief inspector there already and I can see no reason why he should be changed."

I rang off, feeling rather annoyed. I diverted my phone to Mandy's number, locked the house and met Mandy at Waterloo. I told her first about the DOT call and she thought for a bit.

"The Secretary of State must be under terrific pressure to change Bob, Peter. You probably would be the ideal choice."

"No thanks. I don't think I want to be regimented and have administration and a lot of people working for me. I want to be free."

"So I've noticed."

I kept my head down and said nothing.

We walked to Mandy's flat and sat down and relaxed. I had been running around for weeks and at last I could relax, sit down and do nothing. Mandy disappeared and came back wearing shorts, a pullover and two gin and tonics.

"You'll freeze."

"Not for long. I've turned the central heating up and you can keep me warm."

"I'd like to take you out for a meal."

"That's very sweet of you but you really do need some rest."

"I'm not sure with your plan I'll get much of a rest."

"Well we shall just have to see." She smiled at me. "I've decided this week-end to do what my clients do for a change and shelve our problems, Diana and all."

I woke up in the middle of the night. It was cold. The central heating was off. I had my arms round Mandy, she was keeping me warm, or was it the other way round? I was wide awake. What was it that Carol had said 'an old friend of Dick's. She had called Richard 'Dick'. On Golf Hotel's voice recorder, 'Dick' was sitting in the middle seat. I had assumed it was Dick Tremlett, the off duty Captain but of course Richard Trentham would have known Harry from GAPAN. I remembered the visit to Richard in the hospital. What had he said? *'Peter. The hijackers.'* and *'I tried to tell…?'* Was it Richard who was in the jump seat and who Harry had called 'Dick'? I remembered that Richard's shoulders were badly broken. By the shoulder straps? Another thought struck me as I suddenly realised what Richard might have wanted to tell me. He might have noticed something wasn't quite right. Perhaps he'd seen a warning written somewhere or perhaps a 'GPS' enunciation on Charles Tumbrill's display instead of 'GESS'? I did not know enough about what the displays would show with the wrong boxes fitted and I was not about to ask Roger. Roger would have mentioned it to me for sure if there had been something extra to see? As far as I was concerned the matter was closed. Nothing useful would be gained by further investigation. I finally got back to sleep.

We got up very slowly luxuriating in having nothing to do. Mandy finally got out of bed to make up a tray and have breakfast in bed and read the papers. I picked up the FT to read my article but the main headline made me wince "LARGE AIRCAFT NOT SUFFICENTLY SAFE". The article was written by Jim Akers and really went to town on how, at the moment, large four engined aircraft were designed to the same certification standard as small aircraft like the BAe 146 which only carried about 100 passengers. He had taken my remarks in my article on higher standards being required and started criticising the EASA for not heeding the advice of experts like myself and Anne Moncrieff. He wondered whether in view of the size and complication of the new systems it would be advisable to re-introduce three crew members. Akers also felt that Cat 3B landings should not be permitted with these large aircraft until Enhanced Visibility Systems were available.

I could not really fault the article but I knew that the fall out would affect me since I would be accused of advocating putting up aircraft costs and operating expenses. I knew the arguments were going to start and go on for a long time since airlines didn't like paying more than they have to and ???safety costs money. However it was quite clear that if only the regulators had listened to Anne Moncrieff all those people on RWA 573 would still be alive.

Chapter 11

The phone rang. Mandy was still in the bathroom and I picked up the phone.

"Peter."

I froze. It was a voice from the past which I had tried to forget.

"You were marvellous."

I heard Mandy coming back and put the phone down.

"Who was it.?"

"Oh. Just a wrong number."

A Flight Too Far

EPILOGUE

Could it ever happen?

'Flight too Far' and its technology is set a few years ahead of the present day, January 2006. The four safety themes underlying the story are firstly, the change in Europe of the responsibility for the certification of modern aircraft, from their national authorities to an unsupervised centralised organisation. The second theme is the coming use of satellite navigation systems to enable aircraft to land in hazardous weather conditions such as extreme fog. The third theme, which affects the first two themes, is the all pervasive presence of software and the need for immaculate design and operation. The fourth theme is questioning the logic of the present certification requirements which have basically the same design standard and operating rules for all aircraft, regardless of size.

Certification of aircraft is a fundamental task to ensure the safety of air travellers. There is no such thing as absolute safety. Taking into account statistically all the perceivable risks, an aircraft has only to be 'safe enough'. Each National authority has its own regulating organisation to formulate a set of design rules that try to ensure an acceptable safety level for civil aircraft. For example, the United States of America has the Federal Aviation Administration and, until recently, in the United Kingdom, the Safety Regulation Group, previously the Air Registration Board, had the responsibility for certificating aircraft. These regulating organisations have similar requirements but, inevitably, there will be important differences which often result in arguments between the national authorities when they are certificating each other's aircraft. The big change in Europe is that all the national authorities have now lost the responsibility for certificating new aircraft coming onto their own national registers, since a new supranational authority has been formed to do the task on behalf of all the individual national authorities, the European Aviation Safety Agency, which is an agency of the European Union. It's legal position is not entirely defined, in that it is not clear whether the Agency, for example, can be sued. All new aircraft entering Europe to go on to an EU country's register must be certificated by the EASA and national certification cannot be withheld by an EU country if EASA has certificated the aircraft.

The UK in the past had an organisation called the Airworthiness Requirements Board which used to monitor the work of the Safety Regulation Group and this had the effect of ensuring that all decisions by the SRG were very carefully thought through. In the case of the EASA, there is no equivalent of the ARB and history shows that an organisation without supervision can be subjected to political and marketing pressures. Even with 'auditing' there is no guarantee of correct procedures, as can be seen in the EU itself; without proper monitoring the situation is very worrying since safety is involved. In fact the only check and balance on the EASA is, surprisingly, the USA's FAA. If the requirements of these two major certification organisations were to drift apart it would make the certification of each other's aircraft very difficult and there would be many arguments, perhaps even involving the World Trade Organisation, if protectionism was suspected.

The European certification scene is a changing one but there has to be a concern over European accident investigation under this new certification regime, since the accident investigation organisations are national ones and are likely to remain so. Because accidents are often appalling disasters, no EU government would ever accept investigation by a supranational body under the aegis of the European Union, particularly as commercial pressures are never far away. The problem here is that if the accident is due to a fault in the certification rules or procedures, the local national authority can claim, quite correctly, that the matter is outside their jurisdiction. At the same time, the EASA will be very reluctant to disclose or admit any defect in their procedures. The current arrangements therefore could result in some very unsatisfactory arguments in the event of a serious accident.

Another interesting change, this time in the aircraft navigation scene, is the advent of satellite navigation systems which can provide landing guidance to aircraft. The United States Global Positioning System has been available for many years but it has never been satisfactory as a stand alone navigation system for civil aircraft, since it is basically a military system and does not meet civil safety requirements in the respect of failures. The European Galileo satellite system is just starting but will eventually be operational and will be a basically civil system, suitable for sole source en route navigation. Conceptually these satellite navigation systems can also be used as approach aids to airfields anywhere in the world, providing all the necessary airfield details have been entered into the database of the aircraft's navigation system. Furthermore, the satellite systems can be used for landings providing the accuracy of the satellite information has been augmented with a local measurement system. GPS has a Local Area Augmentation System and the Galileo system, if it is to be used for CAT 3 approaches, will almost certainly have to have an equivalent.

Epilogue

There is a significant difference between a landing system using ILS, with its vertical and horizontal beams as references, and a landing system using satellites. The ILS accuracy is determined by the national air traffic authority and by the positioning of the transmitting antennae, whilst the approach accuracy of a satellite system depends on the combined accuracy of the satellite system plus the design and integrity of the aircraft on-board system software. The path in space for the aircraft to follow is computed entirely by the software in the aircraft and relies on the complete accuracy of the airfield information in the database. The national air traffic system has responsibility for the airfield lighting and the runway itself but has no responsibility for the path which the aircraft is following to reach the runway threshold.

As has been mentioned, software is used not only in enabling an aircraft to make an approach and landing but also in the actual flying of the aircraft. The days of the aircraft controls following the position of the pilots' input lever, the control column, have long since gone. This is a situation well understood by aircraft designers and the certification authorities but, despite all their efforts, ensuring that software is 'absolutely safe' is not that simple. Nevertheless, in order to make aircraft as efficient as possible and therefore competitive, aircraft designers are relying more and more on computers and the software that drives them. This is a challenge not only for the designers, but also for the certification authorities.

The final theme of this book is to point out that at the moment the certification rules for large aircraft are basically the same as for smaller aircraft, not only in the design requirements but also in the operating rules. The unpalatable fact is that up to now all aircraft types have accidents, for all sorts of different reasons. It is suggested that the rules for large aircraft, able to carry so many people, may need to be reviewed to try to prevent these aircraft from ever having an accident. It may be necessary to have more than two pilots on the flight deck and the equipment standard on these large aircraft may have to be to a higher standard, for example a synthetic visual landing system may be required so that the pilots can see the ground, whatever the weather. Airlines would not like any of these changes but safety has to be paid for.

Aircraft design does not stand still. There will be more and more technical challenges in the future. This book takes a snapshot at the challenges in the immediate future. Peter Talbert will have to work hard to keep up!

A Flight Too Far

ALB
January 2006

A Flight Too Far

Epilogue

A Flight Too Far

Printed in the United Kingdom
by Lightning Source UK Ltd.
123579UK00001B/104/A